"A delightful book for our times showing us that no matter how many walls humans put up between each other, we are inter-connected by history, by land, and by the best in us."
— Ivelisse Rodriguez, PEN/Faulkner Finalist, author of *LOVE WAR STORIES*

"In SISTER CITY Ian Woollen holds up a mirror between Indiana and the Yucatán, and the reflection is an imaginative, funny, compelling, and beautiful world. These are characters and stories, peoples and places, that stay with you because Ian Woollen is a storyteller and shaman, an enchanter of new forms of community and empathy, a novelist who has composed poetic consejo for our time."
— Fred Arroyo, author of *THE REGION OF LOST NAMES* and *WESTERN AVENUE AND OTHER FICTIONS*

"Pick up this quirky, warm-hearted book. Start reading, and soon, as an idiom-challenged tour guide translator puts it, "all your troubles will be in your behind." Author Ian Woollen is deep, wise and droll as ever in this humane, hip, and humorous new novel."
— James Alexander Thom, author of *ST. PATRICK'S BATTALION* and *FOLLOW THE RIVER*

"The communities in Ian Woollen's sharply observed SISTER CITY share more than a name—Cave City, Indiana, and Ciudad de la Gruta, Mexico. A cast of memorable characters move back and forth between the two. History, culture and love all come into play as politics threatens to end the cities' twenty-year relationship. Woollen's take is both humorous and affectionate, while unsparing of those who put ambition before people. Readers of John Nichols will welcome Woollen's work."
— Gwen Florio, award-winning author of *SILENT HEARTS* and the Lola Wicks mysteries

"In this rich, ambitious novel, Ian Woollen lays out a grinning ziggurat reminiscent of the great Kurt Vonnegut, who also took things to the limit. This is a tale of two cities like we haven't seen and when it builds to a crescendo it involves a thousand things. A thousand and two. An unabashed conversation of all the issues we call home!"
— Ron Carlson, author of *FIVE SKIES* and *RETURN TO OAKPINE*

"Two stories interwoven of fictitious rural cities, one in Yucatán, one in Indiana, whose inhabitants will attack or defend their cities' historic bond against a grim political perspective. Seeking glimpses of self-determination in the spirals of time, these endearing characters remind us of what matters to any society: a sense of community, all the more when in the form of first-rate storytelling."
— Fer de la Cruz, Yucatecan poet and author of *SEVEN SONGS OF SILENT FIREFLIES*. Winner of the Mérida International Poetry Prize.

"Not since the Midwestern sly satires of Sinclair Lewis has main street and malocchio been in better hands. The deft Ian Woollen takes the form even further. This exquisite novel is a border-crossing (literally) gothic grotesque of a new orderly disorder. Something quite sublime!"
— Michael Martone, author of *BROODING* and *THE MOON OVER WAPAKONETA*

"Laughs, thrills and chills as a motley set of colorful characters learn to see and navigate the web of relationships that tie people and places together. A transnational Milagro Beanfield War for our times."
— Peter Guardino, Ph.D., award-winning author of *THE DEAD MARCH: A HISTORY OF THE MEXICAN-AMERICAN WAR*

Sister
City
A NOVEL

Ian Woollen

coffeetownpress

Kenmore, WA

coffeetownpress

A Coffeetown Press book published by Epicenter Press

Epicenter Press
6524 NE 181st St. Suite 2
Kenmore, WA 98028.
www.Epicenterpress.com
www.Coffeetownpress.com
www.Camelpress.com

For more information go to: www.coffeetownpress.com

Sister City
Copyright © 2021 by Ian Woollen

ISBN: 9781603813525 (trade paper)
ISBN: 9781603813532 (ebook)

LOC 0002020934894

Printed in the United States of America

IN MEMORY:
Pep Sobrer, friend and guide.

Acknowledgments:
Heartfelt thanks to all the people who helped bring this manuscript to life. Truly, it could not have happened without you.

0.

Zero. The starting point, the baseline void of zero. A mathematical concept of nothing that is, in fact, something extremely powerful. The idea of zero allows its Mayan originator, a tattooed wizard atop a limestone pyramid in the buzzing, tropical jungle two thousand years ago, to think about time in a big way. The Short Count and the Long Count, going forward with lots of zeroes. The implied trajectory of cyclical return in base twenty, seen graphically in the shape of the numeral itself, a shell, an orb, that mirrors the shape and motion of its true creator, the Sun. Ever proceeding, ever returning.

Thus ruminates retired Professor Ignacio Morales, muttering under his pipe-smoker's breath. He lectures math students in his head during his afternoon walk beside the old city wall of Ciudad de la Gruta. On the shaded side of the street, it is still over ninety degrees. He proceeds through the west gate and on out around the Jaguar Pyramid. "For some, zero is a lucky number. For others, a negative description of their personality."

His former students joke about Ignacio Morales' attempts to attach psychological import to numbers, especially in his annual Double Zero speech on the eve of the university's major sporting event, the Sister City soccer game against Southwest Hoosier State in Cave City, Indiana. The *gringo* goalkeeper always displays a red double zero on his jersey, in direct provocation to his Mayan opponents.

The professor pauses to wipe his perspiring forehead. He clears his throat and fantasizes about a lecture on the complexities of Riemannian zeroes, a fresh wand of chalk at the ready. His suit and trouser pockets contain stubs of the stuff. He imagines the ancient mathematician scratching equations into the ground with a spearhead, surrounded by admiring warriors, or using precious cacao beans as counters. Ignacio deems himself a worthy descendant, though only one quarter Maya on his mother's side (if such really matters to identity).

The afternoon sun shines down from atop the Jaguar Pyramid with a polynomial force of the fifth degree. The professor reaches for the handkerchief in the pocket of his linen jacket. He dabs his rheumy eyes.

"*Buenas tardes, señor.*"

"*Hola, mi amigo.*"

"*¡Qué calor!*"

"*¿Cómo va?*"

"*Muy bien, gracias.*"

Ignacio smiles and acknowledges the daily greetings from the *turbulencia* in the street. Neighbors in folding chairs and shop owners waving from behind their counters and the hammock vendors with their carts. Laundry flapping on the balconies. His neighborhood is an architectural relic of the 19th century *henequén* boom, an era when nearly all the marine rope in the world was made from Yucatán sisal, before the advent of synthetics.

Ignacio steps carefully on the broken sidewalk, shuffling along with his cane, a modified pool cue with a silver handle attached. The cane is a gift from his late friend, Delmar Butz of Cave City, Indiana. Oh, how he misses Delmar, that colorful boob.

Ignacio doffs his straw hat to the tamale lady at the corner of Centennial Park, to the nurses smoking cigarettes outside the cancer clinic, to the one-eyed operator of the shoeshine stand at the bus station, whom he has known since childhood, but can't remember his name. He pauses to avoid a loud motorcycle, stacked high with birdcages, and a priest carrying a floppy fish in butcher paper. He eases around the line of schoolchildren at the Meteor Museum. Ignacio waves to the aproned cook, a distant cousin on his father's side, reading a magazine in the alley behind the bakery, Pandemonio. The place is popular with the university crowd.

Every day at 4 p.m. or thereabouts, Ignacio stumps through the *palmas*-lined avenues of his ancestral city with the blinking, bemused gaze of a reclusive, intellectual bachelor who has just emerged from eight hours in the dim, teak-panel study of the Morales mansion. Rumor has it that the professor is working on a grand equation. Using the Mayan numeric system, the shell zero and the dot and the bar, he is attempting to solve the end-times mystery of 2012. What was supposed to happen? What might still happen? The expat regulars on the sidewalk stools of La Sombra Azul, the barrio's busy cantina, catcall their interest:

"Cracked the secret yet, professor?"

"Would a tequila help?"

"Betting big on the Reds this weekend."

"We miss your *beisbolista* friend."

The professor pauses and bows and summons his lecture voice: "I grieve for Delmar too. Gone twelve years now. My heart still aches for Delmar Butz. And, as for my research, gentlemen, please trust that should there be a breakthrough, you will be the first to know."

Delmar Butz is the dead person, the shadow force. There is always one behind the scenes, a recently deceased individual who continues to exert a wave of influence, both overt and covert, among family and friends. He was killed by an aggressive melanoma, probably caused by too many years on the spring training practice fields without sunscreen. Delmar didn't have time for sunscreen. He was a busy man. As kids and adults, Delmar Butz and Ignacio Morales enjoyed a profound bond, and a twelve-year absence still qualifies his death as recent. Their friendship transcended cultural differences and led to the establishment of the Sister City accord between their two towns. Twelve years without Delmar is a drop in the bucket. Twelve years without Delmar is barely a glimpse of the plumed bird in the forest.

A recurring dream of Ignacio's: He and Delmar together in a New England boarding school as awkward teens, pouring a failed chemistry experiment down the toilet and running away as it explodes. The Headmaster orders them into his office and inquires, "Ignacio Morales and Delmar Butz, is it true that you have eliminated a bowl?"

The sister city relationship between Ciudad de la Gruta and Cave City, Indiana officially began at the turn of the century, at the beginning of the new millennium. Thanks primarily to Ignacio and his *gringo* friend, scion of the Butz Quarry fortune. They led the effort, assisted by Ignacio's opera singer consort, Señora Calatrova, and Delmar's wife, Glodene, "A beautiful woman blessed with a sense for the ridiculous." That's how Delmar first described her to Ignacio: "Her hair is woven into a thick, elaborate braid that looks like it could be put in the oven and baked."

Delmar enlisted his Mexican friend in the wooing campaign, because Delmar was not the smoothest operator. Ignacio would offer a selection of verses from some lovelorn Yucatecan poet that made Delmar sound both passionate and erudite.

Glodene worked as the reference librarian at the Cave City Public Library. Delmar had a soft spot for librarians. From an early age, he believed them to be omniscient creatures who magically intuited what their patrons needed to read, which for him was usually biographies of baseball players.

Glodene, of the coiled auburn tresses, was and is and will remain forever beautiful, in a retired librarian-esque way. Brave, too. She smuggled in multiple rounds of laetrile and other non-FDA-approved substances after her husband's melanoma diagnosis. Delmar endured eighteen months of chemotherapy and radiation before departing. Though Delmar did not think of death as a departure. An avowed atheist and skeptic, Delmar finally came around to a broader view, after many post-prandial conversations with Ignacio and Señora Calatrova. Yes, death is a joining, a full joining. A vase of his ashes has joined the overflowing ashtray and pipe stand on Ignacio's night table.

Both Ignacio and Delmar grew up as math-nerd kids from backwater, old-money families. In 1966, at age fourteen, they were shipped off to the same boarding school in Massachusetts. At roll call on orientation day, Delmar caught the similarity in the names of their hometowns. Cave City and City of the Cave. Delmar stopped in at Ignacio's dorm room that afternoon and gawked at a silver-framed photo of the handsome Morales mansion and quipped, "Looks like you people have more money than Carter's got liver pills." The friendship evolved from a joint interest in shooting pool, to figuring out the mathematical explanations for the physics of the trick shots they practiced for hours on end, instead of going to class.

In their mature, globetrotting years, Delmar and Glodene Butz visited Ciudad de la Gruta many times. They drank and danced at La Sombra Azul, showing off their sliding, gliding Arthur Murray moves. They traveled in Latin America frequently, a part of Delmar's job as a statistician and baseball scout among the Mexican leagues for the Cincinnati Reds.

More on that later, as Delmar liked to say.

Today, Ignacio's walk is more than a routine constitutional. The professor is on a mission to share a letter with Señora Calatrova at the *teatro*. Her sculpted bust graces the lobby entrance. In a land of distinctive noses, hers stands out, like a piece of downspout that has broken loose from the overhang of her brow, lying upturned on her face. In retirement, the blue-haired diva teaches piano lessons in the rehearsal hall and resides in a basement dressing room. The *teatro* remains damaged from the latest hurricane, a fierce Category 5 that reached miles inland. Tour groups peek in on her dressing room lair. Señora Calatrova waves to them with a hand fan from her hammock. Her fan also doubles as a weapon, an insect whacker, a mosquito killer. Quick as lightning. Smash. The wall is dotted with her handiwork.

The letter that Ignacio, huffing and out of breath, delivers to the *teatro* is from Glodene Butz in Cave City. It is very disturbing. Glodene writes with a fountain pen on flimsy, folded blue paper. Her graceful penmanship suffers a bit from the onset of elderly shakes, and a touch of nervous, widow-worry has crept into her overall tone of late. But all that is not enough to explain away her dire alarm about the upcoming Sister City Referendum.

Señora Calatrova reads aloud, with a resonant, reedy mezzo: "Dear friends, alas, such dangers as Delmar never would have imagined are upon us. We must take a stand..."

Two decades ago, to appease a few grumps on the city council, the original Sister City agreement mandated a renewal every twenty years, via a referendum vote in both cities. Until now, everyone had assumed that the referendum would be a rubber-stamp matter. A lively, broad-based *intercambio* exists between Cave City and Ciudad de la Gruta. Student groups travel back and forth twice a year. Several joint business ventures flourish, including Sister City Tours and a gang-wear clothing outfitter that keeps the teens employed. Of note recently, the development of Flamingo Estates, a retirement community for the growing number of retirees who can't afford to hang it up comfortably in the States. And, of course, the annual soccer game.

According to Glodene's sources, the Sister City referendum, upcoming next spring, will not be an easy rubber stamp. The political climate is in turmoil. No more go-along-to-get-along. Ugly winds are being whipped around by an ambitious Sheriff who is running for mayor and calls the Sister City agreement: "The *worst* deal ever made."

1.

Flight time from Boston to Indianapolis lasted two hours and twenty minutes. It felt like a million years to Winnie Marsh, and a million miles. She leaned against the window in Row 17, just behind the wing, and stared down through puffball clouds at the sinuous surface of an alien planet below. Fly-over country. The antipodal Midwest.

She squinted and scanned, hoping to spot an earthwork, the Serpent Mound or the Great Circle Mound. Recalling an extra credit question from an exam she proctored last year, working as a TA for an undergraduate archeology course at Boston College. It was a question about the prehistoric Ohio mounds. Seen from the sky, these striking structures were possibly interconnected, sending joint messages up to the celestial spirits. What kind of messages? Most of her students hemmed and hawed and narrow-mindedly complained – hey, human flight didn't exist back then.

Or, as one droll stoner suggested, perhaps the messages were intended for extraterrestrial visitors – Martians, bring something to read!

Indeed. Winnie reached for the in-flight magazines and flipped desultorily through the fashion ads. She heard a sneeze behind her and another sneeze from across the aisle. She feared the invisible, nefarious world of microbes. She mouthed a silent prayer.

Beside her, Chad O'Shaughnessy slept, curly head tilted, mouth slightly open. Winnie envied Chad's cat-nap skills and his ability to ignore the sneezes and the occasional buzz from his phone. He slept through the safety announcements and the rattling drink cart service. He slept through the commotion in the front of the plane mid-flight, an asthma attack in the first-class section.

Beyond the tip of the plane wing, an anthill city appeared below in the bright, distant cornfields. Indianapolis, Indiana. The plane's descent was underway. Winnie prayed for a safe landing and for courage and strength and a sense of humor and whatever else she would need to go forward. "Please make sure your seatbelts are fastened and your tray tables are latched." When the jet touched down, tail first, it bounced twice, three times. The chatty co-pilot came on the intercom and said, "Welcome to Indianapolis, folks, the land of the long runway. We should have you to the gate in a few minutes."

In Row 17, Chad sat up abruptly and ran both hands through his reddish blonde mop and turned to Winnie for a wink or a smile, but found only wide-eyed apprehension. It was livestream now. IRL. The landing jarred loose a bit of their Eastern smugness. No more jokes to their Boston friends about learning to speak Hoosier, or cheering for the Colts, or going to the video store.

"Come on, Professor," Chad said, scratching his soul patch and forcing a grin, "the land of the long runway awaits."

Winnie stalled, digging into her purse for Chapstick. She applied it fervently. She tightened her ponytail bun and reinserted her standard #2 pencil, regularly used as a lecture pointer, pill counter, magic wand, and, during her childhood in church choir, a music marker. The bumpy landing still fluttered in her stomach.

"We don't have to do it," Winnie Marsh said, "We could take the next flight home."

Home had been Boston, Massachusetts for both families, the Marshes and the O'Shaughnessy clan, for over three hundred years. No relative had ever moved farther west than Albany. This was an uprooting. This was an exile. Chad and Winnie were relocating to Cave City, Indiana for Winifred Marsh, Ph.D. to begin her first job out of grad school as an adjunct lecturer in the Folklore Department at Southwest Hoosier State University. In the academic field these days, beggars can't be choosers. She would have to swallow her pride and hopscotch to a position back east.

The consensus among friends and family was that there was no way could she manage this ordeal alone. They viewed Winnie as a delicate bookworm, despite her penchant for devouring lobster bare-handed. Chad, the on-again-off-again boyfriend since high school, had been recruited as a willing accomplice with a new title: fiancé.

Chad was a masters-level recovering pothead and newly minted addictions counselor. He was eager to clean up the big world, the same way he'd cleaned up his little one. Go slow, stay low. His NADAC certification would travel, his supervisors assured him. No need to worry about a gap in the resume. Their official engagement made the Indiana move more palatable for both families. Their mothers could focus on a grand Boston wedding next summer. Their fathers could raise an extra glass at the golf club to the adventurous, soon-to-be-newlyweds.

Both families, despite some skeletons in their closets, boasted long traditions of service and accomplishment. The list included an inventor of steam engine valves, a noted abolitionist, and a bishop. Winnie's mother was a former president of the Junior League. Chad's father was the official Statehouse lobbyist for the fishing industry. He also occupied the Catholic diocese's seat on the regional fishing council, because let us not forget that 'cod' rhymes with 'God.' Each generation was expected to at least *try* to make a mark. Thus the 'Go West, Young Couple' banners at the banquet hosted by Winnie's parents last night, and the many toasts about pioneer spirit.

How much did Winnie and Chad know about Cave City, Indiana? Not a lot. Chad's mother's bridge partner, an Evansville native, had informed Winnie at the banquet, "A good conversation starter out there is, 'How does your mama like your hair?'" The town lay somewhere between Evansville and Terre Haute, on a tributary of the Wabash River. Guidebooks mentioned coal mines and limestone quarries. Google searches mentioned an Indian mound site and an annual summer theater attraction, a historical drama about Abe Lincoln's boyhood years: "Indiana made Lincoln a man. Illinois made him a lawyer." The town hosted a Persimmon Festival in the fall, featuring a special event, the Pigeon Hill Outhouse Race. The Southwest Hoosier State athletic teams were known as the 'Frackers.' The female athletes were 'Lady Frackers.'

The most popular restaurant was Happy Dan's Hot Dogs. This was a good sign. Winnie recognized Happy Dan as a character from the Tall Tale lore of the 19th century prairie. Chad suggested that Winnie could write something about Happy Dan for an academic journal. Their faculty apartment had been selected from some fuzzy online photos on the Buena Vista Residences website. The Spanish name was a bit perplexing, until the leasing agent explained that the apartment complex fronted a monument plaza from the Mexican-American War, a circle of benches around an obelisk and a statue of General Winfield Scott standing on General Santa Anna's head. Or, something like that. Basically, Winnie and Chad were operating sight-unseen.

A blunt morning sun poked through the windows of the jet. The plane slowly turned and pulled up to the gate. In the front of the cabin, two medics with a gurney carried off the asthma attack passenger. Winnie pulled down the shade and clutched at her forehead. She grumbled, "I have a headache. Can we just hang here until the aisle empties out?"

A passing stewardess paused and leaned in and asked, "Is there a problem?"

Chad O'Shaughnessy said, "It's an existential issue. Might take a minute or two."

Chad took Winnie's other hand and gently massaged her palm, while the plane began to clear. He tugged at her hair and nibbled on her ear and whispered, "Time to get the girls together." This was a reference to Winnie's standard buck-up phrase for assembling her many sides. Bookworm Winnie. Playtime Winnie. Somewhere-on-the-Spectrum Winnie. 'Professor' Winnie was the newest member of the internal girls club.

Professor Winnie groaned and sighed. "Fuck, okay." An early adopter of the F-word to counter her delicate flower reputation, Winnie used it to express everything from annoyance to profound awe. Her nervous breathe on Chad's cheek felt like a moist, warm snail's foot reaching out into the unknown. "Okay, let's go."

He kissed her forehead. They scooted sideways into the aisle and lifted their belongings down from the overhead bins. Leather purse, book bag, backpacks. Chad tightened his lantern jaw and thrust it forward and commenced to lead them forth into their pioneering engagement.

As they exited Terminal A into the main concourse, they heard a lilting voice on the intercom announce: "*Bienvenidos a Indianápolis, damas y caballeros, una comunidad bonita y elegante. Favor de no fumar en el aeropuerto.*"

Chad said, "Did we get on the wrong flight? Is this Phoenix?"

Winnie said, "No, it's the Indianapolis *International* Airport. They must think the Spanish bit adds a little flair."

Passing the entrance to Terminal B, Chad and Winnie saw and heard a tearful Hispanic family huddled in an emotional, send-off embrace. It was hard to tell who was leaving and who was staying. Wailing cries of love and loss echoed through the hall. Winnie and Chad paused and silently noted the contrast from the stoic handshakes and kiss-kiss pecks received a few hours earlier in Boston. At the edge of the family huddle was a small girl with a dark, angelic face, and a pink bow in her hair. A face that has been painted a hundred different ways by a hundred different artists over the centuries, each one emphasizing the radiant black hair and obsidian eyes. The face turned and stared back at them, as if in long-lost recognition.

The girl clutched a soccer ball in her arms. Winnie smiled and waved at her, and the girl waved in reply, but in doing so, dropped the soccer ball. It rolled across the crowded concourse. Chad chased the ball and returned it to her. An older brother took the ball and thanked him. Chad channeled some college Spanish: "*De nada.*"

At the baggage claim, Winnie muttered, "I hope that was a good omen."

Chad said, "Me too." He sensed it could be otherwise. He sensed it could mean trouble.

Winnie was referring to their first big trip together, almost a decade earlier. A spring break spree at a Mexican resort with curvy pools and swim-up bars, when they were both more prone to impulsive dives into the deep end of things.

"I'm not going to think about it," Chad said. His turn for an existential hiccup. He coughed and readjusted his grip on the backpack. He closed his eyes and vigorously shook his head.

Cut to a flashback: Chad with a ponytail and Winnie with hair down to her butt as freshmen at the University of Vermont and Massachusetts respectively, partying at a resort in Cancún. Both nursing hangovers. Spur of the moment, they sign up for a day trip bus tour of some Mayan ruins inland. They sit together in the front row of the resort bus, just behind the driver. To avoid a traffic jam on the main highway to Mérida, the bus driver veers off on a shortcut that takes them into hardscrabble back country. Milpa fields and thorny agave. A gravel road bouncing through small villages of low stone walls and elliptical, one-room houses and dirt basketball courts. On the thatched-roof outskirts of an unnamed village, a young girl with black hair and a pink bow on her head and obsidian eyes chases a loose soccer ball into the road and, screech, the front fender of the bus hits her, knocking her bleeding and unconscious into a ditch. A noisy crowd assembles. Several of the men clutch machetes. A three-legged dog hops around the body. Two elderly women wrap the girl in a shroud. The body is still twitching. The bus driver climbs out and launches into heated debate with the men. Chad hears them through the open door and understands enough of the Spanish to comprehend that they are arguing about a payoff, about how much it will cost to allow the bus to leave the scene. Chad steps out and looks down at the girl and she stares back up at him and her dark eyes flutter. He reaches for his wallet and produces three Ben Franklins and it seals the deal. Three hundred bucks for the kid's life, to the relief of Chad's frightened peers. The bus full of spring breakers revs up and continues down the road to visit the *ruinas* at the nearby town of Ciudad de la Gruta. Chad is their hero. But Chad does not feel like a hero. The incident figures thereafter in recurring dreams about his complicity in a secret crime, and his increasing pot and pill consumption.

"A lot of cumulus in the sky today," Chad said.

"Do you want me to go for the rental car?"

"I'll get it," Chad said.

"What is that noise?"

"Cicadas," Chad said.

The August torpor outside the Indianapolis airport grabbed at their skin and the scree of cicadas assaulted their ears. A fat sun ballooned higher above the control tower. Slanting beams generated heat mirages that, from a sidestep angle, revealed gauzy clouds of miniscule, fluttering gnats. Chad and Winnie slapped at the bugs.

"It's a jungle out here."

"I'll go for the car. You wait back inside."

Winnie pointed to Chad's hip pocket and said, "Wallet? Money clip?"

Chad, a chronic loser of wallets and passports and keys, slapped at his chest and hips. "Check, check, got it." He philosophically tried to spin his short-term memory malfunctions as a virtue: non-attachment. "In the big picture, babe, it's only material stuff."

An attitude that Winnie thought was sort of cute, when it wasn't a pain in the ass. "Any word from the Pilgrim Relocation Experts?" she asked.

"Nothing since Vincent's truck picked up our stuff," Chad said.

Their furniture and other worldly possessions were being transported to Indiana by a moving company that Chad had hired because it was owned by a former baseball teammate, Vincent Guglielmo, who was possibly not the best choice, according to the idea of once an addict, always an addict. Vincent had been Chad's first dealer in high school. He had been clean for three years, attended meetings, and exercised regularly at the gym. Chad made a point of trying to help his buddies in recovery, come what may.

Chad's father, reverently known as 'Chief,' had recused himself on the transport decision. Usually, Chief weighed in on every aspect of his son's life. Chief O'Shaughnessy, who wore his Rolex twenty-four seven, tightly monitored all things organizational for his family, including color-coded files for summer vacations. If he could, he would organize the air molecules in the house. Not this time. Not for Chad's move to Indiana. Chief called it a "maturity moment."

Chad's status in the family was still tarnished by his drug arrest five years ago and his guilty plea. Last night, at the end of the banquet send-off, Chief O'Shaughnessy placed an arm around his son's shoulder and shared a piece of family history, previously unknown to Chad, about a black sheep great uncle who had been given a one-way train ticket to Indianapolis in 1912 and never heard from again. This was disturbing. It only reinforced Chad's position, still questionable because of his recent genealogical research. He had sent in hair samples, collected from shower drains at the family Cape Cod cottage, for DNA analysis and had announced in a toast at the banquet that they were all part Neanderthal. This caused Chad's grandmother to choke on her beef tenderloin and Chief to break her rib performing the Heimlich maneuver.

Chad, an inveterate mouth-breather when in deep thought, pondered the fate of his mysterious great uncle and coughed up a gnat and shook off a niggling fear that he too might disappear in Hoosierland and never be heard from again.

Winnie interrupted, "Hello, pal? You okay?"

He snapped to and saluted and stroked her cheek and said, "Back in five with the wheels. Maybe you should try eating a banana or something." Blood sugar could be an issue for Winnie.

Winnie Marsh straddled her suitcase and dug out a banana and a phone from her purse and started scrolling through messages. Many were from her mother, Prudence. The lady with the enormous purse. A graying

Girl Scout who subscribed to the 'Be Prepared' code, Prudence Marsh carried her enormous purse everywhere, hanging from the crook of her left arm, even weighing in at the doctor. *Bing.* Another text appeared from Prudence. She was already suffering from her only daughter's absence and demanding photos and updates on Facebook.

Winnie started to reply, but hesitated. Oh fuck, who used Facebook anymore, except the old folks? Amid last night's many stay-in-touch admonitions, Winnie had tipsily promised to post frequently, and her current posture – balanced on the suitcase with the banana – would make a good selfie. Good as in cute. Good as in amusing. Good as in conveying appropriate self-care with nutrition. But, enough is enough, Mother. We have to draw the line somewhere. Winnie, beset with her own anxieties, felt done with curating her moods to mollify Prudence.

Winnie took the easy way out. Blame it on Chad and his lifestyle scruples. "We're swearing off social media for a while. Sorry. Chad's idea." It was true. Chad had extracted a vow of a social media moratorium in order to experience this new place and this new chapter undiluted. "Sorry, but that's the way it is. We need to respect Chad's opinion on this. It's just one of his phases, like butter pecan." Over and out. Winnie turned off her phone.

Chad honked and pulled up to the curb in a white Chrysler C-300. He popped the trunk and began loading their bags. Winnie's husky voice belied her soft features. She rasped, "Why did you get this big-ass car?"

"Because I like a big ass," Chad said, whacking her on the rump. "Let's live a little."

And for two rippling, wind-in-the-hair hours they did. They cruised at eighty miles per hour down the freshly-paved Interstate-69 toward Evansville, windows open to the sultry air. The radio spouting genuine country music. Chad improvised some lyrics: *"I wanna sniff yoooo all over, baby, better than glue."* They traded smirks that signaled a renewed optimism for their Cave City endeavor.

A post-stoner moment ensued. Another of Chad's recovery quirks: spontaneous utterances that surfaced from a few permanently zonked brain cells. Chad surveyed the busy traffic, three lanes moving at a frantic clip, and announced, "Just like I-95, Professor. Just like home. They got real traffic here too. Huzzah. Ain't it great? Mutually cruising on the razor's edge of catastrophe with complete strangers in speeding pods of steel. Trusting our mortal existence to smoothly pumping pistons and ball bearings. Truly, lemme tell you, fast-lane traffic is humanity's greatest expression of our faith in the good will of others. It's the altruistic gene writ large. Can you feel the connection? We're like one mass organism here. Totally reliant on my compadres in the next lane not to screw us all over."

"That's an interesting observation, dear," Winnie said, glancing at her passenger side mirror and noticing, a quarter mile back, a pickup truck loaded with migrant workers, all standing in the bed, swerving off momentarily into a guardrail in a profusion of sparks and smoke. Chad, eyes front, did not see it, and Winnie decided not to tell him.

Chad sang, "Army beans and Army gravy make me wish I'd joined the Navy…"

He reached for the turn signal and veered off at the next exit. He ran into the Quickie Mart and emerged a few minutes later, complaining that the bathroom was out of order. The clerk had urged him to go pee in the bushes behind the loading dock. It was a cornfield, actually. Following Chief O'Shaughnessy's rule that one must always purchase something in exchange for using the bathroom, even if only a cornfield, Chad carried a bag of chips and two Big Gulp sodas.

Winnie broke open the chips, as Chad accelerated back onto the highway. She resolutely announced, "We are in the boonies."

"So it appears," Chad said and pumped a fist.

"*Must* run away," Winnie said. This was another of her code-phrases, especially towards the end of a semester. She sucked on the Big Gulp soda. A thought surfaced that 'running away' might be a provocative post along with a photo of herself and Chad in matching Colts jerseys, which would certainly annoy her mother and her brother. Winnie often insisted on wearing matching t-shirts as a way to feel coupled.

They passed an exit sign for a town named 'Gnaw Bone.'

"Did you see that?"

"I think so."

"Did any of the guidebooks mention anything about cannibals?" Winnie asked.

"No, there was no mention of cannibals. I'm sure there's a perfectly good explanation for why a town would be named, 'Gnaw Bone.' Just not sure what it is."

Winnie said, "I could make that the first research assignment for my students. Go find the origin of the name 'Gnaw Bone,' Indiana."

They drove on south and west and eyed the expansive cornfields, the undulant highway, and the tall, speckled sycamores with cows huddled underneath, flicking tails at the flies. Overhead, turkey buzzards floated around bulbous thunderheads. A red barn with a collapsed roof featured a spray-painted announcement on the barn door: "LAP DANCES evry fri. nite."

"We are truly in the wild," Chad said.

"Some serious rural action here," Winnie agreed.

Their rubber-necking and straw-sucking gurgles gradually grew into a mutual acknowledgement that this could be okay. Their ability to travel well together might be enough to sustain what was otherwise going to be a risky year. This could be just what they needed, a thousand miles of individuation between them and their preppie families.

Winnie said, "I forgot to tell you about an exchange with my brother last night. I was talking about my dissertation research. How I recently stumbled onto some early family financial records and discovered that a chunk of our inherited dough originally came from rum and slaves in Santo Domingo. When I suggested that we might think about some kind of reparations divestment, he just laughed, like I was making a joke. That dumb-little-sister laugh."

Chad responded, "Making amends. One of the critical steps. I understand."

He reached over and stroked her head and pushed the moment too far. "Maybe we won't come back. We could stay and raise little Hoosier babies."

Winnie harrumphed and returned the gesture with a punch on his arm. It was playful, but – oops – hard enough that she accidentally spilled the Big Gulp into his lap. Twenty ounces plus ice.

"Oh, no. Ouch, sorry."

"My nuts are freezing off. Goodbye Hoosier babies."

Chad turned abruptly onto the next exit ramp, an unpopulated exchange which accessed County Road 62. A couple of lonely billboards stood at the edge of the woods. One advertised the trophy-stuffing services of a local taxidermist. Another featured a law enforcement official on a rearing white horse, with the caption: 'Sheriff Hooker wants to be YOUR next Mayor.' Chad pulled over into the mossy shade of a maple grove. The navigational device on the dashboard of the Chrysler C-300 admonished him: "Mistake. Go back."

Chad barked at the dashboard, "Shaddup."

"What are you doing?" Winnie asked, cautiously. Chad, like his red-faced father, was prone to quixotic temper flares.

"Changing my pants."

He stepped out and opened the trunk and dug through his suitcase for a pair of Bermudas. He pulled off his wet jeans and underwear and threw them in the backseat. To demonstrate his restored calm, he hopped bare-assed around to Winnie's window and mooned her. It lightened the mood. Life was always better in shorts. Chad's fat-thigh, wrestler build never fit well in trousers. At boarding school, Chad was the kid wearing a too-tight blazer and tie-over shorts and docksiders.

Just before reentering the car, he noticed a gray, lichen-covered stone in the weeds beside the road. An old-style mile marker. He bent to examine the incised lettering and reported to Winnie, "Look, just like the ones back home. 'Cave City – 15 miles.' Let's take this road."

To appease him for the spill, and secretly envying his impetuousness, Winnie said, "Sure. Lead on. We're in no rush."

The GPS again bleated, "Mistake. Go back." Chad flashed a middle finger at the device and punched it off.

Winnie admired Chad's looser relationship to technology. It was different from her own indentured servitude to devices. In college, when confronted by worried sorority sisters who were concerned about her rollercoaster thing with bad boy Chad O'Shaughnessy, she explained it as an "opposites-attract vibe."

"Can I ask you a personal question?" Winnie said.

"What's ever stopped you before?"

"Do you really think we can pull this off?" Winnie said, "I'm sure there's a betting pool back in Boston and the odds are probably running 3-1 against."

Chad nodded. "Every baseball coach since Little League has said that I thrive on adversity."

"Right, I knew that," Winnie said, "but I didn't really know that."

"I've had a lot of near misses, but you're the only near Missus who I really dig," Chad assured her with a grin.

They curved south and sharply west again on the two-lane road that hugged the farm perimeters. A train whistle blew mellifluously in the distance. They passed a roadside shrine embellished with two bronzed baby shoes. They passed a scarecrow affixed to a rusting tractor, a sign for the Rushing Wind Bikers Church, and a beauty salon in a garage – 'Timeless Hair Creations.' They passed a hand-painted sign in Spanish for a nearby medical clinic.

"What the hell, more Spanish?" Chad said.

A honk from behind and Chad slowed as their car was overtaken by the pick-up truck with the migrant workers in back, two of them bleeding from head wounds. Chad stared quizzically. Who are those hombres? A couple miles on, another turn south brought a new landscape. The soybean and corn fields ended. Horizontality ceased, as if a historical marker had announced: "The glaciers stop here." The earth's surface creased and sank.

The Chrysler 300 slowed and descended from the tabletop of corn and soybeans down into dark emerald, wooded ravines. The road narrowed and the asphalt crumbled and gave way to gravel.

"Somebody needs to pump in some daylight."

"Good smells," Winnie said, of the forest floor loam.

"Did we miss a turn?" A bent sign indicated that they were no longer on County Road 62. Now they were on Curling Shingles Road.

"Feels like a long time since we've seen another car," Winnie said.

"The next one will probably be a Model-T."

"Or a horse and buggy coming out of that covered bridge."

Another reminder of their home turf. A red timber bridge straddled the banks of a wide, sandy creek. The span was longer than the New England variety and in worse repair.

"Whoa, horsey," Chad said, as he braked and eased down a steep hill and rolled to a stop at the mouth of the wooden tunnel. Cracks of light in the ceiling and walls streaked across the floor planking. Chad switched off the engine.

"Why are we stopping?" Winnie asked.

"Looking for a load-limit sign," Chad said, "I don't know if our rig can make it across."

He stepped out to inspect the venerable structure. He pointed to a long, spray-painted graffiti scrawl that read: "*Vota por la Ciudad Hermana!*"

"More Spanish stuff," Chad called to Winnie.

"What does it mean?"

"'Vote for Sister City.' Are you sure we haven't accidentally ended up in New Mexico?"

Somebody laughed a deep, belly laugh. Somebody under the bridge. "No, but you did somehow stumble into the ass-end of the county."

"Who's there, a troll?" Chad called.

"Be careful what you say. The bridge is haunted," the voice replied.

A splash of waders kicking through shallow water. The troll emerged with a fly rod and feathery hooks on his vest. Another classic, dark-eyed face. The quintessentially handsome, intrepid, soulful Latino male, with a million-dollar smile.

Except this one spoke with an apple-pie twang. "Howya doing? Are you folks lost?" He climbed up the creek bank and laid down his gear and shimmied around in his waders and arranged his hair with a quick finger comb. He walked over and offered a handshake to Chad, who pushed open his car door and slid out.

Chad said, "It appears so. We're trying to find Cave City."

"You don't say. Really?"

"My fiancée has a teaching job there that starts the day after tomorrow."

"Cross the bridge and take the next left. Cave City is just a couple miles down the road. I'm Frank Vigo. I teach at the college."

"Southwest Hoosier State?"

"Yep. Love it or leave it," Frank Vigo said.

"Why do you say that?"

"I've been there a long time."

"Well, Frank, we're only planning to stay for a year. I'm Chad O'Shaughnessy and this lady here with me, Winnie Marsh, she's one of your new hires."

Frank Vigo smiled and stood up straighter and waved.

Winnie, a tad embarrassed at being seen in her dusty travel duds with a lap full of chips and a Big Gulp, eased out of the car and stepped around to greet her colleague. To distract from her nervousness, she reached over to Chad and wiped a sunscreen smudge off his nose.

"Winnie Marsh, pleased to meet you," Frank Vigo said, "I'm in the Folklore Department. I read your dissertation. It was a hoot."

Winnie specialized in the folklore of parties and games in the Colonial Era. Puzzle jugs and fuddling cups. Her dissertation focused on the Dutch in New Amsterdam. They were hard-core partiers. Her choice of specialty is a bit compensatory, because socially, Winnie herself was a chronic wallflower, starting as a kid at her own birthday parties, fleeing to a birds-eye perch at the top of the staircase, and later, in college, the lone figure outside on the porch swing. Admiring it all from a distance, professionally and personally.

"Thank you," Winnie sputtered, "Amusing material is one of the perks of our field."

Frank Vigo said, "New Amsterdam in the 17th century must have been a rollicking scene. The lawsuits for all the broken windows caused by playing golf in the streets. And the emergency order during the lean times requiring farmers to use grain for bread instead of making beer. One can only imagine how things would be different if the Dutch and the Spanish had maintained their hold in North America."

"Speaking of the Spanish," Chad interrupted, before the academic shop talk got too cozy. He pointed to the graffiti on the bridge. "Has there been a recent influx here? What is this 'Sister City' bit?"

Frank Vigo produced another fulsome laugh. It allowed Winnie to better appreciate his compliment about her dissertation. This guy liked to laugh.

Frank answered, "Cave City has a sister-city agreement with a town in the Yucatán, Mexico. It started back at the turn of the century, thanks to some local movers and shakers; Delmar Butz and his friend, Professor Ignacio Morales, and Mayor Rex Blaine, an idealistic young guy who wanted to make his mark. Rex was the first politician in these parts to put on a sombrero and eat a taco. Although now our former mayor is a congressman and doesn't seem to remember ever living here."

Winnie asked, "What's the name of the town in Mexico?"

"Ciudad de la Gruta."

"We've been there," Chad and Winnie chimed. "We've been to the Mayan ruins."

The train whistle sounded again in the distance. Chad slapped at some bugs on his neck. Winnie tightened her hair bun and extracted her yellow pencil and re-inserted it. They shared a furtive, wondering glance that silently asked, "Is this weird?"

Frank Vigo continued, "The Sister City relationship becomes more complicated when you factor in the archeology. Excavations in our local

Indian mound have turned up Mayan artifacts that appear to have come from the Ciudad de la Gruta region. Our sister-cityhood may have actually begun a thousand years ago."

"And what's this about a haunted bridge?" Chad asked.

Frank's mirth disappeared. "Tragic tale," he sighed, "Spanish colonials have been in these parts since the 1600s. When, as Winnie is aware, Spain controlled everything up the Mississippi, my family a case in point. I grew up in nearby New Madrid. Of course, you remember the famous Revolutionary War hero, George Rogers Clark, who took Vincennes from the British while having a love affair with a señorita, whose brother was the Governor of the Spanish Territory."

Winnie swallowed and said, "Actually I'm a bit vague on the Old Northwest."

"No problem. Fast-forward to the 1890s and the Spanish-American War, and the beautiful daughter of the college president here. She shocks the town by committing suicide at age nineteen. Standard burial practice at that time allows the family to dress the body at home for placement in the casket. And in doing so, the president's wife discovers that her daughter is pregnant. Suspicion and angry rumors abound. The girl had recently been seen in the company of the Spanish professor at the college. He was a young gentleman, also from New Madrid. They were seen courting right here on this bridge. A mob forms and drags him from his classroom and they lynch him from the crossbeam at the far end of the bridge. Right over there."

"That's awful," Winnie said.

Chad squinted through the tunnel to the dim opening at the other end, as if the body might still be dangling from the beam. "Do you think our car can make it across?"

"Sure, if you go slowly. And, if you don't mind giving me a ride back to town," Frank said, "I'll show you the way and help get you settled."

Chad answered, "Good, thanks. And, by the way, I'm from Boston, so I have to ask – did you catch any fish?"

Another deep belly laugh. "Only you two," Frank said.

In the winding creek, still waters were running deep. Crayfish and a swirling cloud of minnows, a few bluegill and, lower down, fat, whiskered catfish hovered at the bottom, near a previously undiscovered trove of flint-knapped spear points embedded in slick clay.

Cut to: the white Chrysler C-300 rolling across the dim, creaky bridge. Slivers of daylight morph into ghosts. Figures slip through the cracks in the planking. Mayan traders and early mound builders and Indian hunters and the college president's daughter and the hanged Spanish professor. All flowing around the car, but invisible to the car's occupants, as Chad drives slowly, unblinkingly, through the dim tunnel toward an arch of green light on the other side, creating the impression that Chad O'Shaughnessy and Winnie Marsh have no clue what they're getting into.

2.

Nearby, on the same creek, another arrival after a long journey via the Wabash tributary and the Ohio and Mississippi rivers. This one by canoe, a thousand years ago, long before motor cars and the covered bridge. The early Mississippian and Hopewell peoples having expanded out from the caves to build platform mounds with conical temples and a chief's lodge on top, with granaries and round houses and corn cribs below, along with drying racks for fish and animal skins, especially eel skins. Fatty eels that swim up the rivers, annually, like Mayan canoes. The eels are an important source of nourishment. Their strong, shiny skins are prized for making belts and necklaces, popular trade items with the Maya.

This Hopewell village is enclosed on three-sided sides by a daub and wattle stockade that fronts the riverbank. The oblong mounds surround a central plaza that is used for assemblies and for the ritual playing of the chunkey game. It is a style of urban planning originally inspired by their Mesoamerican visitors.

Cook fires breathe ribbons of smoke into a glistening cobweb morning. The sun sends long probes into the Oracle Cave. Birdsong fills the forest, the co-co-coo of mourning doves. The village rings with expectant shouts and whistles as it prepares for the Maya travelers from across the big water. Per instructions from the excitable Priestess Dawn, who has recently dreamed of her beloved Mayan counterpart, Priestess Moon. She senses her approach. Both are young, butch, single, 'third-sex' beings whose priestly status wards off unwanted male advances. Their main job within their respective tribal hierarchies is to chant, to sing each day into existence. To inflate the sky each morning with prayers directed from the heart. And then turn the job over to the night person, the star chanter, usually a long-in-the-tooth elder who doesn't sleep much anyway.

Children and dogs frolic at the water's edge. Scouts climb high in the oak trees, up onto the sky-burial rigs, loincloths flapping. They yell an alert. Everyone pauses and turns at the sound of a collective murmur. Everybody looks out beyond the sandbar and sees the clouds parting to admit a radiant light show. Streaked, bent, rainbow-like arches extending down from sky to earth. Hoops of light connecting all things and all beings and all time.

Out there, just beyond the laundry station on the sand bar. Here they come! A cheer for a convoy of outriggers nosing around the bend, paddling around the point. Blue jays and cardinals swoop down in greeting and ogle the sturdy vessels and the short, stocky Maya paddlers who have survived the long journey from the Yucatán. One personage in particular is visible at the front of the lead canoe, wearing a feathered headdress, singing full-throated, arms outstretched.

Clad in a ceremonial robe given to her by Priestess Moon on the last visit, Priestess Dawn runs down from the temple mound and wades quickly into the channel, waist deep, toward the embrace of Priestess Moon. She leans in for a tight squeeze and *splash*, over they go, along with several baskets of gifts. Quickly retrieved, amid gales of laughter from all.

At least, that's how I imagine it. The vaporous 'I' cogitating in a hundred-degree heat trance. Sipping tequila in my dim, steamy, expat cave. La Sombra Azul in Ciudad de la Gruta. The Mayan name for it: *Aaktun kaaj*. Cave Village. The town from whence Priestess Moon embarked, once upon a time. Picturing the joyous meeting between the two soulmate Amazons, both recently orphaned. Gazing down on their village festivities, as if from one of my circling drones.

Like all expats, I am prone to fits of nostalgia. And lately, I look back on my 1970s childhood in southern Indiana as a gauzy Eden. Back when we foster child urchins still played jump-rope and used firecrackers to blow up G.I. Joes and Barbie dolls (a prelude to my later career) and ran barefoot in the woods and climbed trees and explored the caves without certified guides, where we not only hunted for arrowheads, but actually found them. Back when I, the vaporous 'I,' watched black-and-white westerns on TV and believed that white hats meant good guys and black hats meant bad guys.

Full confession. I am not really like all expats. I am not one of the retired or disabled oilmen who frequent the cantinas here, complaining that their seven-year honeymoon is over. It usually takes about seven years for expats to start asking: What am I doing here? Complaining that Guatemala is cheaper. Opining that the Yucatán, being a peninsula, functions more like an island, meaning that the native population, though outwardly warm, remains coldly suspicious of foreigners.

I have a nickname. They call me 'El Drone.' A few people recognize my scarred face. I am the mayor's right-hand mystery man. I live in semi-hiding, a sort of nomadic Witness Protection Program that keeps me out of the clutches of the narcos and my former employer, the DEA. The mayor moves me around between several weed-infested, abandoned mansions scattered around the city, structures leftover from the green-gold henequen era. I run the mayor's 'Eye in the Sky' drone program, souped-up quadcopters with Zenmuse 4K cameras. Also, as an erstwhile Hoosier, I function as a political advisor for the Sister City referendum campaign. Granted, there are a few ethical concerns with my surveillance drones, but they have reduced criminal activity, particularly the nine to five kidnapping business. Rich kid grabbed on the way to school at 9 a.m. Parents informed via text from the kid's phone, along with information on the drop. Parents hustle to the bank for cash. Kid home for dinner by 5 p.m. The mayor's ratings are way up, for now.

The mayor of Ciudad de la Gruta also has a nickname, El Plástico. It is a bit more prosaic. He is named for his do-gooder habit of walking daily from his home in the old barrio of Santa Lucía to his office at City Hall, picking up plastic bottles along the way. Just a few of the millions of flattened, crinkly plastic bottles that line the streets of every rural town around here. In Priestess Moon's era, they would have been pottery shards and they might have had a purpose in firming up the roadbed. Today, we have the recycling program, which is another of El Plástico's initiatives. Any enterprising *pobre* with a cart or a burlap bag can gather up bottles and take them to the recycling center at the airport and receive a hundred pesos in return.

Would Priestess Dawn and Priestess Moon be able to recognize their respective home turfs today? Both limestone karst topographies remain unchanged, as do the hills and *colinas*. Ciudad de la Gruta is not far from the Ruta Puuc. Limestone is everywhere in both locales. Schools, churches, fire stations, post offices, chunks of slag in the alleys. Cave City and Ciudad de la Gruta. The Yucatán limestone was used to build the Mayan temples at Chichén Itzá and Uxmal. The stone from Cave City was used to construct more modern temples, the Empire State Building and Yankee Stadium. A fitting coincidence that the town of my youth and the town of my midlife crisis are made of the same stuff. Both are places where time stopped, as the saying goes.

Correction. This is not a fair description of these two burgs. More like Time swerved to avoid an errant cow or pig or an escaped flock of backyard chickens and ran into a ditch and splintered into a thousand different pieces, reflecting aspects of last year, last century, last millennium.

Viz: The Saturday farmers' market on the courthouse square and the Sunday flea market on the *plaza grande*. Blind people selling brooms on downtown street corners. Avenues in both towns closed off for pedestrians and bicycles on the weekends. Happy Dan's Hotdogs in Cave City and Lourdes' Taco Stand in Ciudad de la Gruta. Both grilling meat outside the wrought-iron gates to the cemeteries. And there is always some poor guy on a curb, hunched in that archetypal pose – the squat. The squatters watch the diminishing trickle of commercial life in the town centers. A couple pool halls and shoe repair shops and sporting goods stores holding on. And also a storefront Visitors Center, where an elderly volunteer hands out Sister City bumper stickers and keychains. And don't forget the mutual fixation on corn. The Corn Queen. The Maize Princess. Everyone loves a teenage beauty pageant. Giant silos smack in the middle of both *centros*, beside the railroad tracks. Closed drive-in movie theaters and failing strip malls on the scrubby edges of the industrial zones. And the improvised Friday night parade on Main Street and Avenue Hidalgo, when the farm boys and the *campesinos* cruise by in mud-splattered pick-ups, waving and whistling to the lovers draped together on the sidewalk benches. Women in both towns known by their recipes, Señora Tres Leches Cake and Mrs. Persimmon Pudding. My foster mother long reigned as Mrs. Cornmeal Mush. Let it harden, cut it, fry it.

Both cities are island-like hives, surrounded by quasi-impregnable terrain, hot tundra and second-growth forest. Their civic governments, ancient and modern, before the invention of air-conditioning, retreated to the caves in the hot summer to hold council meetings in the cool, rock chambers. And, at least once a year, citizens are forced to organize search parties to rescue overly adventurous youngsters who stray from the spelunking tours into the dank tunnel recesses.

The walls of both cave systems feature paint-blown ochre silhouettes of prehistoric hands and also diagrammatic petroglyphs that, even as a child, I sensed were actually maps of the snaking waterway route between the two regions. Recently, a graduate student in archeology at Southwest Hoosier State, a Native American woman named Night Snow, has confirmed my hypothesis in a published paper. The petroglyphs are roadmaps. Her work was picked up and reprinted on the Sister City website. We are not exactly contemporaries, she and I. Night Snow is younger, in her early thirties. I knew her only by reputation, before I left town. In addition to her spelunking skills, teenage Night Snow was known for making Cave City men out of Cave City boys. Oh, she was a daring red fox.

More on that later.

3.

The Elbow Room was the Cave City equivalent of La Sombra Azul. A town and gown watering hole, equidistant from campus and the courthouse square. Pressed tin ceilings with a collection of NASCAR bobble-heads displayed above shelves of liquor bottles. Originally a speakeasy, the Elbow Room was an institution, revered by all, except the sangria drinkers who complained that the bartender mixed Hawaiian Punch with Sprite.

After a quick tour of the Southwest Hoosier State campus and a stop at the Buena Vista apartments, Frank Vigo invited Chad and Winnie to the Elbow Room for a late lunch. The campus, originally the site of a seminary, is a typical assemblage of classroom buildings and dormitories, situated around the library and the chapel, with quads and diags and brick walkways shaded by stately beech trees, whose longest, lowest limbs were supported by carved crutches.

Amid the move-in activity at the Buena Vista apartments, there was no sign of the Pilgrim Relocation truck. Chad texted and phoned Vincent Guglielmo twice, without any response. Winnie's stomach growled her annoyance. The ever-present cicada screeching sounded like a thousand loose fan belts. Frank directed their attention to the Mexican American War Memorial. They walked around the pigeon-covered statuary. Chad tried calling Vincent again. Nothing. The sun glared overhead like an interrogation lamp.

Frank said, "Not to worry. Let's go eat some lunch and your furniture will be here when we get back."

"Do we walk or drive?"

"It's just a few blocks. We can walk. I'll show you the courthouse square too."

As they entered the revolving front door of the Elbow Room, located in a former Grange Hall, a corn-silk blonde waitress turned from a customer and whistled greetings. Another waitress scurried off to clear a booth at the back. This was apparently Frank's regular booth. Make way, folks, for a popular guy. Patrons and staff nodded greetings as Frank and Chad and Winnie paraded to the far corner. Frank exchanged high-fives with former students at the bar.

"Do they have a sandwich named after you?" Winnie asked.

"Not yet," Frank said, "Unless you count the frankfurter."

Frank's booth was located next to a public telephone. They sat down and Chad swiveled and reached over for the phonebook, hanging on a chain.

"Calling a lawyer?" Winnie said, still perturbed about the moving van delay. Vincent had personally guaranteed that his driver and the truck would be waiting upon their arrival.

"I'm checking for an O'Shaughnessy," Chad said, "Remember Chief's story last night about the family black sheep who was exiled from Boston to Indianapolis."

Frank Vigo laughed and said, "You might be in luck, though not good luck. There is an O'Shaughnessy who lives out in the county. Brakeless Eddy, he's called. A dangerous dude. Runs a brake repair shop in his barn. Goes off his meds every so often and comes in here packing heat and rants about his great-grandpappy being cheated out of an inheritance back in Boston. If he's your relative, probably best to be avoided."

Winnie grunted and said, "Sounds like one of Chad's family." She perked up as she eyed a platter of onion rings and frosted mugs of root beer in the next booth.

"That's what I'm having," she said.

"The root beer is home made," Frank said, and signaled for a round.

"This place reeks of local color," Chad said.

"'Reeks' being the operative word," Frank agreed. He turned and responded to several more howdys from the row of customers at the long, zinc bar. A doctor in surgical scrubs and a striking woman with eagle feathers woven into a black braid.

"You still have Indians here?" Chad asked.

"A token few," Frank nodded.

"What tribe?"

"Mostly Shawnee."

"Descendants of the mound builders?" Winnie asked.

"That one is harder to figure," Frank replied, "No one really knows what happened to them."

Chad said, "My buddy, Vincent, our furniture mover, ascribes to the theory that they were taken away in a spaceship."

"Yeah, I've heard that theory," Frank said.

"Vincent is a junkie," Winnie said, "You think that'll be his excuse when our truck disappears – that our furniture was taken away by a spaceship?"

Chad put a hand on her arm. "It'll be okay. I'm sure the driver is just stuck in traffic or something."

Frank redirected the conversation. "That Indian lady over there. Her name is Night Snow. She's in the archeology department. You'll meet her eventually. She's a fixture."

"Frank, it seems like you're kind of a vortex person," Chad said, "You know everybody."

Frank shrugged and shook his head. "Not really, it's just that I'm the token gay. I'm the gay faculty member. I'm the gay school board member. I'm the gay guy on the board of the neighborhood association. And people want to know me so they can think they're open minded."

"That can be a little lonely," Winnie said.

"True," Frank said and tried to laugh it off, but this laugh didn't come as easily.

Winnie raised her root beer mug. "Here's to you, Frank. You've been very kind to us and as long as we're here, you've got a friend."

"Thank you, Winnie Marsh," Frank said.

Winnie borrowed one of Chad's lines. "Come on, Frank. When somebody toasts you, look them straight in the eye, or else you'll have seven years of bad sex – "

"I'll take it," Frank said quickly, and they all laughed.

Winnie and Frank veered off into a conversation about prepping for the first day of classes and an upcoming faculty meeting. Chad gazed off at the other figures lining the bar, including a robed priest. He tried to think about his own job prospects, or lack thereof, and he also imagined Brakeless Eddy among the crowd and wondered if there was any merit to his inheritance beef. Would Chad's family ever admit it? Would Chief ever deign to meet Brakeless Eddy? Probably not.

Chad sipped his root beer. He overheard Frank Vigo mention his role as faculty advisor to the Southwest Hoosier State Ballroom Dance Club, which involved driving the team to competitive dances at Vincennes and Evansville. Chad knew what was coming next. Side step, slide, step...

"Honey, this is our big chance. We can finally learn how to rhumba," Winnie said.

Chad forced a nod and a grin. Learning to dance was a self-improvement project that Winnie, the chronic wallflower, and Chad, the tough-guy-who-doesn't-dance, had often discussed as a worthy goal, but it wasn't high on his list at the moment.

"I need to get a job first," Chad said, somewhat illogically.

"What kind of work are you looking for?" Frank Vigo asked.

Friendly as hell, this Frank guy. Hard not to like, but Chad shook his head. It was still hard to refer to himself a counselor, due to a case of rookie imposter syndrome.

"Just tell him," Winnie said.

Chad disclosed the basic information about his counseling degree and the addictions focus.

Winnie chimed in, "People have always opened up to Chad. They tell him all sorts of personal things. I think that it's because when he listens, he tilts his head like a dog. Clients are always saying to him, 'I've never told anybody that before.'"

Frank Vigo responded with statistics about the increase in opioid and meth abuse among the student population and the townies. It was even worse out in the county. He offered encouragement that Chad's services were sorely needed around here, except for one glitch. The university's social work program produced an annual crop of counselors who gobbled up the agency jobs. Frank pointed to the robed priest standing over at the bar and said, "You should talk to Father Mike. He's got a huge flock, many of whom self-medicate with substances, because they can't afford anything else, and he's making referrals all the time. Would you like me to introduce you?"

"Go for it," Winnie said, "This is your chance."

Chad rubbed his red soul patch and looked down at his shorts and bare knees and said, "I'm not exactly dressed for an interview."

Frank said, "Not to worry. Underneath that robe, Father Mike is probably wearing shorts too. He's a new priest who gives sermons based on Star Trek theology, in an attempt to fill the pews with a younger crowd. Whenever he hears any scoffers, he exclaims, 'For God's sake, wake up, you're on a spaceship this very minute, and we're all hurtling through the Milky Way.'

Chad reached over and squeezed Winnie's hand and said, "Okay, no time like the present. Let's do it."

Just as he started to rise and scoot out of the booth, a loud clatter sounded from the street. Horseshoes on pavement. A hefty man in a law enforcement uniform and a white cowboy hat on a chestnut horse rode up to the door. A small woman perched on the saddle behind him. Two deputies with video cameras ran alongside and circled the scene. The horse snorted and stamped. The man doffed his white cowboy hat to the cameras and twirled his mustache and pulled his right leg over the pommel and slid down and deftly lifted the petite woman off the horse. She was slathered in make-up and costumed in a bright *huipil*.

"Behold our illustrious Sheriff," Frank Vigo explained to his lunch guests, "along with his current girlfriend, Chica, who everyone calls 'Malinche' behind her back. You know, the lady who allegedly betrayed Montezuma. Sheriff Hooker squires Chica around town to demonstrate that he doesn't hate all Latinos. They must be doing a campaign commercial. He's running for mayor."

"A low budget commercial," Chad said.

"We saw a billboard by the highway," Winnie said, "'Sheriff Hooker wants to be YOUR next mayor.'"

"Right. The subtext being, 'and not THEIR Mayor,'" Frank said.

Cameras rolling, the Sheriff nodded and waved and proceeded to enter the revolving door of the Elbow Room with his painted girlfriend and the cameramen in tow. Perhaps the goal was to capture some hearty, man-of-the-people footage. Oops, the revolving door stuck on the Sheriff's gut and jammed and pinched Chica's calf and she began to cry.

"This is definitely not in the script," Winnie said.

"I don't think there is a script," Frank said. He gestured toward the kitchen. Two Latina waitresses emerged, carrying trays of mugs and food platters. Their eyes bulged as they caught sight of the Sheriff. They hesitated and started to retreat. Flustered and reddening, Sheriff Hooker forced his way through the front entrance. The plexiglass in the door cracked. Boom! The waitresses reacted in fear. They screamed and dropped their trays and began to run for the rear exit.

Sheriff Hooker stumbled free from the encumbering door. Ignoring Chica's plight, he responded instinctively and blew a whistle and lumbered after the escaping waitresses, demanding to see their papers.

This action brought Father Mike into the fray. The peach-fuzz priest reared back from the bar and yelled, "Go pound sand, Sheriff Hooker. I thought we had a deal – no arrests in public places." Father Mike threw off his robes, revealing jean shorts and a Sister City t-shirt underneath. He gave chase after the Sheriff.

Frank Vigo sighed glumly. He slumped back into the booth and said, "Maybe we can all go to church on Sunday and I'll introduce you then."

"That would make my mother happy," Winnie said.

Up and down the bar, a period of stunned silence gave way to a cacophonous debate that sprang up between the supporters of Sheriff Hooker, advocates of a firm stand against the parasitic illegals and their employers, the roofing and drywall contractors, one of whom bluntly claimed, "Hey, we hire these people because they work hard for cheap, and 'Hoosier' originally meant 'hard worker.'"

Chad leaned over and whispered to Frank, "I follow the news and I'm aware this is a big issue, but why is it such a harsh, hot-button topic out here in backwoods Indiana?"

Frank swallowed and replied, "Long story. First, there's the black market in wild ginseng. The immigrants are cutting in on the old boys' harvests from the state forests. And, there are also some leftover grudges from the Mexican-American War."

"You've got to be kidding," Winnie said.

"This area was ground zero for the recruiting of the Second Indiana Volunteers, otherwise known as the 'Fleeing Indianians,' because they broke and ran at the battle of Buena Vista in 1846. Let it be said, the Volunteers had been betrayed by their own government with imperialist promises of land and booty, instead receiving only disease and hunger. Somewhere far down in the collective Cave City psyche is a deep fear of Mexicans and a distrust of Washington, D.C., making them vulnerable to a rabble-rouser like Sheriff Hooker. There is a painful, historic memory here of getting their asses kicked by the Mexicans on the first day at Buena Vista."

"And the Mexican-American War plaza near our apartment is an attempt to erase that shame?" Winnie asked.

"Yes, but don't say it too loud," Frank nodded.

They watched as the Indian woman and the doctor in blue scrubs spun and slid off their barstools and eased out through the broken front door to aid Chica, small as a minute, crumpled on the sidewalk.

4.

On the other side of town from La Sombra Azul in Ciudad de la Gruta, on the south side of the *plaza grande,* stands the historic city hall. Long ago, it was the royal governor's residence, before the capitol moved to Mérida. First, one must notice the carved horses. Inside the three-storey central courtyard, above the columned entrance to the mayor's office are two carved, wooden steeds. They sit on either side of the mantle above the doors. These horses are iconic figurines that were popular items in the colonial era, many produced in workshops around Ciudad de la Gruta. On top of one horse rides a bishop and underneath, being crushed by a raised hoof, is a lowly Indian. On the other horse rides a prince, and underneath, being crushed by a raised hoof, is a lowly *campesino*. Blatant, raw celebrations of political authority, the power of church and state. The current occupant of the mayor's office, El Plástico, leaves the carved figures in place above his door to remind him daily of how far his country has come. Or, on some days, how far there still is to go.

El Plástico, muscular arms akimbo in his signature white cotton *guayabera,* paces back and forth across the tiled floor of his spacious, top-floor quarters. He pauses beside the arched window that fronts the plaza, the window recently marred by a bullet hole. Must have happened last night? He peers quizzically through the small-bore hole. The dusty town simmers below. His domain, his civic body. Main arterials dotted with yellow, ageless city buses, chugging hither and yon, destinations scrawled in soap on their slanting windshields. On one street corner, an old hippie with a parrot on his shoulder charges tourists a buck for a photo with the green bird. On the opposite corner, student protesters recite their chants against the Sister City referendum. *O, ye children of little faith,* El Plástico thinks.

The city hall was originally constructed from the stones of a Mayan temple on the site. The huge chunks of limestone also form the building material for the nearby church, situated traditionally at a right angle across the main plaza. The re-purposed limestone walls of city hall are pockmarked by bullet indentations, a potshot patina in the soft stone. A local tradition that is supposed to be symbolic, a way for disgruntled citizens to register their dissent. According to the tacit rules, one does not shoot at the venerable, arched window, because that is more dangerous and requires repair work.

El Plástico makes a mental note to ask El Drone to review yesterday's surveillance video. Perhaps it will reveal the culprit. El Plástico strokes his unshaven chin and stares at the hole in the window and wonders if the pistol shot was simply errant – someone drunk in the night – or if it carries a specific message for him. Hanging above El Plástico on the paneled walls, a long row of dusty, gilt-framed portraits of former mayors gazing down quizzically at this poor upstart. How in heaven's name did he join our austere club?

"*Vientidós,*" El Plástico grumbles. One of the local *dichos*, a wisdom saying: Nothing that can't be solved with a .22.

El Plástico knows from experience that all politicians garner a few enemies. And, truth be told, El Plástico has thrived on having a personal enemy, a nemesis, by the name of Ramón Puentes. A dark angel with a reptile grin, ever since childhood. Ramón's pink tongue darting out from perfectly sculpted lips. On the school playground, on the soccer field, at exam time, auditioning for seasonal work as a tray-spinning *vaquero* dancer on a cruise ship, always battling Ramón Puentes. A smart guy, a wily foe. Ramón impressed fellow students and teachers with his Pickle Science demonstrations, in chemistry class and at parties. Relying on the conductive properties of the pickle brine, Ramón would dramatically cut a lamp cord and separate the wiring and touch it to either end of the pickle, until the vegetable fluoresced and exploded.

But a *veintidós* is not Ramón's style. El Plástico cannot think of anyone currently so upset with him as to shoot at his window. Except his lovely, avaricious wife, Mercedes. She is still stewing over his refusal to take the TiendaMax bribe. The Yucatán's big-box superstore. The TiendaMax bribe offer (for a hefty tax abatement and rezoning of the *centro*) was recently delivered in person by Ramón Puentes, in his latest incarnation as the

TiendaMax rep for this region. Mercedes also remains resentful of El Plástico's decision to forego the official mayor's residence in favor of his late parents' bungalow in the barrio Santa Lucía.

Or perhaps the .22 culprit is one of the Sister City student protesters down there on the corner. The supposedly educated students. Maybe even the dashing Juan Pablo Chayac in the red beret. My dear boy. He is El Plástico's adopted son, currently estranged. Shortly after Juan Pablo was rescued from a 9-to-5 kidnapping attempt at age eight, his biological parents fled to Spain. Young Juan Pablo threw a vicious tantrum at the airport and insisted on staying behind. He was abandoned at the airport and El Plástico and Mercedes, unable to produce children of their own, became his guardians. Mercedes spoke of it as their civic duty. Juan Pablo was a bright kid and seemed open to receiving El Plástico's paternal, mentoring attentions, until a political awakening at age seventeen. It was marked by a polarizing moment at the breakfast table, when Juan Pablo proudly announced that Diego Rivera was his new favorite painter, and El Plástico replied, "You'll get over that."

Juan Pablo, editor of the student newspaper, publishes articles in support of a fledgling opposition party, the Radical Synthesizers. Exposing El Plástico's fiefdom and decrying him and his Sister City agreement as outrageous examples of blind subservience to gringo cultural imperialism. A hoary complaint that apparently still has influence among the young. El Plástico checks his calendar. Less than six months now until the Sister City referendum vote.

In the busy street below, the group of student protesters chant and wave placards at the passing traffic. 'Divorce the Greedy Sister.' 'Vote NO to Sister City.' El Plástico closes one eye and peers into the bullet hole in his window, as if looking into a telescope lens. He gazes down at the noisy students and smiles wryly at the memory of a bumper sticker he had seen during his first official trip to Cave City, Indiana – 'Hire a teenager, while they still know everything.'

Immediately surrounding the bullet hole in the window shines an intact circle of fractured, prismatic glass. El Plástico adjusts his gaze and spots the familiar, hunched figure of Ignacio Morales walking slowly with his pool-cue cane across the plaza. And, per habit, the old professor stops to engage the students. Ignacio reaches into his pocket and pulls out a piece of chalk and scrawls some numbers on the wall. Illustrating a point about the economic advantages of the Sister City relationship, one hopes. Thank God for Ignacio Morales.

In the distance El Plástico sees the tallest pyramid at the *ruinas*, the Jaguar Pyramid, silhouetted by the descending, oblong sun. He hears the hourly bell clanging in the baroque church tower. Although the origins of Ciudad de la Gruta go back thousands of years, the modern town dates to the 16th century. A Cortés crony claimed the setting reminded him of his hometown near Madrid, and thus the construction of the white-walled colonial architecture and the grid of small parks and the perimeter wall.

The fractured lens in the mayor's window creates a red, crepuscular halo. For a few moments, El Plástico experiences an unsettling vision. His late mother was a second generation Korean Mexican, from the 19th century boatloads of Koreans snookered into de facto slavery on the henequén plantations. She, and her mother before her, suffered from epileptic hallucinations. They were often about winning the lottery, which she never did. El Plástico's mother scratched out a meager living selling *lotería* tickets in the market and providing services as a professional mourner. An important service not to be dismissed. She claimed to feel the full sadness of the community, and people paid for her effusive grief.

El Plástico has inherited a milder version of her epileptic perturbations of consciousness. He derives an ongoing sense of connection to his mother from the condition, but it doesn't make it easier to undergo a seizure. El Plástico rubs his broad forehead and trembles and stares through the bullet hole and suddenly envisions his city covered in blood. Waves of sun-drenched blood in the barrios of Ciudad de la Gruta. Heart pounding, heart wrenching. Violence has been a plague upon this land forever, but in recent years his beloved town has been spared the worst of it. In part due to El Drone and his surveillance devices.

El Plástico winces and his heart tightens spasmodically inside his broad chest. The intensity of it all forces a decision. He has been strongly considering a run for the governorship next year. His supporters and his ambitious wife are urging him to take his career to the next level, even if it means a party switch, from PAN to PRI. His palpitating heart now insists: No, wrong, I must stay here. My job is here. My people are here. Consumed with the blood-call of his birthplace, El Plástico decides in this instant to forego the governorship. However much this decision will anger Mercedes, he must remain and protect Ciudad de la Gruta and the Sister City accord.

A knock at the door. "Enter if you dare," El Plástico says.

"It's just me," a plaintive voice calls, "The glazier. Come to fix the window."

The office door creaks open. A short, balding glazier backs into the room, carrying his toolbox and a new pane of glass lashed in a wooden frame. It is strapped to his thin shoulders. He says, "I'm here to fix your window."

El Plástico fears that his hallucinations have worsened. This guy in front of him appears to be an age-adjusted image of his childhood friend, Gonzalo Sánchez, who ran off and swam the Rió Bravo twenty-five years ago. His teeth still banded with shiny silver, a vestige of his Mayan ancestors' penchant for decorative dental implants. Last heard from in the distant Cave City, Indiana.

The gnarled laborer, sensing the mayor's question, nods and holds up his right wrist, revealing a crude cross incision that matches the one on El Plástico's right hand. "I was afraid you wouldn't want to see me, because you are so important now."

El Plástico spouts, "Gonzalo, nonsense, what are you doing here? I thought you were living the high life up north."

Gonzalo shrugs despairingly. "Deported. A nightmare. Because of a cop who hates Mexicans, but keeps one as his housecleaner, of course. Three months in a holding cell. For nothing, for being a human being."

"That sheriff? The guy who rides a horse?"

"With a deputy running after him to clean up the shit."

Together, they shake their heads at the invidiousness of El Norte.

"And Dolores? Tell me about her. How is your sister?"

In the few moments of hesitation before Gonzalo answers, El Plástico senses something being withheld, bad news that must be hidden from him. More tragedy for star-crossed Dolores. El Plástico again strokes his boulder forehead, as if trying to erase the thought, which only exacerbates his desire to know what has become of his first true love, Dolores. His only true love, really. Returning to him nightly in erotic dreams, more frequent in the past year. His marriage-of-convenience with Mercedes, the beguiling daughter of a semi-corrupt judge, has been revealing itself for what it is: two scheming climbers that attached themselves to each other for purposes other than domestic harmony.

Gonzalo says, "I'd just moved to Cave City to be with Dolores and her son, Enrique. Both of us thought it would be safer, with the Sister City deal. And it was, for a while. But Sheriff Hooker is running for mayor now, and you know what that means. He wants publicity. I got caught in one of his favorite dragnets. Planting a deer carcass on the highway and then lying in wait for the poor hungry Mexican who tries to carry it home for supper. Who knew that eating roadkill is against the law? And, believe me, this sheriff is not stupid. He knows that I am Dolores' brother and that Dolores knows you and he is sending a signal. Nobody is safe from him. Nobody gets a pass."

Looking at these two men side by side, El Plástico in his crisp, clean shirt and the seedy glazier in threadbare work clothes, one would never guess that, as kids, they shot rats at the dump on weekends.

"By the way, how does Sheriff Hooker know that Dolores and I are acquainted?"

"She's very proud of your accomplishments," Gonzalo says, "She boasts about all of us growing up together."

El Plástico pivots away to a side table and pretends to be consulting some papers so that Gonzalo will not see him tear up.

"And who told you that my window needed fixing?" El Plástico asks.

"Your secretary."

"She did? Well, then…"

El Plástico scratches his stubbly chin. He cannot remember informing his secretary about the discovery of the bullet hole. But that doesn't mean it didn't happen. The day before, he'd been joking about '*señor* moments' with the gringo retirees at the ribbon-cutting for Flamingo Estates.

El Plástico reaches into the bottom drawer of his desk and pulls out two shot glasses and a bottle of Habana Club rum. He rarely consumes alcohol, learning his lesson after several black-out excesses as a teenager, as well as in the Navy. He often uses it for other means. Truth serum, for example. Another possible explanation for his window's bullet-hole could be standing right in front of him.

"A drink, old friend?" El Plástico says, recalling Gonzalo's youthful habit of tipsy pranks.

Gonzalo sidles up eagerly and lays down his tools and wiggles out of the straps of his frame.

El Plástico pours out two portions. Gonzalo downs his mouthful. El Plástico feigns a sip and pours another dose for his friend.

"You're looking well, despite everything," El Plástico says.

Gonzalo coughs and grins. "Thank you. I'm afraid the reality is otherwise. In the mirror, I only see a ghost. But, yes, I was always the handsome one. And you were the ugly cuss."

El Plástico nods. "I've learned to make ugly work for me."

"You have truly," Gonzalo says, "They talk about you up in Cave City. They admire how you borrow ideas from other towns. The open-street bicycling days and the recycling program. Dolores takes pride in calling you her childhood amigo."

El Plástico feels another hot blush of emotion on his stalwart face. His memories of Dolores have been squashed for too long.

"I've been trying to revive my father's business, now that he has passed," Gonzalo continues, "It's a lost cause. All his best customers are gone. And young people don't fix anything anymore."

El Plástico feigns another sip. Privately second-guessing his theory about Gonzalo as the .22 culprit, because wouldn't it make more sense for him to shoot out the windows of some minor municipal structure in order to generate business, rather than the mayor's office? Unless he is harboring a jealous wound, unless he secretly resents El Plástico's success.

The mayor again asks about Dolores. "Tell me more about your sister. I think of her often. How is our brave adventurer?"

"Working three jobs. Always exhausted, and she has stopped sending money to our relatives," Gonzalo says. "She never really had much time for me up there. I think I reminded her too much of the past. And, frankly, I owe you an apology. When I left town, I swore I was going north to bring her back. I said I would bring her back to you, and I never did."

"Don't blame yourself," El Plástico says, "And her son?"

"Even worse. Dolores caught him stealing from the trailer where I was living with three other roofers. He knows that none of us use bank accounts and are too scared about *la migra* to call the police if we're robbed."

"Oh, my Dolores," El Plástico muses, and pours another drink for Gonzalo, who has begun to tear up too.

They both pause to gather their emotions.

El Plástico and Dolores Sánchez had been teenage sweethearts, deeply devoted, a very long time ago. Dolores, a precocious explorer of the surrounding caves and *cenotes*, was considered a great beauty in her youth. Her quinceañera is still remembered by many in the neighborhood. The romance ended with a mysterious pregnancy. Mysterious because Dolores and young El Plástico had pledged to save themselves for marriage. On discovering her condition, Dolores impulsively fled from her family and her *novio* and her country. Nobody understood why, until letters began to arrive with photo-booth images of her and the baby. People speculated about the unknown father. El Plástico claimed ignorance. Ostensibly, Gonzalo had followed her a year later in order to ferry them home. One thing led to another and he never returned. Initially crushed by Dolores' disappearance, El Plástico now credits this tragedy with revealing his path to the future: joining the Navy and stopping drinking and discovering his steady leadership skills.

El Plástico edges closer and lays an arm across Gonzalo's shoulder. He sighs philosophically and says, "Gonzalo, do you remember our afternoons together shooting rats at the dump with your father's .22 pistol."

"Fondly," Gonzalo answers, daubing his eyes.

"Do you still have that pistol?"

"Everything else has been pawned. It's the one thing of his I still have."

El Plástico gazes up at the timber beam on the ceiling. Extending his forefinger, he points to the window and traces the path of the bullet that came from the street through the glass and lodged in the beam overhead.

El Plástico asks, "If we dig out the bullet from that beam and send it in for a ballistics test, what do you think we might discover?"

Gonzalo totters against the desk. "I'm sorry, El Plástico. Please forgive me. I didn't think you would even talk to a wretch like me. I've been desperate for work and I didn't know how else to approach you. Please don't call the police. Let me fix your window for free."

El Plástico shrugs and says, "I'd be happy to find you a job, Gonzalo. And, actually, I don't want the window fixed today. The bullet hole has taught me an important lesson. I want to keep it as a reminder for now."

Gonzalo insists, "Allow me make this up to you somehow."

"You can tell your sister that I'd be grateful to hear from her," El Plástico says, "Tell her that I often dream about her at night."

Cut to: Dolores' splendid fifteenth birthday party. Dolores dancing with young El Plástico, known then as Roberto. Teenage Gonzalo and Roberto kick a ball made from duct tape in the streets of Ciudad de la Gruta. Splash! Dolores dives into a *cenote*. Roberto and Gonzalo dive in after her. Drinking cheap aguardiente, Roberto serenades Dolores with trova musicians. If this were a *telenovela*, the dark truth would be shown: Roberto's midnight sexual encounter with Dolores that he blacks out and represses and never speaks of. Her pregnancy and her escape and dangerous crossing to El Norte, ashamed and frightened and fleeing to protect her boyfriend and her family's reputation. The ravages of time showing itself in the transformation to all their faces. Smooth, glowing, hopeful *caras* turning into leathery iguana masks.

5.

An exhausted, middle-aged Dolores Sánchez climbed the stone steps of the church on the Cave City town square. "¡Ay, Dios!" A veteran home-health aide, she was exhausted from a long night shift, massaging the feet of a dying hospice patient, a former dean at Southwest Hoosier State. The patient was now a drooling wreck, and his anguished family was too scared to touch him.

Dolores paused on the portico outside the church, St. Fernando the Fur Trapper. She checked her watch and her phone. No word from her son, Enrique, who probably took advantage of her nocturnal absence to go out paintballing. His latest obsession. Dolores groaned and continued up to the entrance. Her footsteps deliberate and slow in the fog. She is very aware that accidents happen to people who try to function at this level of fatigue.

Dolores entered the chapel of the Redskin Madonna and slid into the front pew. She crossed herself and assumed a position of prayer and dozed for a few minutes. Before the stare-down commenced. This is what her faith had come to, stare-downs with the Virgin, who never blinked. A form of commiseration over the troubles that illegitimate sons create, a form of sharing a conception secret.

Dolores prayed that Enrique had at least remembered to feed his parrot, and himself. "Dear God, how is it possible to *forget* to eat?" Dolores prayed that Enrique would snap out of it and realize how important baseball is for a scholarship and call his coach and apologize for quitting the team, or getting kicked off, depending on the story.

She checked her watch again. She was ten minutes late for the next job, the apartment job, assisting new tenants with move-in at Buena Vista

Residences. No problem, not to worry. The new tenants were still waiting for their moving van to arrive. Her follow-up was just a formality anyway, management wanting to appear involved. And the young couple had seemed okay with the layout the previous day, shepherded by Frank Vigo, who laughingly introduced Dolores to them as the town's best salsa dancer (although Mexican style *cumbia* was her favorite).

Dolores groaned and swallowed two aspirin dry. When was the last time she had danced with anyone?

She felt a familiar hand on her shoulder, a gentle squeeze. "Hello, Father Mike, you're in early today," Dolores said. He was always sneaking up on her, padding around the church in his socks.

"Bless you, Dolores. How are things with Enrique? I tried to speak with him after Mass last Sunday. Hoping to get him interested in my new satellite stargazer live feed, but he ducked out the back."

Father Mike sat down in the pew beside her and stretched his long legs out into the aisle.

"He still won't talk to the baseball coach," Dolores said, "I don't have any clout. If I threaten to take away his phone, for example, he threatens to report me to ICE."

"Oh, he wouldn't do that to his mother."

"You've never seen him in one of his rages. He gets so angry at me. I don't understand why. He blames me for leaving Mexico when he was still growing in my belly. Then he refuses all my offers to send him to meet his relatives in Ciudad de la Gruta."

Expressing sympathetic frustration, Father Mike tugged at his hair and twisted it and said, "Come on back to the flight deck. Let me show you my star link."

He referred to the head priest's office as the 'flight deck.' Why seeing the star link was relevant at this moment, Dolores did not know, but Father Mike's enthusiasm was infectious, as always.

"I brought some donuts for the family in sanctuary," Dolores said.

"Bless you. Let's deliver them," Father Mike said.

Dolores followed him down a carpeted hallway to the back of the church. Father Mike was unofficially allowing a Salvadoran family to hide from the immigration police in a large utility closet, without informing the church board. He gave the *rat-tat-tat* secret knock at the door and whispered, "Food from a friend." The door opened a crack and one arm came forth and Dolores handed over the bag of donuts. She said, "My partner is baking again this afternoon. I'll bring more *pan* on Tuesday."

"*Gracias*," said a faint voice from within.

She followed Father Mike back up the carpeted hallway to his office. He motioned for her to sit in a leather wingback chair in front of a TV monitor. On her left, atop his desk, a gaggle of family photographs. To Dolores, they looked like something from another world. Proud, well-fed farm people hugging their new seminary novitiate.

"Do you have any coffee?" she asked.

"I can make some."

"Please," she said.

He waved a remote control at the TV screen and padded off to the kitchenette. Presto, blinking stars and planets and rings of Saturn as seen from NASA satellite footage and the Cassini explorer and the Mars Rovers appeared on screen. Father Mike returned with coffee and activated the laser pointer in his remote control and briefly waxed about the vastness and the light years and deep time in the Next Generation.

"Beam me up. Don't you think Enrique would like this?" he asked.

No answer from Dolores. She was slumped in her chair, snoring.

Father Mike touched her shoulder again.

Dolores opened her puffy eyes and started speaking softly, as if directly from a dream. "It wasn't about distance, when I was out there. Out in the campo with my brother, Gonzalo. And my *abuela* explaining the names and the shapes and the messages of the constellations. The Stingray-Paddler and the White Bone Snake. It was about closeness. The stars so close, we could touch them. Reflected in the water of the *cenotes*."

"Remind me, what is a *cenote*?"

"You call them 'swimming holes.' In the Yucatán, they are deeper, straight down in the limestone, holes created by meteorite strikes long ago."

"What kind of messages did your *abuela* talk to you of?" Father Mike asked.

"Creating an opening," Dolores answered, "an opening to the *inframundo*."

"What do you mean exactly?"

Dolores yawned and shook her head and smiled at his curious but pointless questions. She searched in her jacket pocket for a painkiller with caffeine. "I have to get to work," she said.

"Go in peace," Father Mike said.

Dolores exited the church and descended into the morning mist and crossed the street mid-block. She walked past the Justice Building, which also housed the county jail, stepping gingerly across the chalk missives scrawled on the wet sidewalk to the inmates above, "*Sin miedo*" and "*Te quiero,*" letters bleeding together in the mist.

She passed the storefront corner office of Reginald Beek, Esq., a.k.a Immigration Lawyer, in the First National Bank building. She stopped and backpedaled and peered in the plate glass windows. Perhaps it was finally time to make an appointment to find out about legal papers, so her son could not threaten her with deportation. She gazed in at a plush, professional office with a big mirror and framed prints of birds and several potted plants and a busy desk with stacks of files. The immigration attorney maintained the transparent decor of the original bank tenant; the president's office clearly visible to the street, so the customers could know and trust that he was hard at work.

Except that as far as Dolores knew, no one had ever actually seen Reginald Beek, Esq. at work in this office, nor had they spoken to him. No one knew if he really existed. Several of Dolores' friends had called and made an appointment and had been met in the waiting room by a secretary wearing a dust mask who demanded a five-hundred dollar retainer. After filling out a stack of papers, they heard nothing back for months. When they telephoned to ask for an update, the secretary acted surprised and claimed that Reginald Beek, Esq. was closely monitoring the progress of their application through the labyrinthine bureaucracy of governmental departments in Indianapolis and in Washington, D.C. Surely from experience with the messy bureaucracies in their own country, they should understand the complexity of this process and be more patient. The implication being, of course, that a complaint could bring retribution.

Dolores' focus shifted to the reflection in the plate glass of her puffy eyes and haggard face. She reapplied some lipstick and dug out the apartment staff ID nametag from her purse and attached it to her blouse. The fog swelled and thickened around her. The legendary fogs of Cave City, also known as Devil Farts. Reputedly exacerbated by fracking and coal mining, seeping up from underground caverns and smelling of the planet's intestines. It was gross and tantalizing.

She walked on toward the Buena Vista apartments, across the Mexican-American War Memorial plaza. Rain puddles on the porous limestone slabs of the plaza brought forth a different odor, a special mix of geo-aerated scents that reminded her powerfully of the *zócalo* in Ciudad de la Gruta at the start of the rainy season. Oh, soul swoon. A flock of waddling pigeons and a grandmother watching three toddlers do what toddlers do with pigeons, here and on *zócalos* everywhere. The toddlers traipsed toward the birds and the birds waddled away until the toddlers got close enough to trigger a loud flutter of wings. And the toddlers giggled with glee and wanted to do it all over again, as if this was the most satisfying experience in their life. For some, it would be.

Dolores felt a disturbing combination of thrill and resentment that her heart could be catapulted so quickly back there, after decades of trying to forget, to erase the colors of the clothes and the music of her father, the bicycling knife-sharpener's pan-pipes in the street, the *cenotes* and the starry *campo*. She wondered indulgently what Roberto was doing at this moment. She wondered about her hapless brother, Gonzalo. She tasted a hint of key lime soup in her dry mouth. One of the dishes from her youth that she regularly cooked for Enrique and that he refused to eat. Why did he get so angry at her attempts to connect him to his Mexican heritage? She stared up at a wet, gray limestone obelisk, lined with the incised names of the fallen, lost sons of other heartbroken mothers.

Dolores reached the far side of the plaza and trudged across the hazy avenue and turned into the Buena Vista parking lot.

Which is where she heard the first sounds of the fight. A plaintive howl.

Two foggy figures up on the second-floor balcony. Alarmed sobs and shrill imprecations. The two new tenants from the day before, still only partially visible, their voices sounding very different now. High shriek, the international code for distress. The young woman laying it all out to the world.

"Our moving van stolen! Please tell me it's not true. Our moving van with my antiques and collections. You entrusted my antiques to a junkie, Chad. How many brain cells do you have left in your skull? What were you thinking? Toad of toads."

More shoulder-shaking sobs.

"You were just trying to help out your old boarding school drug dealer. You probably still owed him money. You probably sacrificed my possessions to pay off a drug debt. And then to tell me 'hey, babe, it's all insured.' You *are* a Neanderthal. No amount of money could ever make up for the loss of my sleigh bed and my dresser and my great-grandmother's rocking chair. I should have listened to my sorority sisters. They were right about you. Narcissistic butthead disorder. And you want to somehow keep this a secret from my parents? How's that going to happen? You just don't want Chief calling you a loser, yet again. And what about when my mother comes out for a visit, how are we going to keep this from her?"

Winnie collapsed against the balcony railing to catch her breath, words devolving into whale sounds.

Chad repeated, "I didn't hire him to pay off a drug debt and Vincent didn't steal the van. The driver disappeared with it, and Vincent is still trying to locate him."

Dolores Sánchez carefully mounted the fire stairs to the second-floor balcony level and approached the open door to Apt. 2B. She joined a few concerned neighbors, other junior faculty, academics clutching briefcases and water bottles off to their first day of classes. Not a pantsuit in the crowd.

"What's happening here?"

"Their moving van was stolen."

"Our furniture was stolen," Winnie sobbed.

"It wasn't my fault," Chad insisted.

"From the parking lot?"

"No, the truck driver disappeared off the radar on the way out from Boston," Chad explained.

"Is that a siren?" Dolores said.

"I hear horse hooves."

"Did you call the police?" Dolores asked.

"No, we just found out," Winnie sobbed.

"Watch it, folks," a neighbor said, "Sheriff Hooker to the rescue."

"He'll showboat somehow. Try to get his picture in the paper."

"Please tell me this is all a dream," Winnie said.

Chad turned and recognized Dolores at the back of the crowd of onlookers. "Hello, Dolores. Sorry, we didn't mean to create a disturbance."

Give the red-haired gringo credit for at least remembering her name. Dolores nodded and whistled and clapped, trying to get Winnie's attention. Dolores had witnessed a few domestic disputes in her life, and participated in some of her own, especially with her unrepentant, unruly son. This one deserved a prize. The young lady was impressive. Full throated expression, her hands choreographing her anger and hurt.

"Don't try to blame it on me!" Winnie said.

Dolores pushed forward and offered Winnie a hug. The girl fell onto her shoulder.

Chad cringed and swiveled. A wrestler trying to avoid a pin. He was down for the count. Hampered by the cardboard tray with two large coffees he was clutching. His usual policy during Winnie's squalls was to let her tire herself out. This time she seemed to be gaining strength.

"Fuck Vincent Guglielmo," Winnie said.

"Horse hooves getting closer," someone said.

"Okay, let's all move off the balcony, please," Dolores said.

Bracelets jangling, Dolores kicked into Latina-superpower mode, meaning, *get out of my way, people*. Any contact with Sheriff Hooker was to be avoided. Unsure of what else to say to the young *profesora* and her man, Dolores resorted instinctively to touch. She stepped in between Winnie and Chad and reached down and grasped her hand and his elbow.

The cardboard tray of coffees spilled on the floor. *Mierda*, all in a day's work.

Dolores cleared her throat and tried to evoke the eloquent, sharp-tongued spirit of her other employer, Mrs. Glodene Butz. Weekend shifts as a lady-in-waiting for the grand dame widow of Cave City. Glodene Butz always knew what to say, even if it wasn't always polite. Dolores blurted, "Quiet down, it's not like you're the only people ever to arrive in these parts with nothing."

"Hunh?" Winnie mumbled.

"I could tell you plenty of stories about people arriving here with literally nothing. But now is not the time. Come with me, please," Dolores said.

Winnie and Chad continued in Dolores' grip, as they moved inside the apartment. For Chad, the elbow hold felt strangely familiar, like a referee at a wrestling match stepping in at the end to declare a winner by raising one of the wrestler's hands and holding the other in consolation. And probably it was Winnie's hand that would be raised, but maybe this exotic referee who had suddenly appeared between them with a soulful gaze would recognize that Chad was the real winner, because he didn't lose his temper and hit anything or yell like Chief.

The siren blared again, closer.

"*Hola, amigos.*"

Frank Vigo appeared out of the fog at the door, all ready for school. Jacket and tie and shoulder-strap case. He and Dolores stared at each other and raised and lowered their eyebrows a few times. Frank understood the urgency of doing something before Sheriff Hooker showed up.

"How about some pancakes?" Frank said, "Remember our plan to go out to breakfast?"

Dolores countered with an alternative: "You take the señorita to breakfast, Frank, and I'll take this gentleman downstairs to our warehouse where we keep the furniture that other tenants have left behind, and he can pick out a few items."

"Good idea," Frank said, and offered a handkerchief to Winnie.

She waved it like a white flag. "Okay, okay, okay. Sorry, I freaked out," she gasped.

Dolores tugged on Chad's arm, pulling him toward the door. "You, mister, please come with me. I'll show you some nice, comfortable furniture. Amazing what people leave behind. You can pick out a couch and some chairs and a bed. Whatever you want. I'll explain to the manager. It'll be okay."

Chad followed along obediently through the fog. The bracelets on her wrist stirred up a different association. A stoner flashback: early teenage years, the era when all his friends' parents decided they must hire a nanny and not just any nanny, a *foreign* nanny from Latin America. Chad would show up at his friends' houses and encounter these Latin American women, lovely, hearty apparitions, often not that much older than him. They'd communicate with their hands, often reaching out to touch him, to emphasize something they were trying to share in their rudimentary English. And so Chad, age thirteen, tried to learn some rudimentary Spanish to reply in kind, and maybe this explained his motivation for taking Spanish in high school, instead of Chief's insistence on Chinese.

"*Lo siento, señora,*" Chad mumbled.

"*Paciencia,*" she said.

Dolores led him down the exterior fire stairs and around behind the mechanical room to a musty, cement-block garage, full of couches and futons and loungers. A dust-cloud beam of daylight pushed through a dirty skylight. The place smelled faintly of pot. Chad had a nose for it. He sat down on the end of a red leather sectional. Still shell-shocked from Winnie's meltdown, he lapsed into a form of speech often used by his mother in the face of his father's tirades. A protective, robotic politeness.

"Thank you very much. You're very nice. I know you don't have to do this for us."

Dolores sat down at the other end of the red sectional, savoring a rare expression of gratitude. And so unlike the daily guff from her son. Dolores smiled and nodded, as if they had just been introduced at the social hour after Mass. She took a deep breath, relieved to have avoided Sheriff Hooker. She imagined Glodene Butz spouting one of her favorite *dichos*, "What goes around, comes around." Even though she wasn't entirely sure what that expression meant, she repeated it. "What goes around, comes around."

Chad mumbled, "Right. Comes around and bites my ass."

Dolores said, "No, no. You and your lady are just going through an upset. It will be better when you get settled."

"You think?" Chad said.

As if he really seemed to care what she thought.

"Yes. Where did you move here from?" Dolores asked.

"Boston, Massachusetts. A world away. My fiancée hates being gone from her hometown. She misses her family. She misses her friends. That I can understand. She feels like a stranger in a strange land."

"Tell me all about it," Dolores said stoically, "I've been here over twenty years." This loosened things up enough for Chad to ask where she was from and for Dolores to answer truthfully.

"Ciudad de la Gruta."

"Oh, the Sister City."

"Not for long, I'm afraid."

"We heard about the referendum from Frank Vigo. We saw the graffiti on the covered bridge outside town. You don't think it will pass? Why?"

Dolores stepped over to the window to make sure the sheriff had departed. She tilted her head and stared up at the dusty skylight and sighed. "Why don't you go ask Frank?" she said.

"I'd like to hear it from you," Chad replied.

Again, oh, this young man was asking for her opinion and seemed to genuinely want to hear it, the same way that Enrique, as a little boy, used to ask for his mother's advice on homework. But that was so long ago now and she had almost forgotten that she did have her own opinions. Trusting that God, that dark Trickster, often worked in a mysterious manner to bring strangers together for unknown reasons, Dolores coughed, and, emboldened by the *profesora*'s vociferousness and channeling Glodene Butz, she replied:

"The sisterhood is fine. The sisters of Cave City and Ciudad de la Gruta are strong and alive. The teachers in the grade schools, Miss Lampson and Miss Ibeniz, they set up weekly Skype sessions between classes. The kids have pen-pals too. The sewing guilds and the quilters designed a Sister City flag. If it was up to the women, no problem, we would work things out. It's the men that are the problem. Prideful, strutting roosters. Discrimination among Latinos is just as bad, you know, just as bad among our own people who vote against their own best interests. Why don't you ask Frank Vigo about that?"

As a rookie therapist, Chad was slowly learning about these quicksand moments: asking a seemingly straightforward question and then realizing he had stepped into a deep hole.

"You clearly have strong feelings about this," he said.

Dolores, embarrassed at her intensity, changed the subject. "I have a son about your age, a few years younger."

"What's his name?"

"Enrique. He goes by 'Ricky.'" Dolores said, "He's got big troubles. Not like you. Yours are small trouble."

"What kind of troubles?" Chad asked.

"Drugs and stealing and also kicked off the baseball team," Dolores said. "Busted for pot. Expelled from school. Six months in juvy. It's some kind of unhappiness, I think. Something his mother cannot cure. Something about me leaving Mexico before he was born that never settled within him. I offer to buy him a ticket to visit our home country. I tell him, go to your room and don't come out until you can smile. But, he says no."

"What position does he play?"

"Pitcher."

"Why did he get kicked off the team?"

"Refusing to bunt."

Chad nodded. "You mean, he can swing a bat?"

"He pitches, and he can hit the ball too," she said.

Chad straightened and turned and spontaneously shared some of his own intensity. He said, "I've been there. I got through it. He can too. In fact, believe it or not – and a lot of people who knew me back then still don't – I am a newly trained addictions counselor."

Dolores crossed herself. This is why God brought them together.

"Please, young man," she said, "Will you talk to my son? Perhaps you are the one he needs. All the counselors we've seen just want to put him on more drugs."

Chad scratched the back of his neck, as he slowly shook his head, not as a negative response. More a clearing-the-fog shake of the head. His fight with Winnie was still swirling inside him. He owed Winnie big-time, and he owed her more than an apology. The moving van theft was a major fail on his part. It might help patch things up if he could announce to her that he had secured his first client in Cave City.

Chad said, "I appreciate your confidence, Dolores. No guarantees, but I'll give it a shot. By the way, speaking of drugs. It smells like weed in here."

Dolores said, "The maintenance crew uses this area to party."

Chad slid his hand down between the couch cushions and came up with a mints tin. He knew exactly what it contained. Two or three half-smoked roaches. Wham, the craving hit like a lost moving van. He was on the spot. Hello, Higher Power, wherever you are. He would have to do the right thing, but first – where does this come from – waves of insidious craving. Craving for release, relief, escape, just a couple tokes. Craving some perspective on the larger questions. Like how, as Chief would say, had he ended up bitch-slapped and blue in Bumfuzzle, Indiana? The imagined first rush of pleasure quickly giving way to a kick of paranoia. Old-style reefer madness paranoia, marijuana as the south-of-the-borderline personality temptress. Dolores' jangling bracelets, driving him nuts. All exacerbated by long ago visions of the little Yucatán girl with the bow in her hair hit by the tour bus. As if she is calling to him across time and space, as if she is summoning him to a reckoning. Ding. The meter has run out. The return of the repressed. Three hundred measly bucks only buys so much time. It was just hush money. Hush, little girl. Hush, other world. Hush to everything thrown under the bus.

Chad pulled out his wallet. He hadn't lost it yet. He fished around inside and produced a newly printed business card for Dolores. She smiled and clutched it to her wrinkled bosom.

6.

Ignacio Morales puffs on his pipe and gazes at the rows of numerals scrawled on the smudged, slate chalkboards of his high-ceiling study. 9.8.0.0.0. Trying to find some meaning in the Mesoamerican Long Count dates, beyond the literal interpretation. 9.1.1.10.10 or March 19th, 457 A.D. He is determined to find some meaning beyond the inexorable cycles, all leading forward and around and back to zero, predicting eventual cosmic destruction. Or, to put a more positive spin on it, predicting the Second Law of Thermodynamics.

"Ignacio, my dear, get your head out of the clouds and pay attention to your guest," Señora Calatrova says. She reaches up to lightly finger the necklace of brown moles on her chest. Quite beautiful, really. An odor of marmalade emanates from her skin.

Ignacio loves that smell. He puts down his chalk.

Señora Calatrova has taxied over from her lair in the *teatro* to the Morales mansion for tea and flan and to discuss the Sister City referendum and the recent letters from Glodene Butz.

"Excuse me," Ignacio says, "I was just ruminating on the possibility that twenty-years is in fact the natural life cycle for a Sister City deal and that we have to accept its inevitable demise with the hope that a future generation will resurrect it."

Señora Calatrova counters, "My views on this topic are well known. Don't be an old poop. Delmar would be turning over in his grave to hear you talk like that."

"The eternal gringo optimist," Ignacio nods, "that was Delmar. Always ready to rack 'em up for a new game, after I'd beat him."

Teacups and saucers wobble on the side of a carved walnut billiards table, along with Glodene's blue stationery. Outside the west windows, a tireless afternoon sun stands guard.

Señora Calatrova dabs her lips with her napkin and shifts in her chair and adjusts her leather bodkin, complete with holster and dagger. She still wears the costume of the leading role that made her famous. For years she was the foremost interpreter of Lieutenant Nun, from the popular opera of the same name. Based on a 16th century account of a transvestite nun who escapes from a Spanish convent and becomes a notorious brigand and gambler in the New World, her celebrity in Mexico increasing with the rise of the 'women-assassins' genre. She once received a worshipful shout from the upper balcony at the Festival Cervantino, "Lady, thy sins are forgiven!"

"Do you think we should alert El Plástico?" Ignacio asks, "With Juan Pablo and the students out there protesting Sister City daily on the plaza, you'd think that the mayor's office would be aware of the situation."

"Good question. I don't know. El Plástico lives in his own little bubble," Señora Calatrova says, "Currently enamored with his fancy drone program. He thinks it shows him everything there is to see in this town. As a matter of fact, Juan Pablo Chayac is a piano student of mine. A very talented young man. And really, in his heart of hearts, he is not opposed to Sister City. I think Juan Pablo is just flexing his wings against El Plástico's influence."

Ignacio tamps on the bowl of his pipe and relights it. "Perhaps Juan Pablo is the one we should talk with. If Juan Pablo knew that Sister City was really in jeopardy, he wouldn't speak out against it so harshly."

"Agreed. We could invite him in to be interviewed on our radio program," Señora Calatrova suggests.

"I don't understand. How would that help?"

"We invite him into the studio after a concert to talk about music and the benefits of music education and we get him to publicly acknowledge that our exchange programs with Cave City are thriving and useful. Like the choirs in the nursing homes, for example."

"It's worth a try," Ignacio says.

In their retirements, Señora Calatrova and Ignacio Morales, lifelong *aficionados* of classical music, co-host a radio program as part of the monthly broadcast of the local symphony orchestra. Their portion of the program is a form of post-game show. Sometimes interviewing section leaders: "It sounded like the woodwinds got a little behind in the second movement, but sorted things out and got back in the fray by the end of the third movement. Can you comment, please?" Sometimes reminiscing about Señora Calatrova's illustrious career; backstage gossip and so forth, like the time she was singing for a young Venezuelan conductor who conducted by waving his hair around as someone yelled, "It generally goes better if you look at the score." Sometimes telling jokes, including Delmar Butz's favorite musical quip. Q: What is the difference between a symphony orchestra and a bull? A: In a symphony orchestra, the horns are at the back and the asshole is at the front.

Delmar was a worldly man, but not particularly cultured.

"Every morning I hear Glodene's voice in my head, counting down the days till the referendum vote," Señora Calatrova says.

"Remind me. How many are left?" Ignacio asks.

"One hundred and fifty-two," she says.

Ignacio returns to the chalkboard and starts breaking down the number into x times the square root of...

7.

"Vincent, you scumbag, where's our truck? And don't tell me the aliens took it," Chad hissed into his phone. Trying not to wake Winnie.

"It's not your truck. It's mine. My vehicle. I stand to lose big here too, Chad. This isn't all about you. God, what a week. I haven't slept since Tuesday."

"Save the bullshit. You promised us, man. You promised us our furniture would be waiting."

"I warned you about moving out to the middle of nowhere. They still eat squirrels out there, and have spelling bees, and cut mazes in cornfields. Have you seen any UFOs yet?"

"Don't, Vincent. Don't do it. Don't try to put this on me. Take some responsibility," Chad said.

"Could be a karma thing with all her stuff."

"Please, no, stop."

"She and her family have some really old baggage."

"Vincent, you're talking about my fiancée."

"Her furniture. I'm talking her furniture. All those antiques. Like the belongings themselves didn't want to leave the confines. Like they belong here in Boston."

"Are you trying to tell me the truck never left Boston?"

"No, it's just that my runs don't usually go farther than Pittsburgh," Vincent said.

"Right, yeah. We talked about that. And you said you have a driver who grew up in Owensboro, Kentucky and knows exactly where Cave City is."

"It turns out there's a Cave City in Kentucky too, and he thought that's what we were talking about."

"You're in contact with the driver?" Chad asked.

"Not exactly."

"How not exactly?"

"I got a text from his probation officer."

"I'm losing patience here, Vincent. Are you saying that you entrusted our possessions to a felon?"

"Come on, Chad. Don't be a hypocrite."

"I asked you a question."

"You can take the redneck out of the country, but... you know the rest. Apparently, the driver cut south at Wheeling on a detour to attend a family reunion."

"Wherever that is."

"These country boys are unpredictable. They have gut affiliations that we city boys just don't understand."

"You're sounding a bit enamored."

"Chad, you're the one who taught me that people often get more conservative when they get sober."

"Always sucking from the hind tit, Vincent. I'm hanging up. Call me back when you can tell me our truck is on the way."

"It's my truck, man."

Chad said, "Goodbye for now."

Chad, sleepless, lay beside Winnie on the lumpy futon that he and Dolores had dragged up from the storage room. Winnie stirred briefly and mumbled, "Everything okay?"

"Nothing to worry about," Chad said, his voice rippling with forced equanimity. It was 2:30. It could not possibly be 2:30. There must be some mistake, some flaw in the space-time continuum that had emerged since the last time he looked at the clock. Chad rolled off the futon and padded out to the balcony to look again at the stars. Both he and Winnie were surprised by the minimal light pollution in Cave City. The player-piano scroll of stars each night inspired them to hope for a better tomorrow.

In the intervening weeks since the moving-van crisis erupted, Chad had worked hard to establish a functional ceasefire with Winnie. He dipped into his recovery bag of tricks and adopted a contrite, fake-it-till-you-make-it mode. He rubbed Winnie's shoulders frequently. He avoided phone calls from Chief and did everything he could to make the apartment habitable. Two BarcaLoungers and a futon frame were moved up from the storage area. Chad ventured forth to the strip mall and shopped for basic replacement supplies: sheets, towels, toiletries. He set up a bank account at Old Union.

Their social media moratorium helped to create a protective shield of denial. If it wasn't posted online, it wasn't really happening. Winnie sent out a few texts to let people know they were still alive, but no more.

Twice daily, Winnie used her stress-reduction breathing exercises. She focused on the start of the new semester. She spoke briefly on the phone with Prudie, assuring her mother that Cave City was a lovely college town, and revealing nothing about the van theft. She'd always thrived on the back-to-school energy of August and she was glad to see its local manifestations. Kids with lunchboxes and matronly crossing guards and sales on school supplies and the sounds of marching band practice. Adopting a modified version of her mother's queen-bee autopilot, Winnie made lesson plans while taking long baths and plucked her eyebrows. Every morning, she shot herself out of the cannon. Breakfast was a hard-boiled egg. She ate it standing over the wastebasket, sprinkling salt between bites.

Winnie used the gregarious Frank Vigo as a third wheel buffer. Frank went along with it, out of concern for his new colleague. Winnie invited Chad to join them everywhere. "Frank and I are going to Happy Dan's for lunch. Do you want to come with?" "Frank is showing me Mound Park this afternoon after class. Do you want to see it?" "Frank and I are going to hang up posters for Sister City at the Student Union. Do you want to help?" "Frank is taking me to the tango club. Do you want to try it? The Christmas party is apparently great fun, and by then you'll be a regular dancing bear."

Chad swallowed his frustrations and signed up. The tango club was torture. Worse than two-a-day preseason baseball workouts. The club met in a dusty banquet hall above the Elbow Room and danced to recorded music. Step forward. Step back. Ouch. Turn. Bump. Side-step. Bump. Sorry. Slide forward. Bump. Oop. Sorry.

Chad tried to follow up with Dolores Sánchez on the counseling for her son, Ricky. It made sense to do it. He should do it. But Chad's rookie doubts prevented him from making the call. He literally got the shakes. Fortunately, Dolores re-initiated the contact, after Ricky was busted again for truancy.

They scheduled an appointment for the following Thursday. The plan was to meet at Dolores' home. Sort of intervention style, sort of social-work style, sort of a way to gather more information on the situation, and obviously more convenient for Chad, who didn't have an office and wasn't cool with Dolores' idea of meeting at the church. Sure, substances and spirituality are always connected, but Chad didn't want to play that card yet.

On Thursday morning, before heading off to Dolores' place, Chad walked over to the sporting goods store on the square and bought two new baseball gloves. The entire inventory was marked down for a 'Back to School' sale. He also bought two bowling balls, cheap. An early birthday present for Winnie. He intended to prove that he could take the initiative on a shared endeavor that did not involve Frank. His idea based on the impression that bowling was a popular couple activity in the Midwest. One shiny blue ball and one shiny red ball, each one with a case, hidden in the back of the bedroom closet.

Chad showed up a half hour early at Dolores' trailer. He wanted to be on the premises before Ricky arrived home from school. Chad overestimated how much time it would take to hike out from campus, past the carillon tower and the classroom building where Winnie and Frank were teaching, past the athletic fields where the soccer team was practicing, and on through several residential blocks of foursquare and saltbox houses, side yard gardens full of late season zinnias and tomatoes and Queen Anne's lace. A couple of urban deer munching on the vegetable patches. He counted nine Sister City yard signs, and also spotted two more, at a distance, being stolen by a large person in a leather skullcap. The person tore the signs and deposited them in an alley dumpster. Chad saw a kid draped on a porch swing, legs up on the railing, waving with a bare foot to the passing traffic. He passed a funeral home that doubled as a wedding chapel and cut diagonally through Mound Park and behind the strip mall, half of the buildings boarded-up and vacant, and the Dollar General, where he had earlier purchased underwear and socks.

Chad crossed the river on the narrow pedestrian lane of an iron railroad bridge. On the other bank, a purple thistle patch covered with monarch butterflies. He saw a marker for Oracle Cave, a half mile up the hill. Chad checked the map directions on his phone. He veered left into the trailer court, Riverside Homes, i.e. the floodplain where Dolores lived with her son and her partner. Their small garden by the front stoop was laden with tomatoes and peppers and zinnias. A scrawled sign above a metal bowl said, "Water for our dog friends."

Dolores Sánchez stood waiting at the front door, as if sensing his early arrival. "You found the way all right?"

Chad nodded, "I followed the tomatoes."

Dolores smiled and, quoting Glodene Butz, said, "Two things money can't buy: true love and homegrown tomatoes. Fortunately, in this house we have both. Let me introduce you to Rosa."

A throaty hum sounded from behind her and a rotund, bouncy woman stepped out and ignored Chad's outstretched hand and went straight for a wet kiss on Chad's cheek.

"Rosa's form of lip-o-suction," Dolores said.

Clearly, they were desperate for Ricky to get some help.

Dolores ushered Chad into a small, bright, immaculate living area. The shelves were lined with elephant figurines. All colors, all sizes, all materials, all with their trunks raised.

"The raised trunk of the elephant is a symbol of good luck," Dolores explained.

"We'll probably need some," Chad said.

Laid out on the floor were votive candles and a Day of the Dead altar. Chad noticed his business card among the many items displayed. "Isn't Día de los Muertos in November?" he asked.

"Year round in this house," Dolores said. "A memorial for all our friends who have been deported."

A birdcage on a stand in the corner housed a ruffled, green parrot. "Hi, fella," Chad said, "Can you talk?"

"He sometimes says strange things. Parrots are known to be very long-lived. We inherited the bird from an old Poblana woman who immigrated in the 1980s. Rosa and I cared for her when she passed away. The parrot occasionally squawks, 'It's morning in America.'"

"Probably something he heard on TV," Chad said.

"But Rosa, no, she does not talk," Dolores said, gesturing toward her partner, who smiled and hugged Chad again. Her fingernails were long and lacquered and encrusted with fake diamonds.

Dolores explained that she and Rosa had met on the job, their other job. The home healthcare job, working the night shift with the bedridden dying. Switching out catheter bags and administering sponge baths and deftly assisting with the mortal transition. Over time, they had developed a seamless teamwork, instinctively knowing the other's next move. The intense, physical intimacy of sharing so deeply, and so frequently in the final passage became a shared, personal intimacy between them. Communicated exclusively with eyes and touch, because Rosa was mute, completely mute.

"She doesn't need to talk. She says it all with her face," Dolores said.

Rosa could express anything with her glowing, cheese-ball mug. A Guatemalan who had made her way north atop the notorious train, The Beast, she had not always been mute. On that trip she had apparently experienced something that rendered her speechless. Rosa and Dolores, known professionally now as the Silent Angels, were a sought-after team among hospice families. The Silent Angels were full-service, often going above and beyond. Their most recent case involved an elderly cancer patient, desperately hanging on until her daughter could fly in for a goodbye. Alas, the patient expired an hour before the taxi arrived from the airport. Dolores dimmed the lights and fluffed a lot of pillows and Rosa climbed into bed with the deceased patient and, hiding under the blankets and pillows, was able to manipulate the deceased's flabby arm, as the daughter ran into the bedroom and knelt beside the bed, such that it looked like the elderly woman was bestowing a blessing just before her last breath.

Rosa pointed to the coffee pot in the kitchen and Dolores asked Chad if he wanted a cup. "We make it strong here," Rosa's face said.

Chad accepted and almost gagged on the first sip. He persevered with the thick brew, which pleased Rosa. It tasted like licorice. She smiled and padded back into the tiny kitchen and returned with a bowl of yellow pabulum.

"It's called maatz. A sacred food of the Maya," Dolores said, "A power food, sort of like what your pioneers called 'corn pone.'"

"Good stuff, Rosa, thank you," Chad said.

Dolores asked, "Things are better now in the apartment with the *profesora*?"

"A little better, with your help," Chad nodded, and gobbled the maatz. "This is seriously good stuff. Surprisingly rich."

The parrot squawked and said, "It's morning in America."

"Rosa's maatz is very rich," Dolores agreed, "Even Enrique will eat Rosa's maatz."

Rosa smiled proudly and gestured toward the plastic sack full of two baseball mitts that Chad had brought and placed beside the front door. Her smile shifted to a mischievous grin, as if she knew exactly what Chad was up to.

"I'm prepared for anything," Chad said. "I know the kid is a baseball player. Anything else I should know about Ricky before we meet?"

"Oh, where to begin?" Dolores sighed. "A young man with too much to say. He's like a type of summer squash that's popular around here, 'Early Prolific Straightneck.'"

Rosa pointed down to a blurry photo in the Day of the Dead floor display. A winter scene, a middle-aged man and a small boy squatting beside two rotund snowmen.

"He was close to his uncle, Gonzalo, who was arrested this summer and sent back to Mexico," Dolores said, "My brother promises everything to everybody. He promised Ricky that he would come back, but we all know Gonzalo is not coming back, although Ricky is just now figuring that out."

"Speaking of good stuff, there has to be some about Ricky," Chad said.

Dolores didn't miss a beat. "Plenty of it. Enrique is an old soul. A deep soul. But that's his problem. Soul loss. Our ancestors knew a lot about soul loss. And the main job for their healers was to retrieve lost parts of a person's soul. That's what we want you to do. We want you to retrieve the lost parts of Enrique's soul."

Rosa nodded affirmatively and wiggled her fingernails.

"Okay," Chad said. "I might need another bowl of maatz for that."

Brakes squealed and an engine backfired as Ricky pulled up outside in a dinged-up El Camino. Young Ricky, in his Baja hoodie with his piercings and tattoos and his wing-in-flight nose climbed out of the car and slammed the door. Before he had gone two steps, Chad charged out of the trailer, leapt down off the front stoop, and hurled one of the baseball gloves at him. Fast-pitch underhand style.

Ricky caught the glove against his chest with a forearm.

Chad ordered, "Gotta break these in."

To any baseball person, this was irrefutably true. Chad produced a fresh ball and an off-speed lob. Ricky opened his glove palm up and allowed the ball to fall into the pocket. He slapped it against his thigh and instinctively tossed the ball back.

The intervention was happening. Trust the process. Chad fired a chest-high return and dropped into a catcher's crouch. A bit of a risk, in that it looked like a submissive position, but one that required an appropriate response from anyone who considered himself a pitcher.

Ricky slapped the glove a couple more times and slowly began his wind-up. Chad betrayed a faint smile. There was definitely hope for this kid. Ricky's wind-up was graceful, displaying balletic poise and internal resolve with a high kick flourish. He threw a bullet and Chad lost it for a second in the sun.

Pow, ouch, hurt so good. Ricky was trying to knock Chad over. Sorry, kid, try again. Twenty times, back and forth. They both worked up a visible lather. Ricky's dark laser eyes glared over the edge of his glove, staring in hard, picking his spot for the next delivery. Chad remembered the stare of the dead Mexican girl long ago and hoped that his actions here could somehow be redemptive.

Dolores and Rosa and the green parrot looked out from the trailer window.

Breathing heavily, Enrique paused and strode forward, as if coming down from the mound for a conference. Chad rose from his crouch.

"Who are you, mister?"

Chad, speaking as much to himself as to Ricky, proffered a variant on an AA *dicho* that felt right for this moment. He said, "I am the catcher you have been waiting for."

8.

Actually, the Mexican girl hit by the bus long ago is very much alive. Age eighteen now, seriously disfigured, she walks with a limp and a crutch. Her face contorts around two broken cheekbones and one eyebrow distended in flash-frozen horror at seeing the oncoming bus too late. She still wears a colorful hair bow. She goes by the name, "Dotcom." A popular name in remote Yucatán villages where cyberspace is still just a magical rumor.

I meet Dotcom in La Sombra Azul. She lives in Ciudad de la Gruta now. She visits my corner table. We eat *pok chuc* and other traditional Mayan dishes. Pork this and pork that. She talks to me because I look her directly in the eye. Most people can't bear it. Her face is a scary mask. Her *campesino* parents didn't know what to do with her. They and four other children and an aunt and two cousins inhabit a traditional oval Mayan house, with a sheet metal roof and a dirt floor. They speak the Yucatecan Mayan dialect and work the fields. After the bus accident, Dotcom lay in a coma in the village medical clinic for many months, almost a year. In a small room where the two nurses on break watched dubbed re-runs of Star Trek. Dubbed into Spanish, except for the Klingon, which sounds very similar to Yucatec Mayan.

Dotcom emerged from the coma early one morning, speaking Klingon. "*QaStaH nuQ? Nuqneh!*" She returned to school and latched onto languages. She also studied in the bookmobile that comes to the village on Tuesdays and Thursdays, an El Plástico initiative to the outlying hamlets. The bus accident knocked around Dotcom's brain, such that she became a language savant.

She yaks on about the stick figure characters in her dog-eared textbooks. There is a Doña Marta and Don Pedro who live in Mexico City and discuss preferences for spices and appliances and the weather in the *subjuntivo*. There is Tim and Sally Jones and their son, Chuck, who live in Chicago and discuss shopping and sports in the *pretérito*.

Dotcom's parents and the village elders admire and fear Dotcom's gift and her eerie, traumatized gaze, as if she is a beatific demon. In an act of communal revulsion masked as charity, they raised enough money to send her away to study at the Jesuit school in Ciudad de la Gruta. She inhabits a small apartment near the railyard silos with Carlota, a great-aunt. Tía Carlota is a laundress who picks up extra cash by dancing at La Sombra Azul on burlesque nights for the tourist *viejos*.

On Saturdays, the courtyard at the bar becomes a dance hall, with the house *orquesta* playing old-style salsa. The music is slow and easy. The tunes are from an era of white suits and dresses, before air-conditioning, when folks didn't want to work up too much of a sweat. Tía Carlota arranges for young Dotcom to work at La Sombra Azul as a translator. Dotcom wears her plaid school uniform skirt and blouse and pink hair bow. She translates the sweet nothings between the dancers and the generally well-behaved Midwestern geezers, who travel down on charters organized by Sister City Tours.

Occasionally, she'll limp over to me to clarify a new word or phrase, such as "tuckered out."

Knowing that Ciudad de la Gruta will never attract the type of tourists who frequent Cancún and the Gold Coast beaches, El Plástico and Sister City Tours pitch weekend getaways to a niche market of Hoosier retirees. The hundreds of retired engineers, mechanics, and factory workers from the school bus plant, just south of Cave City. Many of the sturdy vehicles they manufactured are still operational, with odometers topping four-hundred-thousand miles, still running the third-class routes in the rural regions of Mexico.

Sister City Tours, leveraging the intense loyalty of these workers to their product, arranges for them to ride these routes and even to drive their old buses. They eat a catered lunch in the bus company garage and, later, enjoy an evening burlesque show with mature dancers of their own ripe age. Carlota is one of the most popular caddies, though make no mistake, Carlota leads.

Dotcom handles her translator duties well. She is calm and professional. The gringo clients remind her of the duffers back in her village, the *viejo* squatters who believe that staring at the road all day is *doing* something. She understands that her job also includes being a confessor. She takes a few liberties with vocabulary and poetic spin, and occasionally goofs up on idiomatic phrases, such as: "Soon all your troubles will be in your behind."

Here are a few more examples of Dotcom's translations. Old Mechanic to Carlota: "Madame, you are the embodiment of the eternal life force. You have roused the long dormant yeast in my heart."

Carlota to Old Mechanic: "Thank you, good sir. I am so grateful to have a chance to converse with you, because you are obviously the richest man in the room."

I pay for Dotcom's meals and also give her extra cash for information gleaned from the Cave City retirees about the political situation in their town. Being relatively new here, Dotcom is unaware of my reputation and checkered past. She thinks 'El Drone' refers to my monotone voice. She thinks I'm just a sentimental expat eager to hear the gossip from home.

Just yesterday, after an encounter between Dotcom and a talkative former line worker, I learned more about the precariousness of the Sister City referendum and the loss of an important supporter. Not that El Plástico and I aren't aware of the difficulties facing the vote, thanks to Ignacio and Señora Calatrova. Sadly, Sheriff Hooker's candidacy appears to be gaining ground. We had been counting on an ace in the hole: the former Cave City mayor, Rex Blaine, who signed the original Sister City agreement. We have all been counting on him to speak up in our favor, now that he is Congressman Blaine. Surely, Congressman Blaine would ride to the rescue to save his creation. Apparently not. Last week, Blaine gave an interview to the Indianapolis Star and called the Sister City agreement a "youthful mistake" and a "naive misunderstanding of the complexities of employment" and "a dumb ploy for better food in southern Indiana."

There's more. The retired line worker also tells Dotcom that the current mayor, Ralph Rosewater, a plumber by trade, is ignoring the Sister City referendum. Instead, he is devoting all his energy to securing a Cave City exit on the new Interstate 69 extension. Many motorists complain that there is no place to pee on I-69 between Indianapolis and Evansville. Mayor Rosewater is betting his reelection chances on landing a new highway exit and establishing his fair city as the place to pee on the interstate. Rosewater claims the Sister City referendum is too divisive, too risky to bring up at election time. Better to let it die a natural death from lack of attention, or from what he calls a "pocket-veto."

Terms like "pocket-veto" are tough for a translator. Dotcom enjoys dissecting the vagaries of the lingo, such as the Spanish verbs that change meaning in the past tense. After hours, Tía Carlota joins us and we chat about other topics. I know all about Dotcom's recurring dream of a red-haired male figure with gold coins in his eyes driving a bus, which is why she never rides the city bus and insists on stumping across town to the club after school. Always followed by dogs. Tía Carlota and Dotcom are big believers in street dogs as protector spirits.

Dotcom observes about herself, "I am like a yogurt container with the fruit on the bottom, Mr. Drone. My good parts are hidden and have to be stirred up."

Tía Carlota teases young Dotcom about her fixation on her textbook 'friends,' Marta and Pedro from Mexico City and Sally and Tim and Chuck from Chicago. In Dotcom's mind, they have all recently migrated to a retirement home for language textbook characters, a beach resort near Cancún where they lounge in rocking chairs and compare notes on their careers as cross-cultural icons.

And, yes, Dotcom also knows about my invisible friends, Priestess Dawn and Priestess Moon, my fantasized indigenous stereotypes. Dotcom peppers me with questions and draws me out on the backstory. *How did they first meet?* As kids at a large convocation of tribes at the nearby city of Cahokia. *What were their parents like?* Both sets of parents were prominent leaders, organizing discussions on trade routes and medicine and the beans-squash-corn diet. Their folks got on well together, smoking pipes and sipping hooch. *What did the girls do for fun?* The girls played the bead game and gambled on chunkey and they shared stories about taming animals. *When did they become orphans?* The great city of Cahokia, home to fifteen thousand souls, was mysteriously destroyed by disease and famine and who knows what else. And both sets of parents died in freak accidents. Priestess Moon's father, a high Maya dignitary, slipped on a wet spot at the top of his temple, on those jarring, steep, narrow-rise steps, and fell down the ziggurat cliff and broke his neck. *What happened to Priestess Dawn's father?* He was killed by a copperhead snake at the mouth of the Oracle Cave, perhaps as divine retribution for telling the tales during summer months, which was forbidden. Their mothers died of grief. *How did Dawn and Moon stay in touch?* Seeking solace together, they managed to send and receive messages through an aerial, migratory songbird system similar to carrier pigeons. The Mississippian tribes were eager to hear the latest Mayan legends, usually funnier and more provocative than their own, involving dwarves and naughty women subverting the social order.

Dotcom drills me with her mangled eye and flips into a surprisingly acute doubtful mode. "How can we be certain the mothers died of grief? Isn't this all just our own make-believe?"

I order up another drink and a flan. The bells from the nearby church sound the hour. "To some degree, yes. I hear similar accusations from the sabbatical anthropologists who pass through town on their way to the *ruinas* and find their way into my corner here. They lecture me on the dangers of claiming any sure knowledge about these early peoples and their fixations on blood and human sacrifice. I understand the point. We must be careful and not get swamped by our own projections. However, ten minutes later, those same academics are buying a round and toasting the Human Family."

Dotcom raises her glass and bangs it against mine and launches into more questions. She demands an account of Priestess Moon's outrigger canoe journeys across the Gulf, and up the Mississippi. She wants details on the annual tribal festival. A riotous talent show, kind of like the county fair. Dancing, lots of drumming, weaving, juggling, swimming, spear-chucking and other feats of agility. Seated atop a woven-vine dais, Priestess Moon and Priestess Dawn cheer and perfect an early version of the royal wave.

Dotcom picks up on the priestesses' growing political power as a result of increased trade between the peoples, and the Mayan engineering assistance on the platform mound project. *Who is allied with them and who isn't? Who is opposed to the annual powwow and why? Do Priestess Moon's teeth have the turquoise implants? Was her forehead squeezed flat as an infant? Are they in love? How do they define 'love?' Do Dawn and Moon have dogs as pets? How many words for 'dog' are there in the group of languages we call 'Mayan?'*

The dog question gives me pause. One of many secrets in my life: I was one of those kids who never got over the death of their first dog. I surreptitiously hand down scraps to the mangy strays that follow Dotcom into La Sombra Azul. Maybe not so surreptitiously. Dotcom spots me doing it and again drills me with her evil eye and says, "You feed them, Mr. Drone, because you yourself are a stray."

Cut to: dog skeletons in a royal tomb, and live dogs roaming the streets of Ciudad de la Gruta and Cave City. A drunk outside La Sombra Azul sings to a mutt with hanging dugs, "A man with money pays the dog to dance, while a poor man dances like a dog." The Maya bred dogs as a food source and honored them as guides to the afterlife. The hairless *k'ik'bil pek* and the *cux* and the *tsom*. Portrayed in the sacred *PopolVuh* as important creatures that revolt against cruel treatment by the emotionless Wooden People of the Second Creation, thus instilling in subsequent human generations a sense of respect and dutiful care for dogs. And instilling in subsequent canine generations, who today discretely roam the barrios of Ciudad de la Gruta, a moderate level of trust that offerings will be found, that the proprietors of the *taquerías* will save a few tortillas and deposit them on the curb nightly, and that on rainy days car owners will check before driving off, to make sure a dog isn't sleeping underneath the vehicle. Meanwhile, up north, the Carolina dog and other pariahs served as watchdogs and hunters and herders. Bigger bodies, closer to wolves. In Cave City today, their rugged descendants can be found in half-drowned litters by the river or raiding compost piles in the back alleys. One of them, a young, mangy coon dog, trots out from around the Mound Park excavation site and follows along behind a whistling guy who has just crossed the train bridge, swinging a baseball glove in one hand. The dog thinks the whistle is for him.

9.

"Yip, yip, yip," barked the dog.

Chad O'Shaughnessy, whistling a tune from tango class, was returning from his third encounter with Ricky Sánchez. Their meetings were still all about baseball and still a bit awkward. Dolores and Rosa pushed the *maatz* and the strong coffee. Ricky was suspicious of Chad, worried that he could be an undercover officer. In the case notes, Chad charted a little progress in the conversation department. Drinking Cokes on the concrete slab patio after throwing and discussing baseball-as-life metaphors. Today's truth: never swing at the high, stinky cheese, and watch out, because life throws a lot of high, stinky cheese.

And then this thing with the hound. Jeez, the dog would not leave him alone. Prancing in circles and nipping at his pantlegs, and suddenly a vertical leap, straight up into Chad's arms. The dog licked his face. Cute, but a pain in the ass. Phew, down boy. Chad dropped the dog. He wiped the sweat and dog-lick from his face with a bandana.

"Go on. Get away."

The dog did not comply. Chad checked for a collar and a tag. He found nothing except bristly scruff. Chad sat on a stone bench at the entrance to Mound Park and pulled out his phone. He speed-dialed Winnie and it rang four times and went into voicemail. Chad dialed again, their private signal for "pick up, please." She answered and said, "I'm in a meeting."

"Sorry to bother you, but I've got a problem."

"You finally figured that out?" Winnie commented.

"Hey, you must be having a good day," Chad said. He fended off another leg nip from the dog. "It's a canine problem actually. I'm down at Mound Park, coming back from throwing with Ricky again, and this mutt has just appeared and won't go away and I don't know what to do."

"You're calling to ask my advice on this?"

"Yes, you have a Ph.D."

"Thanks, that's nice."

"Do I call Animal Control? Is there an Animal Control here? I don't want the critter euthanized. I mean, he is kind of a funny guy. A real d-a-w-g."

"Yip, yip, yip."

Winnie said, "Look around. The owner might be in the park."

"I'll do that, but what if I don't find anybody? What if I have to bring this guy home with me?"

The dog chimed in again. "Yip, yip, yip."

"How bad does he look?" Winnie asked.

"On a scale of one to ten, maybe a seven."

"Are we actually talking about adopting a d-a-w-g?" Winnie said.

"It sounds like it, which is crazy," Chad said. "The last thing we need, while I'm trying to find a job."

"Ask around the park," Winnie said, "If no luck, we'll deal with it. It seems like the universe wants us to learn how to deal with things. Wait, what...just a second... I'm in Frank's office and he has an idea."

Of course, she was in Frank's office and, of course, Frank had an idea.

"Frank says there's a neighborhood association meeting tonight, and if you haven't found the owner by then, we could go to the meeting and take the dog and somebody might recognize him."

"That's a plan," Chad said.

"If you bring that dog home, I am not giving him a bath," Winnie said.

"Nobody is asking you to give him a bath," Chad said.

Chad surveyed the Mound Park landscape. Mothers pushing strollers on the paved paths that wound around the tiered elevations. Joggers and skateboarders and an elderly man doing tai-chi on the tennis court. Chad backtracked around the far side of the Snake Mound, toward a group of smaller mounds that were still undergoing excavation. The dog followed at his heels. He approached the roped-off excavation site. Canvas tents and a portable tool shed and lots of sifters and trowels and rakes.

The door to the shed opened and an official-looking person emerged, a distinctive figure. Chad recognized her from the Elbow Room. She was wearing overalls and a white hardhat over dark braids with bluejay feathers inserted in the braid knots. A nametag on her denim shirt read, 'Night Snow.'

"Is this your dog, by any chance?" Chad asked.

The dog barked, "Yip, yip yip."

"Nope, not mine," Night Snow said.

"You sure it's not your dog?"

The woman flared her nostrils and closed one eye. "That's an interesting idea. You think maybe this is, in fact, my dog, but I am experiencing an episode of temporary amnesia and I don't recognize him?"

Chad shrugged and said, "I'm just kind of desperate to get him off my hands."

"No collar, no tag?"

"I was walking over the bridge, and he shows up and seems to think he belongs to me."

"One of the cave dogs."

The dog barked, "Yip, yip yip."

"One of the what?" Chad asked.

Night Snow pointed to the forested hill across the river, behind the train bridge, and Dolores' trailer court. "Up there in Oracle Cave. It's a local myth. A pack of wild dogs lived in the cave, and according to the legend, every so often one comes down and attaches itself to the loneliest person in town. Are you lonely, fella?"

"That's sort of a personal question, isn't it?" Chad said.

"Pretty simple, pretty straightforward," she said.

"I am a newcomer, it's true, a displaced person, just moved here from Boston," Chad said.

"And you're still probably adjusting to the heat and humidity," Night Snow said.

"Days like this, we throw back in Boston. We go to the shore."

"Out here, you have to take what you get."

Changing the subject, Chad gestured toward the nearby stakes in the ground and said, "Tell me what's going on? Some kind of archeology dig?"

Night Snow knelt down and patted the canine. She nodded and explained, "A chronically underfunded project of the archeology department. Of which, I am currently the only employee, being the proverbial, perpetual graduate student who has never finished her dissertation. What's happening right here, specifically, is that we're uncovering the foundations of the stockade wall that enclosed the entire area and, wow, so intricately constructed, the way it was designed is really clever… um, sorry, I can get totally absorbed in this."

Chad knew the feeling and, poof, it triggered one of his zonked brain cells. Something burst, maybe a residual from the baseball discussion with Ricky. Unable to contain it, Chad said, "The relentless flow of time. The next pitch. On and on. People will do anything to sidestep the passage of time. Some burrow into the distant past. And then, of course, those futurist geeks, trying to stay ahead of time. Meanwhile, in places like this, you can't help but sense the gaze of these amazing predecessors, peering over our shoulders at our starchy, consumerist excuse for a civilization."

The woman closed one eye again and peered at him and stood up. "Seems that we just went from zero to sixty," she said.

"Like a curveball went right by and left me staring. A touch of bipolar mania. I probably should be taking some medication for that," Chad said, and changed the subject again. "Your name is Night Snow. Where does that name come from?"

"Indian. Shawnee."

"You're a real Indian? I've never met a real Indian."

"You want to take a selfie?"

"No, but we should probably take a photo of this dog. He doesn't appear to be more than a year old. There must be a listserv or something we could post the photo on to find its owner."

"We? Oh, am I involved here now?"

"Maybe you're the lonely one, Night Snow."

"Watch out, getting personal," she said.

The dog said, "Yip, yip, yip," and made a big leap. Chad cradled him in both arms.

Night Snow patted the dog's head and reached back into the tool shed and grabbed a coil of rope. She said, "If you're that desperate to get rid of him, I'll take him to the pound for you."

Chad shook his head. "I'll keep on looking. May I use that rope for a leash?"

She handed him the coil and said, "Bring it back later, if you can. We're on a tight budget here."

Night Snow held the dog, while Chad tied the rope around his neck.

* * *

Winnie Marsh was drinking coffee with Frank Vigo in his office, on a break between classes. A fact she did not disclose up front on the phone, because lately Chad was acting jealous of Frank's attentions. Winnie had to remind Chad that Frank was gay and not interested in her sexually. Rainbow flag on the wall. Wow, such a handsome man.

Although not at this moment. Uncharacteristically morose, Frank sat at his desk and stirred his coffee with a finger. Slumped and exhausted, he exuded gloom.

"If you need a dog crate, I can loan you one," he said.

Winnie tried to lighten his mood with a chuckle about Chad. "Maybe picking up dog poop will prepare him for changing diapers," she said.

"Excuse me, what? Please don't tell me that our new hire is taking maternity leave," Frank said.

"Chad is in no position to become a parent. We've just been joking about having kids. For now, he's mired in his job search funk and feeling guilty about the moving van theft. I'm doing better with it. The theft gives me permission to let go of old stuff, both literally and figuratively."

Frank mustered a smile and said, "Good for you."

Winnie added, "At first, I was really worried about becoming a teacher, about standing up in front of all those people. It lasted about five minutes on the first day of class, and ever since I'm large and in charge. I love my seminar room."

Frank said, "Your student feedback is very positive."

Winnie stepped closer and put a hand on his shoulder. "What's up, Frank Vigo? It's too early in the semester to be so stressed out by school. Did you get some bad news about your tenure file?"

"I am not optimistic on that front. The administration frowns on my political involvement, and, honestly, they have me by the short hairs. Tenure or not, I'm a homeboy with nowhere else to go."

"So, what is it? Why the long face?"

"You don't want to know," Frank said. He shifted away from her touch and stood and moved over to the window.

His office overlooked the soccer practice field, an expanse of green and yellow grass marked by patches of mud. Down below, the Frackers were running laps out around the bleachers. A whistle blew. The coach yelled and the players ran over to the bench. They guzzled water from barrels and poured it over their heads and circled around the coach, who motioned toward the fieldhouse for a special guest to approach. The ubiquitous Sheriff Hooker astride his horse, chewing on gum and the edge of his mustache.

"That guy again," Winnie said.

"You don't want to know," Frank repeated.

"Why do you keep saying that?" Winnie asked, moving to his side.

"I don't want you to be implicated," Frank said. "I'm already in way over my head."

"Implicated in what?"

"In that nightmare, down there," Frank said, and pointed to Sheriff Hooker on the soccer field.

"Our wannabe next mayor," Winnie said.

Frank explained, "Hooker's son is on the squad and the soccer coach invites the Sheriff to their practices to give pep talks about the big game coming up in November with Ciudad de la Gruta. Trying to turn what should be a friendly, connection-building match into a do or die showdown with an enemy."

"There's trouble in Cave City..." Winnie intoned.

"Exactly," Frank said, "You and Chad are just here for a year. You should enjoy it and get the most you can from the teaching experience."

"And otherwise not get too involved," Winnie said.

"Savor the chance to be a pond skimmer. Enjoy the Persimmon Festival. Go see the Outhouse Race."

"I am not even going to ask what an 'Outhouse Race' is," Winnie said, "I don't want to know."

"Check out Dinky's Amish Auction Barn."

Winnie said, "An hour ago you suggested that we go to the neighborhood association meeting tonight. Are you saying we shouldn't?"

"At your own risk," Frank sighed. "I'll be there to hear a presentation from a new advocacy group called Parents with Boundaries."

The alarm clock jingled on Winnie's phone. "Time for class. Gotta go." On the way out the door, she added, "We might take you up on that dog crate offer."

Winnie strolled across the leafy quad to her seminar room in Tippecanoe Hall. Large, but cozy. Burnished, lemon-waxed oak panels supporting a colorful plaster mural that wrapped around the upper walls. Sharp acoustics. No need for amplification. It was just right. Winnie prepped and occasionally napped in the back row alone, before and after class. She showed up early and stayed late. It was *her* place, the apartment being in such limbo, full of castaway furniture.

In her seminar room, Winnie was able to forget about the moving van disaster. She gazed around her space with pride. It was her professional launching pad.

The quaint mural depicted timeline scenes of Indian hunters and traders and pioneer wagons and the New Madrid earthquake, and the founding of the modern Cave City. Each panel had been patiently explained to her by Frank Vigo. Begun as a utopian society in 1805 by the Arborites, similar to the Shakers but with a Germanic tree-spirit angle, the town struggled to attract newcomers. Then the Arborites hit on a clever idea: legalizing quick divorce. Come and stay for sixty days and get unhitched. Couples traveled westward on flatboats, down the Ohio River and up the Wabash. Cave City became the Reno of the early frontier. Many newly liberated folk stayed on in the region to farm. The painter, reputedly a student of Frederic Edwin Church, had a sense of amusement. The main panel highlighted a freshly unhitched pioneer couple dancing and waving their divorce decree, which fit right into Winnie's lecture on the folklore of celebration. Frank had explained that before retiring to his hometown in the 1860s, the mural painter had been an assistant to Frederic Church on the trip to South America that resulted in *The Heart of the Andes*, the picture that made Church's reputation and also his fortune (by charging a quarter a head to see it in his New York gallery). This painter followed his example and made his own fortune creating a series of sensationalist Aztec temple paintings that featuring beheadings and other bloody barbarities. He hauled them around in a covered wagon to fairs throughout the Midwest and charged a dime a person to stare at pictures that inadvertently perpetuated the bloodthirsty reputation of the savages.

As Winnie's students wandered into the seminar room, they greeted her with cheery hellos. Winnie smiled and greeted them by name. "Hey, Angel." "Hello, Brittany." "Hey there, Kevin." Dr. Winnie Marsh smiled again, to the entire room. She had ignored her department chair's advice about not smiling until Columbus Day. She was popular with her students, despite being strict about phone use. Many were jocks, who thought they had signed up for a gut class. Right out of the gate, Winnie demanded a no-phones policy. Frank Vigo cautioned against it, but Winnie stood firm. And, lo and behold, her grungy undergraduates cooperated and acted relieved to be device-free for an hour. They liked her first assignment, a research project on the origin of the town, 'Gnaw Bone,' and her second one too; go home and gather four jokes from your relatives and analyze what they signify about your family. The kids listened respectfully and took notes and participated in discussions about the similarities and differences between the study of Folklore and History. Winnie exhorted them to get out of their heads and *feel in their bodies* how Folklore is the living subconscious of the culture. Whereas *Hist*ory, as the word implied, was a stale archive of male privilege and bluster. Not the typical oratory they were used to hearing.

Take the early 19th century Tall Tales about Happy Dan, for example. The students enjoyed this one, many of them eating frequently at Happy Dan's Hotdogs. Winnie came armed with research and illustrations from the library. Turns out all the Happy Dan stories are a variant on the Good Samaritan. They involve Happy Dan making the best of some misfortune that comes from a misguided attempt to help a hayseed pioneer in distress. The piquant moral of the stories underlies the present-day social behavior marketed as 'Hoosier Hospitality' – be nice to strangers, but not too nice.

The students responded with appreciative grunts of *way cool*.

Such that Winnie began to think: yeah, cool, maybe Midwestern kids are raised differently and maybe a Hoosier baby idea is worth considering.

When Winnie got home from class that afternoon, she found Chad shampooing the dog in the bathtub. She walked in just as the rinse phase commenced. Predictably, the dog shook and sprayed water and soap bubbles everywhere.

"Welcome to the funhouse," Chad said.

"He is one ugly mutt," Winnie said, "Have you given him a name yet?"

"I was waiting for you. Can you hand me a towel?"

"Oh, that's tricky. Allow me to name him so I'll get attached."

"It's a *her* by the way," Chad said.

"Are we still taking *her* to the neighborhood association meeting tonight?"

"That's the idea."

"Smells good in the kitchen. What are you cooking?"

"A simple dish, beans and rice, but with a little seasoning kick, thanks to Dolores and Rosa. The barter system has its benefits."

"Frank says he has a dog crate we can borrow. Let's stop at his house on the way over."

They ate a quick meal. The dog lay curled peacefully on the floor under the table. Chad shared some details from his session with Ricky. How he tried to prompt the kid to talk about having not only one but two undocumented mothers, and how he seemed to want to respond to that, but couldn't find the words. Ricky's body language, an exaggerated salute, when setting the next appointment hinted that he wanted to try again. And Winnie shared some details from her conversation with Frank, about his concerns for them getting in too deep.

Chad said, "It seems like we're already there."

Winnie said, "Exactly what I was thinking."

The dog said, "Yip, yip, yip."

Frank Vigo's residence, ten minutes away, was an old farmhouse, circa 1850. As the city grew it had gradually been surrounded by more modern dwellings. Frank claimed to have evidence that the house was once on the Underground Railroad. As might be expected from a gay, tenure-track academic, the place was decorated tastefully. The living room featured a framed collection of circus posters (Frank had written a book on them) and Eames chairs and matching porcelain lamps and brass andirons in the fireplace.

The metal crate was waiting in the front hallway. Along with Frank, looking even more down. Dribbles from dinner colored his shirtfront.

Chad asked, "Did you once have a dog?"

Frank shook his head. "My parents did. I like dogs, but it's too much for me. The crate is just one of many things I couldn't throw out after they died."

Chad reined in the eager mutt, tugging on the rope leash. Winnie asked, "How long have your folks been gone?"

Frank started to answer, but was interrupted by a loud thumping from upstairs. He pretended that no one heard it.

"Let's scoot to the meeting," he said, trying to shepherd Chad and

Winnie toward the front door, "It would do me good to get some exercise."

Thump, a crash, then crying and a wail.

"Oh, no," Frank said. "Here they come."

"What's going on up there?" Winnie asked.

"You're about to get implicated," Frank sighed.

"We can take it," Chad said.

"I hope so. Let me fill you in now, before they come down," Frank explained, "Two little ones. Nina and Paulo. Their parents were deported to Guatemala over a month ago and I haven't heard anything from them since. I'm afraid they may be in danger. They asked me to keep the children, so ICE wouldn't separate them into foster homes or send them to the camps. It doesn't look like the parents are returning…leaving me stuck in a serious predicament."

"This is why you've been so tired," Winnie said.

Frank nodded wanly. He climbed the steep front staircase and opened a door to the upstairs hallway and down rushed two fireball four-year olds, followed by their babysitter for the evening, Rosa. What Frank didn't say was that he had been having a side fling with Nina and Paulo's father, Héctor, just before the arrest and deportation.

Perhaps because Winnie was the same age as their mom, perhaps because her smiling face was so warm and inviting, the kids went straight for Winnie's embrace. She hugged them both tightly.

Babysitting is a tough job when you can't speak. Rosa winced and shrugged her apologies to Frank for being unable to contain the kids. They, at least, promptly forgot their tears when they caught sight of the dog. The dog jumped and yanked the leash from Chad's grip, and a happy, sloppy, squeal-filled wrestling match spilled from the hallway into the parlor.

The adults hurried in after them to corral the chaos. Chad said, "I guess she is a cave dog. And now we know who she really came for."

"How do you know about the cave dogs?" Frank asked.

"I met Night Snow in the park this afternoon."

"She knows the lore," Frank said.

"You didn't tell me about her," Winnie said.

"Not to worry. You'll see her again at the library," Frank said.

Rosa made shooing hand motions that indicated she had the situation back under control and that they were to leave and go on their way. Frank hugged her and wished her good luck. The dog remained with the children.

* o o

Together, Chad and Winnie and Frank ambled the several blocks to the public library, unhurried and unencumbered by a dog. Gazing at the evening sky, a spontaneous decision had been made. They would make a couple 'lost pet' posts, and if the mutt went unclaimed, Winnie and Chad decided to keep it, for the sake of the kids. Somehow they would work it out. The sky, saturated with an imminent sunset, glowed purple. Carillon bells rang out the hour. Streams of pedestrians approached the ivy-clad building. Smokers loitered in the parking lot.

Outside the main entrance, a familiar circle of figures waited, including Night Snow and Father Mike and also Dolores. She was attending to an elderly personage in a wheelchair, Mrs. Glodene Butz, her head bundled in a silk scarf.

"Glodene, you seem to have met with some kind of barbering misfortune," Frank Vigo said.

"Backed into a roll of flypaper at the Historical Society," Glodene said, "Dolores had to scissor me free."

Frank made the formal introductions. Chad and Winnie were officially presented to the inimitable Glodene Butz. She offered up a powdered hand. Chad bowed ceremoniously and kissed her protruding knuckles.

"So glad to meet a young gentleman with some manners," Glodene said.

"If my otherwise useless father taught me anything," Chad said, "It's that one must know how to charm an old lady."

"Oh, my dear boy, you were doing so well," Glodene said.

Night Snow flared her nostrils and closed one eye and peered at Chad. She said, "Hello, again. Welcome to the cabal."

"We're missing Dr. Crane," Father Mike said.

"I hope he hasn't gone off on a bender," Dolores said.

"That doesn't usually happen till Halloween," Frank said, "an anniversary reaction to his divorce from Dr. Madero."

"What's the cabal?" Winnie asked.

Night Snow deferred to Glodene for an answer. "Our mayor, Ralph Rosewater, is a well-meaning nincompoop who has completely dropped the ball on the Sister City referendum. My late husband, Delmar, is sweating bullets up in heaven. We are a group of concerned citizens who have vowed to save Sister City."

A sign-up sheet went around the basement conference room and ended up with forty or so names on it. All makes and models of people. Glodene Butz was not the only elder in a wheelchair. The other one was lugging an oxygen tank. Night Snow pointed out the reporter for the Cave City Splinter, tapping at his laptop.

"The Cave City what?" Winnie said.

Glodene explained, "The name of the newspaper goes back to the Arborites, when the sidewalks were made of wood. This wasn't a wealthy town and shoes were a luxury item, and at the end of a typical day, many citizens spent time picking splinters out of their feet."

A crewcut moderator with a pair of sunglasses hanging off the back of his head called the meeting to order. A dreadlocked secretary read the minutes from the last meeting. Old business, new business, basic democracy. A gas station that had petitioned to add a carwash. A discussion about a request for a variance to build a granny flat. Some residents felt it was a disguised attempt to foist more student rental space on the neighborhood. A motion, and a second, to approve the date for the annual fall clean-up. An update on options for dealing with the urban deer influx. A reminder about a new regulation in the Noise Ordinance, expanding the hours to call in complaints about porch parties. A problem that should improve as the weather got colder. A motion, and a second, for a unanimous vote *against* installing a cellphone tower in Mound Park.

Murmurs and rustling as a latecomer in a cowboy hat appeared through an exit door and slid into the back row. Sheriff Hooker, in civilian clothes, his double-wide girth expanding over two folding chairs. No deputies. No horse. Pretending to be incognito, cleaning his fingernails.

"What's he doing here?" Chad whispered to Frank.

"Not exactly sure," Frank Vigo answered.

"How did he get to be Sheriff anyway?" Chad whispered.

Dolores hissed, "A pact with the devil."

"You mean, like a Faust thing?"

Night Snow leaned in and whispered, "First, he got elected County Coroner because nobody else wanted the job. Exploiting a loophole in the law that says the position does not require a medical license."

Father Mike whispered, "And then, shocker, several people who he had pronounced dead came back to life, and that actually created a positive vibe for him."

Frank added, "He dyes his hair with tobacco juice. Creates a shiny sheen and a helluva stench."

Glodene whispered to Chad, "Psst. What do cowboy hats and hemorrhoids have in common?"

"I can't imagine," Chad said.

Night Snow said, "This is one of her late husband Delmar's lines."

"Sooner or later, every asshole gets one," Glodene cackled.

Night Snow added, "She tells it every chance she gets."

The moderator opened the floor to a well-dressed trio sitting patiently in the front row, sipping from water bottles. A group with a seemingly innocuous name, Parents with Boundaries, and four obedient kids in tow. "Stand and say hello, kids." Their spokesperson was a tall, pole-thin woman with a puffy perm that looked like a serious case of bagworm.

She tapped on the microphone and harrumphed and proceeded to deliver an infomercial on the importance of safe and secure learning environments for our children, while the kids passed around printouts. She handed the microphone to her colleague, who regurgitated the same speech with a shriller tone. They were adamantly opposed to the Sister City school programs. Next, their closer. A retired gym teacher put it right out there: demanding the elimination of any public classroom program that included online contact with the Mexican schools in Ciudad de la Gruta, and the firing of teachers who promoted such boundary-blurs.

Sheriff Hooker stood and stuck two fingers in the corners of his mouth, producing a sharp whistle. This elicited more applause from a dozen or so attendees who didn't want to get on his bad side. Sheriff Hooker recited, "And as for teaching the Spanish language to our precious little ones, if English was good enough for Jesus Christ, it's good enough for our kids too."

"Now we know why he's here," Winnie said to Frank.

Frank simultaneously nodded and shook his head in dismay. "This is the kind of crap we're up against."

The cabal glanced among themselves to determine who would deliver a rebuttal. "Somebody needs to tell the teachers in Ciudad de la Gruta about this," Dolores whispered, "and also warn El Plástico."

"Yes. Can you do that?" Glodene asked.

"The teachers, no problem," Dolores said, "I can get word to them through Gonzalo, but for me to contact El Plástico personally…"

"Understood, don't worry. I'll handle him," Glodene said.

When the applause died down, the moderator opened the floor for comments. Winnie surprised everyone by jumping up and grabbing the microphone. Was she trying to prove that they deserved a place in the cabal? Was she trying to impress Frank? This was definitely not wallflower Winnie. She yanked the pencil out of her hair and pointed it directly at the Parents with Boundaries trio.

She started off with a plea to the town mothers and the town fathers, about nurturing their core community, about the importance of diversity and good public schools for avoiding population drain, for keeping local couples who might otherwise move away to bigger cities, for attracting new young couples, such as Chad and herself, who will be starting families soon…the inference being that the cruel, constrictive policies of Parents with Boundaries would not be a drawing point. She shifted to some personal comments about growing up in a family that only recognized Europe as a foreign land worth any attention, completely ignoring Mexico, our wonderful southern neighbor…

She did not make it to the finish line. Something happened. Something welled up inside and her voice faltered, she handed the microphone back to the moderator and returned to her seat and began to choke up.

"It's okay, babe," Chad whispered, patting her knee.

"I'm implicated," Winnie said. "I can't go back."

"What do you mean?"

"I just kept seeing their faces, Nina and Paulo, coming down the stairs at the house," she said, "Nina and Paulo. I can't unsee those faces."

10.

Countdown to the Sister City Referendum vote: 101 days. Hard to justify taking any time off, but El Plástico needs a break. Sunday afternoons, El Plástico and El Drone take a weekly boat ride out on the Gulf, before their regular Monday meeting in the mayor's office to discuss campaign strategy and to view the latest drone footage.

They drive sixty kilometers north across the flat, steamy scrubland to a small port. Halfway there, the highway rises over a hill that reveals an expansive, green jungle vista, with the blue ocean in the distance. El Plástico keeps his vessel, his one self-indulgent luxury, berthed in a secure marina. His status as a former Navy midshipman and a bureaucratic connection through El Drone (who he met during a joint operation with the DEA) allowed him to purchase a decommissioned patrol boat. A light weight, shallow draught doozy. A Polaris class fast-assault craft. Dual 685 hp diesel engines with ducted water jets. Top speed 40 knots. Decelerates to a full stop in 2.5 boat lengths. A truly agile boat that can perform sharp turns at high speed, which is what El Plástico and El Drone enjoy doing. They barrel around the bay and bounce through the whitecap chop. No talking, no thinking about civic affairs or the Sister City referendum. Pure here and now, stinging gusts of spray on their grinning, weathered faces. Sun-screened jowls and yellowing teeth and gold bridgework bared to the wind for a stomach-churning hour, out and back.

Except on the occasions when El Plástico's wife comes along. Behold the demure Mercedes, a sphinxlike beauty, with a penchant for bug jewelry. The boat is named for her. *Xtabay*, a legendary Mayan ghost temptress. Mercedes loves tricking people into mistakenly reaching up to brush the cockroach off her blouse collar, only to discover an expensive, onyx scarab.

Mercedes lounges, splayed out in a folding chair, near the bow with a drink, waving to the other boaters and the beach crowds. While El Plástico throttles down, cruising wake-less in and out of the harbor. El Drone acts as deck steward, serving Mercedes food and beverage. She delivers agenda orders, such as, "I want to see a whale today. You promised me a whale last time, and there wasn't one."

"*Cariña*, you're whining on my yacht. There is no whining on this yacht," El Plástico says.

On these trips, to pass the time, El Plástico and El Drone stand back at the helm and delve into philosophic prompts. They converse as sparring partners, taking turns at the wheel, two embattled public-sector veterans, mired in the grind, each requiring a sharpening of their dulled edges. Topics range widely, from physical changes in their aging bodies; "I only get little whiffs of things now. I don't bathe in smells the way I used to," to the merits of the Mexican Constitution versus that of the United States; "Our Mexican document is designed to be supportive of a multiparty electoral system, it just hasn't worked out that way so far."

On the merit of Juan Pablo Chayac and the student protesters' criticisms of the drone program: "The scientific definition of a fluid is anything that takes the shape of its container and so it is also with the fluidity of our communities. A citizenry requires clear containment to actualize its freedom."

On ways to die: "Would you rather have a heart attack or a stroke?" Pause. "Either one, just no kidney stones."

On cultural appropriation: "How come every phone book in North America contains businesses with names like Aztec Roofing and Aztec Plumbing, but you never see Mayan Roofing or Mayan Plumbing?"

On Sister City campaign strategy: "Our biggest problem is the local voting public's anger at the madman in Washington, D.C., which gets conflated with the referendum, so our people think a vote against Sister City is a protest vote against Washington."

On marriage and dogs: "Is it true that a single man lives like a human being and dies like a dog, while a married man lives like a dog and dies like a human being?"

El Drone, of course, sticks up for the dogs.

Recently, El Plástico avoids any direct discussion of his marriage, ever since his decision not to run for Governor. According to Mercedes, that decision "killed their baby." A certain type of power couple, Mercedes and El Plástico have struggled for a decade with childlessness and infertility, a condition that El Plástico privately thinks at least exonerates him in the matter of Dolores' pregnancy, and in compensation, their political ascendancy has become 'their baby.' Frustratingly unclear as to what activity could replace the governorship as common ground between them, especially with each coming from such different sides of the socioeconomic tracks. Previously, their joint parenting of the young Juan Pablo Chayac had provided some sense of connection. These days Mercedes goes out alone, spending a lot of unexplained time away from the house. Or rather, a lot of time explained as, "I was at the *doctora.*"

That is, counseling sessions with psychologist Milena Madero, which predictably triggers some underlying machismo insecurities for El Plástico. He knows Dra. Milena Madero. He knows she has recently divorced her gringo husband from Cave City, Dr. Rufus Crane, who she had met before medical school, when he was still in the Peace Corps. And El Plástico fears that Milena Madero is subconsciously implanting animosities toward Cave City into his suggestible wife. His fallback position is to splash on more bay-rum aftershave every morning, her daddy's brand, because Mercedes purports to like it.

On Mondays from 7:30 to 9:00 a.m., El Plástico and El Drone review the week's highlight video reel in a windowless room full of monitors and electronic equipment adjacent to the mayor's office in city hall. They drink black coffee and munch on *pan dulce.* The highlights are selected by El Drone, knowing the mayor's security tastes. First is any footage that is directly crime-related. Ever since the installation of the circling Eyes in the Sky, crime stats in Ciudad de la Gruta are down. The drones provide high-resolution footage of traffic flow throughout the city, replayed in slow motion and telescoped via software, revealing exactly what kind of vehicle is traveling exactly where and when, to and from a crime scene, before and after. Presto, a freeze-frame on the getaway car and its license number. Last week's footage yields new information on a troubling tourist scam, two trucks from Veracruz delivering 100% acrylic *rebozos* that were being sold on the street as 100% pashmina.

Next, scenes of pedestrian life in the roiling anthill of the polis. El Plástico takes a voyeuristic pleasure in watching this show, as if observing a laparoscopic tour inside the urban body. The streets are veins and arteries and, throbbing like a heart, the busy *plaza grande* and its aortic fountain. The bird's-eye perspective also providing a glimpse down inside the hidden courtyards and overgrown *jardines* and shadowy, columned, inner passages that are invisible from the street level. A typical block in Ciudad de la Gruta is twice the size of one in Cave City, because of the agglomeration of peeling, shuttered facades on the front of interior dwellings cobbled together from old stables and servant quarters in the rear, where a segment of the population, a form of modern cave-dwellers, avoid the sun and the oppressive heat by never going outside.

And there, look, on this particular Monday, just past the bus station, El Plástico's childhood friend, Gonzalo Sánchez, begging on a street corner. A donation cup and a cardboard sign in his lap.

El Plástico sighs and says, "Oh, poor Gonzalo. Remind me, I have to do something for that guy. He is Dolores' brother."

El Drone makes a note and asks, "What kind of something?" El Drone knows about Dolores from their boat discussions and the rare occasion when El Plástico joins him at the corner table in La Sombra Azul.

"I'm not sure, some kind of job."

"His sign is in English. What does it say?" El Drone asks. He manipulates the controls to zoom in on the piece of cardboard. It reads: "Need Directions?"

El Plástico chuckles and says, "He's trying to make a few pesos off his English skills and an odd local custom –"

"Dotcom has told me about that, the giving wrong directions thing."

"It is considered impolite, when asked for directions, to say that one does not know the way. Instead, people will give wrong directions, rather than say that they don't have an answer – to the tourists just off a bus."

El Drone pours more coffee and suggests, "You could make him an official Direction Giver. Make it an official city position. The Direction Giver of Ciudad de la Gruta. Give him a little kiosk on the corner and pay him fifty bucks a week."

"I like that," El Plástico says, "Let's continue with the video. I still have a half hour before meeting with the deputy council about the exact wording of the Sister City ballot."

Other bird's-eye selections follow recognizable figures in the streets. Familiar characters whom El Drone knows will elicit some commentary from his boss. The quadriplegics on their mats outside the church, and the gray-haired hippie who has switched out the bird on his shoulder for an iguana. Dotcom and Tía Carlota buying vegetables at the market. The retired mathematician, Ignacio, stumping past the church with his pool-cue cane toward the copper-clad roof of the *teatro*. They watch Ignacio turn into the delivery alley and proceed around back, where a woman, wearing what appears to be a Queen of the Night costume, flutters down the fire exit stairs and kisses him three times.

"He's going to visit his girlfriend," El Plástico says.

"The old diva who lives in the dressing room?"

"They do a radio show together on the community station," El Plástico says.

"Is she really his girlfriend? The expat gossipers at La Sombra Azul would like to know more about that."

"Señora Calatrova is our version of Cave City's grand-dame, Mrs. Glodene Butz, except without the money. Every town needs one. In fact, the two women are close friends, which creates a problem for Ignacio, who is in love with both of them, but out of respect for their friendship and the memory of his friend, Delmar Butz, who was Glodene's late husband, Ignacio will never reveal more than a gentlemanly fondness for either."

"Perhaps they could all have a threesome," El Drone says.

"Spoken like a depraved bachelor who sleeps with his dogs," El Plástico says.

They zoom in on a shadowy figure carrying a briefcase near the student protesters on the square. This could be a problem. The return of Ramón Puentes in dark glasses and a business suit. El Drone has seen him before, and has heard El Plástico jokingly refer to him as "my nemesis." Maybe not so jokingly.

El Plástico groans, "I didn't know Ramón was back in town. Carrying a big wad of cash, no doubt. There's money inside that briefcase. Stacks of bills. Covered with his fingerprints. Ramón loves the feel of money. Last time I saw that briefcase, the contents were being offered to me as a bribe, here in my own office. I wonder who he's offering it to now."

"The TiendaMax bribe?"

"Their corporate honchos want a zoning variance to build a superstore on the downtown plaza. Ramón is their regional rep. Before that he was a venture capitalist, a financing whiz-kid who set up a cable TV channel showing spectacular car crashes, and then he concocted a lucrative microlending fund that suckered in thousands of dollars from do-gooder gringos. However, when his investors started wanting to visit the little seamstress shops and organic avocado farms that they'd supposedly helped start, Ramón had to leave town quickly. And, going back further, he was always my rival at the *colegio*. In a way, I owe my competitive side to him. We battled for everything. He even tried to date Dolores. Wait, slow it down, play that part again…"

Backwards and forwards, slow motion. El Plástico and El Drone watch a dim Ramón Puentes, smoking a cigarette, a gold bracelet on his wrist. He paces in circles under an arcade across the street from Juan Pablo Chayac and the other student protestors. Ramón doffs his cap twice, three times, possibly a signal to the student leader.

"Is the briefcase for the students? Is he funding the Sister City protests?"

"Maybe TiendaMax thinks that if they defeat the Sister City referendum, we'd be more open to their demands."

El Drone reaches down inside his boots and yanks up his floppy socks and clears his throat and announces, "There's another clip I have to show you that also contains some footage of Ramón. I'm torn about it. I really don't want to show it."

"Why not?"

"For one thing, it's going to feel like being hoisted on your own petard. I mean, regarding video surveillance. Maybe I should destroy it. Maybe it's my job to protect you from this." El Drone dimly realizing that what he's asking for is a clearer definition of their relationship.

"Run it," El Plástico says, cracking his knuckles.

The clip starts innocuously enough, a view down on the barrio Santa Lucía and El Plástico's house and Mercedes sunbathing topless in the little tile patio of their courtyard. A peek they've enjoyed a few times before. This time, there is something different. Prompted by a loud honk from a black Ford Escape idling on the street in front of the house, Mercedes stands up, throws on a wrap and grabs her purse. She hurries out to the carport. She climbs into her own car, a red, vintage Galaxy and backs down the driveway and turns into position behind the black Escape. It pulls away and she follows along.

"Run it back again and give me a closer look at the other car," El Plástico orders.

"Guess who," El Drone says, "Betrayal times ten."

The driver of the Escape is invisible, except for one arm hanging out the driver's side window with a cigarette and a gold bracelet on the wrist.

"Ramón, no. If this is what I think it is, I am going to beat him into the ground like a surveyor's stake," El Plástico snarls, and hurls his coffee cup against the wall.

"I was afraid you might react like that," El Drone sighs and looks down at the fragments of the coffee cup. He sees the fragments of El Plástico's reputation as a steady leader.

"I am going to have to act. He is moving in on my wife. It's the code. I'm going to have to gut him. I'm going to have him drawn and quartered. My voters will expect it. If this affair comes out and I don't do something, people will think I'm not a man," El Plástico snaps, "You have to help me figure this out, Señor Drone. You used to knock off people all the time, right? How do I do this?"

El Drone flips on the overhead lights. "Listen, slow down, I really don't think your reputation, or your political future, or the Sister City vote will be helped by committing murder. I mean, look what happened to me. Yeah, I offed a lot of bad hombres for the DEA and ended up with a nervous breakdown. I regret every one. They eat at me like worms."

"What can I do?" El Plástico says, "I should have followed my father's advice. He claimed that you must always have three women, because having only one woman is a problem and two women create problems, but having three women creates options."

The nearby church bells sound the hour.

"I'm not sure that would really help either," El Drone says, "Let's go for a walk. Let's go pick up some plastic."

"I don't want to pick up any damn plastic," the mayor says. "I want to know where those two cars were going. Do you have that clip too?"

"The hotel by the airport."

"I am seriously going to have to do something. I'll electrocute him like one of his fat pickles."

El Drone kicks into gear. "We need a do-over, boss. Reschedule your meeting with the deputy council. We'll take your truck and drive up to the coast and head back out on the boat. Let's start this week all over. Let's get back out on the Xtabay."

El Plástico and El Drone gather their things and cancel the rest of the morning. They speed off in a city truck, but halfway to the coast they get stuck behind a festival procession, four hundred marchers covering the narrow highway carrying a giant bier and crucifix. It is not Holy Week. What gives? El Drone rolls down his window and yells for an explanation. The Saint's Day of the nearby village, someone yells back. El Drone urges the use of the vehicle's siren and flashing lights. El Plástico resists, transfixed by the congregants, one face in particular, one young woman singing a song that reminds him of teenage Dolores. His own Saint Dolores. Singing a popular song he knows only too well, "La Peregrina," with poetic lyrics by Luis Rosado Vega, a lover's lament over a geographic and cultural divide. Its final refrain, a plea:

O wanderer who left her native coast…
Don't forget the ardent heartbeat of this land
Don't forget the fervent yearning of my love.

Cut to: El Drone and El Plástico climbing aboard the *Xtabay*. They cast off from the dock and hit the throttle and point the boat straight out to sea. Sun sparkles ricochet off the water. The wind claws at their hair. El Plástico's eyes fix fiercely on the horizon. He fantasizes about Dolores and running away to be with her, his true love. Almost like one of his epileptic hallucinations, he sees an animated GPS chart that shows him piloting the craft directly across the Gulf and up the Mississippi River to find his Saint Dolores in Indiana. To reclaim his heart and his past and his pride. He also sees a sweaty blur of bodies, Mercedes and Ramón, and their revenge sex in the airport hotel. Tearing at each other's clothes. Mercedes robotically in complete control and Ramón desperately trying to keep up. Mercedes' elbow knocks off his dark glasses. His briefcase falls open on the bed, spilling out clouds of cash. Colorful bills. Their naked limbs writhe and kick the loose money. The door has been left ajar. The unlocked door to the room creaks open. The maid, Tía Carlota, enters. She is carrying in an armful of clean towels and sheets. Tía Carlota eyes the chaotic bed scene and, without dropping her load, deftly reaches for a five-hundred peso note floating through the air. It would serve them right.

11.

Chad had wrestled with his job search. Slim pickings. Frank Vigo was correct about all the agency positions being taken. Chad applied for an NPI number and registered at CAQH Credentialing and read the Sunday classifieds in the Cave City Splinter. Winnie urged him to design a website. He shaved off his red soul patch and walked downtown to the spinning pole at Buddy's Barber Shop and suffered through one of Buddy's hatchet jobs. He taped a business card on the mirror wall, along with the real estate brokers and insurance agents. "You want it cut like we do it here, or like wherever you come from?" Buddy asked.

"Like you do it here," Chad answered. The result made him look like he had a court date. It was humbling.

At Winnie's suggestion, he strapped on a necktie to start the day. A disguise to feel employed. He sent out resumes and made cold calls and heard nothing back. He knocked on agency doors and left his business card at the hospital stress ward and detox center. And heard nothing back. With a little prodding, Father Mike referred a couple parishioners, actually scheduling the intakes and offering office space at the church.

Cancel. Cancel. No-show. Cancel.

Still nothing definite from Vincent about the moving van theft. It was a black hole. Vincent continued to claim his driver had temporarily gone AWOL. Chad finally fessed up to his father about the situation, hoping his attack-dog dad would jump on the legal and insurance stuff. Chief O'Shaughnessy scoffed and threw it all back at him, calling it a "maturity moment." Chad could not bring himself to call the police and file a lawsuit against an old teammate.

Chad's job struggle dragged on into September. He tried to hide his increasingly depressed moods from Winnie. She was cruising on all cylinders. Her internal girls-club appeared to be doing really well. She loved her teaching and her playtime afternoons, shepherding Nina and Paulo and the dog to the park. The children named the dog, 'Bongo.' At night, they enjoyed stargazing together on the sleeping porch at Frank's house.

Chad didn't want to bring Winnie down. He looked through the wedding magazines, sent by Prudence, and tried to make positive comments. "Your mom is pushing traditional vows, instead of writing our own," Chad said, "I guess it would be easier. What do you think?"

"I think we should do whatever we want," Winnie said. "That is, unless you want me to take a vow of poverty."

Chad heard this as a subtle dig at his unemployed status.

Frank suggested looking farther afield to bigger markets, Vincennes or Terre Haute. A gig there would involve a commute, and more time and more energy. Chad was starting to feel short on both. Maybe he should just ride out the year, tacking up Sister City flyers on telephone poles and helping Frank register student voters and babysitting Nina and Paulo, who had started calling him 'Shad.' They giggled contagiously when he made his lip-sucking, fish-face in response.

Chad occasionally participated in the daily rumbles with the kids and the dog, buying ice cream treats from the vendor in the park. Nina and Paulo got it into their toddler heads that every day was Bongo's birthday, which required a fiesta. They liked shopping for fishing lures online with Frank and Chad, favoring the ones with bright, colored eyes. "If I am fish, I bite on that," Paulo said.

They visited with Night Snow at her archeological dig in Mound Park. She wowed the kids with newly unearthed treasures, a chunky stone and an adze head. She also set them up for exciting discoveries of their own, by hiding arrow heads in the bushes and directing Chad to assist their search.

Some of these discoveries backfired, spontaneously making the kids cry, for reasons which Night Snow and Chad theorized might have something to do with their missing parents. Still no word from anyone in Guatemala, and, strangely, the kids never asked about their parents. The cabal members in the loop about Nina and Paulo agreed on a lame ruse; that if Nina and Paulo did start posing questions, they were to be told that their parents were away on a long trip. Nobody was quite sure what to do when the kids started referring to Frank and Winnie as 'Mommy' and 'Daddy,' and Chad as 'tío Shad.' The unspoken hope was that Dolores and Rosa would volunteer to take them long-term, but God knows they already had enough on their plate with Ricky.

Chad also became accustomed to Sunday afternoon sinners-mass at St. Fernando the Fur Trapper. The pews dappled with colored light from the stained glass windows. Outside, the wayside pulpit displayed folksy teasers such as, "Been Missin' Ya." Chad listened to Father Mike, the boy-priest, welcome his flock and proudly announce his appointment as special advisor to the Southwest Hoosier State Astronomy Club. Father Mike sermonized about Star Trek and the heavens. He tried to relate outer space exploration to the local immigration situation, with mixed results.

Chad initially pegged Father Mike as an endearing, guileless, red-shirt sucker, and figured the Catholic Church must be reaching far down the bench these days to staff its rural parishes. Father Mike began every sermon by intoning the Trekkie call to worship: "Captain's Log. Stardate: 2347. The corner of Third and River Street, outside the cemetery and Happy Dan Hotdogs..." And on the next Sunday, "Captain's Log. Stardate: 2356. The Persimmon Festival. A unique event on this distant planet, featuring the Outhouse Race..." A clever ploy actually, because it brought people to church to see if he would mention their business or their neighborhood.

As the days slowly got shorter and darker, the tang of decay in the air, Chad's temper and moods worsened. Hints of migraines flashed like a check engine light. He began to consider going to confession. To unload on Father Mike about the cravings and the recurring pot dreams, exacerbated by one of Night Snow's finds in the excavation, a small, jade one-hitter pipe. Chad walked daily through clouds of pot smoke in the student ghetto near his apartment and the tantalizing smell hijacked him back to a succored, self-medicating prehistory. He recognized it was getting dangerous when, waiting for Winnie to come home late one evening, he wandered down to the furniture storage garage behind the apartment building and tested the door knob, just in case someone had left it open, just in case that tin of half-smoked roaches was still hiding under the red sofa cushion. And, yes, it was open. Chad slipped into the dark storage area and eased down onto the red sofa. He worked a hand slowly down under the cushion. Hello, stinkin' thinkin'. Hello, relapse. So, this is how it happens. He'd always wondered exactly how his unraveling would go. A brief mental battle ensued and ended in a pyrrhic victory, a brilliant rationalization that it would be okay to just smell the roach. To just squeeze it and hold it up to his nose and savor the scent.

Fortunately, this triggered a flashback to his arrest. It was not a good memory. Driving across the Tobin Bridge after an outdoor, battle-of-the-bands concert with a load of ganja and a few suspicious types, including Vincent Guglielmo, who pointed out the flashing lights of the patrol car cruising along beside, signaling to pull over.

Officer: Do you realize how fast you were driving?

Chad: Seventy?

Officer: No.

Chad: Eighty?

Officer: No.

Chad: Ninety?

Officer: No. Five miles an hour, son. Five miles an hour on the Tobin Bridge.

A lot was being bottled up, mostly to protect Winnie, and himself too. Without intending to hurt him, Winnie could take advantage of these states, winding him up and watching him spin and crash into invisible walls. Her vow of poverty line still bugged him.

Confession might be a good first stop, before a return to a twelve-step group. Take it to confession, as Chief always advised, meaning: don't talk to me about it. Bottling things up was the O'Shaughnessy way and confession was their one outlet. Chad tried to imagine how he would tell Father Mike about his anxiety and his envy of Frank and Winnie's relaxed style with the kids. He heard Father Mike's probable reply through the grill of the confessional, "Beam it up, friend. Beam it up to Jesus."

He imagined telling Father Mike about going out to lunch, alone, yesterday at Happy Dan's Hotdogs. In a corner booth, eavesdropping on two guys from Butz Industries at the next booth, hemming and hawing about hernia trusses and the differences between first and second shift workers at the quarry, airing a gripe about parking spot hierarchy, given management's official hands-off policy. The second shift's attitude looser and less respectful because those people still think their jobs are stepping stones to something better, to something *else*, whereas the first shift gang are lifers who accept the unspoken parking spot rules. And on to a discussion of the bus factory's plan for retooling to RV production, playing to the new demographic of yahoos who sell their home and buy a rig and hit the road in an RV because the collection agencies can't find them on the road. And Chad thinking, what the heck, maybe I should try that.

Mustering his depleted mojo, Chad still managed weekly sessions with his one client, Ricky. His barter arrangement with Dolores and Rosa yielding yummy catfish tacos made with Frank's weekend catch. Chad and Ricky would throw the baseball for half an hour and then drink a Coke, sitting in plastic lawn chairs at the back of the trailer under a weeping willow tree. Every few minutes, Ricky nervously shifted his oversize Reds cap forty-five degrees, from front to side to the back of his head. His impassive, sculptural face resembled an image, magnified a hundred times, of a seahorse. If Rosa was home, she'd bring out a plate of *galletinas*.

It took a while, but Ricky's conversation slowly evolved from grunts and shrugs to phrases like, "I'm not as dumb as they think." Chad carefully served up some self-disclosure, modeling himself as a cautionary tale for teenage jocks who think they can get away with anything. He shared his own experience of playing stoned and refusing to bunt, of getting benched. Another unexpected source of help: Chad's ability to recall arcane stats on the Cincinnati Reds, the oldest team in the majors and Ricky's favorite. A big boost came on the day that Chad, having learned from Glodene Butz about her late husband's scouting career, arrived with a selection from Delmar Butz's baseball card collection, many from the era of the Big Red Machine.

Chad tried to keep their conversations simple, and occasionally include some Spanish terms. Likes and dislikes. Hopes and fears. Regarding Spanish, they both admitted to a fondness for the 'no fault' construction of screw-ups. 'I' did not drop the ball. No, the ball dropped itself from me. *Se me cayó la bola*. Eventually another of Ricky's interests emerged: music. To Chad's surprise, it was bluegrass music, not hip-hop or ska. Enrique Sánchez liked bluegrass and was learning to play the banjo. He wanted to start a Latin bluegrass band with a fiddler buddy from juvie, who still had six months on his sentence.

"Latin bluegrass?"

"A hard sell, but I think there are possibilities," Ricky said, "We're calling our band, 'The Undertakers.' We're aiming to build on the death angle."

"The death angle?"

"Common ground. Mexicans have their Santa Muerte, and my mom and Rosa at their hospice caregiver jobs are the Silent Angels. The gringos love their death dirges too. You know, 'Daddy's dancing skeleton done visited last night from the great beyond...'"

"I got an official letter in the mail the other day, saying that I had been pre-approved for death," Chad said. "Some kind of life insurance pitch."

"My point exactly. It's everywhere," Ricky said.

"Okay," Chad agreed, "but you'll have to be ready for the guff."

Ricky beat him to the punch. "The guff about banjo players being idiots. How do you know when the stage at a bluegrass concert is level? Because the banjo player is drooling out of both sides of his mouth. Enough of that. I've lived with that since kindergarten. People have been making fun of me since I was in diapers."

Chad began to encourage Ricky to open up about his experience of 'family,' broadly defined, including animals, his parrot, superheroes, Batman, and the deportation loss of Gonzalo. Slowly and intermittently, more backstory emerged, because everybody knows everybody's business in Hispanic families. Ricky shook his head, as he described how his mom turning lesbo only added to his confusion about his origins. He knew he was conceived in Ciudad de la Gruta, but not much more, having refused a trip to Mexico to visit his grandparents before they died. Initially, there was a story about his unknown father being a musician at her fifteenth birthday party. This got hazy when Gonzalo, tipsy on wine, twice blurted that he never really believed it. Ricky struggled hard with that obfuscation, because the girls in his high school who didn't know who had fathered their kids were sluts, and did that mean his mother had been a slut?

"She claims she left Ciudad de la Gruta to make a better life for me," Ricky said. "Maybe she was just running away from her own troubles. Maybe my life there wouldn't have been so bad."

Chad, relieved that Ricky could speak the thought, answered with a fist-bump, and wanting to stick up for Dolores, he added, "Honestly, so what if she did leave for her own reasons? That doesn't mean she didn't do it for you too. She took action. She made a change, just like you. People can change."

If only it were true, Chad thought, on the trudge back to his apartment. He did not sleep well that night. Winnie phoned him from Frank's house to inform him that the kids were having a rough time and she was going to stay with them, because Rosa had to go in to work a night shift for hospice and Frank needed a break. Alone in bed, Chad trembled through a dream about their stolen furniture, about the truck driver thief cavorting on Winnie's rocking chair.

Ricky Sánchez unwittingly reversed the roles at their next session. It was unseasonably hot and both Dolores and Rosa were away at work. The door to the trailer was locked. Chad waited for Ricky on the front steps. He stood and stretched and tapped on the window at the parrot cage. The bird squawked in response, "It's morning in America." Ricky drove up and coasted to a stop. He climbed out, swearing.

"Something wrong with the car?"

"Brakes just went soft, a couple blocks back. She's been needing new pads for a while. Can I ask a favor?"

"Sure, what is it?"

"Cheapest place to fix it is out in the county, but I hear they can be kind of rough on Latinos. You mind riding out with me?"

"No problem," Chad said, secretly welcoming the distraction and a spin in an El Camino, even though somewhere in the back of his mind he heard a supervisor questioning the client-therapist boundaries here.

Ricky put on his flashers. He drove slowly and punched in some traditional Yucatecan trova tunes. It was cool. Two guys in a car, driving around, listening to music. It felt good, this riding around. Chad tapped his foot and swayed his head. In the old days, the right music could change a dark mood.

Ricky hummed along to the quaint strumming and the harmony singing of the trio. He said, "For some reason that my mother won't explain, this song always makes her cry." "La Peregrina" again.

O my wanderer of lovely, charming face,
Don't forget the ardent heartbeat of my tropics
Don't forget the fervent yearning of my love.

Chad hummed along too. "I can understand getting emotional about a song like this," he said. It all felt bittersweet. Riding around in Indian summer and cruising past the soccer fields. Heading on out of town over the bridge, admiring the hills and ravines, resplendent with early onset ochres and oranges. The sun was a tawny ox, dragging time across the sky. They rattled across the wooden-covered bridge that Chad remembered from his first day in town. They passed a corn maze and a haunted barn, dressed up for Halloween.

They passed the Rushing Wind Bikers Church and the rural medical clinic for the *trabajadores*, where Dr. Rufus Crane, recognizable in his blue scrubs, walked in a circle around a picnic table, stuffing a sandwich into his mouth.

"This is Dr. Crane's place?" Chad asked. "This is where he fights the good fight?"

"Seven days a week," Ricky said.

Chad spotted Dolores' car in the lot. He asked, "Is your mom hurt? What's her car doing there?"

Ricky said, "She works part-time out here on Thursdays and Fridays, filing forms for Dr. Crane. It's another one of her jobs."

"She works everywhere," Chad said.

"Right, she works everywhere," Ricky repeated.

A tractor hauling a flatbed piled high with hay bales, and belching diesel from its stack, passed them tightly on a curve. Ricky, afraid the hay bales might tip over on them, swerved and the car almost went into a ditch.

"Oops, sorry. We're about there," he said, nervously.

"You okay?" Chad asked.

"I should have brought a baseball bat for protection."

Chad said, "You really think it might get physical?"

"No telling with this guy," Ricky said.

The El Camino slowed and made a curve around a long hedgerow of jewelweed. Beside the road, a series of four homemade signs announced: "I got a gun / Pretty and pink / It made the bad guy / Stop and think."

Chad shook his head and spouted, "Yeah, made the bad guy stop and think there's some latent homosexual tension here and this dude secretly wants a pink dick in his holster."

Ricky laughed and said, "You're sick, Chad, but I like that about you."

He turned into the driveway and came to a stop in the muddy parking lot of Brakeless Eddy's Brake Repair.

Chad finally figured it out, wham, and his heart started beating like a paint mixer. Brakeless Eddy's Brake Repair comprised a garage building with two bays and an office and an auto junkyard in back beside a small farmhouse. The parking lot was bordered with rusting, antique tractors. Chad began to cough, a spasmodic cough.

"*You* okay?" Ricky asked.

"I hope so," Chad said.

Brakeless Eddy O'Shaughnessy, sheathed in oil-stained coveralls, wandered out from the office and approached the driver's side window. "Hello there. Nice rig. What can I do you boys for?"

"My guaranteed muffler fell off and I need pads and there's maybe a leak in the line," Ricky said.

Chad remembered Frank Vigo's warning and prepared himself for the worst. He coughed again.

Brakeless Eddy produced a tissue from a little packet in his breast pocket and handed it to Chad. "We don't guarantee nothing against falling off, but not to worry. We'll get you fixed up," Brakeless Eddy said, "and by the way, you may have heard, I had a guy working here until a week ago, who carried a big chip on his shoulder about Hispanic folks, and when I found out what he was doing to my customers, I fired him on the spot. My wife's Honduran and her people and my own, we was all newcomers here not that long ago."

Breathing a little easier, Chad wiped his nose and said, "Thanks. You want us to drive on into the garage or roll her?"

"Put it in neutral. Let's give her a push," Brakeless Eddy said, and whistled for his mechanic.

Together, they all maneuvered the El Camino into the bay and onto the lift. Ricky and the mechanic gazed up at the underbelly of the car. Brakeless Eddy said, "My man here, Roy, is a wizard. He'll teach you everything you need to know about your set-up."

"Can I stay and watch?" Ricky asked.

"Fine with me," Roy said.

Brakeless Eddy and Chad O'Shaughnessy retired to the cracked, vinyl loungers around the desk in the office. On the desk lay a hunting rifle, in the process of being cleaned. Raccoon and skunk pelts hung on the wall behind him. Two shelves above the window featured other treasures from the forest, several racks of antlers and a stuffed coyote. Brakeless Eddy poured them both coffee and fingered an unlit cigarette. The insurance calendar on the door was a year out of date.

Brakeless Eddy dabbed at his broad face with a red bandana. Tiny specks of red cloth stuck on his chin stubble. He said, "I wander into town once a month or so, but I don't think I've ever seen you before. Are you new here? With the college or something?"

Without revealing his name, Chad nodded, "My fiancée is teaching at the college." And he added, "We came out from Boston."

Brakeless Eddy nodded and chewed on his cigarette. He turned toward the grimy window and stared out across the junkyard, seemingly trying to focus on something very far away. He said, "My grandpa hailed from back east too. On my dad's side. Story goes he was given a one-way ticket from Boston to Indianapolis at age twenty-one, just after his pop died. Worked as an elevator repairman up in Indy, a fitting job for a guy with severe bipolar disorder, as my doctor would say. Up and down. Up and down. Every generation tries to get away from it or send it away. My dad moved to Cave City to take a coal mining job when he graduated high school. Just a different elevator, going down in the ground. Fortunately, there's medication that helps me a lot."

Chad jumped up from his chair. Or, as he imagined telling Ricky in Spanish afterward, something *jumped me up* from the chair. And the scales dropped themselves from his eyes, and his stomach flipped itself over.

He said, "Can I bum a smoke?"

"Take a couple," Brakeless Eddy said and shoved the pack toward him across the desk. He recommenced cleaning the rifle.

Chad paced and unrepentantly filled his lungs and blew out the smoke, dragon-style, and did it again. He stepped over to the window and peered out at the junkyard and some distant features telescoped themselves into focus. Brakeless Eddy was on target. This grease monkey relative was right on target. Chad could see it now. His ancestors had tried to send the bipolar disorder away, expel 'it,' and when 'it' wouldn't leave subsequent generations alone, they tried to explain 'it' away as Irish moodiness. The ups and downs of the O'Shaughnessy men. Oh, they're just moody, just the Irish blues. Resisting any formal diagnosis and treatment, because O'Shaughnessy men don't want to blunt their brilliance. Reach for the bottle, or in Chad's case, the wee pipe.

He lit a second cigarette, internally debating whether to reveal his name, or just disappear after Ricky's car was ready and maybe not even tell Winnie. It was a confusing, bilious internal debate. What's the big deal about revealing a shared name? Why did that feel like committing an irrevocable act? Brakeless Eddy wasn't such a bad guy, at least when he was taking his meds. Maybe that was it, another version of Step One, yet again. Over and over, how many times admitting to the powerlessness, the up and down, up and down.

Brakeless Eddy said, "You look like you swallowed something that don't agree with you."

Chad said, "Guess what my last name is."

"I'm not good at the guessing shit," Brakeless Eddy said.

"I'm an O'Shaughnessy. From out east. And I think we might be related. The night before I flew out here, my dad finally told me that one-way ticket story," Chad said, "I'd never heard it before."

Brakeless Eddy spit and chuckled, "Hello there, cousin, or whatever you are. I shouldn't be surprised. My wife won't be surprised. She's been telling me for a couple years that what with everybody getting so obsessed with genie-fuckin-ology, it was only a matter of time before one of you boys showed up."

Cut to: Chad's relapse that same night, alone in the apartment. Winnie is not home yet. Chad sneaks down to the furniture storage area and hungrily inhales all the roaches, without thinking. Zombie-faced, he floats back upstairs to discover that he's locked himself out of the apartment. Immediate punishment from the Higher Powers throws him into a paranoid tailspin. He slinks off into dark streets and wanders past St. Fernando the Fur Trapper. He backtracks to avoid Father Mike, who is out on the roof with a telescope. Chad flutters like a moth outside the eerie night-light glow from the storefront office of Reginald Beek, Esq., Immigration Lawyer. He wanders across the Mexican War plaza. All the way down to Mound Park and Night Snow's archeological dig. Chad attempts to climb the 'no trespassing' barrier and, whoa, is confronted by Night Snow, holding a weapon, a prehistoric spear. She explains that occasionally she picks up extra cash, working overtime as security for the site, because of the market in stolen Native American antiquities. Chad explains nothing. He clutches his temples in both palms. A train whistle sounds in the distance. She asks if he needs help. He flees and gets lost and an hour later finds himself crouched in the bushes, peering in the living room window of Frank Vigo's house, staring at Nina and Paulo and Rosa and Bongo and Frank and Winnie, all playing a version of an old-time children's game: Ring Around the Rosa, with Rosa standing in the middle, swinging her arms. Ashes, ashes. Chad falls down.

12.

Couples therapy in Ciudad de la Gruta is like couples therapy everywhere. Hard work, with a nod or two to local healing traditions. Dra. Milena Madero is known as a practitioner who will try anything. She wears three pairs of eyeglasses, one on top of her head, one pair of silver half-rims perched on her nose, one hanging from a gold chain on her chest. A voluminous presence, she draws from a grab-bag of therapeutic, *curandera* skills. The walls of her office are covered with framed degrees and certifications, mirrors of all shapes and sizes, and shelves of Mayan artifacts, tiny carved figurines and glyph fragments.

Milena Madero, formerly married to the hyperbolic Peace Corps doctor, Rufus Crane, has been around the track. Another day, another encounter session. She is not at all intimidated to be sitting across from the mayor of Ciudad de la Gruta in her consulting room. They are awaiting the arrival of her mercurial patient, Mercedes. A beam of sun from a skylight falls on the empty chair next to El Plástico.

"I wonder what could be keeping her," he says.

"You know the old saying about bullfights and burials being the only things that start on time in our country…"

"Punctuality is usually one of her strong suits," El Plástico says and adjusts his pressed, white *guayabera*.

"Perhaps she wants us to have a few moments together," Dra. Madero suggests, "She wants to give you a chance to get a few things out. Is there anything you'd like to share, to help me get on board, before we begin the couple work."

El Plástico croaks, "Maybe Mercedes is out there squeezing in another tryst with that asshole, Ramón."

Unfazed, Dra. Madero suggests, "Let's give her the benefit of the doubt. She really was quite touched that you finally accepted her invitation to come in."

El Plástico shifts nervously in his chair. Scooching away from the spotlight beam that is slowly moving towards him. Silently cursing El Drone for talking him into this nonsense as a way to avoid a scandal. And nobody mentioned that Dra. Madero's new office, post hurricane, is a mere two blocks from the plush *palacio* of Mercedes parents', where she has fled from El Plástico's accusations. Mercedes is still denying everything, claiming the date with Ramón was a ploy to defuse his TiendaMax machinations.

"Free association. Is that what I'm supposed to do?" El Plástico asks.

"The floor is open."

"It's nice to see you again," El Plástico says politely, starting over. "You're looking well."

"Thank you," Milena Madero replies. "You flatter me. The years have added a few pounds. I like to think of weight as systemic. There's only so much mass in the world, and if one person loses some weight, then some other person gains it. I see myself as carrying these pounds on behalf of all middle-aged women."

El Plástico pats his paunch in reply. "Right, understood."

They had met years before, for several sessions when El Plástico and Mercedes were seeking help for young Juan Pablo Chayac. Despite the brevity of his kidnapping, the kid was traumatized by it and also by his own parents abruptly fleeing the country. He had attached himself to his perceived rescuers, El Plástico and Mercedes, as surrogate parents, thanks to some solid family work with Dra. Madero.

"I'm very grateful for your help with Juan Pablo. He's all grown up now and doing quite well."

"So I hear from Mercedes, and see in the newspapers," says Dra. Madero, "A soccer star at the *colegio* and an outspoken student leader."

"A bit too outspoken, if you ask me," El Plástico says.

"A developmental phase, I'm sure," Dra. Madero says.

"I know it is painful for Mercedes too," El Plástico says "for him to disavow us."

"Could be an underlying issue that we should talk more about together."

"He apparently wants to become a journalist, a very dangerous profession these days."

"A brave young man. A truth teller," Dra. Madero says.

"He does have a silver tongue," El Plástico agrees.

"He takes after his mentor."

"Now you're flattering me. He puts me to shame," El Plástico says, "What are all these mirrors, by the way? I don't remember them in your old office."

Dra. Madero answers, "Our Maya ancestors thought that mirrors were windows to the other world."

"They knew how to make mirrors?"

"Using crushed bits of hematite."

"I hope we can get a glimpse into the otherworld of Mercedes and Ramón," El Plástico grunts, glancing again at his wristwatch.

"Or into your own," Dra. Madero counters gently.

Does she know about my seizures, El Plástico wonders, has Mercedes told the doctor about my seizures? Sliding back into his chair, he tries to give himself permission to feel for once, at least for the next hour, that he is not in charge of the meeting.

"Marriage is a crucible," Dra. Madero says.

"Yes, and speaking of which, I believe that you were once married to Dr. Rufus Crane of Cave City," El Plástico blurts out.

"That's correct."

"You still have a research project together?"

"We're looking at the active ingredient in the Mayans' psychoactive herb, piziet, and also into their psychoactive use of reptile skins to see if it might have benefits for post-traumatic symptoms."

"What happened to your marriage with the gringo doctor? Why did you two split up?" El Plástico blurts again.

"Excuse me, but why would this be relevant?"

"I want to know if you think there's a fundamental incompatibility."

"Between who?"

"Tell me if you think the Sister City arrangement is fundamentally flawed. That there's a fundamental incompatibility, and that our antipathies with the gringos just go back too far, that it is impossible to achieve anything constructive."

Milena Madero switches out the half-rims on her nose for the ones on top of her head, as if trying to gain some perspective on a session becoming more complicated than she had anticipated.

"Mercedes frequently mentions how dedicated you are to your work, but I need to remind you that we are not here to talk about that. We are here to talk about your relationship."

"Do you think Sister City is a dead end? The referendum vote is fast approaching."

"I'm not sure my political views…"

"Because if it is, if I really am fighting a pointless, uphill battle to recertify Sister City, maybe I could let that go and return to the idea of the governorship. That would please Mercedes, wouldn't it? That's what she really wants. For me to be governor and for us to leave and move to the capitol. But, you see, what she doesn't understand is that a run for governor creates a new set of problems with the PRI and the Morena people. They pretty much leave me alone out here in our little pueblo, but if I were to run for governor, that would necessitate cutting a deal with the party's honchos."

Milena clears her throat and says, "Señor, truly, you might benefit from someone to talk to yourself."

El Plástico interrupts, "I talk to El Drone."

"And who is El Drone?"

"An expat gringo who could really use some of that psychoactive stuff you're developing, otherwise very *simpático*."

A shuffle and a light knock at the door. Mercedes slips in from the waiting room and slides into the empty chair, like a student late for class. She is dressed in jeans and a sweatshirt. No lipstick and no bug jewelry, her hair still wet from a shower.

Has she been eavesdropping?

She leans in toward El Plástico and confides, "I've been trying to get the *doctora* to prescribe me something for months, but she says I'm a healthy person. Can you believe it? Wouldn't it be so much easier if I could just take a pill?"

El Plástico feels a slight easing of tension. He realizes that Mercedes is as nervous as he is. Her lower lip hangs down like an open glove compartment.

Dra. Madero pauses for a few moments of recuperative silence and reaches over and rings a chime. Once, twice, three times, like starting a yoga class. It gets her clients' attention. She stands up from her chair and orders, "Up, up, come on now. Let's activate the body-mind. Let's wake up that body-mind."

Eyeglasses rattling, she demonstrates a few tai chi moves. She swings her arms into a C-curve. El Plástico and Mercedes hoist themselves up and awkwardly follow suit. "Once, twice, that's it, good." Dra. Madero invites El Plástico and Mercedes to sit back down and catch their breath and prepare for an awareness exercise. "A simple one, but challenging in its own way."

Dra. Madero directs them to turn and face each other and gaze into each other's eyes, resisting the urge to turn away, resisting the urge to break the contact, breathing through the anxiety in their stomachs, allowing the intimacy of seeing and being seen to take them to a shared connection from which the session can begin.

Adding a message explicitly for El Plástico: "Resist the urge to knit those dark brows into that famous politician's glare that is used to vanquish your debate opponents, because this is not a debate."

Adding a message explicitly for Mercedes: "Resist the urge to staunch those tears, if they're coming just let them flow."

Mercedes shakes her head, no. Enough is enough. She opens a palm toward El Plástico, silently demanding the handkerchief she knows he always carries in his back pocket. She dabs her eyes and blows her nose and tosses the handkerchief back to her husband.

"If your tears could speak, Mercedes, what would they say?" Dra. Madero asks.

"I can't pretend anymore."

"What do you mean?"

"You grow up thinking adults are in charge, and then you become one and realize that nobody knows shit," Mercedes announces, "Likewise, you grow up thinking the politicians are in charge, and then you get into the game and realize they make up the rules as they go along."

El Plástico snorts a gruff agreement.

"Tears are not usually so conceptual," Dra. Madero comments, "They're usually expressing something more emotional. More basic."

"I miss my *cómplice*, my partner in crime."

"Your what?"

"That's what she used to call me," El Plástico says.

"And what kind of crime would that be?" Dra. Madero asks, "By the way, I hope we're not testing the confidentiality laws here."

"Not at all," Mercedes says.

El Plástico explains, "You know the saying, 'this feels so good, it should be a crime.'"

Dra. Madero smiles and switches out her glasses again. "Are you saying that you two once depended on each other for reliable pleasure and self-soothing?"

"But then I discovered that my husband is a bigamist," Mercedes says.

"Excuse me?"

"Already married to his work, long before we met. Eighty hours a week. An obsession to wall himself off from real life."

"You used to admire me for it," El Plástico grumbles, "and we did collaborate on a few successful projects, and there was our parenting of Juan Pablo."

"We were just speaking about him," Dra. Madero says.

Mercedes sighs. "Our one true baby. Little did I know it would be our only baby."

"This again, my fatal flaw, my lack of manhood," El Plástico snaps and swivels to knit his brows at the mirrors on the wall.

Dra. Madero, seeking a reset, adjusts her eyeglasses and gazes theatrically down upon her clients' torsos. "Let me just describe to you what I'm seeing," she says.

She delivers a florid picture of their internal geography, with an emphasis on metaphorical details about their organs, arteries, viscera, the blockages in their hearts and so forth. In hopes of eliciting an expanded description of their internal emotional states.

"I see a blue, juvenile butterfly in your liver, struggling to break out of its chrysalis," she says to Mercedes.

Mercedes is having no more of this today. Not even from her longtime therapist. Mercedes considers herself to be a modern person, above all this hocus-pocus. Indeed, she studied economics at the university, and despite her own issues with spending, was the driving force behind El Plástico's effort to eliminate *la mordida*, by paying the police force a decent wage so they wouldn't have to resort to bribery.

Her lower lip trembles. Tearful sobs return.

El Plástico reaches over and touches her arm. "We were talking about Juan Pablo when you came in. I was about to mention my idea for bringing him back into the fold, by offering him the job of writing a Sister City Manifesto. All Mexicans love a good manifesto. He could make his mark with it."

Mercedes shakes her head. "Knowing Juan Pablo, it might make him angry and only drive him further away from us."

"Ignacio and Señora Calatrova think it's worth a try," El Plástico says.

"Old Guard sycophants," Mercedes sputters.

Attempting to maintain some control of the session, Dra. Madero returns to her X-Ray eyeglasses. She peers pointedly at El Plástico's belly and says, "I see a black snake curling up inside your spleen."

El Plástico nods imperceptibly. He knows the snake well. Turning around and around on the question of fertility. All the medical tests inconclusive. The faint snake turning it over and over, as if from light years away in the universe, whispering the possibility that his sperm worked well enough with Dolores, that his seed once did the deed, though he has no memory of it. Or there was some kind of chemical exposure during the Navy years, and this or that could exonerate him in the Court of Infertility. But no way is he going to open that can of trouble, and risk revealing where his true heart lies.

"Obviously, we're not going to fix anything here," El Plástico says, "I think what we're really looking for is some kind of negotiated ceasefire, some kind of annulment."

Mercedes chimes in, "The church's concept of annulment, crazy as it sounds, does have a certain logic to it."

"What kind of logic?" Dra. Madero asks.

"Same as with an arranged marriage. If the arrangement is faulty, void it," Mercedes says. "My father sold me to the highest bidder."

"You really believe that?" El Plástico asks.

"No, not literally, but we each thought it was a fair exchange. I was supposed to get a rising, honest, ambitious politician whose career would carry me out of this dusty flyspeck on the map," Mercedes says, "Then my husband decides not to live in the mayor's house and not to run for Governor and abandons our bed every dawn to walk around gathering up plastic bottles."

"And what were you supposed to get?" Dra. Madero asks El Plástico.

Silence. A throat-tightening cough.

"Tell her. I'd like to hear this," Mercedes says.

More silence. The black snake turns, and the skylight sun burns down on his head.

"Connections and compliance from the Old Guard?" Mercedes prompts.

"I was a poor kid from the barrio, an urchin who did not follow his father's footsteps in the circus and instead went into the Navy, because I wanted a fix," El Plástico interjects, "I lacked confidence and self-esteem. I wanted connections, yes, in the sense of feeling a part of life, instead of being an outsider."

"Speechwriter drivel," Mercedes says.

Dra. Madero intercedes. "The important thing is to realize why the deal broke down. Why it wasn't enough for both of you. Childlessness is an excuse. The deal broke down because you are human beings and you require a more genuine, personal relationship with a partner. You need to understand that about yourselves, or you'll go out and make another bad deal."

"With a real criminal from TiendaMax," El Plástico says.

"I don't know what you're talking about," Mercedes says.

"Oh, yes, you do. Be honest with me. That's all I want," El Plástico pleads.

"You just hate Ramón because he's your childhood enemy. He was smarter than you in school and a better soccer player than you," Mercedes sobs, "Ramón doesn't hate you. He's voted for you in every election."

El Plástico throws up his arms. "So I should be grateful that he stole my wife?"

End of session. El Plástico storms out.

In an attempt to calm his nerves and restore some faith in himself and his mayoral calling, El Plástico returns home and dons a hooded monk's robe. Despite the heat, he goes out to walk the streets anonymously. The hooded robe is his father's *lucha libre* costume. His father wrestled as the Fallen Friar in the traveling circus. Since *lucha libre* is traditionally a family affair, everyone expected his son to follow in that business, which is partly why El Plástico's moniker stuck. The term not only refers to his recycling efforts, but also a description of his character – a sort of superhero resiliency, flexibility, with a hint of brittleness.

El Plástico draws visceral inspiration from his robed, fly-on-the-wall rambles, like he does from the drone footage. Joining the crowds on the Avenue Hidalgo and watching the small Maya women hawk their bright garb, he checks on the dominoes game that runs continuously in a back stall at the *mercado*. Smells the day's catch at the fishmonger. Occasionally notes a code violation. He drops a few pesos in the basket of the sketch artist drawing portraits of tourists in Centennial Park. He laughs at a scrawled note taped on the rear window of a dinged-up Jeep: "Will trade for a tricycle or a fat *mestiza*." El Plástico thrives and revives on the city's pulse.

He admires one of the Sister City posters on the side of a city bus, part of the new campaign to both promote the Sister City referendum and to channel the voters' anger against Washington. The posters feature smiling, friendly faces of normal, everyday Cave City citizens. In this one is a corn-silk blonde waitress at the Elbow Room, paired with a poetic couplet: '*Un voto por mí es un voto contra el loco de allí.*"

Striding by the bus station, he tests the effectiveness of his disguise by slowing and shuffling past Gonzalo at the 'Official Directions' booth. Gonzalo perched on a stool, reading the sports pages. Gonzalo often attended the Fallen Friar's wrestling matches when the circus was in town. Light and shade. Bus traffic tintinnabulations. Does Gonzalo recognize El Plástico? No, okay, good.

This afternoon, El Plástico's anonymous ramble takes him to the Speaker's Corner in Centennial Park. As luck or fate or pure chance would have it, Juan Pablo Chayac is in action, waving his bullhorn and preaching against the Sister City referendum. Looking youthfully roguish with a thin, fuzzy beard and his red beret. He shakes his arms and scares off the pigeons from the heads of the statues. Juan delivers a fiery address about the cultural infantilization of Mexico due to North America's fetishization of the pseudo-primitive. "Whenever you see the word 'folkloric,' instead see 'propaganda,'" Juan Pablo says.

El Plástico appreciates his strong delivery, but struggles to comprehend the full message, other than its implicit call for a big man with a big stick. The student demonstrators applaud fervently. El Plástico fidgets and sweats inside his robed disguise. Maybe the students know something he doesn't. Maybe his thinking on the subject has been stunted by delusions of common ground, between himself and Mercedes and the gringos, and also with Dolores?

Fresh from the therapy session, his raw doubts worsen when he glimpses Ramón Puentes in the black Ford circling the park. Mentally poking at an old wound, El Plástico exacerbates his self-doubt about the apple ever falling far from the tree. A spoiled daughter of ill-gotten wealth, Mercedes held his impoverished childhood against him. Once she teasingly referred to him in a magazine interview as 'El Cheapo,' a pejorative version of his nickname still in use among his detractors.

The black Ford slows and stops. The tinted driver's window descends. Ramón Puentes, who also attended many *lucha libre* events as a child, recognizes the hooded robe disguise. He points his manicured forefinger at El Plástico and yells to the students, "Look, over there! A spy in your midst! The mayor!"

El Plástico turns and offers a fist to Ramón.

A few rowdy students take the bait. Voicing a new, cruder twist in their Sister City critique, they brazenly accuse El Plástico of being a cheapskate who sold out the city to a poor gringo sister, instead of a rich gringo sister. "We want Chicago! We want Dallas!" they chant, "Say NO to El Cheapo! Say NO to Cave City!"

Exposed and humiliated, El Plástico yanks the hood from his head, feeling as close to rage as he'd felt since discovering Mercedes' affair. Ignorant ingrates! How quickly a full stomach erases the memory of struggle. How quickly these kids have forgotten the hurricane and its devastation. Block after block in shambles. And their Cave City *compadres* – Doctor Crane, Frank Vigo, Glodene Butz and Night Snow, even some of the soccer players from Southwest Hoosier State, delivering truckloads of relief supplies within three days, driving round the clock, more efficient than the *federales* and the Red Cross.

Breathing heavily, El Plástico channels his ire into his real super power, the El Plástico dagger stare. The oft-photographed, conversation-stopping stare. Frequently seen in city council meetings and televised campaign debates, honed long ago in childhood by hours of staring contests with Ramón Puentes. Deep-set, shapely sockets, inherited from his father, surrounded by portentous brows, a black-hole glare from eons away that swallows planets. The oncoming light at the end of the tunnel that really is a train. Tight slits of eyeballs aglow like a predator at midnight.

To his credit, Juan Pablo recognizes the hypocrisy and the crude offense in the student jeers and calls them off. The demonstrators disperse and the black Ford disappears and El Plástico's internal hurricane subsides. Taking off the monk's robe, he crosses the street to Pandemonio and orders a double espresso. He receives a few enthusiastic *holas* and slaps on the back from other patrons, and, sipping the coffee, he remembers Dra. Madero's suggestion that he find someone to talk to. At first, thinking of

La Sombra Azul, only a few blocks away, but still not ready to forgive El Drone for recommending the therapy session. He recalls another of his bedrock sources of support, the elderly diva, Ignacio's girlfriend, lodged in the Opera House.

Señora María Inez Patricia Gómez Calatrova. A solid member of the Old Guard, who has championed him and Sister City from the beginning. Retired now, teaching piano and voice lessons to private students in the back of the Teatro de Reyes, a mansard marvel, built just before the Reform and badly damaged in the hurricane. The eccentric crone. She and Glodene Butz. The flame keepers of the secret matriarchy. The *abuelas* really do run the show here.

Señora Calatrova's father, Francesco Phillipe Cárdenas María de Rocha, the renowned tenor, lies buried in the orchestra pit. He was assassinated during a performance of *The Fairer God* on the night of February 4th, 1976. An impassioned operagoer rose from his seat in the balcony in response to Señor Rocha's signature aria as the captive Montezuma, before the execution scene. The audience member pulled out a pistol and shot the singer. Explaining it later as a mercy killing, so Montezuma couldn't get it from the Spaniards. The young señorita was a chorus-singer at the time. The girl ran out from the wings and cradled her mortally wounded father and heard him say: "Forgive that man. I die happy. This is the greatest praise a singer could ever receive."

María Inez Patricia Calatrova subsequently takes many lovers but never marries (except once briefly, or so the story goes, which is why she's called 'Señora'), choosing to remain her father's daughter to the end. The elderly opera singer continues to reside, appropriately enough, in her father's dressing room, propped up in bed beside the piano, wearing moth-eaten costumes, waving a hand fan, killing insects. To generate some additional income, she works two days a week at the music store on the plaza, in the sheet music department. She sits at an upright piano and plays the customers' selections, so they can hear the piece before purchasing it. She also accepts tips from the tour groups in the opera house and from her *fanáticos* and friends, including Ignacio. Everyone knows to bring flowers.

El Plástico arrives with a dozen roses from the shop on the corner (his mother would have chosen the appropriate color, but her expert knowledge has been lost to his generation). Ignacio is already present, paying court and providing an audience for Señora Calatrova's current student, who is none other than… Juan Pablo Chayac. He must have come directly from the demonstration for his weekly piano lesson. Have they arranged for this meeting? Are they waiting on El Plástico? Is this a set-up?

Several tense moments ensue, as pointless introductions and reintroductions are made. To buy time, to assess internal fight-or-flight data. El Plástico feels like the dumb rat in the maze. To make chitchat, he asks about the binoculars hanging from Ignacio's neck.

"In my old age, I have taken up bird watching," Ignacio says, "It was Delmar that got me into it. On the way over here, I saw a painted bunting."

"He and Delmar shared a bird list," Señora Calatrova says, "If one saw a bird, the other put it on his list too. The logic defies me."

"Delmar was very good at describing colors and wing structure," Ignacio says, "And, yes, there are many North American species that I have seen thanks to Delmar, though I have not actually seen with my own eyes."

Señora Calatrova laughs and turns the focus back on El Plástico and Juan Pablo. "You two rare birds know each other," Señora Calatrova says, not as a question, but as a pointed reminder. A rippling trill in her voice. Everyone in town knows their history. Both of them, the mayor and his adopted son, seem visibly eager to acknowledge it.

Juan Pablo bows from the piano bench. He readjusts his beret and says, "Papá, hello. I apologize. I'm sorry again for that scene in the park. Sometimes my people go a little too far. That Dallas, Chicago bit was absurd."

"Apology accepted," El Plástico states, "I'm glad to see you're still studying piano." Suddenly all his anger melts into an urge for a bear-hug.

"Of course. Thanks to you and Mercedes. You're the ones who got me started on it," Juan Pablo says.

"Not too bourgeois a hobby, even for a budding revolutionary?" Ignacio teases.

"Any excuse to spend time with the Phantom of the Opera," Juan Pablo replies and bows to Señora Calatrova.

"I was saddened to hear that you might be boycotting the Sister City soccer game," El Plástico says.

"No! Please tell me it's not true," Ignacio says, "We need all our best players. Those Cave City teams are getting better, now that they have so many of us living up there."

Señora Calatrova reaches into her bedding and extracts a thick envelope from under a pillow. She says, "We have been discussing the Sister City situation."

"I was reminding Juan Pablo that there is a long tradition of switching sides in our politics, an honorable tradition, nothing shameful about it," Ignacio says.

Señora Calatrova waves the envelope like a baton. "And I was describing this alarming letter from our dear friend, Glodene, who is very concerned about the future of the Sister City agreement. She writes about a crazy official on a horse –"

El Plástico nods. "Sheriff Hooker. Running for mayor. Used to be the coroner. The horse is a publicity gimmick, as is his Latina girlfriend. They call her 'Malinche.'"

"Maybe you should start riding a burro around town," Ignacio says.

"Also, there is a group called Parents with Boundaries who are trying to undo everything we have built for the children, including my choirs. The joint school choir concerts that we stream online."

"This I have not heard about," El Plástico says.

"Are you worried about the Sister City vote?" Señora Calatrova asks.

"More so every day."

"Especially with Juan Pablo here working against us," Ignacio says.

"Glodene reminds me that in our original agreement there is a termination clause which states that *both* cities must vote against renewal for Sister City to actually be voided," he adds.

"I'd forgotten, yes. Why did we do that?"

"The businesspeople wanted it for protecting investments in joint ventures."

Juan Pablo Chayac finally chimes in, "But that effectively binds each city to an international accord. That means we are operating as independent city-states. Washington and Mexico City will never stand for that in reality."

"Unless we make it a cause célèbre," Señora Calatrova cackles and winks. "And you like a good cause célèbre, Juan Pablo, don't you?"

"And how would you accomplish that, Señora?" Juan Pablo asks.

Key change. Señora Calatrova shifts the trill in her mature singer's voice to a minor edge. "El Plástico has an idea for stirring things up with a Sister City Manifesto. Our people love political manifestoes. And we can make it worthwhile for you to change sides. We call upon your eloquence. We call upon you to become the author of the Sister City Manifesto."

"What exactly would this document say?" Juan Pablo asks.

Señora Calatrova directs her envelope baton toward El Plástico. His cue, his chance to reestablish their bond.

El Plástico stands and raises his chin and speaks:

"Something like...Whereas, it turns out that two hundred TV channels are too many channels, and whereas this antic, fragmented, post-truth world has become so addled and confused and addicted to sensationalism and racist hyperbole and round-the-clock marketing, and whereas blind loyalty to nationalism and greed has become an impediment to humanity, and whereas federal governments have become inept cesspools of incompetence and corruption, and whereas everybody knows that small municipalities like ours must rely on self-determination, and must do whatever we can to preserve our dignity and our core downtowns, thus... thereby, accordingly, we the citizens of Ciudad de la Gruta, Yucatán and Cave City, Indiana believe it to be incumbent on ourselves for the purpose of our mutual survival and, oh yes, 'the pursuit of happiness,' to hereby reaffirm our joint commitment of sisterly support to the pursuit of our joint happiness no matter what those motherfuckers in Washington or Mexico City think about it..."

Ignacio erupts in applause. "I can't wait to see Sheriff Hooker's reaction."

"He might fall off his horse," Juan Pablo says.

Later that evening, in his un-airconditioned student apartment across from the basketball courts in Centennial Park, Juan Pablo Chayac sits alone and considers this interesting offer. From the open window, he watches a group of noisy kids playing basketball, running full court. Youngsters who don't yet have the ability to rise into a jump-shot motion, so they chuck the ball up with a side-arm thrust. Kids at the chrysalis age that Juan Pablo was when he was abducted and El Drone's surveillance copters saved him.

The Sister City Manifesto idea does have a specific appeal for him. And, historically, the Mexican people do resonate with the manifesto form. It would definitely broaden his audience, beyond his 2500 followers on Instagram. The resurgence of his bedrock loyalty to his birthplace and his soccer team begins to sway his political loyalties. He feels it well up in his throat. Though he assumes he will ultimately refuse to participate in the manifesto project, he feels flattered to have been asked to join.

He places a pillow on the floor to meditate. He sits cross-legged, in a half lotus. Juan Pablo, a regular practitioner per the advice of Dra. Madero, trusts that his meditation skills will lead him to some clarity on an honorable way to withdraw. Breathing pointedly through the base of the spine, the belly, the heart, the throat, the crown of his head. "My body is in the universe, the universe is in my body, and together my body and the universe combine. . ." But this evening his flow is interrupted by a clatter of ideas for the Sister City Manifesto. Implicitly trusting that El Plástico would give him the creative latitude, Juan Pablo finds himself breaking his breathing sequence every few seconds to reach for the notebook in his shirt pocket to jot down a thought. *We are optimists locally and pessimists globally...*

Cut to: Juan Pablo Chayac at his desk, tapping at his laptop, writing and editing the Sister City Manifesto. He prints a draft and makes corrections. He emails drafts to El Plástico and El Drone and the cabal in Cave City. They assemble in Mrs. Glodene Butz's brick Victorian manse, an annex to the Historical Society, where the retired librarian volunteers part-time, identifying the faces in the boxes of crinkly photographs that people bring in from their attics. Night Snow, Dolores, Chad, Winnie, Frank, Dr. Crane, and Glodene all confer. Everyone offers ideas. El Plástico and the gringo cabal email their comments and corrections back to Juan Pablo, and he makes further revisions that result in a twelve-point bulletin. It is published jointly online on the Sister City website and in the local newspapers, and on hundreds of social media pages used by immigrants to stay connected across borders. The ham radio clubs in both towns talk it up. The Sister City Manifesto is picked up by BBC Mundo as a human interest story. Sheriff Hooker first hears about it from Chica, who sees it on the Spanish-language channel out of St. Louis and thinks it is fake news. Sheriff Hooker does not fall off his horse, but he does throw a beer bottle at his TV set. "This means war," he fumes.

13.

Sheriff Hooker, back from work, purred and stroked Chica's head as she pulled off his boots. He allowed himself one hour and forty-five minutes in his lounger, after cantering home from the Justice Building and stabling his horse in the garage. He lounged from 7 - 8:45 p.m. Schedules were important, especially with the campaign heating up. Only three months until the Sister City vote. Healthy balance was important too. Sheriff Hooker was a balanced man. He kept half of his savings in mutual funds, and the other half in his mattress. Like his father before him, he clipped coupons and sprinkled flax seed on his Cheerios.

Sheriff Hooker resided in a ranch house with a satellite dish the size of an asteroid in his front yard, just beyond the industrial park. Above the front door, a horseshoe, nailed up in a U to catch the good luck falling from heaven. The location was barely beyond the city limits, so stabling a horse in the garage was technically legal. The neighbors were too afraid of him to complain about the smell and the manure he used as compost for his garden. And nobody complained about the clang of horseshoes banging against iron posts in the backyard on the weekends.

Chica, such a sweetheart, looked comfortable in her harem pants. It amused him to watch her chase flies with the vacuum cleaner and eat freezer frost with a spoon on the hot days. Still so enamored with the miracle of modern appliances. She helped him lift his sore doggies and assume a semi-horizontal position in front of the new TV. A flat-screen replacement, after the beer bottle incident.

The Sheriff nodded to the framed photograph on the wall of his son. Tiny Hooker, shown crouched in goal for the Frackers soccer team. Chica brought the Sheriff a fresh beer. They heard a volley of crow caws from the backyard.

"Any presents from our crow friends today?" Hooker asked.

Chica had been finding odd deposits on the patio, gasket rings and shiny .22 casings. "They are not my friends," she said.

"Why's that?"

"There's madness in birds," Chica said.

"No more than us," the Sheriff said, "You wouldn't believe what I had to deal with today, a guy trying to rob a gas station with a fire extinguisher."

Usually, Sheriff Hooker knitted or crocheted for a half hour before supper. A skill learned from his mother, as a way to relax efficiently and economically. He knitted baggy sweaters and scarves as gifts for Chica, to express his appreciation for her efficient and economical preparation of his nightly meal: mac and cheese, with beans and bacon, and one shake of Tabasco.

The Sheriff was all about economy and efficiency, the result of being the offspring of postal workers. His father, a mail carrier for thirty years, walked his route backwards so as not to undercut the union's time quota. After he died, they found a lifetime supply of golf pencils in his dresser drawers. Who knew? Knit one, purl two. Sheriff Hooker considered it an achievement that he could allow himself one hour and forty-five minutes in the lounger, without falling asleep like his dad.

Chica brought him a shot glass of his mother's cure-all, vodka infused with garlic. Right on schedule. "Thank you kindly," he said, "how is Hazel today?"

"She's looking very pretty," Chica replied.

"I'll be down to see her a little later," he said, "I have to write a short obit first."

Writing obituaries for the newspaper was another of Hooker's well-balanced habits acquired during his tenure as County Coroner, an above-and-beyond service that made him uniquely qualified for public office. The Cave City Splinter had cut back on staff and eliminated their in-house obit writer, forcing grieving families to produce their own obituaries. Mr. Hooker the Coroner, acquainted with most of the families in the area, offered his writing skills to the survivors of the deceased individuals whom he had pronounced dead, and remained dead.

His writing style had a vernacular appeal. Local folks who might otherwise struggle with penning these summary paragraphs came to him with requests. It was an easy, efficient way to make a hundred bucks on the side, quickly funneled into campaign donations. When concentrating, he curled his lips and chin up toward his nose. The breath from his nostrils made his mustache flutter.

After a short illness, and a long, ball-busting marriage to his high-school girlfriend, who finally skipped out on him last year, Floyd Smith kicked the bucket in the comfort of his own bed, surrounded by at least a couple of his known offspring. So long, Floyd. In his prime, Floyd was one of the best mushroom hunters in the county, most protective of his secret spots. Lord knows, you didn't want to cross him on that. Floyd worked as head auctioneer at Dinky's for twenty years. Honestly, nobody ever understood a word of what he babbled on about up there, but Floyd sure knew how to move a lot of crap out from people's barns. And don't get between Floyd and the dinner bell! The man liked a good ham steak, with mushrooms on top.

That should do it. After eating supper and ten more minutes in the semi-horizontal position, Sheriff Hooker rose from his lounger and went down to the basement to say goodnight to his mother. The stairs creaked ominously. Chica accompanied him, a step or two behind.

Chica was responsible for maintaining Hazel's hair and makeup. An important job, because Hazel represented all that was good and noble and worth wrapping up in a flag. Hazel had been dead for three years, and lay at peace, wrapped in a stars-and-bars shroud, inside a large freezer that Coroner Hooker had installed in his basement to handle the stiffs that were occasionally brought directly to his door.

Hazel still looked just like mom. She hadn't aged a bit. Sheriff Hooker had always intended to bury her in the graveyard behind the Pentecostal church, but just hadn't gotten around to it. Then came the run for Sheriff and Mayor, and Hazel had become a sort of unofficial campaign advisor. She had always known what was best for her son and she was never shy about saying it. *You gotta fix that hitch in your giddy-up.* Sheriff Hooker, gazing down at her freshly painted smile in the freezer unit, was somehow able to intuit what her advice would be regarding the various challenges faced by his upstart mayoral campaign. *Remember those consultants with their so-called improvements at the Post Office, well, your dad knew how to backstab those college boys...*

"Hazel, there must be a way to counter this Sister City Manifesto business. It's been spreading like wildfire," Sheriff Hooker said and extracted a newspaper clipping balled up in his pocket. He read aloud from Clause

#9, "'Whereas our two communities are linked by deep bonds and loyalties which cannot be broken by ignorance and fear and the propaganda of bigoted, corporate oligarchs, and whereas we collectively act to resist the erosion of our identity by globalization...' What am I supposed to do with this baloney?"

He cocked his ear, listening for a reply, and nodded and looked to Chica for confirmation. Chica was forced to play along, as if she had heard something too.

"Communism! That's right. It's godless communism. We fought it once, and we'll fight it again," Sheriff Hooker said.

To him, all words ending in 'ism' were confounding threats, to be despised. He added, "Oh, and that's a good idea too... We use it to get the attention of the party headquarters and they give us advice on voter suppression techniques and schedule a national candidate to give a speech downtown against Sister City communism and in support of yours truly and raising more money. And we all get our pictures taken eating barbecue with the candidate. How about that, Chica?"

Chica reached over to stroke Hazel's cold forehead. She liked to eat barbecue, but she did not like being photographed in ugly sweaters.

14.

Back when Coroner Hooker was writing obituaries for the bodies dropped off at his door, it wasn't just about a public service. It was to further his political views. The young coroner had hard-nose convictions and he used the obits as a way to spread them. Case in point, my poor parents, two crackhead cases dropped off in the night. Two teenage crackheads that Coroner Hooker eulogized as examples of all that had gone wrong with the godless U.S.A. Spewing blame on the Mexican cartels that smuggled in the drugs that killed these two stupid kids. And mentioning me, as a poor orphan, left to be raised in a foster home at the county's expense. I felt the effects of his pen firsthand.

"Mister Drone, you were an orphan, just like your priestesses?" Dotcom asks, sipping her juice.

"Yes, exactly." I cradle my head in my hands.

"You don't look like you've been sleeping well, Mister Drone," she observes.

"I'm like a log in the fireplace that has to constantly be turned over to stay lit, and in the morning I'm just a pile of ashes," I yawn.

"Is something wrong? Why can't you sleep?"

"I'm worried about the referendum vote. I'm worried the Manifesto may not be enough."

Dotcom is becoming adept at dragging information out of me during our confabs at La Sombra Azul. The more she chats with the Cave City retirees at Dance Hall nights and with Ignacio on his afternoon visits, the more she is getting involved in the Sister City struggle. She's often the first to hear the news from the front, like Sheriff Hooker's recent endorsement by the national head of his party.

Dotcom urges me to convene a strategy meeting between us and the Cave City cabal. For emphasis, she wags her carved wooden cane, a gift from Ignacio. Countdown to the vote: 87 days. Dotcom enjoys feeling part of an in-crowd. She listens to every radio broadcast of Ignacio and Señora Calatrova, and she wants to meet the Star Trek priest, Father Mike, who, according to Dotcom, is now in trouble with his board and the archdiocese for publicly declaring St. Fernando the Fur Trapper to be a sanctuary church.

Honestly, I've been thinking a lot about Cave City too, while lying awake at night. The expat returning to his native turf. I imagine going incognito. A homeless shadow, living in the Oracle Cave, right there with the spirits of Priestess Dawn and her tribe. As a kid, I was caught up in the Young Brave bit, along with Tomahawk, my dog, a fine hunter. We went after rabbits and sold them to restaurants. My nickname then could have been 'Straight Arrow'.

I was determined to be the opposite of my ingloriously dead parents. I was determined to right the wrong of their misguided lives. Unaware of any contradictions, I was one of those rah-rah schoolboys on field trips to the Tippecanoe battlefield, celebrating victory over the dark-skinned Other. All this during the War on Drugs. Teenage Straight Arrow fell for it whole-heartedly. That was going to be my battle. I signed up to get those narcos down there in Cartel-Land. Signed up to get them for the crack epidemic and killing my parents. Police Academy at Vincennes and a degree in criminology from Southwest Hoosier State, and on to Washington for training with the DEA. Before going undercover as a Mormon missionary in Chiapas. I looked the part. I was a technology advisor, wiretaps and such.

The specialty in drones came later, after I figured out how to arm the small copters. My reputation among the narcos benefited from a curious mythological coincidence, a minor bird god in the Aztec pantheon, a hawk dealing death from the sky. Just like my weaponized drones. I inspired a lot of bunker building. The narcos saw me as a serious badass. In reality, I was a numb button-pusher, blindly removed from the consequences of my actions. I operated inside a mobile command unit that was hauled around on an armored flatbed trailer. My flying devices had a range of thirty miles. Other than that, no official limitations. I was free to fire on anything remotely suspicious with daisy-cutter style, cluster explosives.

I did that relentlessly, adding notches to my existential gun barrel in the name of Old Glory. And then going out to party with the local señoritas. I felt like a conquistador. It was the *piñata* life. The *piñata* having been my only exposure to anything Mexican as a small child, thanks to Delmar Butz who sponsored an annual party at the Boys and Girls Club. What a blast. Indulging in destructive tendencies, bam, and being rewarded with a shower of candy. Later in my *piñata* life, I blew up people and their houses all day and celebrated my tally all night. Until one day in transit, by chance, our flatbed convoy drove me by the site of our latest attack. It was a small ranch outside a pueblo in Chiapas. Because of the distance from the town, no one had come out to clean up the mess. All the bodies. Women and children and old men and dogs and animals. It was just a normal, rural community. It was not a narco cell. I had blindly destroyed many innocents many times over and I never had to see it. One dead dog in particular reminded me of my childhood pet.

Maybe that's why I feed the strays here in Ciudad de la Gruta. And buy lunch for Dotcom in my AWOL sanctuary in La Sombra Azul. She could easily have been one of my victims. I wax on about Priestess Dawn and Priestess Moon, like the hippie standing over at the bar, who believes he is the reincarnation of Quetzalcoatl. The U.S. authorities leave me alone, because I have not publicly ratted out the drone attack program. And the Mexican authorities, wary of my loose cannon status, respect El Plástico's protective cloak. Currently, I am staying at the airport hangar that also houses my drone equipment, while I repaint the copters and cameras in brighter colors. Feedback from the mayor's latest survey indicates that the local citizenry, inured to subtle repressions, enjoy the fact that my drones resemble dragonflies in the sky. Dragonflies are good things. They eat mosquitoes.

Dotcom and I hide out in our respective fantasy dimensions, both of us in exile. Maybe she's right about my fixation on Priestess Dawn and Priestess Moon and their successful, albeit brief, joining of their two limestone worlds, and my attempt to go back home again and do it all differently.

A week later. Dry palm-frond husks scratch across the dusty tile courtyard of the cantina. A gauzy sun floats on a cloudbank. Autumn temperatures are starting to diminish a bit. Dotcom sucks an apple juice with a straw and tilts her crooked face toward me and asks, "Do Priestess Dawn and Moon have voices?"

"You mean, literally, in my head?"

"Where else?"

"I suppose so. In fact, they both are starting to sound a little like Señora Calatrova."

"What do you mean?"

"That little trill in her throat."

Dotcom laughs and says, "Mine too. All my people are all starting to sound like you and Ignacio and Tía Carlota and Señora Calatrova."

"That's a good sign," I say.

"A good sign of what?"

"A sign of feeling connected, part of a group."

Dotcom sighs and says, "Do you think I'll ever know what it is to be in love? Could a man ever fall in love with me?"

"Just a matter of time," I say, "It would help to get rid of that pink hair bow."

"Oh, no. It's attached, like an appendage," she says.

Dotcom raises her glass towards mine, to practice a new ritual, taught to her by Tía Carlota and the dancing retirees.

"Toast, but not like bread toast," she says.

"Toast, but not like bread toast," I say, "Here's to you and your lucky stars."

"And to the red-haired man on the bus who saved me," she says, "with the gold-rimmed glasses."

"And to the referendum," I add.

"El Drone, do you think it would be possible for you to contact Priestess Dawn and Priestess Moon and ask them to do something for Sister City?"

"Are you serious?"

"Something to stop Sheriff Hooker."

"Do you mean fast-forwarding into the future?"

"As usual," Dotcom clucks, "I'm several steps ahead of you."

I nod and raise my glass to hers again. A welcome breeze flows in, rustling the leaves of the ceiba tree in the courtyard. Dotcom has been instructing me on its many uses. The sacred tree of the Maya.

"Do you know any of the townspeople coming for the strategy session?" she asks.

She is referring to the upcoming Sister City convocation, now officially scheduled next month by El Plástico, a gathering of civic leaders from both towns to discuss the fate of the referendum, with Dotcom hired on as translator.

"Only Glodene Butz. It's hard to believe she's still alive. When I was a kid, she and Delmar drove around town in a golf cart, with frilly Acapulco decorations, circa 1966. She was always loud and proud for Mexico, because of her baseball scout husband."

"Señor Delmar," Dotcom intones, "The spirit of Señor Delmar seems to be very active."

"Glodene is a force to be reckoned with too. She still sits on the board of Butz Industries, the family business that funded Delmar's baseball career."

"She is what is called a *battle-axe*?" Dotcom says, showing off some new vocabulary.

"Don't tell that to Ignacio," I whisper, as we turn and see the stooped gentleman push through the front gates, along with a mangy *perro*.

Dotcom giggles and attempts to wink. "Oh, *she's* the other girlfriend he wants, but he thinks he can't have her?"

"She's the widow of his best friend."

Dotcom and Ignacio have been getting acquainted. He recognizes a like-minded obsessive in her. Ignacio stops in on his afternoon strolls and pays his respects to the disfigured savant. They have been exploring the topic of baseball, new territory for Dotcom. Basic vocabulary: *jonrón* and *lanceador* (although Mexicans just use *pícher*). Dotcom knows little about the game, but she wants to be able to talk baseball with her dancehall clients. As one might expect with two such minds, Ignacio and Dotcom dive into Delmar's theoretical musings on the origins of the game. Why it is so popular in North and South and Central America? Delmar believed that baseball is living proof that underneath the surface split between North and South, there is a more fundamental unity. He believed that the bat and ball are echoes of the tribal game of chunkey, and that the layout of the field mirrors an ancient Mesoamerican village. The pitcher's mound at the center of the game is the Temple Mound, the bases are the dwelling units, the base paths are the literal dirt paths that existed between these features of the village, and the outfield walls are the stockade. It sort of makes sense. Dotcom takes it a step farther. She sees the game as a pan-tribal gauntlet of inclusion and exclusion, the job of the fielding team being to put 'out' the individual batter, who is being challenged by the pitch, by the hurled challenge from the Temple Mound to prove his worthiness in navigating the ways of the village.

Today, Ignacio Morales wiggles his cane in greeting at Dotcom. He pauses first by the bar to respond to the needling from the expat regulars: "*Holá*, Professor, any luck with the Grand Equation? Have you cracked the code?"

Ignacio nods gravely. "Gentlemen, I have big news. It's an algorithm based on the root of 1492."

"When Columbus sailed the ocean blue?"

"Very astute, sir."

"And? What does it mean?"

"We're screwed," Ignacio says, with a straight face.

"Oh, no. What's going to happen?"

"The Second Coming."

"Of Jesus Christ?"

"No, the conquistadors. Only this time the conquistadors are coming from Outer Space."

He waits for the crest-fallen, expat drunks to choke on their silence, then grins and stumps on over to our table, where Dotcom gleefully awaits him, knowing the joke was really meant for her.

15.

In the spring of 1849, Ignacio Morales' great-great-grandfather, on his mother's side, the pure Maya side, had been fighting in the Caste War against the Mexicans at the siege of Mérida. Noticing groups of swarming ants, the traditional signal for the spring planting, he left the battle to return to his village to help put in the corn crop. And nobody thought anything of it.

In the spring of 1862, in the middle of the American Civil War, Delmar Butz's great-great-grandfather, who would go on to found Butz Industries, noticed bluebirds flying north across the Tennessee sky after the Battle of Shiloh. He walked away from his rebel battalion in the middle of the night. He hiked to Cave City to help plant the corn crop. And nobody thought anything of it.

Back in his study after his constitutional, Ignacio shakes his head and rubs his chest. He has been feeling out of sorts lately. Surrounded by chalk numerals on the walls, he fears that he has overly internalized his research into the Grand Equation. He eases down into a slipper chair, rubbing circles on his chest.

Señora Calatrova sits down beside him. She smokes a cigarette in a long holder. They are planning the upcoming Saturday radio broadcast and drinking hot chocolate, ferried in by a maid.

Señora Calatrova drapes a forearm up over her forehead to block the sun from the west windows. It looks like a pose, a swoon. She wears a bemused and bereft diva expression that appears to be asking: What will our vile enemies throw at us next?

She says, "Let's do a show about teaching opera singers to act. They never get enough instruction in acting. I ask my students to both sing and act out the scenes they bring me. Yesterday, I'm with a young soprano who specializes in tragic roles. I have to stop her and inform her: sorry, you've made a common interpretive error, on the line where you soar and sing about having been happy once. The problem is that you actually looked happy, and it's a common mistake in the middle of great trouble to sing a line like that and appear happy, except the character is *not* happy."

"Truthfully, neither am I," Ignacio groans.

"What is it, my friend?"

Ignacio tries to explain his physical and mental quandary. The transcendental numbers have become too much. He points to the chalk-covered blackboards. "I keep coming back to zero. The numbers keep coming back to the Big Bang equation, t=0. Time equals Zero. I think that's what it was all about for the Maya. Not in the sense of absolute emptiness or division by zero or the end of time. Although, of course, their mathematics were always intimately connected to periodic collapse. Their Doctrine of Cycles. It was more that they reached a point of recognition that, as my quantum physics colleagues now understand, time is actually discontinuous. There is no flow. There is no forward line. Time, such as it is, exists only in discreet, random, free-fall units. The Maya were able to foresee our descent into this post-timeline staccato limbo of extreme relativity, of not-knowing, of not having a thread."

"And this is a problem for you how?" Señora Calatrova asks. She leans in and gently strokes her distinctive nose, as if summoning her genie.

"My heart feels like an arrhythmic time-bomb. I seem to have taken this all in too far, not only as an idea, but as a physical reality. I feel like an old movie projector, sputtering through life at twenty-four frames a second. I've lost the illusion of the flow of experience. I go out for my walks and everything is a herky-jerky, molecular collage."

Señora Calatrova waves her cigarette holder and says, "Fantastic, very interesting, Ignacio, grand upon grand." Always a fountain of positive regard, so engrained in the women of her generation, she gushes on, "It sounds like an exciting modal shift, like a piece by Lavista. Let's talk about it on the next radio show."

Ignacio winces and forces a smile, trying yet again to trust in his chalky calculus and its promise of a defined infinity. He puffs a dark cloud from his pipe.

16.

Countdown to the Primary Election in Cave City: 79 days.

A billboard appeared at the edge of campus, at the far end of Tecumseh Avenue, picturing brown-skinned drug addicts with needles in their arms, swarming over the border wall. Paid for by Parents with Boundaries. The cabal responded by taking up a collection (with Glodene providing matching funds) and they put up a billboard out by the highway exit that featured photos of Hoosier exchange students climbing up the Jaguar Pyramid and a picture of Mexican exchange students climbing over the Snake Mound and the caption, 'We Go Way Back Together.'

The caption was Chad's contribution. His only positive contribution in weeks. Recovery is recovery is recovery, whether in Mexico or Boston or Cave City, Indiana. A gradual process, one day at a time. There are a few local variants in Cave City involving meth and moonshine, dental issues and infected, calcified nose bumps caused by drinking from mason jars.

Obviously, Chad O'Shaughnessy needed to return to a recovery group. It was obvious to Winnie, at least. Whenever he changed his passwords, something was up. And when he stopped doing his basic 25/25/25 exercise routine.

Chad could still summon his game face for appointments with Ricky. He could still pretend to function with Frank and Paulo and Nina. At night on the sleeping porch, he tried to channel Father Mike and teach the children about the stars and outer space.

"The sun itself is a star."

"A daytime star?" Nina said.

"That's right."

"Is inner space a thing too?" Paulo asked, "or just outer?"

"Sure, you each also have a universe inside," he said.

"You're just trying to scare us," Nina said, the skeptical one.

"Point taken," Chad said, "the inside universe can be scary."

"When that happens, I crawl under my bed," Paulo said, the stoic one.

"That's a good idea," Chad said.

Back at the apartment, a lot of tight-jaw grimaces and staring at the wall. And the annoying feeling of always having a hair on his tongue, and trying to pluck it off, but finding nothing. Chad knew from vigils with his grandparents and several pets that 'turning to the wall' was never a good sign, in animals or people.

"Why are you changing your passwords, Chad?" Winnie asked again.

"I don't know. I didn't like the old ones."

"Is it for security reasons?"

"I've already forgotten the new ones. I think they were the names of Indian tribes."

Winnie usually handled his depressive dips with encouraging, buck-up blinders. This episode was different. She noted the loss of appetite and the uncharacteristic sighs. He gave up on tango class, and stopped putting on a tie in the morning. No more out-of-the-blue, poetic expostulations on random topics such as Nina and Paulo's fascination with hide-and-seek. He lost interest in board games. And, a major clue, he lost interest in sex.

"Chad, do you remember telling me about Chief's birds-and-the-bees talk?"

"Yep, the 'man-in-the-boat' talk."

"Chief's term for clitoris, 'the man-in-the-boat.'"

"Typical of him to make it a male entity."

"And what did Chief advise about the man-in-the-boat?"

"'You have to keep the man-in-the-boat laughing.' I know, sorry. Just don't have the energy."

Meanwhile, Winnie and Frank were going forward into the fall semester. Frank Vigo was back in top form. With the cabal's assistance on the home front, Frank was able to reengage his latest research project: a study of local *retablo* paintings. Outsider art images that are a pictorial tradition among newly arrived *indocumentados*. Each person creates a picture with paints or pencils or pen on paper or cardboard or wood that symbolizes one's gratitude for the safe passage across the border. It was all Frank talked about anymore, at the dinner table, at the Elbow Room. After school, he knocked on doors in the Latino ghetto, the motel rooms with six guys inside. He took photos and interviewed patients at Dr. Crane's clinic.

"It is folklore happening live," Frank said, hoping to stimulate some response in Chad during pizza night with the kids. "There's a new phenomenon occurring. I'm starting to see the exact same image appearing over and over in *retablos* from this area, a tunnel. I'm calling it the 'spirit tunnel.' Maybe you'd like to come with me to do some field work, to help out?"

"Good for you, Frank. Very nice," Chad replied. He tried to rise to the occasion. "I could help take the kids fishing tomorrow."

"Yes, all go fishing with Shad," the kids yelled.

"Sounds like fun. I could use a break," Frank agreed.

Unfortunately, the fishing adventure only exacerbated Chad's sense of incompetence. No good deed goes unpunished. Rubber boots, floaties, sunscreen, a green mesh net. They drove out early to the covered bridge. The kids were mostly interested in chucking rocks at tadpoles. It all went pretty well at first, or rather, nobody got hurt. A lot of catch and release in the sandy creek, and Frank coaching the kids about hanging in till they landed a 'keeper.' Finally, Paulo and Nina both got a strike. Two shimmering trout. The kids were thrilled. Chad felt okay too. Mission accomplished, until the next morning. The adults gathered for breakfast. They fried the two fish on the stove and called for Nina and Paulo to come downstairs to eat their catch. Sudden cries and lamentations sprang out from their sleepy faces. They ran over and attempted to embrace the dead fish on their plates. Nina and Paulo thought the word 'keeper' meant they were keeping the fish as pets.

Hard to spin Chad's unshaven lethargy into anything constructive. He blamed it on the encounter with Brakeless Eddy, which had stirred something he couldn't describe, and which nobody in his family wanted to discuss. On the phone, his father laughed it off as "just your luck." The elevator image haunted him, or so Chad claimed. Up and down. Up and down. He remembered being frightened of the elevator in the Back Bay office tower, going up to his dad's office on the fortieth floor. And with good reason, he now realized.

Chad lapsed into minimal contact with friends and family. He stopped trying to reach Vincent. Everything needed an apology. Sorry for squeezing the toothpaste wrong. Sorry for my socks on the floor. The weather didn't help. Swirling, yellow clouds of wet leaves mirrored his mood. Leaves on the windshield of Ricky's car, like tickets from the autumn police. Chad spent the shorter days and longer nights streaming the Red Sox on WEEI sports radio and complaining about the bullpen.

"Forget about the Red Sox," Winnie said, "We live *here* now. Get your sulky ass to an AA meeting. If there isn't a Narcotics Anonymous meeting, AA will do."

Yes, okay, babe. "Have a good day at school. Say hello to everybody for me." Back to bed to watch the numbing TV galaxy of city council meetings on the community access cable channel, staring at the byzantine proceedings for hours, Mayor Ralph Rosewater presiding in double-breasted seersucker, taking up his highway exit plan and refusing to talk about the Sister City referendum.

The sticking point for Chad was his slowness in recognizing that basic mental-health hygiene was reason enough to go back to a 12 step meeting. He rationalized that because his relapse was a onetime event, he didn't need to do anything about it.

"Bullshit," Winnie said. "Get a grip. Therapist, heal thyself." She wouldn't give up on him, dammit. He finally acquiesced.

"That's a very handsome t-shirt you've been wearing for the last five days," Winnie said.

"Okay, okay, I'll go to a meeting."

But, how to find the right group in this town? On the following Sunday, Father Mike began his sermon with a Captain's Log description of an AA group called the Shivering Denizens who met at the public library. Chad made a note, prompted by a sharp elbow from Winnie. Usually, a 12 step group with enough gumption to name itself was good, and he knew how to get to the library. And if somebody recognized him…back to square one. Been there, done that.

My name is Chad and I am an addict.

He showed up late for a noon meeting in the basement of the landmark building, and hovered outside reluctantly, hobbled by a few last-second qualms. What if the person to recognize him was Ricky? Chad had been encouraging him to check out a teen NA meeting. How would Ricky feel about discovering that the catcher he had been waiting for was also an addict? Chad paced in circles. The Higher Power thing was a problem too. Knowing how the process works can sometimes be an impediment to it.

A door to the basement stairwell opened and a familiar figure appeared and grabbed him by the arm. "Come on, Chad. The meeting is inside."

It was Night Snow. She was all business, crow feathers in her braids today.

She hauled him into a large, windowless room full of men in overalls and three-piece suits, electricians and academics, and one guy in a bathrobe and pajamas with a toothpick behind his ear. Someone tried to pass a bottle of water to the toothpick guy and he complained, "The only thing I hate more than bottled water is tap whiskey." There were women in overalls and professional attire, paralegals and vet techs, and one lady in a flannel nightgown, who grabbed for the water bottle, and complained, "I am dryer than a burnt boot."

No sign of Ricky, thankfully.

"Take a seat. You'll be okay." Night Snow said. She gently tugged at his arm. Chad descended into a chair beside her. She handed him a cup of coffee. The scripted litanies had a stabilizing effect. Recovery is recovery is recovery. "All God's children gotta come from somewhere. And nobody thinks well of you, if you can't think well of where you come from," said the moderator, another familiar figure from the cabal gatherings. Dr. Rufus Crane, attired in his standard blue scrubs.

"What's he doing up there?" Chad whispered.

"A lot of doctors are pill heads," Night Snow said, "Before he started the clinic, he got fired from the hospital emergency room for handing out too many free samples."

Over the bumpy course of the next week, with two meetings a day, Chad listened to the same hair-raising accounts of ruin and hitting bottom and rising from the ashes that he'd heard a thousand times before, with some local variants involving predatory deputies in Sheriff Hooker's drunk tank.

And he met the Crazy Girl again. She was a fixture on the scene, appearing at all the recovery groups and rehab establishments that Chad had ever attended. Initially, he gravitated to this sleek wraith's confluent magic like a moth to flame. Flamboyant declamations of injustice and abuse, and showy displays of scarring, and guzzling hand sanitizer, and sex in elevators and mechanical rooms. The Crazy Girl had it all. At least now he could recognize her, a bit rougher around the edges this time, a little older.

It was Night Snow. She was the latest incarnation. The eyes and hair and unlaced hiking boots and a new nose-piercing and the feathers bit. Turns out she'd been valedictorian at Cave City High and gone east to Dartmouth College on an American Indian scholarship, during their messy mascot debacle, before getting expelled for too much firewater and cocaine consumption and uppity AIM provocations and behavior unbecoming a Shawnee.

"I was Exhibit A in Buffalo Bill's Wild West Circus for smokin' Indian chick run amok off the reservation. Because I messed up so much at being Indian in the present, now I focus on Indians in the far past," she said.

"I don't have to guess why you always wear long sleeves," Chad said.

"Sliced myself up pretty bad," she said.

Chad nodded and said, "I'm too narcissistic to cut on my fair skin. But I have self-administered some internal scars. The latest thanks to an encounter with a guy named, 'Brakeless Eddy.' You know him?"

"I know *of* him," Night Snow said.

Chad sighed and rubbed the spot under his lip where his soul patch used to be and said, "Can I ask you a favor? I'm going to need a sponsor. I'm going to need someone to air this out with. I'm not doing a very good job of it with anyone else, even though that's supposedly my field. You ever been a sponsor?"

"Yes, I'll do that for you," Night Snow said and patted his shoulder.

Winnie was aware of Chad's vulnerability to the Crazy Girls, but she also knew that Chad needed help now. She shelved her trepidations and went along with Dr. Rufus Crane's official suggestion that Night Snow become Chad's sponsor. Winnie knew and trusted Dr. Crane from the editing sessions for the Sister City Manifesto. Though a little suspicious of Rufus' pious, Peace Corps demeanor and the blue scrubs costume, she gave her blessing after checking it out with Frank Vigo. Frank vouched for Night Snow's long-term sobriety. They had driven a supply truck together down to Ciudad de la Gruta after the hurricane. Frank also hinted that if Chad got on board with the program, it might prompt Dr. Crane to hire him as a therapist out at the clinic.

"Rumor out there is he needs somebody to work regular hours as a counselor," Frank said, "He's been trying to hire a shaman, but apparently shamans do not work regular hours."

Slowly, a healthier routine emerged. After his noon AA meeting, Chad walked to Happy Dan's Hotdogs to buy takeout sandwiches. He proceeded to lunch with Night Snow, either at the Mound Park dig, or at her job in the archeology department on campus. She maintained the diorama exhibits of stuffed animals and papier-mâché trees and forest Indians huddled around cook-fires in the far past. Some days, Chad brought peanut butter and jelly sandwiches from home.

Night Snow liked to jaw about her visits to Boston during college, stealing sculls for rows on the Charles River and several hazy weekends on Cape Cod. "I spent a month in Provincetown one night." She claimed to be a dedicated Patriots fan, which Chad found hard to believe.

"Indians and football go way back," Night Snow said, "We developed the first trick plays. I still buy tickets whenever the Patriots play the Colts up in Indianapolis. They're coming in January this year. Let's go together."

It was good medicine overall. One day at a time. Chad relished talking the shop talk again. Fake it till you make it. In her capacity as sponsor, Night Snow added a few of her own recovery mantras: "Joy and suffering are not opposites. Cynicism is the opposite of joy, and callousness is the opposite of suffering."

"Wait, I'm not sure if the original Cynics back in Rome would agree with that," Chad said.

"I'm frequently wrong, but never in doubt. I mean 'cynicism' in the modern sense," she said.

"As in, not caring about anything."

"Yes, that would be the clinical description," she said.

"My favorite diagnosis," Chad said, laughing aberrantly, a pent-up laughter.

It became their private line, to be inserted after any basic observation. "The sky is sure blue today."

"Yes, that would be the clinical description."

Chad was surprised to feel their recovery disputations creating a no-drama bond, which was physically deepened by Night Snow's close-talking style. A few breathy inches between mugs. The fluctuations in her thoughts, like the bouncing flight path of a towhee. "Are you aware that the air we're breathing is the same air that my tribal ancestors breathed five thousand years ago?"

"Is that why it smells like onions?"

She chewed on her sandwich and smiled. "The early tribes harvested wild onions for sure. They're depicted in that scratched-up tablet of hieroglyphs leaning in the corner."

He squinted and followed the line of her pointing finger to the far wall of the 'Staff Only' workshop area, over behind the diorama exhibits. "Something you just found in the mound dig?" Chad asked.

"That particular tablet has been on display here since I was a kid. Lately, I've been examining it more closely. I made a rubbing last week," Night Snow said. "Look at this..."

She reached under her work desk and pulled out a tracing-paper scroll and unfurled it. Four rows of panels in exquisite, Mayan cartoon style.

"The original comic book artists," Chad said.

"There's been a lot of speculation about contact between the Maya and the Hopewell tribes. The standard rap on archeological interpretation is that it's one part science and three parts imagination. Some scholars think this tablet may have come over from Cahokia, over near St. Louis. If you examine it closely, it seems to be depicting a convoy of canoes carrying a Maya woman, a goddess or princess, to meet a Hopewell woman figure, waiting for her on the shore at the bend in a river. And it looks a lot like the sandbar bend in our own little river. I know the locations of sandbars in rivers can change, but the following panels seem to be showing preparations for a feast, inside a cave."

Chad stared and said, "Is it okay to touch the stone?"

"Sure. Do it."

"I feel like a blind man reading Braille for the first time."

"It is an experience," Night Snow agreed, "when you actually feel the ancestors in your fingertips."

Slowly stroking the stone, Chad said, "If this is true, it certainly refutes Sheriff Hooker's position about unwelcome newbies."

Night Snow nodded. "They were here long before us. I was thinking we could use this image as a logo on our next Sister City billboard."

Winnie, still a bit nervous about Chad's many hours with Night Snow being a codependent trap, eased up on her concerns. Everyone was seeing progress. Winnie and Frank noted Chad's improved story time efforts with Nina and Paulo. Instead of merely giving in to their demands for bedtime stories with play-by-play accounts of World Series games, Chad initiated his nightly "Tales from the Tunnel" series.

Chad's stories were inspired by Frank's work on the *retablos*. The main symbol in the *retablos* for a safe journey north was a tunnel shape. Frank described a recurring tunnel image, a tunnel between a quarry swimming hole in Indiana and an open *cenote* in the Yucatán. Picture a full moon. Picture a popular quarry in Cave City, alongside a deep *cenote*. Picture an underground tunnel connecting the two, which on certain nights, when the moon is just right, can magically transport people from one place to the other, underneath the border. "A pneumatic tube version of the 'underground railroad' myth," Frank called it.

Chad used the concept to improvise nightly adventure stories for the kids. Sometimes with animals swimming back and forth. Sometimes children in little rafts.

"Tell us another Tale from the Tunnel," Nina squeaked, from under the covers.

"Are you sure? You don't think I'm just trying to scare you?" Chad asked.

"Yes, but I like it," Nina said.

Winnie was getting to know Night Snow personally and that loosened things up too, woman to woman. Over onion rings and root beer at the Elbow Room, they invented a basic intelligence test for men: can he discern patterns in the silverware drawer? Night Snow employed the tried-and-true conversation starter, "How does your mama like your hair?" And Winnie went with it, surprising herself with an effusive discourse. "As a matter of fact, a lot. Too much. Mother made me grow it out this long as a kid, because it reminded her of her favorite doll. She used to comb my hair, and the doll's hair, one hundred strokes every night."

Winnie tacked up a photocopy of the glyph rubbing on the door to her office, and invited Night Snow to her seminar as a guest lecturer, with artifacts. The show-and-tell format can still go a long way with college students. She also appreciated Night Snow's ability to give Chad a compassionate what-for when he missed a meeting.

"Bottom line, I want to know, how do you do it?" Winnie asked Night Snow, "How do you stay clean and sober? What's your secret?'

They were walking the rails-to-trails path to Mound Park that bisected the university and ran beside the town wharf along the river. Winnie and Chad and Night Snow and Frank and the kids running ahead with the dog.

"Traditionally one does not give out an answer to a wisdom question, without concrete proof of the seriousness of the questioner," Night Snow said.

"How about a cartwheel? I used to be able to do cartwheels," Winnie said.

"I'd like to see that," Frank said.

"Winnie was an Olympic cart-wheeler in grade school," Chad said.

"I bet the kids would like to see that too," Frank added.

Winnie handed the dog leash to Chad. She demonstrated a schoolyard special. Up and over, two times. "Yip, yip, yip," Bongo barked. The kids clapped and wanted her to do it again.

"Very impressive," Night Snow said, "The answer to your question is prayer. I pray, Indian style."

"What characterizes Indian style?" Winnie asked, pausing to catch her breath.

"We pray with eyes open, because you have to see the blessings from the Creator," Night Snow said, "and also with hands out and open to show that you're not holding on to any old stuff."

"I think the buzzword for it nowadays is 'mindfulness,'" Frank said.

"I've never been able to get the hang of it. Tried everything," Chad said.

"We Indians are at an advantage," Night Snow said.

"Why is that?" Frank asked.

"The sacred drum in our chest."

"I've got one too somewhere," Chad chimed in, thumping his chest, "first, I have to find it."

"Exactly, paleface," White Snow countered, "Most of you guys have a heart that's completely hidden, but bleeding all over the place."

"That about sums it up for him," Winnie nodded.

"Yes," Chad said, "that would be the clinical description."

Leaf storm, all the colors. Orange, yellow, purple, brown. Fire bushes flaming red. Skeletal branches swayed against the evening sky. Pumpkins glowed on the porch steps. A hard frost. Daylight failing and the frost taking its toll, withered chrysanthemums and borage and other ghostly reminders of the shredded Veil. Stench of fallen paw-paws and persimmons crushed underfoot. Halloween. All Souls. Day of the Dead and Hanal Pixán, the Mayan festival for the departed. This brief season of mortal mutability and lawlessness. Roving bands of miscreants that include Ricky, smashing pumpkins and toilet-papering the oaks on the square and egging windshields in the faculty parking lot at Southwest Hoosier State.

Hoping to build more rapport between the foursome, Chad invited Night Snow to join him and Winnie and Frank for a Halloween outing with the kids. The weather predictions were favorable. Cool, but not freezing. They met for supper at Frank's house and feasted on catfish tacos.

Nina and Paulo had been wearing their angel costumes all day. Angels with LED light halos. They insisted on rigging a halo for the dog too.

"Treekortreet. Treekortreet," Nina and Paulo repeated, practicing what they thought was a one-word invocation.

"Do you think they'll be frightened when we run into other kids dressed as goblins and monsters?" Chad asked.

"No, tío Shad," the kids boasted, "We'll fight them."

"Angels aren't supposed to fight."

"I wouldn't worry too much," Frank said, "They're genetically wired for the presence of spirits."

Winnie said, "Yesterday at naptime, I was singing that lullaby from church. 'Listen more closely to things than to beings...' And the next thing I know, they're walking around the house with their ears cocked to tables and chairs. And I said, 'What are you doing?' and they said, 'We're listening closely to the things.' I asked, 'Are you hearing anything?' and Nina answered, 'Yes, I'm hearing my grandmother in Guatemala.' So, I asked, 'What is she saying to you?' Nina goes, 'She's telling me to send food.' 'What about you, Paulo, are you hearing anything? He goes, 'I'm hearing my grandfather in Guatemala.' And what is he saying to you? And Paulo, who copies everything his sister does, with a twist, says, 'He's telling me to send pizza.'"

Frank shooed the kids away. "Go put on your shoes."

He whispered to the adults, "The thing is, they've never met those grandparents. The family down there are farmers. All the kids know is that you-know-who left because of a famine. Two years of harvests destroyed by military raids."

"Any word yet from you-know-who?" Night Snow whispered.

"Nothing, and I'm fearing the worst."

"Treekortreet, treekortreet," the kids squealed, returning with shoes on and swinging their empty candy bags. The dog jumped up and chimed in, barking.

"Okay, team, time to go," Frank said.

"Wait, my phone is ringing," Chad said, "It's Dolores."

"Tell her the fish tacos were great," Night Snow said, "especially seasoned with epazote."

"Hello? What? Ricky did what?"

Dolores sounded worried. Ricky was on the loose again, cross-dressing as a bearded cheerleader in a fright wig for Halloween. Perhaps to spite his mother and Rosa, or just stoned stupid. Dolores and Rosa had appealed unsuccessfully to his patron saint, Batman. They had asked Ricky to please consider the consequences of being spotted in a stolen Cave City High cheerleader uniform, and not to risk all the progress that he'd been making with Chad. The parrot screeched in the background.

On the phone, Dolores said, "I called to warn you that he and his dropout friends are headed over to Frank's neighborhood, where the candy haul is better."

"We'll be on the lookout," Chad said.

Hats, gloves, coats, scarves. A bright moon peeked out from behind the bare trees. They slowly squired the two little LED angels and the dog through the neighborhoods surrounding Mound Park. After an initial period of shy hesitancy, the kids got the hang of marching up and down front steps, opening their candy bags to receive their manna and together piping the seemingly magic words in their high voices, "Treekortreet."

Frank and Winnie took turns hovering close behind at each door, ready to sweep the kids up in a hip hoist and carry them off, while Chad and Night Snow preempted any overly probing questions about the provenance of these little creatures with thanks for the sugar haul.

Frank and Night Snow reminisced about the supply truck convoy to Ciudad de la Gruta after the hurricane. Driving straight through, seventy-five hours, door to door. Dr. Rufus Crane in the lead truck. Handing out little white-cross pills to keep everyone awake, and advising, based on his Peace Corps experiences, that they ignore any military contingents attempting to flag them down on the highways. Night Snow owned up to one embarrassing moment. She was really hungry and she ordered guacamole at the undamaged restaurant on the plaza and felt irritated when it didn't come in a few minutes, because how hard can it be to pour out some guacamole from the jar in the fridge, and when it did finally come, she took a first bite and realized, oh, they made this guacamole from scratch.

"Do you remember that old lady who refused to be evacuated from the theater?"

"Señora Calatrova, the diva," Frank said.

"Dr. Crane is an opera buff, so he just let her be."

"But not his ex-wife," Night Snow said.

"That was a different story," Frank said, "the unflappable Milena Madero."

"He tried to win her back by dancing a *pasodoble* on top of the truck in front of her office," Night Snow said.

"It didn't go so well," Frank said, "This was before he got sober. In fact, that's why we have to watch out for his annual relapse. It was about this time of year."

"He lives just a couple blocks up and over," Night Snow said. "That loud music we're hearing? Could be coming from his place."

The toreador march from *Carmen* wafted through the chilly evening, along with the sound of a gravelly, solo male crooner.

Frank and Winnie and Night Snow and Chad and the two kids rounded the corner and beheld the great doctor himself, halfway down the block, channeling his inner bullfighter. Arrayed in a sombrero and polka dot boxer briefs, a plastic sword sheathed in a bathrobe belt, and holding out a red towel as a cape, Dr. Rufus Crane pranced up and down his porch, bellowing the toreador melody. Interspersed with plaintive cries to his ex-wife, Milena. And also intermittently sermonizing on the dubious benefits of the Peace Corps and the false equivalency of peace with homogeneous economic development…

"He is on a bender again," Frank said.

"Drunker than seven Sioux," Night Snow said.

"I wish there was something we could do for him," Winnie said. "Chad, any ideas for an intervention?"

"Let me think a minute."

As other moonlit groups of children and parents approached the house, Dr. Crane waved his red cape back and forth, daring them to come closer. And, when none did, he seized his plastic sword and punctured another bag of candy bars and hurled fistfuls of candy towards the sidewalk.

Mini-size bars. Almond Joy, Baby Ruth, Snickers. They littered the sidewalk and the curb. It was very appealing to Nina and Paulo and much easier to gather up directly, but just as they began to reap the harvest of Dr. Crane's bender, a loud band of hooligans charged out from the dark bushes across the street with the same goal in mind.

Ricky Sánchez and his pirate crew carrying pillowcases full of booty.

They were immediately recognizable, thanks to Dolores' tip. The little kids screamed. Nina scampered behind Winnie, and Paulo jumped behind Chad's leg and clutched it tightly.

It felt endearing to Chad, to be chosen as the kid's protector, and also motivating. The intensity of Paulo's squeeze on his knee helped to clarify the necessity of a strong response to Ricky's invasion. He reached down for Paulo and carefully shifted him over into Frank's waiting embrace. Chad stepped forward out of the dark to confront Ricky in the cone of light from a streetlamp.

Arms thrown up in exaggerated consternation, Chad shouted, "Enrique, stop. This is Little League, please."

Ricky froze at the sound of Chad's voice. The other hooligans scattered. Ricky remained paralyzed and muttered, "I didn't know you'd be here."

Chad said, "That's no excuse for terrorizing these kids. You know Nina and Paulo. You've babysat for them." To mitigate the shaming, Chad stepped closer and put a hand on Ricky's shoulder and said, "Let's go over and calm them down with an apology and you can fill their bags with some of your candy."

Ricky complied as best he could. He stammered an apology to the other grownups. The kids, staring wide-eyed at the fright wig and beard and cheerleader's uniform, cautiously accepted his sugary reparations.

Dr. Rufus Crane peered out at them from his porch and waved his plastic sword and yelled, "Ain't you ever wanted to see a toreador in all his gory glory?"

"He's as bad as me," Ricky said.

"Huddle up here," Chad said to the assembled group, "I do have an idea for some guerrilla action."

He pulled Ricky aside and whispered into his ear. Ricky nodded resolutely, getting the signal from his catcher. They turned and started toward Dr. Crane's house. Chad waved the group forward and quickly whispered instructions back to the others. He and Ricky strode ahead.

Ricky jumped out into the glow from Dr. Crane's porch light at the base of his front steps. Dr. Crane halted his bullfighter prancing to stare down at this figure in an equally strange costume. Chad and the others remained off in the dark, behind a pile of leaves. Ricky launched into his own cheerleader prance, kicking up his hairy legs.

"Gimme an O," he said.

From the darkness, an invisible chorus responded, "O!"

"Gimme a V."

"V!" shouted the chorus.

And so forth.

"What does it spell?" Ricky called.

"OVERDOSE!"

"What?"

"OVERDOSE!"

"What?"

"OVERDOSE!"

Dr. Rufus Crane stared in horror as Ricky proceeded to enact a death spiral. Clutching his throat and pounding on his heart, Ricky slowly sank to the ground. He kicked his legs and shook his arms in a final, mortal spasm. Out of the dark appeared two little angels with LED halos. The angels carried brown, crinkled leaves from the pile, back and forth, and slowly buried the dead cheerleader's body.

Dr. Crane watched in silence. He turned and slipped on a spilled beverage and fell prone onto the porch. He grumbled, "I hereby forego my prepared remarks and will entertain questions from the floor."

Paulo squeaked, "Isn't it past your bedtime?"

Dr. Crane rolled and crawled back into his house and turned off the porch light. And, one by one, all the other lights inside his house went dark too.

Cut to: Nina and Paulo upstairs in their bedroom at Frank's house. A full moon shines through the window onto their bed. They slide stealthily out from under their covers and onto the rug, where they divvy up their Halloween candy and load it into two pillowcases. They open a dresser drawer and pull out their swimsuits and yank them on and carefully tie their shoes. They grab two kid-size fishing poles. Each child carries a pillowcase bag on their shoulder. Nina pushes open the bedroom door and they attempt to quietly descend the staircase and exit the front door of the house, without being noticed by the adults still congregated in the living room. No such luck. *Hey, where do you two think you're going?* "We're going to Guatemala to bring this candy to our grandparents." *Oh, yeah, and how do you think you're going to get there?* "We'll take the Spirit Tunnel."

17.

Juan Pablo, sweating profusely, douses his face and neck with water. He stays on after the Ceiba team soccer practice to continue honing his corner kick, a sharp, high looper around the near post. Keep your head down. Don't forget the follow-through with the arms. That's it. Juan Pablo slices another spinner off the upper post into the onion bag. Sweat drips off his chin. It feels good. He remembers the raucous cheers from the Mexican fans at Fracker Field in Cave City. Why had he ever, for a single moment, thought he could boycott the Sister City game? No way. Too much fun. An official one-day amnesty that allows everyone and their gringo friends to come out of the woodwork and party and enjoy a game together and savor the hope that someday this could be the norm. Both countries' flags flying together on one pole, and the band playing both national anthems.

In the rusty bleachers at midfield a lone figure sits in the top row. Ignacio Morales, pausing for a rest on the way back from his walk. Ignacio pounds his cane on the metal flooring and calls out in his faint, fervent, old-man voice, "¡Campeones! ¡Campeones! ¡Olé, olé, olé!"

Juan Pablo shifts to the other corner and tries his left foot. The sun throws long shadows off the nearby pyramids. Bang. Off the far post and into the net.

The popularity of his Sister City Manifesto has brought scorn from the radical diehards and celebrity with the general public. Friends and teachers, among them Ignacio and Señora Calatrova, are urging him to consider a career in politics, which is the last thing he desires. He still wants to speak out, still wants to be a voice, but not *against*. Enough with being *against* the status quo. A voice *for*, but *for* what? Something bigger than his own privilege.

Juan Pablo has just published a 'man on the street' profile of Gonzalo Sánchez in *The Extra*, the local newspaper. The focus is on his deportation story. They met at Pandemonio for the interview. He bought Gonzalo a mango juice and an empanada and watched him devour the food. Like somebody might steal it away if he doesn't shove it down fast enough. Juan Pablo invited Gonzalo to compare and contrast the nuts and bolts of survival here and in Cave City. Does the Sister City accord provide any protections to the undocumented? Sound recorder running, but not getting much initially, because so much of Gonzalo's existence is automatic and without words. The hungry man stumbling through various reiterations of, "You do what you have to do to stay safe, and it's sad how a group of men living together in a motel room can just watch each other disintegrate. You try to stay out of trouble and find work. You get a phone number and you call the number until somebody answers, because even at the bottom of the ladder it's still all about who you know, and you do the work and if you stop to think too much, that's a problem."

Juan Pablo redoubles his efforts on the high, spinning corner kicks, so that this year he can bring his best game. Keep the head down. Don't forget the follow-through with the arms…

Behind him, a car approaches. He hears the sound of brakes and a door snapping open.

"Nice shot, kid. Come over here for a minute. I'd like to talk to you."

More an order than a request.

Juan Pablo reaches for his water bottle and drinks and turns to see a coiffed businessman in sunglasses leaning against the chain-link fence. Shadows from the chain-link splay like fish scales on the ground. A black Ford Escape idles behind the man. Someone waiting in the backseat, a woman. Juan Pablo gathers the soccer ball under his arm, and steps over to the fence.

"Remember me? I'm Ramón Puentes," the man says.

"Hard to forget," Juan Pablo says.

"A nice arc you've got on that boot. I used to be a *futbolista* in school. In fact, I'd hoped to play professionally. Do you mind?" He opens his arms, wanting to hold the ball.

Juan Pablo politely places it in his hands. Ramón Puentes slowly rotates the ball, gazing down at it like a crystal orb, falling into a moment of sentimental absorption. "I played a couple positions, goalie and center back, and was equally good with my left foot as my right. El Plástico and I competed for starting roles back in the day. But, you know, one thing leads to another..."

Juan Pablo drapes a towel across his head and takes another drink.

Ramón lights a cigarette and gets back on script. "I mean, let's face it, everything we were brought up to believe in has to do with bettering yourself within the economy. It's all about competing within the economy, and as for games and the comforts of life, you get that when you can. I was lucky enough to be offered an important management spot with a growing company. And I am proud to say that TiendaMax has expanded every year for the past decade. We've added five thousand jobs this year alone for the good citizens of towns like Ciudad de la Gruta. Life has a way of taking you in unexpected directions. Of course, you know well what I mean. You've recently gotten a dose of that."

"No, I'm not sure what you mean," Juan Pablo says.

"How much did they pay you to switch sides?"

Juan Pablo stiffens and shakes his head. "They didn't pay me. El Plástico and I engaged in some discussions and I came to realize that we share some common ground, especially in our beliefs about decentralization."

"And what about those monthly checks that have been coming to your student organization? Don't you think the people who sent them are feeling betrayed by your about-face, and don't you think they are still expecting something for their money?"

"Who is that?"

"The Radical Synthesizers, among others."

"What are you asking?" Juan Pablo asks. He glances over at the figure in the backseat of the car. Looks like Mercedes, but he's not sure.

"Some information at least. Now that you're on the inside, perhaps you could tell me the exact time and location of the upcoming meeting with the group traveling down from Cave City," Ramón says.

Juan Pablo shrugs. "I don't know anything about that. I've got soccer practice here every day, until we fly up there for the Sister City game."

Ramón chuckles, "You'd better look into it. Or life may be taking you in another unexpected direction."

Ramón Puentes pulls a penknife from his trouser pocket and ceremoniously opens the silver blade and thrusts it repeatedly into the soccer ball.

Juan Pablo stares incredulous at the desecration. Ramón laughs a hyena laugh, tongue darting, and tosses the slowly deflating sac back to Juan Pablo. He catches the ball and cradles it like a wounded animal.

The rear passenger door of the black Ford opens. A dyed-blonde harridan emerges, elegance incarnate, except for her red-faced fury. Juan Pablo recognizes his once-upon-a-time parent, who he had written off in his revolutionary phase as an elitist zombie.

Mercedes rushes over to the fence and launches into Ramón. "Stop, no, you promised no violence. You promised me. You told me you just wanted to talk with Juan Pablo. How dare you threaten this boy like that! How dare you lie to me! You're nothing more than a slimy hitman. You never really wanted me, did you? You just wanted access to El Plástico. And as soon as I left him, I was worthless to you."

She spits on Ramón. He spits on her.

Ramón spouts his hyena laugh again. "Look at this – a couple of dabblers. A couple of convenience shoppers, wanting traitorhood without consequences. You two deserve each other, and don't think the powers-that-be are just going to roll over and write off Ciudad de la Gruta as a meaningless backwater. Oh, no. There will be a reckoning."

Ramón retreats to his car and peels out. He abandons Mercedes, sobbing against the fence. "Don't worry. I won't let that bully hurt you," she says to Juan Pablo.

Juan Pablo briefly thinks, *is this some kind of good cop-bad cop routine?*

Mercedes reaches out to give him a hug. Or rather, to demand one from her once-compliant foster child, who played 'Happy Birthday' for her on the piano and liked to sit in her lap on the bow of her husband's boat. Juan Pablo leans over the fence and cautiously opens his arms. They move closer into an embrace that awkwardly avoids the fence. Juan Pablo feels another tectonic shift in his perspective, the fence of their differences being surmounted. As if now he is the grownup, rescuing her from a kidnapping.

Ignacio watches from across the field. He rises slowly and slips away, knowing that he must report this directly to El Plástico.

18.

Dr. Rufus Crane was a proud perfectionist who had suffered deep humiliations in his career, including being fired from the hospital and being divorced by his Mexican wife because she could not stomach, after repeated attempts, the bad food, bad weather, and bad manners of southern Indiana, and the limited popcorn toppings. Milena Madero consumed her weight in popcorn each week. Like many Mexicans, she spread all kinds of unholy crap on her nightly bowls. Stuff that Rufus, in turn, just could not condone. He was a stickler. "What most people eat with brown sugar on top, I eat with salt, pepper, and bacon drippings," Rufus had told her on their honeymoon. He thought that should have made everything clear.

And now, out of necessity, Rufus Crane was being forced to interview a rookie therapist who had never held a counseling job and who had humiliated the good doctor on his own front porch on Halloween night. Admittedly with cause, and using an interesting technique.

The rookie was fifteen minutes late, going on twenty minutes. One demerit against him already. Rufus Crane lit a cigarette and turned back to his paperwork.

Chad O'Shaughnessy got lost crossing the wrong bridge out of town. He had borrowed Frank's car to drive out to Dr. Crane's rural clinic for the interview. He was sporting his lucky tie. The meeting should be a slam dunk. Rufus had let it be known that he was curious about Chad's out-of-the-box style and thought it could be suitable for his population. Chad sucked coffee from a travel mug, wedged in his lap, as he drove out into frosted ravine-land. He questioned whether this rural, missionary gig was really a good fit. Rufus Crane was unpredictable. Maybe better to get a job online as an independent contractor for one of the mental-health apps.

Chad was not concentrating fully on the road when he heard a siren and glanced up in the rear-view mirror and saw blue lights spinning. Trouble ahead and trouble behind. Oh, Jesus, Mary and Joseph and all the Saints. Having just crossed the river, Chad breathed through a memory of his Tobin Bridge arrest and looked for a safe place to stop. He pulled over into the gravel lot at Mount Trashmore, the former city dump that had recently been covered over with topsoil. A few picnic tables and playground slides sprinkled on top. Mayor Ralph Rosewater had designated it a public park, but no one went there because of the smell. According to Night Snow, the mayor had been inspired by early theories about the Indian mounds being trash heaps.

The police vehicle rolled to a stop behind him. Two large figures in the front seat. Sheriff Hooker and a look-alike version, wearing a leather skullcap and stuffing his face with a Whopper. The uniformed Sheriff hoisted himself out of the car. He lumbered toward Chad's vehicle. Frank's vehicle, technically. That is what had caught the Sheriff's eye, he explained, pulling his mirrored sunglasses down to the tip of his nose. As a dedicated public servant, he just wanted to make sure Frank Vigo's car wasn't being stolen.

"I recognized Frank's Subaru," Sheriff Hooker said, "but I don't recognize you."

"I am a friend of Frank's, and he loaned me his car so I can go to a job interview."

"Where at?"

"Dr. Crane's clinic."

"With all those wetbacks?" the Sheriff said, chomping his gum.

"That's not a term I use," Chad said.

"Can I see your license, please?"

"Was I speeding?" Chad asked, opening his wallet.

"No, I just wanted to make sure you wasn't a car thief. And to show my boy how to make a traffic stop. That's my son, Tiny. He's starting for the soccer team this year. And FYI – today is National Take Your Kid Who Wants to Be a Cop to Work Day."

"That's nice. Nothing wrong with a little nepotism," Chad said. A nervous joke.

"Nepo-what? An 'ism'? I hate 'isms,'" the Sheriff said. "How about you give a nod hello to my son."

Chad waved to Tiny, who briefly put down the Whopper and waved back.

Chad, trying to stay calm, said, "Aren't you usually on a horse?"

"Mare's in the shop today, getting new shoes. This license is from Massachusetts. What are you doing in these parts?"

"My girlfriend teaches at the university and, like I say, I'm going for a job interview."

"You one of them outside agitators?" Sheriff Hooker asked.

Chad said, "I wasn't aware that we have outside agitators in Cave City."

"Oh, they're 'a comin.' What with that Sister City Manifesto all over the internet, and Election Day coming up. It's just a matter of time. Are you registered to vote here?"

"As a matter of fact, yes, just changed my registration last week." Chad did not say that he'd done it as part of Frank's registration drive among the students.

"I'll let you go this time. You be sure to remember Sheriff Hooker on Primary Day."

"Okey dokey," Chad said.

That was odd and funny and not funny, Chad thought. He tried to shake it off. He drove carefully on out into the county past broad, bare fields and rows of hay bales. On out beyond the Butz Quarry and the piles of slag stone. Despite the cold, a group of bare-chested collegians were starting their weekend early by leaping from the high lip of the quarry into the waters below. Yelling huzzahs at each splash. *Enjoy it while you can,* Chad thought.

He slowed to the posted 20 mph for a small crossroads community where giant tractor wheels served as lawn ornaments. Overhead, the honk of migrating geese and a broken-yoke sun. No time to think about the weirdness with Sheriff Hooker. Fifteen minutes late already. He reached into his shirt pocket for the paper with Night Snow's handwritten directions. Turn right after the abandoned gas station, back on track.

Another siren in the distance. Chad arrived at the clinic and pulled in behind an ambulance. Two low, concrete block buildings with window air conditioning units and a prefab barn attached, via a glass breezeway. The ambulance driver yelled to a nurse, "Logger, chain-saw laceration."

Chad waited in his car until the hubbub subsided.

Fortunately, Dolores Sánchez was working reception. She explained the situation to Chad in her incantatory Spanglish. Dr. Crane would not be available for at least another hour now. And not to worry about the moaning in the adjacent examining room, or the other patient, head wrapped in bandages, asleep on a cot in the corner of the reception area. Or the nurse running past the window.

"This place is a war zone," Chad said.

"Among other things," Dolores added, crossing herself respectfully. She was putting up holiday decorations. She carefully extracted ceramic figures for a crèche from a cardboard box.

"Guess who just pulled me over?"

"Our *caballero gordo*?"

"Along with his not-so-tiny son."

"That kid bullied Enrique all through grade school. 'Hey, Ricky, who's brown and fries up a lot of chicken? It's Colonel Sánchez, dummy.'"

Dolores crossed herself again and changed the topic with an easy manner, perhaps intuiting Chad's nervousness about the setting and about Dr. Crane. She invited Chad to help string Christmas lights in the front window. *Sí claro*, it was a little early in the season, but Dr. Crane was a big believer in the theory that holiday decorations boost kids' test scores, because they feel connected to larger cultural narratives, however flawed. Enrique's latest report card, which he actually brought home from school, was a case in point. Straight B's.

"Good to hear," Chad said.

"Rosa gives you a lot of credit too," Dolores said.

"Thanks, but how would you know? She doesn't talk."

"Every week, she writes out her prayer list, and your name is always on it."

"Glad to know somebody is thinking of me," Chad said.

Dolores plugged in the lights. They pulsed red and green and white. She directed Chad to the large bulletin board on the wall beside the restroom, festooned with flyers and announcements. She gave a fuller explanation of what she meant about the *clínica* functioning also as a community center with poetry readings and pitch-in events.

"That man on the cot is one of our regulars at the open-mikes," Dolores whispered.

The bandaged guy groaned and sat up and groggily began to recite a poem that had come to him while he was dozing, about migrating geese and field workers. Emotional material, the geese in the sky like letters, spelling out a message of hope to the lonely migrant workers below. "Pretty good for right off the cuff," Chad said.

When Dr. Crane finally appeared and summoned his prospective rookie counselor back to a private office for the interview, Chad felt a little steadier in his gut and a little closer to: I want this job.

Dr. Rufus Crane, wearing blood-stained scrubs and a surgical mask down around his neck, appeared lost in medical pondering. He tugged on his gray ponytail. He pointed Chad toward the folding chair beside his desk. An oak tree outside the cracked window clung to a last few leaves, one branch scraping the pane. Dr. Crane lit a cigarette, even though there was already one burning in the ashtray. He and Chad stared at each other for a couple seconds...a couple seconds too long.

Rufus Crane said, "Haven't you ever seen a doctor who smoked?"

"Uh, no, actually," Chad said

"It's the least of my problems," Rufus said, "Besides, tobacco is a man's best friend. Who said that originally?"

The interview had begun.

"Sounds kind of Native American," Chad said.

"It does, yes, but this one is from a Spanish filmmaker who made a popular movie in Mexico called *Los Olvidados*. You ever seen it?"

Chad shifted in his chair and scratched his neck. "Let me think. I was a jock in college and I took a lot of movie classes..."

"Just tell me what the name means."

"*Los olvidados*," Chad said, "The Forgotten."

"*Correcto*, so you know a little Spanish?"

"A bit."

"Enough I hope for this job. You don't need to be fluent. These folks all know some English."

"*Espero que sí.*"

Rufus Crane turned to the oak tree and blew out some smoke and dropped into reflective mode. "In El Salvador, back in the Peace Corps, I remember a silly Hollywood flick coming to town and all the local kids picked up a line that they repeated to the gringo tourists, 'Goodbye, my lover...'"

Chad nodded and suggested, "They should have added, 'Go buy me lunch.'"

Rufus smiled. "I'm interested in your methods. Working with this population, you'll need something special."

"I try to think of intervention as a kind of performance art," Chad said.

"Tell me what you know about the epidemiological paradox."

"The, excuse me, the *what*?"

"Epidemiological paradox," Dr. Crane repeated. He inhaled and exhaled a cloud of vexation. Outside the window, a different nurse ran by. "Curious statistical phenomenon with Mexican immigrants. In some ways their health is better than one would expect for their average socioeconomic bracket. In others, worse. For example, the second generation with addictions. The Mexican kids of hard-working immigrant parents, who often have done well financially. The children are extremely vulnerable. They have unexpectedly high rates of addiction and depression. Why do you think that is?"

Chad stared at his hands. "Dolores' son, Ricky, for example?" he said.

"Prime example," Dr. Crane said.

Chad pointed to the window, buying time. "That's an oak tree," he said.

"Um, yes, it is."

"We have them in New England."

"Wonderful. You're not answering my question."

Chad chewed off a fingernail. "It's about uprooting."

"Say more."

Chad said, "I just moved out here from Boston. Me and my fiancée. We're sort of homesick. And my homesickness is probably only one thousandth of what it feels like to leave a native country. And the immigrant Mexican parents don't have time to feel it, because they're busting their asses to make a living. So the next generation gets stuck with the mourning. The kids, who don't have any new roots yet, suffer the loss of the old roots for everyone."

Dr. Crane grunted and stubbed out his cigarette. He stood at the sound of another ambulance pulling in from the road. "That's good. We'll give it a try. I can offer office space out there in the annex and fifty percent of the basic fee. I don't charge much. And I must warn you that a lot of your work will end up being pro bono."

"I'll brush up on the Spanish," Chad said and stuck out his hand. "When do I start?"

"Next week, but first, another job. We need your help with the Sister City trip to Ciudad de la Gruta. What with Glodene being in a wheelchair now, and Dolores unable to go, we need you to come along as Glodene's assistant. You have a passport?"

"If I can find it," Chad said.

Driving home across the orange and brown mottled countryside, with a few early holiday lights and musky whiffs of wood smoke, Chad felt a curtain opening. The curtain of autumnal decay that could no longer conceal the human comedy playing out in the isolated communities scattered along the route. Chad found himself thinking about the social contract. He never thought about the social contract. He drummed on the steering wheel and whistled a mishmash of Latin bluegrass tunes. Cresting a hill, he came upon a view down into Brakeless Eddy's junkyard, and a blinking, neon rent-a-sign.

Brakeless Eddy had added a new business venture. The blinking sign on the road outside his repair shop announced, "Eddy's Deer Processing." Chad impulsively turned in and pulled up beside the garage office. A few raindrops fell on the windshield and splattered into tiny paw prints.

He climbed out of the car, leaving the driver's side door open and the engine running, in case he might need to make a getaway. He waved hello to Roy in the garage. Chad wanted to tell somebody, anybody, that he had landed a job. His first real job as a professional, not counting his practicum work.

Brakeless Eddy sat in his office with his boots up on his desk, cleaning his rifle, almost the same pose as when Chad had left him. His cluttered office made cozy by a glowing space heater. On the counter, a half-eaten box of Russell Stover chocolates, with a sticky note affixed that said, "No spit backs."

"Welcome, cuzzie," Eddy bellowed. The man was in a good mood, possibly a super-sized good mood.

Chad stood at the door and saluted. Runs in the blood, apparently. Whatever it was that had Chad O'Shaughnessy on edge about being related to this grinning paragon of humanity suddenly dissipated. Chad said, "I saw the new sign out front. You're cutting up some venison?"

Eddy said, "Been doing it as a hobby for years and finally decided to try to make a buck on it. No pun intended. Not that it's easy, mind you. Open *The Joy of Cooking* to the carving section, you'll find: "Carving is a difficult and subtle art, not easily mastered." What brings you back out to our gobble neck of the woods?"

Chad answered, "I just got a job out at Dr. Crane's clinic. I landed a job, and it occurred to me, since I'm going to need some wheels to show up there on a daily basis, that you might be able to give me a tip on where to find a decent used car?"

Brakeless Eddy grinned and replied, "No problem. I always got a couple decent beaters on hand, because, you know, people drop them off for a brake fix and then don't have the money to pick them up and whatnot. I'll just give you one. We got to celebrate that new job of yours. How about we go deer hunting together? You ever go hunting back east?"

Chad shook his head. "I've never fired a gun in my life."

"Nothing like it. A mystical experience. We'll head out in the woods just before dawn. I know a couple perfect blinds deep in. Things are different in the forest. A hunter can get disoriented in the middle of the forest the same way a sailor can get disoriented in the middle of the ocean. My wife, Juanita, she's one of those caravan gals who came up north looking for a green card. Offered to pay me to marry her. At the time I was kind of broke, so I went for it. Actually, it's turned out okay. I used to act kind of goofy with the girls. I had a stupid pick-up line. Are you my mother? That's what I'd ask. Are you my mother? I thought it was funny, but not many of the girls did. Until Juanita. She looked at me and snickered, "Yes, and you've been a bad boy and deserve a good spanking." That Juanita, she's something else. Get her blabbing and she'll go about her people and their tales. Her latest is about the *nagual*. She claims everybody has an animal double out there in the wild, and whenever something happens to your animal double, it happens to you too. And it all sounds like a bunch of hooey, until you're out in the middle of the forest, perched up in a tree at dawn and the moon is still shining and the stars too and the sun pokes up pink and yellow and red and you start to see things and you start to hear things, like a bobcat on the prowl."

More on that later.

19.

Countdown to the vote: 68 days. Ballots printed and poll-workers recruited.

In Ciudad de la Gruta, the news that Ramón might be stalking the upcoming Sister City conference causes a relocation debate. The plan had been to lodge the Cave City contingent, like any business group, in the Hotel Grande on the plaza and use their banquet room for the meeting. El Plástico talks to Juan Pablo who talks to Mercedes who talks to Dra. Madero who talks to Señora Calatrova who talks to Ignacio who talks to me and Dotcom at La Sombra Azul, and then I hear from El Plástico that the plan has changed.

Personally, I prefer ignoring the perfidious rat, but El Plástico doesn't want to take any chances with his nemesis.

Ignacio reluctantly offers the use of his family's hacienda ten miles outside of town. It is a historic structure, comprising a single row of magnificent, high-ceilinged rooms, with a kitchen at the end and verandas on both sides for shade in the morning and the afternoon. The hacienda had been the site of weekend fiestas for Ignacio and his friend, Delmar, along with Glodene and Señora Calatrova. After Delmar died, the place was shuttered and put in mothballs. Ignacio could not face going there ever again.

Señora Calatrova convinces him to change his mind. She soothes Ignacio's reluctance, assuring him that closing the hacienda had been a grief reaction, an attempt to stop time, to mummify Delmar and their friendship, and that it had only led to paralysis. And that Delmar would want this gathering to occur for the good of Sister City.

The advantage of Ignacio's hacienda is plenty of open space and an on-site *cenote* for swimming and an airy perch on a slight rise with a view of the distant *ruinas* and the city. A mile of flatland visibility in all directions makes it hard for Ramón Puentes to sneak up on us. And it's closer to the coast, so El Plástico can take the guests up for a boat ride on the Xtabay, if they desire.

The problem is getting the house opened and cleaned and supplied in time for the imminent arrival of the Cave City crew. Everyone contributes what they can. Señora Calatrova orders flowers. Dotcom and Tía Carlota set up the catering. Juan Pablo and I organize transportation from the airport. I get the electricity working and wire up some exterior cameras.

Tía Carlota is the real leader of this phase. Steadfast Carlota, the face of toil. Other than her dancing at La Sombra Azul and a Mass on Sunday afternoon, she is consumed by the laundry business. A brightly woven *rebozo* always draped around her shoulders, not for fashion, but for the shawl's utilitarian function as a tool. Fetching laundry from the downtown hotels, and the airport hotel, washing, drying, folding, returning laundry in loads that often ride balanced on her head. Her sense of familial duty to Dotcom extends only to providing room and board. She gives little else in the way of warmth or conversation. Dusting shelves together at the hacienda, I overhear Dotcom ask her, "Do you think it would be possible for a man ever to fall in love with me?" Tía Carlota responds, "No, and that's the way you want it."

Dotcom is eager to learn more about our visitors, especially Night Snow, a real live Indian who had not been exterminated in the genocide of the North American tribes. Dotcom offers the opinion that at least Mexico, for all its faults, didn't explicitly try to wipe out the indigenous peoples. Tía Carlota, from the kitchen, counters with her grim opinion: "No, we're just doing it more slowly. Killing the Maya one at a time with racism. Why else do you think the suicide rate is so high here?"

On the night before the arrival of the Cave City assembly, we are still working at the hacienda, sweeping and dusting and pulling sheets off the furniture and the billiards table, making final preparations. Tía Carlota directs everyone with blunt orders. Little by little, we make progress. Carlota verbally checks things off the list.

The group converses cheerfully between rooms. Ignacio tells stories about Delmar, the baseball scout, during their tipsy, sentimental weekend visits, clownishly demonstrating his methods for teaching young players how to slide, throwing himself into the dirt, head first.

Señora Calatrova arranges red, yellow, pink and white carnations in crystal vases. She and Dotcom add blooms from the elderflower and bougainvillea that surround the old plantation house, placing vases on the windowsills and the wooden wall studs where the hammocks used to hang. Señora Calatrova chimes in with her memories of Delmar and Glodene at Ignacio's weekend-long bashes that apparently often ended with nude bathing in the *cenote*. Its curative waters again extolled by the powder-skinned diva. She says, "We're almost done here tonight. How about a 'skinny dip', as my friend, Glodene, would say? The water is very soothing."

Ignacio agrees and says, "With Glodene in a wheelchair now, she won't be able to join us this time."

El Plástico and I hear this from outside the kitchen. And chuckle. We are carrying out the patio furniture. We trade glances that silently express an admission that perhaps we have been naïve about the extent of Ignacio's involvement with Señora Calatrova and Glodene.

"Sounds like back in the day these folks knew how to have a good time," El Plástico whispers. "*Sabían divertirse.*"

"We'd better keep an eye on them," I say.

Away from the city, the sky is resplendent with a panoply of glowing, 40-watt stars. A crescent moon and a planet, Venus. In the distance, I can see the spotlight at the *ruinas*. It is trained up onto the Jaguar Pyramid. I imagine a much earlier visit to Ciudad de la Gruta from Priestess Dawn and her retinue traveling from her riverside village a thousand years ago to take in the Late Classical splendor of Priestess Moon's temple city. There was much more of a disparity between the two locales back then. Priestess Dawn stares agog at the architecture and the bright murals and the flamboyant textiles. She is paraded and feted and celebrated in the royal box at the ball court. Her best friend shows her as good a time as Ignacio later does with Delmar. Including a ritual ingestion of psychedelic mushrooms atop the skybox in the ball court, watching a game not unlike soccer. Joyously hallucinating into the future, they envision a distant era when their two peoples will meet for an annual festival, traveling aloft in flying boats, like birds.

I whisper to El Plástico, "Watch out. We don't want anybody ending up in the hospital before our northern friends arrive."

We can see the lights of the soccer stadium where Juan Pablo and the team are practicing, day and night now. After a series of recent conversations with him at La Sombra Azul about the Sister City transportation arrangements, I admire the way Juan Pablo has integrated his about-face experience. One must shed a skin. I came to realize that my switcheroo is incomplete. I have not really changed sides. I just went AWOL from one battle zone and turned up here in Ciudad de la Gruta in a similar role, perpetuating a righteous enactment of a normalizing gaze with my drone surveillance, in hopes of corralling humanity's baser instincts while my own remain unidentified.

Cut to: Ignacio and Señora Calatrova disappearing into the master bedroom after the chores are done. They reemerge on the veranda in the star-studded night, clad only in bathrobes. Dotcom and Tía Carlota hurry over to alert El Plástico and me. We follow at a distance, just in case the elderly duo needs help. Ignacio and Señora Calatrova shuffle across the garden to the nearby *cenote*. They carefully descend the spiral stairs, hewn from the limestone, into the cavernous silo. The fluid darkness echoes with their groans and giggles. Stars and the moon float on the rippling surface. The two wrinkled bodies assist each other with disrobing and, naked together one last time, they slide gaily into the silvery waters of senescence.

20.

Chad was eager to join Dr. Crane and the cabal on the two-day trip to Mexico, but he felt skittish about traveling without Winnie. She had agreed to stay in Cave City with Nina and Paulo and cover Frank's classes. Both Chad and Frank urged her to reconsider, over lunch at the Elbow Room.

"Winnie, I know you like your teaching and feel committed to your students, but cancelling a couple classes is no big deal. The dean won't mind. And Dolores and Rosa can take care of the kids and the dog," Frank said.

Winnie thought about it for a minute. "What if we go down there and catch dengue fever?"

"The chances are small."

"Up here you could get a tick bite and Lyme disease."

"That doesn't help."

"You'll meet some good people," Frank said, "Ignacio and the crew."

"We can't just rely on Dolores and Rosa for everything. I think we take advantage of them," Winnie said.

"Are you looking for reasons not to go?" Chad said.

"No, I'm just nervous," she said.

"Nervous about what?" Chad said. "Your mother?"

"Exactly. You figured it out."

Winnie shrugged and threw up her hands. She had begged off the Mexico trip because her mother, Prudence, had announced a sudden swoop-in from Boston the following week. The visit would require a lot of forethought and Winnie had purchased a spiral notebook to make preparations. Half of it full already.

"How are we going to hide the moving van theft from her?" Winnie said, "Did your dad tell her about it, by the way?"

"I swore him to secrecy," Chad said, "Chief is at least reliable that way."

"And the fact that I've done nothing about wedding plans for months? Absolutely nothing," Winnie said.

"Aw, come on, Winnie," Chad pleaded, "I'll get on the case with Vincent again. How often do we get a free ride to visit our old haunts south of the border?"

"Sorry, we're not college kids anymore. I can't just drop everything. And it's not a pleasure trip. You've got serious business down there. Besides, I'm not comfortable in small planes," Winnie said.

"I don't want to go without you," Chad said.

Winnie scooted over and kissed him on the cheek.

"I'll hold down the fort. You all go and have a good time."

It sounded like a blessing, but felt more like a brush-off.

The blustery morning of the departure, a flurry of last-minute packing. Chad still had to find his passport. It finally surfaced in the back of his sock drawer. Winnie assisted him in the ritual pat-down, to make sure he wasn't forgetting anything else important.

"Wallet?"

"Check."

"Clean underwear?" Winnie asked.

"Check."

"Good man. What about duct tape?"

"Thanks, yeah."

"Why do you always take duct tape on trips?"

"I don't know. It's a Chief thing."

Chad grabbed a roll of duct tape from the kitchen and threw it in his backpack, just as Night Snow pulled up outside their apartment and honked.

"Intestinal support?"

"I'll rely on yogurt. It's only till Friday. Back soon, babe."

Though even as he said it, he sensed that this conversation with Winnie would be an ancient memory by then. It might even be forgotten.

Outside, the wind blew up a scrim of leaves. Sunbeams quivered behind them. Night Snow popped her trunk and waved to Winnie on the balcony. The car trunk was full of charts for the strategy meeting, rolled into cardboard tubes. Music flowed from her dashboard speakers, drums and flutes. Night Snow offered a fist-bump as Chad slid into her car.

Chad grumbled, "I didn't have any luck convincing Winnie to come."

Night Snow turned down the music. "Do you think she's onto us?"

A typical Night Snow line. Chad took a moment to steer into the emotional skid of her suggestiveness.

"I'm really pumped about this trip," Night Snow continued, "I haven't been out of town since forever."

"Apparently Frank has been designated our chaperone," Chad said.

"No problem," Night Snow said, "We'll find him a cute boy or a señorita."

"No señoritas for Frank," Chad said.

"Last time we were down there, he was still swinging both ways," Night Snow said.

"That is news to me," Chad said.

Night Snow downshifted into third gear. "Speaking of chaperones, have you been briefed on dealing with Glodene?"

"Dolores gave me a tutorial," Chad said. "No sharp turns in the wheelchair and make sure she doesn't release the brake."

"And you have to play Scrabble and let her win."

"I can do that."

The rest of the way out to the municipal airport, Night Snow discoursed on her ideas for the Sister City canvassing and on Glodene and Delmar Butz.

"Delmar thought of himself as a latter-day Ambassador Poinsett."

"The flower guy?" Chad said.

"When he was still alive, Delmar used to pay for hundreds of those Mexican Christmas flowers to be distributed all around town during the holidays. And, by the way, Glodene and Delmar were not childless, as many people think. They have a daughter who lives in Los Angeles and hates Cave City and never calls."

"Speaking of unknown family," Chad interrupted, "Tell me more about yours."

"Not now," Night Snow said, "Not until we know each other better."

"What about previous relationships?" Chad said, "You've never opened up about that either."

Night Snow swallowed and spoke slowly, "The last one was with a professor in the sociology department who thought he knew what I needed and gave it to me on a platter and when I didn't fall on my knees and accept it the way he thought I should, he decided I was a bitch, but he never did ask me what I really wanted. It was sad. He was the first truly sophisticated scoundrel I'd ever dated. I'd dated other scoundrels before, but with them it was more a genetic condition."

"What *do* you really want?" Chad said.

Night Snow thought for a moment and answered, "What with all the ripping up of treaties, I used to want to rip up the Treaty of Greenville and revive the Ghost Dance. These days, I'd be okay with forty acres and a mule."

She drove through the open gate onto the runway of the Cave City airport and straight out onto the tarmac, where the rest of the party awaited them beside the Butz Industries' corporate jet, a Bombardier XC3.

Glodene Butz, Father Mike, Dr. Crane, Frank Vigo, and a member of the city council, Willard. He doubled as the pilot. Chad recognized Willard from the community cable TV broadcasts of the council meetings. He was the one councilman who always stayed awake in the meetings. A good habit for a pilot, Chad thought.

Greetings and vigorous handshakes ensued, fed by excitement for the journey ahead. They loaded luggage into the belly of the plane. Willard pointed to a dark cloudbank approaching from the west and urged a quick departure.

Before take-off, Glodene asked for a prayer from Father Mike. The young priest, inexplicably arrayed in full cassock, improvised a prayer for safe travel, especially travel to third-world countries. As he rattled on, it became clear that Father Mike, who sermonized on outer space and inter-galactic voyages, had never set foot on an airplane and had never been out of his home state. He climbed aboard and retired to the back of the plane, near the bathroom.

Dr. Crane tried to keep him occupied by confessing his own trepidations around the possibility of seeing his ex-wife in Ciudad de la Gruta. "We're still business partners, you know, and I have to remind myself to be very businesslike."

Chad and Frank and Night Snow worked to hoist and secure Glodene's wheelchair into her spot at the front, just behind the cockpit. "Thank you, it usually takes a few brutes and a bulldog to get me into this plane," she said, "This will be fine, thank you."

Glodene's polished face, with a high, reflective forehead, took the shape of a perfect oval. It reminded Chad of the oval windows in the front parlor doors of many of the older houses in Cave City, and he imagined that, looking inside her, one would see a fabulous room with nowhere comfortable to sit.

As a longtime board member of Butz Industries, Glodene knew the chairmanship drill. The plane was barely off the ground when she called for everyone's attention. "My friends, we are on an important mission. First and foremost, we must convey to our Sister City colleagues an attitude of hope and resolve, in the face of so much negativity about our joint endeavor. As Night Snow points out, the ancient peoples of Ciudad de la Gruta also struggled to maintain their lives in the midst of a dying civilization, and we should be inspired by them."

Turbulence bump. More turbulence bumps. "Seatbelts everybody," Willard called from the cockpit.

"To be continued on the ground in Mexico," Glodene said, and turned to Chad. "If you'll just reach down into my purse there, you'll find my magnetic travel board for Scrabble. You're a competitive chap, right?"

"I can be," Chad said, feeling stirred-up enough by her speech to sense that no way was he just going to let her win.

They flew above the Mississippi River. A direct route that, according to Glodene, followed the flight path of the bird species during winter in the Yucatán; orioles, woodpeckers, tanagers. Frank and Dr. Crane discussed Night Snow's progress on deciphering the tablet rubbings, that she was now grandiloquently calling the 'Cave City Codex.'

Father Mike plugged in earbuds and tried to read a Bible, but trembled, wide-eyed, at each ripple of turbulence.

Chad and Glodene concentrated on Scrabble. Chad got lucky and picked tiles that connected with Glodene's earlier plays to spell out a series of weighty, high-scoring words, like 'marvel.'

"Goodness," Glodene exclaimed, "well done."

"You can beat dumb, but you can't beat dumb luck," Chad said.

"Young man, you are smarter than you are letting on," Glodene said, arthritic fingers reaching for her tiles, one at a time, and finally winning the game with 'lexicon.'

"Thank you, Madame. A rematch?"

"In a minute – "

They turned their attention to Father Mike, who appeared to be on the verge of a panic attack, muttering prayers about *bandidos*.

"Chad, if you'd be so kind as to reach again into my purse," Glodene said, "You'll find a little flask in the side pocket. Pass it back to Father Mike. I think he might need some libation theology."

Father Mike received the libation theology gratefully, too gratefully.

"As my late husband liked to say," Glodene recited, "One tequila, two tequila, three tequila, floor."

Which was promptly what happened, as they started across the wide, blue Gulf.

21.

Winnie showed up unscheduled at Frank's house to help Dolores with breakfast duty for the kids.

"Did the plane get off okay?" Dolores asked.

"I think so. We would have heard otherwise. Are you on to the next job?"

"I'll probably go home for a while and worry about our friends in Ciudad de la Gruta," Dolores said, wrapping herself in a bright, woven blanket, using it as a winter coat.

"They'll be fine. You go get some sleep."

"My problem is that I can imagine everything down there. I can see the little airport and the palm trees along the road into town and the *zócalo* and I can see myself as a girl in the crowd, waving at their motorcade."

"Why is that a problem?"

"Because I can also see my old boyfriend, Roberto. I can see us dancing together. Don't tell Rosa. For such a sweet thing, she can be very jealous," Dolores said. She fastened the blanket around her shoulders with one of the kids' old diaper pins. "*Adiós*, I'm leaving now."

Winnie hoisted Nina and Paulo into their highchairs and filled their bowls and sippy cups with cereal and apple juice. She fed the dog and scurried out to refill the birdfeeder and the suet cage, hanging just beyond the breakfast nook windows. A continual source of fascination for the kids.

"Mommy, a red bird," Nina said. "Look."

"Right, a cardinal."

"And the coo bird," Paulo added.

"That's a mourning dove," Winnie said, "You can also call it a pig with wings."

"A greekle," Nina said.

"Grackle."

"Eating breakfast, just like us."

"More or less."

"All different kinds of birds," Paulo said.

"Mommy, they're sharing the food," Nina said.

"Yes, aside from an occasional fuss, that's right. They know how to share," Winnie said.

"All different colors," Paulo said.

"I want to grow a bird tattoo," Nina said, "on my arm, a red bird tattoo."

"I want to grow a bird tattoo on my leg," Paulo said.

"Tattoos don't grow."

"What?"

"A person called a tattoo artist etches it onto your skin."

"Does it hurt?" Nina asked.

"Probably, a little."

"When can I get one?" Paulo asked.

"Not until you're eighteen."

A few more minutes of birdwatching and juice slurping brought the usual result; Nina and Paulo, still in pajamas, falling back to sleep, slumped in their high chairs.

Winnie poured more coffee and sat with them in breathy silence. She checked her phone for any messages from her mother or Frank or Chad, who had, in fact, forgotten his phone in the apartment. Winnie had tucked it in her purse for safekeeping. No messages appearing, she allowed herself to slip into a satisfied reverie. Not entirely sure why. The contentment on the kids' faces, the sunlight in the breakfast nook, the unexpected awareness that with Chad and Frank gone, it was okay. Left here on her own, and surprise, it was okay.

Winnie was on her own in Cave City, Indiana, and it was perfectly okay.

Except for the small matter of her mother's upcoming visit and the unresolved van theft. Winnie considered a sudden bravura return to social media. A selfie with the sleeping kids that would somehow convey to the world that Dr. Winifred Marsh, Ph.D. was doing just fine, thank you, out here in the middle of nowhere, and could effectively deal with whatever needed her attention. First, more juice and a banana. Riding a wave of confident autonomy, Winnie tiptoed off to the living room and reached into her purse and dug out Chad's phone. She knew his current password and got into his contact list and found Vincent's number.

"Wake up, Vincent, you scumbag."

"Oh, hello, Winnie. Funny, Chad calls me the same thing."

"How about 'master of the futile?' Would that be better?"

"I don't know what that is."

"Try looking in the mirror," Winnie said.

"Did Chad put you up to this? Is he tired of insulting me by himself?"

"Where the fuck is my furniture, Vincent?"

"I thought you had supposedly reached some level of acceptance about this, some kind of detachment."

"Did Chad tell you that?"

"I just need a little more time, Winnie. I've been in touch with your driver. He took a detour to a family reunion in Kentucky and ran into a kissing cousin and her car broke down and she was in some kind of trouble and needed to get out of town, so he gave her a ride to Little Rock. Unfortunately, he has been hocking a few pieces at consignment shops along the way, but I think I've tracked all those down."

"Vincent, my mother is coming to visit next week. And Chad and I, being the detached and accepting ostriches that we are, have so far managed to hide this situation from her. But that may no longer be possible. Do you know what my mother will want to do to you, Vincent, when she finds out my antiques have been stolen?"

"If she's anything like Chad's mother…"

"Exactly. Have you ever read *Beowulf*?"

"It sounds familiar. I think I saw the movie."

"This guy, Beowulf, has to struggle with a monster. But, as it turns out, that's not the worst of his problems, because after he finishes off the monster, he has to deal with the monster's *mother*."

"This is like one of your folklore things?"

"Your friend Chad was trying to help you, Vincent. And now he's relapsed. He's back in the program and we're trying to get through it. Friends don't let friends screw them over like this."

"I'm getting your drift."

"Good. I've got to go, Vincent. Somebody is knocking at the front door, and I don't want them to disturb the kids."

"Kids, what kids? You and Chad have kids already?"

"No, Frank and I do."

"Who? What?"

"Forget it. Goodbye," she said.

Dolores sagged against the door. Tears and sobs. Something was very wrong. Mascara-streaked, blanket askew. The dog started barking. The kids woke up, scared by the barking. Winnie ushered Dolores inside. The two women spontaneously kicked into gear. Acting in sync, they unstrapped Paulo and Nina from the highchairs and carried them upstairs to their beds. They backpedaled carefully out of the room, praying the naps had not been permanently interrupted.

Back downstairs in the sunny breakfast nook, Winnie reached for the coffee pot. "Something happened. What is it?" she asked.

"*Más café,*" Dolores said, "The solution for everything. *Más café.*"

"Works for me," Winnie said.

Dolores crossed herself and said, "Rosa figured it out. She read my mind about Roberto. Somehow, she can do that. Not being able to speak gives her the ability to read minds."

Winnie nodded and said, "I remember when Chad was taking developmental psych, he came home from class and did one of his spews. 'Babe, I finally get it. Nature gives us the first eighteen months of life without talking in order to experience what it's really all about between human beings, before language comes along and screws everything up.'"

Dolores tried to smile. "Are you missing Chad? Are you missing him yet?"

"No, as it turns out, I am doing pretty well without him," Winnie said.

Dolores wiped her smudgy eyes. "I can't stop thinking about El Plástico."

"The mayor?"

"My old boyfriend, Roberto. That's his real name."

"The mayor of Ciudad de la Gruta is your old boyfriend?"

"We were very young. My brother, Gonzalo, El Plástico, and me. Of course, he wasn't called that back then. He was my Roberto. And there was also a boy in the neighborhood named 'Ramón,' who wasn't exactly a friend, but..."

"Wait, Gonzalo, your brother. He's the one who got deported?"

"A few months ago," Dolores nodded, tearing up again. "Up here, they called him, 'Gonzo,' which does not really describe him at all."

"That was shortly before we got here," Winnie said.

"It was terrible. Ricky and his uncle were becoming close," Dolores said, "and suddenly he's gone."

Winnie sat up. "Couldn't the mayor have helped somehow? Couldn't you have asked him to intervene?"

Dolores shivered and shook, like she'd seen a ghost. "I don't know. He might have been able to, if I'd asked him."

"But you couldn't ask him."

Dolores shook her head.

"What really happened between you two?"

Dolores shook her head again. "Señorita, all I can tell you is, never make a rash decision out of fear."

Whoosh, a sudden flapping of wings. A quick dispersal of all the birds at the feeder as a fan-tailed hawk descended, like a chopper, talons outstretched.

22.

A thousand and two things happening at once, which is always the case, but doesn't necessarily feel that way. Eyes skyward toward a faint, midday moon, the Orquesta de la Calle, along with the community choir, under the direction of Señora Calatrova, await the arrival of Glodene Butz's private jet in hundred-degree heat in the freight terminal at the Ciudad de la Gruta municipal airport.

As the plane comes in for a landing, Gonzalo steps out on the runway, waving the Sister City banner – a carnation and a peony on a crazyquilt ground – designed by the towns' sewing guilds. The Bombardier touches down and bounces and slows. The plane turns and taxies toward the terminal. Señora Calatrova raises her baton. The band and choir strike up a slightly off-key, though still memorable rendition of "On the Banks of the Wabash (Far Away)".

Captain Willard pushes open the cockpit door and folds down the exit stairs. Cheers and applause. The occupants appear, one by one, smiling and waving, except for cassocked Father Mike, who has to be carried out on a stretcher. He lies unconscious on the ground in full sun. Dotcom stumps forward and shades him with a parasol.

Frank and Chad lift Glodene's wheelchair and carefully place it down onto the tarmac. They pause to catch their breath, before turning to the luggage. Forming a line with the airport staff, they pull out the suitcases one by one from the hold and load them onto a handcart. Pause to wipe sweat onto their shirttails. Frank moves aside and reaches for his phone. He dials and leaves a message for Winnie, to tell her that they've landed safely. Chad overhears and feels annoyed for not thinking of checking in with her. He digs for his phone, and discovers its absence.

El Plástico, in a white, long-sleeved *guayabera*, clears his throat and pulls a copy of his welcome speech from his back pocket. A flock of onlookers and media emerge from the arrivals building. Cameras, microphones. Everyone eager to participate in this event. The Mexican political rally tradition requires food and music and lots of bling. El Drone tosses fistfuls of candy to the crowd.

A series of significant encounters occur. The long overdue reunion of Glodene Butz and Señora Calatrova, fierce angels of their communities. Ignacio is thrilled to see them together. They all helped spearhead the original Sister City agreement, and, by God, they are not going to let it die now. Glodene miraculously rises from her wheelchair. She gives Ignacio a hug and also one to her old friend, who is wearing a gown with a lace train.

Gasps and applause and cheers.

Gonzalo's reunion with the gringos is next. *Hola, amigo.* Embraces from everyone who knew him up north. Frank and Night Snow and Dr. Crane and Glodene. They warmly convey greetings from his sister, Dolores, and nephew, Ricky. Oh, Gonzalo shudders and tears up. He can't help himself, despite his lingering resentments regarding these Cave City elders who should have been able to stop his deportation.

Dotcom hovers over Father Mike with her parasol. She stares at Chad O'Shaughnessy's reddish blonde hair and gold-rimmed glasses. She watches Chad assist the baggage handlers, unloading Night Snow's gear from the plane. A suitcase breaks and Chad comes to the rescue with his roll of duct tape.

When Chad pulls out his wallet to give the baggage handlers a generous tip, a fifty dollar bill, Dotcom experiences a flash of revelation. She points and shrieks, "He's the one! He's the one who saved me!"

Afterwards, El Drone swears that he saw a flash of green light ricochet between them. Whoa, it takes Chad more than a moment to recognize her, one of those more-than-a-moments in which everything shifts into slow motion, including his thoughts. He remembers the pink hair bow. He finally reacts and says in Spanish, "The truth is you saved me too."

More applause and cheers, though only a few people know the reason why. El Drone and Tía Carlota among them. Chad, shocked by Dotcom's reappearance, does not get a chance to respond further, because Father Mike twitches and regains consciousness at the sound of Dotcom's revelatory shrieks, some being uttered in Mayan. To Father Mike this sounds like the Klingon language.

Father Mike, lifelong Trekkie, replies to her in Klingon. "*HIQaH! QaH!*" Dotcom bends down and answers him in Klingon and that sets off an internal landmine for him. Father Mike, hearing the Klingon and seeing Dotcom's disfigured face, and still in a semi-comatose state, woozily believes that he has been abducted by aliens and is now on the Klingon planet.

Father Mike rolls off the stretcher, jumps up and attempts to flee, stumbling towards the open gate at the end of the runway. Dotcom gives Chad a hug, laying her head sideways on his shoulder, and promises in English that they will talk later, after she retrieves the priest and delivers him to Ignacio's hacienda. Using her cane and parasol, she limps off in pursuit of Father Mike, urging El Plástico to proceed with his speech.

A thousand and two things happening at once. Welcome to Ciudad de la Gruta, friends.

The band plays *Take Me Out to the Ballgame*, in honor of Delmar Butz. El Drone tosses more candy to the crowd. El Plástico, trying his best to reproduce Juan Pablo's delivery style, clears his throat again and launches into a short, upbeat speech to honor their guests and convey, ladies and gentlemen, that we are all aware the times have changed and passing the Sister City referendum will require some hard work. But, let's give it our best. "Let us make a unique contribution to the gaiety of nations."

El Plástico nods toward Glodene, from whom he learned that phrase twenty years ago. The gaiety of nations, indeed. Glodene blows him a kiss. El Drone scans the crowd for Ramón Puentes. No sign of him. Dr. Crane scans the crowd for Dra. Milena Madero. No sign of her either.

A local newspaper reporter clamors and waves his arms and demands, "Where is the mayor of Cave City? Does the gringo mayor not support the referendum? And where is Juan Pablo Chayac, the author of the Sister City Manifesto? Does he not support the referendum anymore? And where is our mayor's wife, Mercedes? She is usually here for these speeches. *¿Qué pasa aquí?*"

El Plástico silences the reporter with his supernova stare. El Drone leans over and whispers something behind a raised hand. El Plástico improvises an excuse for the Cave City mayor, Ralph Rosewater, indisposed with gout, which is actually true, and introduces Captain Willard as the representative from the Cave City council. He explains that Juan Pablo is at soccer practice. An important soccer practice, and, good people, his dedication to a Ciudad de la Gruta victory in the upcoming match with Southwest Hoosier State is equally as important as the referendum. More applause and cheers. El Plástico ignores the question about Mercedes.

El Drone decides to cut short the press conference. Acting as master of ceremonies, he begins ushering the group toward the waiting vehicles.

On the far end of Avenue Hidalgo, the motorcade passes the gated entrance to Flamingo Estates and the old train station and the soccer field where Juan Pablo and the other members of the Ceiba team are practicing. The drivers honk at the players. Juan Pablo spots the gringo cabal and jumps up and down, waving both arms. Hey, two thumbs up! The motorcade passes the commercial strip at the other end of the avenue. Subway, Burger King, and the Tulum putt-putt golf course, each green hole a replica of one of the Maya pyramids.

Some of this is new to Glodene. In the lead vehicle of the motorcade, El Plástico and Señora Calatrova rattle on about developments since her last visit. Glodene laps it up.

"Look, lots of bright zinnias at the putt-putt course. My Delmar loved zinnias."

"Originally a Mexican wildflower. The Spanish hated it. They called it *mal de los ojos*."

"Sickness of the eyes."

"No accounting for taste."

"Is the metal scrap yard still around the corner?" Glodene asks.

"Yes, a thriving operation now, with the fluctuations in copper and brass from the trade wars. Steel prices updated four times an hour. A stock exchange for the nuts-and-bolts dispossessed."

"Oh, more zinnias! They're very hardy."

In the next vehicle of the motorcade, Frank Vigo and Dr. Crane and Captain Willard discuss the numbers with Ignacio Morales. The number of newly registered student voters. The number of absentee ballots to be sent to snowbirds. The number of times that Willard has introduced the topic of the upcoming Sister City referendum in city council meetings and has been summarily quashed. The number of precincts and the length of the voting hours. The disparity in the number of registered voters versus those who actually vote. Not so bad in Ciudad de la Gruta. The early poll numbers are still tilting slightly in favor of passage. Sheriff Hooker's national endorsement has brought the attention of *The Indianapolis Star*. Their polling operation has Sister City passing by 4.3 percentage points, just outside the margin of error.

Every few blocks, Dr. Crane lobs in a question to Ignacio about his ex-wife. "How is Dra. Madero these days? Has anyone seen her lately? I know she had to relocate her office after the hurricane, so where is she situated now? I expected her to join us today. Is she meeting us later at the hacienda?"

Ignacio nods and eventually replies, as discreetly as possible, "Her absence today has nothing to do with you personally. I believe it's a professional conflict, involving a couple of patients who may be part of our gathering, thus it would be a bit awkward for her to participate."

"Okay, yes," Dr. Crane groans. Hard to refute that position.

In the third vehicle of the motorcade, as they pass the abandoned drive-in movie theater, El Drone also assuages Night Snow's concern about the absence of Dotcom and Father Mike.

"Shouldn't we have waited for them? Does she know where we're going?" Chad asks.

"Not to worry," El Drone says, "Dotcom knows where we're going and how to get there. The hacienda is just north of town. It's actually not too far from the village where she grew up and where the accident occurred. I've gotten to know Dotcom over the last year, since she moved into town. I know the story of the bus accident and the red-haired person who stepped forth and handed over the money for her long recovery."

Night Snow teams up with El Drone to cushion Chad's shock. She says, "You've never mentioned this. It sounds important. Sounds like you really came through for her in a big way."

Chad numbly replies, "I thought she was dead. I thought I was paying for her burial. At the time, I was high as a kite. Stoned off my ass. I had nightmares about it for years. Handed over the money to pay for her burial. I thought she was dead."

"You were her savior," El Drone says.

Chad shakes his head warily. "Believe me, I am nobody's savior."

"Sober Me Now confronting Stoned Me Then," Night Snow says, "Been there too."

The motorcade honks and swerves around a pack of stray dogs, near the municipal warehouse where El Drone stores his surveillance equipment. They slow and crawl alongside the Old City wall and the busy ticket-booth entrance to the *ruinas*, where Chad and Winnie once shared a picnic.

El Drone says, "You're getting a full dose of destiny today."

Chad downs half a bottle of water. Night Snow strokes his knee and asks, "What's wrong, pal?"

"A full dose of destiny," Chad repeats, "Like it's all supposed to mean something, and I have no idea what. I'm glad to know she's still alive, but it's complicated."

"Destiny is a big thing down here," El Drone says.

"I don't like it," Chad says.

"Why not?"

"Because now you have to live up to it?" Night Snow suggests.

"I'm a cheap con-man caught in a con bigger than I know."

"Sobriety is a con?"

"Consciousness is a con. It's built into the word."

"That is seriously messed up."

"Maybe it's best that Winnie didn't come," Chad says. "Let's just do this Sister City meeting and get back on the plane and fly home."

"You should talk to Dotcom before you leave," El Drone says. "You really do have to talk to her. She'd be crushed if you left without talking to her."

They drive past a crowded La Sombra Azul. The expat regulars on the sidewalk whistle and shout good luck wishes to the motorcade. El Drone rolls down his window and hollers back. "Thank you, fellas!"

"You don't sound like a Mexican, despite your name," Chad says.

"Originally, I'm from the great state of Indiana," El Drone says.

They ride in silence the rest of the way to the hacienda. Each person in the backseat feeling life's undertow pulling them in unexpected directions that they don't necessarily want to go. For Night Snow that means her friendship with Chad is reaching a level that makes it increasingly difficult to be his sponsor. For El Drone, it means acknowledging that after two decades away from Cave City, the place is still home for him too. And at some point, he will have to go back.

Something about Chad's destiny crunch is contagious for El Drone, and thoughts of going home to Cave City seize him like the hiccups. Back home again in Indiana. El Drone hums snippets of "On the Banks of the Wabash" and rubs elbows with all the guests at the hacienda. He spends the first part of the meeting, the socializing and guacamole part, chatting up the Cave City residents about their little corner of the world. Ostensibly acting as a goodwill ambassador for El Plástico and Ciudad de la Gruta by showing a polite curiosity for all things Hoosier, but secretly soaking up every detail of his childhood turf. The tree growing out of the top of the courthouse. The downtown alleys still paved with bricks.

Caterers in traditional costumes pass trays of finger food and *refrescos* made from tamarind. Background music from a guitar trio. Dr. Crane performing translation duties as necessary, in Dotcom's place. He improvises a bit roughly and apologizes for his lack of nuance. "*Disculpe*, I am a bit rusty. I can hear Milena laughing at my mistakes. What is the word for *river*?"

At 4 p.m., after waiting in vain an extra hour for Dotcom and Father Mike to show up, El Plástico calls the meeting to order. The Sister City crew assembles around a long table on the shaded, afternoon veranda. Glodene insists on starting with another prayer. She leads an invocation meant to allay everyone's fears that once they get down to business, the discussion will turn hopelessly grim. She bucks up morale with Señora Calatrova's reminder that, after reviewing the original documents, the wording clearly states that the agreement can only be nullified if *both* cities vote it down.

"That gives us a little leeway. We can focus our efforts on the city most likely to pass it," Glodene says.

"I disagree," Frank Vigo says, "Without a unanimous vote, I think we're in trouble."

"Why did you add that provision?" Night Snow asks.

"So that any joint business ventures would not be undercut," Señora Calatrova trills.

"Do we have any joint business ventures?"

"Several. Sister City Tours and my research with Dra. Madero," Rufus Crane spouts. "I thought she would be here today. We're making progress and we're close to developing a product for clinical trials. Big pharma is getting interested in our work. I do wish she were here."

El Plástico, sitting beside Dr. Crane, leans over and whispers, "She asked me to convey her regrets to you. A prior commitment kept her away."

Dr. Crane expels a sigh. He continues, "Of course, the legality of two municipalities making such a regulation is questionable. Would that provision stand up in an international court of law? I don't know. Probably not."

"Probably not," Frank Vigo repeats, "That's why both cities will have to vote 'yes.'"

Frank offers an assessment of the larger political picture in the United States. Xenophobia resurgent. What should be a routine reconfirmation of an overall friendly relationship between two small towns is now radioactive. He mentions another attempt to contact Congressman Rex Blaine for his support, but the Congressman is not returning his phone calls. El Plástico chimes in and laments the Radical Synthesizers' smear of the Sister City agreement.

"If anything, we need to learn from you," Night Snow says, "Especially how to live under a repressive regime."

Willard updates the group on Mayor Rosewater's cowardly 'pocket-veto' position. He asks if anyone has more polling data. There is a loud collective groan at the mention of polling. The Manifesto provided a significant bump in the approval rating, but it was waning. Frank reveals that he has been conducting informal surveys among the Southwest Hoosier State students and reports a negative thud, a resounding lack of awareness from most of the respondents.

"How do we counter that?" El Plástico asks, "How do we get on the radar and make the case to both our communities that Sister City is worth saving?"

This question elicits a litany of existing cooperative projects. The weekly Skype session between the schoolchildren in Miss Riggins' sixth grade class at Prairie Elementary and the kids in Doña Marta's class at the colegio. The pen pal column printed by both local newspapers, inspired by the longtime promotion of letter writing as a form of social cohesion by the Mexican Post Office.

"But *why* is it worth it?" Ignacio asks, "We must be able to communicate *that*."

"Because it makes city council meetings a little less boring," Willard jokes.

"We have to do better than, 'Vote for Sister City, because it's less boring.' That's not very inspiring," El Drone says.

Seated next to Glodene in her wheelchair, Chad fidgets and seems to want to say something. Perhaps as a way to yank his thoughts away from Dotcom and Father Mike's ongoing absence. He looks to Glodene for permission.

"Your play, Chad," she says.

"Allow me to think out loud," Chad says, "If this discussion was happening in a therapist's office, I would ask you all to step back and consider the Sister City relationship as if we were talking about real-life sisters, because there are many models of sisterhood, many different kinds of sister relationships. You've got your Rich Sister, Poor Sister thing. You got Beautiful Sister, Ugly Sister. What kind of sisters are these two towns?"

"Good question," Dr. Crane says.

A murmuring catatonia envelops the group as collectively their brains search for possibilities. A chameleon scurries across the patio. Two small birds land on the table to peck at pastry crumbs. No one makes a move to shoo them away.

Night Snow blurts out, "Orphan sisters."

"Orphan sisters?"

"Yes, orphan sisters."

El Drone concurs, "That's exactly how I've always thought of them."

"Why orphan sisters?" Tia Carlota asks.

"It appeals to the heart. There's a mythos about orphans. It appeals to the basic human desire to support the underdog," Night Snow says, beginning to unpack her cardboard tubes, "and it's already in the Codex. Let me show you. "

She unfurls the rubbing panels.

El Drone spouts, "I recognize those images. From the archeology museum. I saw that stone on field trips as a kid."

Frank Vigo jumps in, "Orphaned by our state governments, orphaned by our federal governments, and our so-called representatives in Congress; orphaned by the interstate highway system and the death of the railroads, and the exodus of the young. All we have is each other, our Orphan Sister."

"Stick with your Orphan Sister and she'll stick with you," Ignacio intones.

"A good slogan," Glodene chimes in.

"Stick with your Orphan Sister and she'll stick with you," El Drone repeats, "Dotcom would like that. She would approve. What about Father Mike?"

"He would be on board for sure," Dr. Crane says.

Night Snow unfurls more fuzzy photos of the glyphs and pitches an idea for reviving the "Orphan Sister City Festival" that had in fact started a thousand years ago.

"I suggest that, going forward, we schedule the festival every other year, alternating locations. And that we start in Cave City, because the referendum vote there is more in doubt," El Plástico says.

"We should host it right before the election," Frank Vigo says. He makes a motion and Ignacio seconds it and the motion passes unopposed. Glodene offers to donate ten-grand as seed money. "That should be enough to throw a good party," she says.

"No other city in the world can claim to be hosting a festival that is a thousand years old," Señora Calatrova adds.

"I'm thinking ahead to the half-time show at the Sister City soccer game," Dr. Rufus Crane says, "I'm imagining a *lucha libre* demonstration with the Orphan Sisters wrestling an evildoer who just happens to resemble Sheriff Hooker."

This prompts a chorus of laughter from everyone, including the wait staff.

"Quiet, please!" El Drone says. He stands and motions for one of the nearby waiters to come closer. It looks like El Drone wants to call for a round of drinks. Instead, he points to something on the waiter's collar. It turns out to be a small microphone attached to a wireless unit inside his jacket pocket.

"Where did you get this?" El Drone demands.

The waiter nervously answers, "A man with shiny hair and a gold bracelet. Just before we got in the truck to come here with the food. He said that El Plástico ordered it. He said El Plástico wanted a recording for posterity."

El Drone turns to El Plástico and apologizes, "This is Ramón's work. I'm sorry, boss. Ramón outsmarted me. This is my fault."

"Oh, damn Ramón Puentes," El Plástico groans and rises and steps over to the cowering waiter. He taps the microphone and speaks into it. "Ramón, can you hear me? I hope you can hear me. I am sitting here with a special group of people. You and whoever else is behind this, you are not going to stop us. Is it just the money, Ramón? Is that what you're after? Is this really about TiendaMax? Or is the party promising you a job at the top? Or is this about Mercedes and our personal vendettas? Why do we keep after each other like this? I'm ready to be done with it. Remember us as altar boys in church, competing to see who could stand up the straightest and snuff out the candles with the least effort? It is ridiculous for us to be stuck in this feud."

Cut to: Ramón Puentes, wearing headphones, hunching over his digital recording equipment in a messy hotel room. He grimaces and pushes a button at the end of El Plástico's speech. Striking a match, he lights a cigarette and snuffs out the match between his thumb and forefinger. He throws off his headphones and pulls on a hat and exits the hotel room in a huff. He strides a couple blocks beyond the cemetery to a dark cantina, its front window shades drawn tight, which signals a men-only joint. Slow, sad *corta-venas* music plays in the background. A few professional women hover around the bar. Professional listeners, that is. Their job is to listen compassionately to long accounts of woe. They nod and murmur and offer kind words, and score a few drinks in the bargain. Ramón orders tequila. He commences to speak to the female stranger who appears beside him. He unloads his version of the nemesis-hood. His version of the long pursuit, racing El Plástico since forever, both bottle-fed on the male code for career success: be ruthless, without anyone noticing. He got so close so many times, so close to the top. But cruel, unexpected circumstances exposed him. And El Plástico cruises forward, so obviously a snake since the very beginning and yet nobody seems to care. The professional female listener nods and replies, "Take heart, *señor*, there are some people to whom life deals so many bad cards that eventually they are free, liberated, by the extent of their misfortune." Ramón orders another tequila, and one for her too. He asks if she would like to see an electrified pickle fluoresce and explode. "No, *gracias, señor*," she says, "another time perhaps."

23.

Dotcom and Father Mike never make it to the hacienda. They forget about the Sister City referendum. They are having too much fun at the *ruinas*. They climb to the top of the Jaguar Pyramid. Father Mike assists Dotcom with every step. He admires the detailed relief sculptures of fantastic figures. "That one is Old Stingray Paddler," Dotcom says, "and this one is called 'Boniness Spirit Companion.'" They squeeze together under Dotcom's parasol, lost in time and a heated discussion about their favorite Star Trek episodes. Comparing the original series to the Next Generation to the later versions. The topic turns to theology in outer space. Behind them, the crimson sun looms, summoning a joint hallucination of red-shirt saints and language-instruction characters, all awaiting human discovery on a hospitable planet in a distant galaxy, maybe not that far away.

24.

Winnie was surprised by Chad's emotional return from Mexico. Chad heel-kicked the apartment door shut and threw his bag in the corner. He embraced her and wouldn't let go, really wouldn't let go. A five-minute hug, while he vented one of his random brain-spews: "We're so lost in this universe, tiny specks of meta-data. Jigsaws of ego-plasm, the greedy self an increasingly antiquated phenomenon. Except thankfully, you and me, we two specks have found each other. Tiny spores of ego-being floating alone in the soup of time. And it's not a straight line, babe, this time thing. It's weird. So hung up on straight lines. I'm glad we're getting married. I think I finally understand why people do it. Spiders weaving a web. All we can do."

"Chad, tell me more about your trip. I love the idea for reviving the Orphan Sister Festival," Winnie said, realigning her blouse and the pencil in her hair. Happy to see him, yet also exhausted from teaching her classes and Frank's classes and caring for the kids and Bongo.

Chad shrugged and spun and stood on tiptoes and raised his arms to the ceiling and fell back on the couch. An interpretive dance summary.

"She is alive," he whispered.

"Who, what *she*?"

Winnie had never seen him cry more than a few crocodile tears. A line of glistening cheek-rollers slowly emerged as he described the inscrutably striking face of the lame, blind-in-one-eye Mayan girl with a pink hair bow, miraculously returned from the dead.

"Wait, slow down, tell me this again…"

Winnie feared a tawdry confession, a drug relapse with a chamber maid at the hotel, or a torrid threesome with Night Snow. It took a minute for Winnie to realize that Chad was describing the girl who had been hit by the bus on their spring-break trip, many years ago. The girl, Dotcom, had recovered and grown up to become a language savant who could talk to Father Mike in Klingon.

"I thought that bus incident was something I just had to get over. Now it's something I have to live up to," Chad said.

"How do you mean?"

"Destiny is a big thing, according to El Drone."

"El Drone, the mayor's surveillance guy?"

"He's actually a Hoosier boy in hiding. And Dotcom is clearly a person of destiny, especially the way she and Father Mike connected right away and dove into their new life. By association somehow, I am destined for something too. I just don't know what. Getting sober, I thought my main goal was just not being an asshole. Apparently I'm actually supposed to do something in this world. Maybe it's the Orphan Sister Festival."

"There is plenty of folklore on orphans to draw from," Winnie said, "But, be honest, did you relapse? This sounds like a relapse."

"No. That's why it's so confusing. And then you look at Father Mike being so sharp and decisive about his new ministry in Ciudad de la Gruta."

"What new ministry?"

"Father Mike didn't come back with us. He refused to get on the plane."

"Because he hooked up with a one-eyed Mayan who speaks Klingon?" Winnie said.

"They're starting a church together. She claims there is a large demographic, especially among the villages, who will support their message."

"What message would that be?" Winnie asked.

"That during the Ascension, Jesus traveled into outer space, where he is now waiting for us on another planet."

"Jesus is waiting for us on another planet. You're kidding, no, please tell me you're kidding."

"I talked with her and Father Mike for about an hour at the airport before we left. They're designing a website."

Winnie almost gagged. Chad thumped her on the back.

"Father Mike and Dotcom are very serious. You can read all about it at TheChurchofPlanetJesus.org. It should be up soon."

"This can't look good for the referendum," Winnie said, "our local priest running off with a Mexican hussy to start the Church of Planet Jesus."

"Right, there is an optics problem, but she is not a hussy. She's a very intense individual," Chad said. "We talked about the bus accident and she claims that she often thought about me and imagined me living in a Chicago penthouse apartment. She pictured me helping my neighbors, a family named Jones with a kid, Chuck, who likes to talk about sports, and she says that the Church of Planet Jesus is going to designate a list of their saints and that I'm going to be one."

"That's a laugh," Winnie said, "How are we going to explain this to my mother?"

"You mean, speaking of intense individuals?"

The shift in topic brought Chad out of his exquisite swoon. He began to pace. He dug through his backpack and found a small box that contained a pair of silver earrings.

"These will protect you," he said.

"Thank you," Winnie said, "Tuesday morning. She arrives Tuesday and she'll want to go to church and meet Frank and Glodene, and everyone will be blabbing about the Planet Jesus scandal. And it will only make her more skeptical about Cave City."

They moved to the kitchen to make coffee. Winnie modeled the earrings. Chad said, "I should have gotten something for your mom."

"Did you talk to Frank about her?" Winnie asked.

"About Prudie?"

"Yes, about Prudie."

"Was I supposed to?"

"No, he was supposed to talk to you."

"We chatted on the plane ride back. I told him about Brakeless Eddy, that he's not such a bad guy as Frank thinks, that he's got a Honduran wife and she does beadwork that they sell at a booth at the soccer game. We talked about fishing and Cuban cigars. Our previous failed attempts to smuggle in a box of cigars for our fathers. Frank told me about once asking a customs officer, 'What do you do with these Cuban cigars that you confiscate?' And the guy says, 'We burn them, slowly. One at a time.'"

"I'm glad you bonded over cigar talk, but – "

Winnie had her own confession to make. She and Frank had hatched a plan to use his house as the main location for entertaining Prudence Marsh, aka Mother Hen, during her state visit.

"Why would we want to do that?" Chad said, a little miffed to learn that Winnie and Frank were concocting such schemes together.

"Because Mother Hen still doesn't know about the moving van being stolen. That would be a huge black mark against you. Right up there with the time she showed up unexpectedly at your basement apartment and you answered the door naked. And right now, our apartment doesn't look much better than your old one. I'm thinking it's just for a few days. We steer every encounter to Frank's place and the kids. She'll love Nina and Paulo."

Chad grunted a blunt acknowledgment that the plan had some merit. He swung his arms and shook it out. His relationship with Prudie Marsh needed a reset. The incident to which Winnie just referred was only one of many infractions. Violations of golf course etiquette being high on the list. Peeing in the woods and throwing clubs. Sartorial mistakes were not far behind. Wearing shorts to Christmas Eve Mass. Chad's attempts at humoring Winnie's mother always fell flat.

"We can try it," Chad said, "There's something else that would also help, between you and your mom."

"A personality transplant?"

"It would help to let her know directly when she pisses you off," Chad said.

"Why so?" Winnie bristled.

"Because, upon reflection, I've been able to see a few things differently, and I realize that a lot of the stuff I pull with your mom is actually on your behalf."

"On my behalf?" Winnie said, "This sounds like more junior counselor crap."

"You carry around a lot of frustration with her, ever since you were young, but you never do anything about it. You hate her self-censoring, especially when she applies it to you. I want to stick up for you, and so I provoke her – for you."

"For me?" Winnie said.

"I know it sounds odd. I'll try to back off and you try to step forward."

Winnie bit a lip and nodded. "Okay," she said, "Operation Prudie begins. We can do it."

The visit went off better than expected, until the soccer game. The weather cooperated, producing a string of pleasant, late autumn days.

Mother Hen's surgically-enhanced beak remained in joint all week. She arrived outfitted from the L.L. Bean catalogue, as if for a backcountry excursion in the Yukon, except with pearls and high heels and the big purse on her arm. Her twice daily costume changes helped support a cheerful demeanor. She sat in politely on the first planning session for the Orphan Sister Festival and afterwards wrote a check for a thousand dollars.

Prudie Marsh came to Cave City determined to fawn over her daughter-the-professor and everything associated with her daughter-the-professor. As for her crude son-in-law-in-waiting, he could be assiduously ignored. The same way Prudie ignored her husband. Chad ended up as a peripheral entity, sidelined by Prudie Marsh's cloying attentions to Winnie and Frank Vigo and his "charming house" and "these adorable little munchkins." The kids demonstrated their newly-learned cartwheel technique multiple times a day.

Prudie's gushy thing for Nina and Paulo was fed by an obvious, unsuppressed, anticipatory desire for grandchildren. And the kids' gushy thing for her was fed by their unsuppressed hunger for her sugary treats and for an *abuela* replacement. To her credit, Prudie participated. She did laundry and the dishes. She located BounceLand, a warehouse at the edge of Terre Haute, renovated at minimal cost into a warren of trampolines. The space was full of bouncing children in special, rented non-skid socks and a few uninhibited adults. Prudie among them, to Winnie and Chad's dismay. Her pearls and purse and boobs flying in all directions.

"I thought you were joking about the personality transplant," Chad whispered.

"Maybe this is menopause," Winnie whispered.

At church, Prudie took the scandalous news about Father Mike in stride, explaining that his sins were small potatoes compared to the predatory priests in Boston. She attended all of Winnie's classes and gave her daughter a scare by daring to participate in the class discussion. Attired in red chamois and a purple down vest, Prudie Marsh raised her hand at the back of the seminar room and cleared her throat portentously.

Winnie had been lecturing about the formation of urban legends. She gulped and tapped her wristwatch and signaled to her mother to speak, briefly, please.

"I just want to share a thought or two, dear. Hello, everybody, I'm your professor's mom..."

Her students turned and clapped, bless them. Winnie tapped her wristwatch again.

After her blithe introduction, Prudie carefully and coherently shared an interesting observation: in contrast to the Tall Tales of rural legend, which everyone knew to be false, urban legends foster a veneer of truthfulness that many people believe.

Phew, okay.

This created some lively conversation at Frank Vigo's dinner table that night, about truth and falsehood in family legend. Frank revealed a genealogical secret about a revered boat captain ancestor, who, it turns out, had been a slave trader. There was a discussion about Nina and Paulo (while the kids played upstairs), how they would eventually have to digest the reality of their missing family in Guatemala. Curious about Chad's professional opinion, Prudie inquired why he thought the kids never asked about their biological parents? Chad shared a feeling that at some level they did know what happened, but were too afraid to make it conscious. Winnie recounted her discovery from the previous summer of the slave trade roots in the Marsh family fortune. And Prudie Marsh, a bit tipsy on sherry and suddenly all contrite about her earlier refusal to recognize that truth, came out in support of Winnie's divestiture idea. Suggesting they sell the portraits of those bewigged old baddies and donate the proceeds, because she'd never liked them anyway. The colors don't match the wallpaper.

Chad's reputation with his prospective mother-in-law was improving, due to his new clinic job. It was starting well. As predicted, Dr. Crane quickly filled Chad's caseload with fascinating people, wiry hod-carriers, *yarderos*, roofers, farmhands, slaughterhouse meat cutters, and home-health aide workers. They appreciated Chad's attempts to conduct the sessions in Spanish and his intake questionnaire: When was the last time you danced to live music, and when was the last time you felt like an authority? *Dígame otra vez.* They discussed authority, not in the sense of power or toughness, but rather the core meaning of the word, same one in Spanish, *autoridad*, the root being 'author,' and thus the true meaning; who is creating the story here, who is defining this particular situation. It's you, *compadre*, and, please, never give up that ability. They also liked his poetic case notes, an extension of an experiment with Ricky. In order to reshape his clients' expectation that he would simply be giving them advice, as Dr. Crane had warned, Chad took verbatim notes during the session and, right before the end, he would dash off a short poem, compiled exclusively from the client's own words. A takeaway gift from each hour, proof that their *consejero* was not judging or thinking ill of them, and that their own thoughts and ideas were the most important part of the session. Dr. Crane recommended a phone consult with Dra. Milena Madero about therapeutic technique with this population, and out of that conversation came her idea for the talking path. Using a chainsaw for the first time in his life, Chad cut a path in the woods behind the clinic and made benches from the felled timber so that some of the sessions could be conducted while walking outdoors.

Keeping his promise, Brakeless Eddy came through and gave Chad a rusted, functional, green 1992 LeMans for his rural commute. It ran rough and throaty, with a spewing, shaking tail pipe and muffler. Chad and the kids named it the "Green Monster." It started reliably every day. Night Snow gifted him a feathery dreamcatcher to hang from the rearview mirror. She revealed a hitherto unknown affection for Pontiacs. She insisted that Chad take her along in the LeMans on Sister City leafleting runs to the outlying neighborhoods. Although she never allowed him to drop her off or pick her up at her house, claiming it was a sponsor boundary issue. Whatever. Night Snow and Chad occasionally indulged in the local practice of idling in the Mound Park parking lot, to share a cigarette. Buttoning up coats and tightening scarves. Forty degrees colder than Mexico. For some reason, ever since their return, Night Snow was smoking a lot.

"I wish I understood the changes in Prudie Marsh," Chad said, "Back in Boston, she's a cat person, and here suddenly she's all over Bongo, taking him to the vet for a flea bath and a grooming. Whenever I try to bring up wedding plans, she waves me off and says it's not my problem."

"Prudie sounds like a person in recovery, overdoing the making-amends step," Night Snow said.

"What do you make of Frank's super-host mode? Cooking gourmet dinners every night and inviting Prudie to the tango club and insisting that Prudie extend her stay so that she could attend the Sister City soccer game and sit in Glodene's skybox along with the dean and other local dignitaries."

Night Snow said, "I'm guessing it's a faculty recruitment strategy, a ploy to impress Winnie's mother, so that when the department chairman makes a permanent job offer to Winnie, which definitely will happen, because they need to retain her talent, Mother Hen will support it."

"Right, I see it now," Chad said. Or thought he did, blinking away the sun and the smoke in his eyes.

25.

The referendum vote in Ciudad de la Gruta is only a few weeks away, but Dotcom and Father Mike barely seem aware of it. Clutching hands, they walk starry-eyed toward the *teatro*. They exist only for each other. They are oblivious to the shunning from all quarters. They talk stars. They see stars. He calls her 'Dot.' She calls him 'Mikey.' Father Mike extols her beauty to one and all. He enjoys her tactile inclinations, bending to pick up twigs, flower petals, grasses, stones; rubbing them against her face, just to know how they *feel*. He claims that when he awoke from his plane ride coma and saw Dotcom's face and her hair bow, instead of seeing a disfigured human, he believed himself to be on another planet and assumed he was gazing up at an alien queen.

They feed each other. They fan each other. They stop to buy flowers for Señora Calatrova. Father Mike waits outside the dressing room in the basement of the *teatro*, while Dotcom seeks tips from Señora Calatrova on how to make love in a hammock, an act that requires some finesse.

I admire them. Everyone else thinks it's absurd. Dotcom is expelled from the Jesuit school and Tía Carlota kicks her out of her apartment. Father Mike is threatened with excommunication, if he doesn't return to the true church. They make the paper in a feature article written by Juan Pablo, along with a photo of Dotcom cradling Father Mike on the airport tarmac. The tawdry scandal of their relationship does cause trouble for the Sister City effort among the clergy and their adherents. Until this blows over, the Sister City campaign will suffer the consequences.

As for The Church of the Planet Jesus, who knows? Ignacio opines that the public will take it as just another zealot pipedream that the town has seen come and go many times before. Or they could end up sticking around like the Mennonites. El Plástico and I are also worried that Ramón may have sold his secret recording of our hacienda meeting to Sheriff Hooker. That would have consequences too.

I remain partial to Dotcom, my Mayan friend, and young Father Mike, who reminds me of my own idealistic youth. As a stale, dried-up bachelor now, I am surprised to feel so much emotion at their displays of affection. Slowly, awkwardly, painfully, I realize that I am desirous of some affection. I have been locked in a self-imposed ban on matters of the heart, out of the belief that my mortal sins disqualify me, that I am too tainted. "Who would mate with that?" as my foster mother used to say. Worry lines and scar tissue from an exploding drone, a missing tooth, raccoon circles around my eyes. In the mirror, I scare myself.

Twice weekly, I bring food out to Dotcom and Mike at the abandoned drive-in movie theater. They are living in the empty projection booth, sleeping in hammocks and using the 'Mayan toilet.' That's what Dotcom calls it. Drive-in theaters, *los autocinemas*, never caught on much in Mexico. This one was a failed attempt by a former mayor to attract gringo tourists from the coast.

I attempt to intercede with El Plástico on their behalf, arguing that at least bad publicity is still some publicity, which can be important with complacent voters. I tell him that eventually Ciudad de la Gruta will get over its scruples and allow the public's soft spot for a unique love story to prevail.

Turns out, I am not the only one secretly supporting the nascent Church of Planet Jesus. Ramón Puentes is in the mix too. Why won't he just go away? His black Ford shows up again on my drone video. At the drive-in. He is apparently providing money, as he did with the Radical Synthesizers. Father Mike is using Ramón's gift money to rewire the projection booth. Dotcom is ordering custom vestments from a seamstress and printing leaflets for Church of the Planet Jesus services to be held at the drive-in theater.

Ramón's motivation remains a mystery. When I ask Dotcom and Father Mike about him, they shrug and say it's a mystery to them too. He comes on Sunday afternoons and, crossing himself and kneeling in the projection booth, graciously offers up wads of cash.

"Watch out. That guy is trouble. You better be careful with him," I say.

"He claims his family wanted him to be a priest, but his beliefs were always more akin to ours and he just couldn't put words to it," Father Mike says.

"Hard to imagine Ramón believing in anything, other than TiendaMax taking over the world."

"He claims his faith has just been waiting for an outlet," Dotcom says.

"Does Ramón try to tell you how to spend the money?" I ask.

"He thinks new religions are most successful when they incorporate aspects of old religions. He suggests that we tap into the old religion of sports, by doing a Blessing of the Uniforms ceremony before the big soccer game with Cave City."

"I think it's a good idea," Dotcom says, "Blessing of the Uniforms will attract many people."

I relate this conversation to El Plástico at our Monday meeting and we both continue to scratch our heads about Ramón's true angle. El Plástico confirms there was an early period when Ramón wanted to be a priest, when they were both altar boys, and often boasted that he would become a bishop, and there was a lot of family pressure for him to take vows. Maybe he is acting on some long hidden spiritual struggle? It seems far-fetched. Ramón is a lost soul. But, then, look at me. Who knew I had a conscience or a heart?

In our next meeting, El Plástico puts in a phone call to Mercedes, who he hasn't spoken with for a long time. She answers on the first ring. El Plástico clicks on the speaker device for me to listen in, and also to steady himself with an audience. He tightens his lips up around his teeth.

"Mercedes, I know you're disappointed in me," El Plástico says, "and I know that deep down you do support the idea of Sister City, so I'm calling to ask for your opinion on a strange situation."

El Plástico describes the latest dirt on Ramón and the Church of Planet Jesus.

Mercedes harrumphs and says, "Plastiquito, you are losing your touch."

"What do you mean?"

Mercedes laughs outright. "This one is obvious."

"It is?"

"Ramón doesn't have a spiritual bone in his body. It's all about shutting down Sister City. Either for TiendaMax or whoever else is paying him to throw a wrench in your career. He's banking on the ongoing scandal of the Church of Planet Jesus. He wants to perpetuate its infamy, because he thinks it will harm the vote. Especially this idea for the Blessing of the Uniforms, which he assumes will backfire and be a huge embarrassment for you."

Not exactly, no, as it happens. Just the opposite. Over five hundred soccer fan penitents, including Gonzalo and Ignacio, flock out to the drive-in theater to the Blessing of the Uniforms on a moonlit night. They are drawn by the prospect of free food, and the local fondness for this game and the Ceiba team. The air smells like oregano. The projection booth is up and running. Father Mike taps into some really old religion by projecting giant images of Maya ball courts and ceiba trees onto the movie screen, behind a dais where the team uniforms are displayed on mannequins borrowed from Dotcom's seamstress. Juan Pablo Chayac and a few other starters from the team accept the crowd's adulation. An evening breeze moderates the temperature. Dotcom, dressed in her version of Federation robes, raises her hands to the sky, streaked with sunset splendor. Almost like fireworks. Absorbing the divine sky energy into her fingers, Dotcom individually zaps each green jersey and prays aloud for speed and clear passing lanes and field vision and corner kicks. She gets the crowd involved with joint, swaying, arm-waving enactment of the mythic world tree in all its symbolic glory, the *kapok*, the *ya'axché*. "Go, Ceiba team! Remember that a strong tree lives just as much below the ground as above it!"

Ramón stands at the back of the crowd and joins in the veneration. Father Mike passes out free tickets to his promised live-streamed broadcast of the game on the drive-in movie screen. They gain Ignacio's rabid support by closing the ceremony with a giant, projected close-up of the notorious Double Zero jersey worn by the opponent's goalkeeper. None other than Tiny Hooker, the Sheriff's son. The crowd boos enthusiastically.

26.

Gameday in Cave City dawned to the coos of mourning doves and the faint whistle of a freight train. Clear and sunny, with a resolute December chill, which the local fans hoped would be an advantage for their team.

As part of the Sister City effort this year, Glodene Butz paid for two charter planes to bring the Ceiba team, along with relatives and friends. Several families signed up and obtained tourist visas, all close with Juan Pablo Chayac. A striker, Pedro Álvarez, and his parents and grandparents and his little sister. They operate a *zapatería* on the western edge of Centennial Park that supplies the team with shoes. The middle halfback, Alfonso Sillón, and his mother and two uncles and older brother. They reside in a house entirely covered with bougainvillea that makes the place look twice its size in the barrio behind the water tower. And another striker, Mauricio Fernández, and his parents and grandmother and two brothers and younger sister who run a small engine repair shop near the 2nd class bus station.

All the visitors to Cave City were housed at the Indian Mound Motel and fed at the University Commons. The pep rally on campus the previous night streaked the sycamores and beech trees with tissue paper. Shreds fluttered in the morning breeze. The remains of a bonfire on the quad smoldered wisps of blue smoke.

Tailgaters and food trucks and merchandise hawkers arrived early at the Fracker Field parking lots. In recent years, the West Lot had become an unofficial, open-air *mercado* for artists and leatherworkers and jewelry vendors. Brakeless Eddy and his wife manned a booth to sell her beadwork. The East Lot was the outdoor food court, featuring several Latin American cuisines. Good smells all day long. Some of the tamale trucks came all the way from Louisville.

Like one of the circling turkey buzzards aroused by the cooking smells and the prospect of easy prey, Sheriff Hooker hovered astride his horse, trotting around the perimeter of the stadium grounds. Grinning and waving to his supporters, Sheriff Hooker felt buoyed and confident that the Church of the Planet Jesus scandal would prove to be his big break. He had waxed his mustache for this day. Chica scurried behind him, handing out 'Hooker for Mayor' bumper stickers. Using a walkie-talkie, the Sheriff barked orders to his deputies. He directed the setup of traffic pylons and made his authoritative presence known to the stream of vehicles arriving from all directions.

Vehicles packed with eager fans, waving Mexican flags from the back of pick-up trucks. Many of them undocumented, bravely surfacing for a day of solidarity. The drivers and passengers peered warily at Sheriff Hooker and accepted the bumper stickers from Chica. Everyone trusting in the unwritten pledge, originally negotiated with the Chamber of Commerce, that no papers would be checked today. A day of tolerance. A day for the embrace of mutual interests, because this friendly match brings a tremendous boon to the local economy. Why not let the illegals spend their hard-earned money for a few hours? Games at Fracker Field typically drew a couple hundred fans at most. Today was standing room only.

Sheriff Hooker cocked his hat and, trying to demonstrate prideful equanimity, trotted over to greet the arrival of his opposition in a Butz Industries van, fitted out for Glodene's wheelchair. The Sheriff had been hearing about their Orphan Sister halftime show from the maintenance guys at the stadium. Silly stuff. The Sheriff dismounted from his horse, a big production on its own.

The tinted-glass front passenger window rolled down to reveal Glodene Butz's patrician smile. And Winnie Marsh, putting on Chapstick.

"Hello, Sheriff, dear. Looks like we've got a beautiful morning. Although a difficult one for you, I imagine, having to rein in your instinctual grudges," Glodene said.

Sheriff Hooker stroked his mustache and chomped his gum and said, "Ma'am, as usual, I have no idea what you're talking about. It is guaranteed that a large number of the usual suspects will get drunk and cause some kind of trouble that is not covered by the amnesty and I will happily arrest them. What are you doing here at this hour?"

"Setting up my luncheon tailgate. A delicious array of Mexican dishes, which, if memory serves, you're quite fond of eating," Glodene said.

"The chow is a separate matter entirely, ma'am. Would you like a 'Hooker for Mayor' bumper sticker?"

"Sure, an historical artifact," Glodene said.

Winnie reached for the bumper sticker, and winked at Chica in return.

"Who else do you have inside that van?" Sheriff Hooker inquired, squinting into the dim back, where Dolores and Rosa and Ricky huddled together among folding tables and coolers of food and musical equipment. In the middle seat, squeezed tight, Frank and Chad and Prudie Marsh, with the kids on Prudie's lap.

"We have a special musical guest today," Winnie announced, "Our tailgate will feature live Latin bluegrass music."

The term 'Latin bluegrass' caused a pained crease in Sheriff Hooker's forehead. "And these little people? Who might they be?" he asked, zeroing in on Paulo and Nina.

The kids recoiled, as if spotting a wolf in disguise. Prudie clutched them close in her lap. She said, "I am Mrs. Prudence J. Marsh from Boston, Massachusetts and they are with me."

"Sheriff, is Tiny playing in goal today?" Ricky called from the back, redirecting his attention.

"You betcha. Tiny is starting in goal. Our secret weapon. Tiny won't be letting nothing into the net. This year we're going to show them how it's done."

'Tiny' Hooker, as previously stated, was more than a chip off the old block. A behemoth. Too big for the football team because, at four hundred and ten pounds, almost as wide as he was tall, Tiny could not run. He could barely walk. But, installed in the soccer goal, he effectively blocked half the net by just standing still and, as needed, waddled a couple steps to either side to block the other portion of the net.

Tiny was the last one out of the locker room. He waddled like he was on mini-stilts. During the team introductions, his straggling, late appearance on the field in a skintight, custom-made uniform with the emblazoned double zeroes brought cheers and jeers and awestruck gasps from the Ceibas' bench.

A *fanático* carrying an enormous green, white, and red flag ran a full lap around the stadium. Below the scoreboard screen, in the practice area reserved for the marching band, the Southwest Hoosier State Marching

Hundred wore festive sombreros and played both national anthems. Everyone stood. Juan Pablo and his teammates crooned all twenty verses of an abridged Mexican national anthem, along with the Ciudad de la Gruta community choir, directed by Señora Calatrova, in the livestream projected onto the big screen at Fracker Field from the drive-in theater in Mexico. Thanks to a pre-arranged, techno-collaboration between Frank Vigo and Father Mike.

Chad and Night Snow and Dr. Crane manipulated their giant, papier-mâché Orphan Sister puppets from the open windows of Glodene's skybox. They had arrived by separate conveyance with the halftime gear. The puppets appeared to be dancing a tango. At the same time, Winnie and Frank unfurled a large 'Support Your Sister City' banner.

Nina and Paulo squirmed on Prudie Marsh's lap. Too many people, too much noise for the kids. Likewise for Prudie, having been dragged by her husband to too many sporting events over the years. She fingered her pearls like a rosary. Winnie checked in frequently and tried to nudge a conversation between her mother and Glodene.

"Don't worry about us two," Glodene said, "We'll pretend to be a couple old ladies talking about foundation garments."

Extended applause and a spontaneous crowd doing the wave mirrored the moves of the Orphan Sister puppets. Sheriff Hooker frowned and paced in the end zone. He felt a growing sense of alarm. During the team introductions, and as the match began, both sides of the stadium joined in a co-generated enthusiasm for a well-played game. Not the usual competitive scorn for the other team's failings. Sheriff Hooker noted the trash barrels beside the ticket booths filling with his bumper stickers. Campaign money down the drain.

Within the first minute of the game, Juan Pablo and Pedro Álvarez and the other Ceiba strikers started pummeling Tiny with line-drive volleys. Playing full tilt, fueled by national pride, they ignored everything their coach yelled from the bench. The cold air was not a problem. They charged and counter-charged, investing in the long ball. However, the sausage, grits, pancakes and farmers' omelets from the breakfast buffet sat heavily in their stomachs and came up inopportunely on the sidelines during the media timeouts.

The crowd cheered appreciatively for both attack and defense. Fans wearing tricolor flags as capes ran up and down the aisles. Sheriff Hooker stalked the sidelines, yelling at Tiny.

Tiny wore his black, motorcyclist's skullcap and thick pads on his arms and legs to reduce bruising. His fat arms fluttered at his sides, like fins on a whale. He was not dexterous enough to always catch the ball. Shots bounced and ricocheted sharply off him at angles that his fullbacks knew how to anticipate, so that they could clear the ball downfield quickly and buy a little time to pant heavily, until the next assault.

Twenty minutes into the first half, there was still no score. This year's game really did look to be different. And it wasn't just about Tiny Hooker. The Southwest Hoosier State team compromised enough skilled athletes of their own, several of them cousins of the Mexican players, that they did not have to resort to desperate slide tackles and yellow cards.

The crowd roared approvingly. Not only for the action on the field, but also for images projected on the big video screen from the fans in Ciudad de la Gruta. Familiar identifications were being made, as close-up images from the drive-in theater flashed on the big screen at Fracker Field. The Cave City citizens recognized old acquaintances, retirees who had moved down to Flamingo Estates.

"Hey, look, there's Gonzo Sánchez!"

Many residents recognized his metallic grin, his incisors encased in silver. They remembered him selling his sister's catfish tacos at the farmers' market. There's Gonzalo, the catfish taco guy. We miss him. What's he doing down there? Oh, he got deported. Briefly, a chant started up: "Bring back Gonzo! Bring back Gonzo!" Until an irate Sheriff Hooker lumbered up the exterior fire stairs to the announcer's booth and ordered the video feed cut, for security purposes.

Outside in the West Lot, cooking and preparing for Glodene's halftime luncheon, Dolores and Rosa heard the chants for Gonzalo and looked up anxiously. While Ricky, like everyone else, laughed and echoed the cheer. "They're cheering for Uncle Gonzo."

"Yes, I know," Dolores said, crossing herself.

"That's cool."

"Maybe, maybe not," she said.

Ricky, excited by the lively, diverse scene, with partyers throwing sombreros like Frisbees and passersby dropping bills into his banjo case, said, "Mom, loosen up. It's gameday. Nothing is going to happen today. Sheriff Hooker can't touch you today. I'm tired of living with your fear. Really, nothing is going to happen."

"Maybe, maybe not. Look at all those extra deputies posted around the exits. They've got dogs with them," Dolores said. "It's easy for you to say nothing will happen, not being the one in danger."

Ricky grumbled, "That's your standard reply. I wish you would at least talk to that immigration lawyer about how to get papers."

Rosa the Silent stepped between them. She intervened with sign language gestures of peace. A job she'd done a thousand times before. She instructed Ricky to keep playing his banjo, and for Dolores to keep rolling tamales.

Another huge cheer erupted from inside the stadium. A score! For the first time in the history of these games, Cave City had taken the lead, as a result of one of Tiny's unpredictable goal kicks. It was just seconds before halftime. The Ceiba goalie and his fullbacks and the halfbacks had edged too far up the field, preparing to receive another of Tiny's erratic punts and for one last rush before time expired. Tiny's kicking style, after he had caught a shot, usually in the gut, involved a curious sidewinder dropkick. He would turn and fold sideways, and the ball would disappear inside his enormous girth and eventually plop out as Tiny spun all four hundred and ten pounds around and, if lucky, connected with some part of his foot. And the ball would slice or hook or dribble forward. This time, however, it rocketed up and out and up and out all the way down the field, high over the heads of the entire Ceiba team, including the astonished defensemen and goalie. They turned and watched the ball bounce once, twice and roll into the open net.

Up in Glodene's skybox, all pretense of neutral decorum disappeared. "Holy cow," Frank Vigo yelled.

Paulo and Nina had never heard mild-mannered Frank yell. They broke loose from Prudie's arms and jumped down behind Glodene's wheelchair and buried their faces in her fur coat. Winnie ran over to soothe them. Night Snow joined in with exclamations of joyful amazement. Night Snow and Chad, who had come up for a water break before the halftime show, spun the Orphan Sister puppets out the skybox window.

Glodene and Prudie remained unfazed. Really, darlings.

"Too bad your mayor isn't here to see this," Prudie said.

Glodene had just been explaining the political implications of Ralph Rosewater's absence from the game. "Yes, he'd probably have spilled a couple drinks down his shirtfront by now," she agreed.

"Be strong, amigos. We'll strike back in the second half," Chad yelled from the skybox window, channeling the spirit of his Mayan sister puppet. He and Night Snow hoisted their papier-mâché figures and started to move downstairs for the halftime show.

"Why is Chad cheering for the Mexicans?" Prudie asked her daughter.

"Because of Dotcom's resurrection," Winnie said.

"Because he's funny," the kids squeaked.

"Because I'm a damn traitor, a San Patricio," Chad said, lapsing back into tease mode with his future mother-in-law, as he and Night Snow exited the skybox.

"He thinks I'm an old shrew," Prudie confided to her hostess.

Glodene had already sensed that Prudie did not entirely approve of her daughter's choice for a husband. She wanted to support Chad, so she brought up his contributions during their recent trip. "He's a very clever fellow, and a good Scrabble player."

Prudie said, "I've never heard the word 'clever' associated with Chad."

Glodene patted the children's heads and said, "All of us in Cave City are grateful for Chad and Winnie's presence and we look forward to many more fruitful years together."

Though her comment was intended to be a warm affirmation, it unwittingly touched a raw nerve for Prudie Marsh. Her Cave City visit had extended beyond the three-day rule and she was feeling it. Not that the fish had gone bad, so to speak, but her travel supply of Xanax was depleted. Prudie realized how much she wanted to be back in Boston, ASAP. How could Winnie and Chad even consider staying in this backwater town any longer than necessary?

Winnie overheard this exchange and, reading the reaction on her mother's face and her grab for another sherry, directed the children to give Prudie a hug and began shooing everyone toward the parking lot, promising good food.

Dolores and Rosa and Ricky were waiting with the luncheon. Despite his aversion to Glodene's politics, Sheriff Hooker could not resist her delicious chow at the tailgate. He forced himself to pretend to listen to a couple of Ricky's songs, tossed a fiver in the guitar case, and turned his attention to eating.

The Sheriff, like Prudie, was struggling with some unexpected distress. Slowly realizing the extent of his ambivalence about Tiny's shocking goal. Slowly realizing how much he was counting on the Frackers' loss to sour people's opinions toward the Sister City vote. If by some miracle the Frackers actually won this game, people would be more inclined to maintain the Sister City status, so this match could be played again.

Glodene and Prudie arrived from the skybox, assisted by Frank and Dr. Crane, who spotted the Sheriff in advance and deftly signaled to Winnie to pivot and move the kids in a different direction. Plates of steaming food were passed around. Dolores and Rosa accepted many compliments. Ricky circled with a serenade. Above him, a line of unscheduled storm clouds moved in from the west.

Glodene officially introduced Prudie to the Sheriff, who had just spilled a gob of salsa on his rattlesnake cowboy boots.

"I've never met a real frontier sheriff," Prudie said.

"It's a very important position," Hooker replied, "I wear many hats in this town, from dogcatcher to detective to consoler-in-chief to moral guide to true voice of the people."

"Congratulations on your son's goal."

"Oopsie. Hold on, please." Another large gob of salsa splat on his boots. A cascade of oaths and a verse of scripture.

"Handsome footwear," Prudie said.

"Ain't they excellent. You see all kinds of boots here today. Rattlesnake, crocodile even," Sheriff Hooker said.

Glodene said, "Mrs. Marsh is visiting us from Boston."

"Boston, huh? How are the Celtics doing with that coach they stole away from us?"

"Sorry, I don't really know," Prudie said.

"I hope you're enjoying Cave City, Ma'am. Our beaners here sure know how to cook. I'll grant 'em that," Sheriff Hooker said, between guttural bites. "Have you ever noticed that beans smell like sweat?"

Prudie appeared baffled on how to respond, destabilized by the effects of too much sherry and increasing anxiety from the boisterous riffraff surging directly around her.

"Sheriff Hooker is running for mayor," Frank Vigo offered, as a conversation stabilizer.

"Against Mister Ralph Rosewater?" asked Prudie, "I was just hearing about him."

"Sheriff Hooker is some of our best local color," Glodene added.

The Sheriff coughed and countered, "Please, no joking about colored, Ma'am. People know where I stand on the colored. Now Spanish colored, that's another matter."

Prudie Marsh, increasingly discombobulated, misheard his statement about Spanish colored and somehow believed the topic had shifted to Spanish painting. She replied, "Yes, a difficult palette. El Greco can be very disturbing. And the surrealists, Miró and his ilk. Quite jarring. But, honestly, I've come to accept that surrealism is just a part of modern life."

The Sheriff, in turn, feeling misunderstood and confused, responded, "Surreal what? *Ism*? What *ism*? We don't need no more *isms* here in Cave City, ma'am. I'm having a hard enough time with all the meth."

At this instant, *wham*, a spinning sombrero landed between them and knocked Prudie's plate from her hands. It broke on the pavement and splashed more salsa on the Sheriff's boots. Prudie sputtered, "I wish you were doing a better job with these rowdies."

His competency under attack, Sheriff Hooker blew a whistle and yelled for his deputies to chase down the sombrero-thrower. Triggering a plan that was supposed to wait until after the game. A plan to put his mayoral candidacy on the political map. Sheriff Hooker and his deputies, some hired on for this event, broke the unwritten pledge and began demanding to see identity papers. A stampede ensued.

Cut to: the storm clouds unleashing a deluge. Fans jump from the stadium walls, onto the tops of cars parked below. Police dogs bark and pull on their leashes. Paddy wagons block the stadium exits. Sheriff Hooker fulminates on his bullhorn. Chad and Night Snow lose each other in the melee. The Orphan Sister puppets are smashed. Winnie and Frank huddle to protect the children. Prudie goes into a full-blown panic attack. Chad runs interference between a deputy and two of his clients, allowing them to escape. Juan Pablo directs his teammates to shelter in the visitors' locker room. Brakeless Eddy and Juanita's beadwork disappears in the mud. Rufus Crane struggles to shield Glodene, as the tailgate tent collapses. Dolores and Rosa are arrested and put in handcuffs. Ricky attempts to intervene and is beaten with a nightstick. In the drive-in theater in Ciudad de la Gruta, the shocked crowd listens in to the crisis. They are still able to hear it all because Sheriff Hooker failed to cut the audio feed along with the video. A rumble of resentment grows, fueled by the rumor that the game is being stopped in order to cement the gringos' 1-0 lead.

27.

El Plástico and Ignacio and Gonzalo and I retreat to La Sombra Azul, along with many other angry fans from the drive-in theater. An oozing, hydrocephalic sun mirrors our indignation. We share our furious reactions to the "gringo game theft" and mumble threats to boycott the referendum.

"Should we demand a formal apology?" Ignacio asks, "an immediate release of all the detainees? I could bring it up on my radio show tomorrow night with Señora Calatrova."

El Plástico heatedly agrees and says, "I'll be doing more than that, if I find out Sheriff Hooker has arrested Dolores. I'll go up there on my boat and demand their release. I'll take the Xtabay and motor straight across the Gulf and up the Mississippi and Ohio rivers and choke him. If that idiot arrests Dolores, I'll strangle him."

Once again, I attempt to be the voice of moderation. "Negative publicity can be good publicity, but that does not include strangling your political opponents. That would be bad publicity that stays bad."

"At least Mayor Rosewater will have to do something now," Ignacio says.

"What do you mean?" Gonzalo asks. "He'll just sweep it under the rug."

"Because today the Sister City referendum becomes an undeniable, front-page issue and Mayor Rosewater must realize that his fate depends on it. He can't sweep it under the rug anymore. It can't be ignored. The Sister City referendum will become the mayoral election in Cave City. If it goes down in the primary, Sheriff Hooker will definitely be voted in as mayor in the fall."

El Plástico strokes his chin, pulling the skin tightly around the bony tip of his jaw. This is usually a sign that his wheels are turning. "Even if that is true, it won't matter a bit if we can't deliver Ciudad de la Gruta. Our vote is up first, in just a couple weeks."

"Plenty of news cycles before then," I say.

A few drinks later, we relax. I imagine the effects of this upheaval causing reverberations across time that flow backwards and forwards. That Priestess Dawn and Priestess Moon, a thousand years ago, are able to intuitively feel the tension between their two communities in the distant future. I picture Dawn and Moon together in a cave, discussing their own emerging, internecine issues. Priestess Dawn having just arrived in a canoe convoy from the south with a fresh supply of jewelry and pottery, only to find that the local peoples are not so interested anymore, due to the unexpected appearance of some new traders. Traveling downriver from the Great Lakes. Bearded, pale figures from a faraway northland proffering fascinating types of metalwork. The Maya stuff is considered outmoded. Who are these dark-robed creatures and why do they produce nothing with color?

I am also experiencing some of my own personal reverberations in time. While the video feed was operative on the drive-in screen, I saw several familiar faces in the cutaways to the Cave City crowds. My old high school science teacher, for example, from whom I learned that experiments never fail; they only provide information. Hard to believe at the moment. The Sister City experiment sure looks like a failure. It seems hard to glean any useful information from this. I fantasize about my own return to Cave City and to the abandoned quarry where I conducted experiments in blowing up G.I. Joe dolls. I'll go back and dig in the dirt and gather up old doll pieces and try to glue them back together. My stomach grumbles, something more to eat, please.

El Plástico orders up a plate of *botanas*.

"Do you ever want to run away and disappear?" he says.

"Yes, I've done it, but it never seems to quite work out as expected. Where would you like to go?" I ask.

"New Orleans," he says.

"Why New Orleans?"

"Our first Sister City," Ignacio muses.

"We had one before Cave City?"

Ignacio says, "Back in the boom days, the rich people in Ciudad de la Gruta used to send their laundry to New Orleans. Every two weeks. The laundry boat across the Gulf."

"The rich and their dirty laundry," El Plástico says.

Just as Ramón Puentes walks into the cantina, decked out in pinstripes and a cravat. All the regulars and the staff sense trouble and turn to watch the showdown. Ramón Puentes heads directly to our table in the corner, crossing the courtyard like a shadow over the moon. He pulls up a chair and straddles it.

"Would you like to make a deal now?" he asks and flashes his reptile grin.

I glance over at El Plástico's *caradura*. For a moment, I fear an old-fashioned barroom brawl. Ignacio clutches the head of his cane. Gonzalo's fists clench.

"Hello, amigo. A pleasant surprise," El Plástico says, "What kind of deal did you have in mind?"

"With your back up against the wall on this Sister City matter, I'm thinking you could use a little support," Ramón says. He pulls a comb from his breast pocket and runs it back through his brilliant hair.

El Plástico says, "Let me guess. In an unexpected shift, the management of TiendaMax wants to offer Sister City a half million dollars in radio and TV commercials – "

"And print advertising," Ramón adds.

"All in exchange for a big chunk of the town square."

Ramón nods. "You were always the finisher."

"I feel more like a sucker," El Plástico says.

"You are many things, Roberto, but not a sucker," Ramón says.

"In general, no. But with you, maybe."

"I'm waiting for an answer."

"I'll think about it," El Plástico says. "Give me some time."

"There isn't much time left," Ramón says.

Cut to: ongoing reactions to the soccer game debacle. The faces of Ciudad de la Gruta and the faces of Cave City. Confused, worried, angry, tearful. Parents and grandparents at their dinner tables attempting to explain to their children and grandchildren about the violence and the round-up arrests. The oldest person in Ciudad de la Gruta, parked on a stone bench in a sunny courtyard, an *anciano* who has seen it all, including Tlatelolco in 1968, shakes his head and wipes his eyes. The oldest person in Cave City, a great-grandfather with white nose hairs, who worked as a hotel dishwasher in downtown Chicago in 1968, sits on a back porch held up with a car jack. He leans forward and launches a stream of tobacco juice toward the alley.

28.

Dolores and Rosa stood entwined in the holding area of the county jail. Thunder heightened the noise in the building, along with a tornado siren. Rain pelted the small, barred windows. Rosa's painted-on eyebrows arched with nervous anticipation. Dolores' charcoal-smear eyebrows quivered. She muttered prayers. They clutched each other and took turns squeezing expressions of their love. Rosa attempted to shield Dolores from the crush of bodies. The holding cell, packed tight like the proverbial sardine can, was stuffy and getting more so.

Fears of deportation spread among the crowd, along with comparisons between Mexican and American jails. The consensus being that, if there is one universal in this world, it is that all jails suck. Questions and rumors flowed. Would they be returned to their hometowns, or just dumped across the border? Would Dolores have to return to Ciudad de la Gruta? Could Rosa accompany Dolores, or would she be sent to Guatemala? And what would happen to Ricky, left alone to fend for himself in Cave City?

Her worst-case scenario finally happening, Dolores pondered how she could make a personal appeal to El Plástico, without Rosa finding out. Of course, Rosa sensed exactly what her partner was thinking, and her face spoke, "Do it. Find a way."

A loud popping sound and, snap, the electricity cut out. A single emergency bulb glowed dimly. The ceiling fan in the corridor stopped. Someone screamed. Thank goodness for Dolores' enduring streak of fatalistic humor. She giggled loudly, "It's just like being on the subway in Mexico City." Everyone knew what she meant and they started to laugh. The tension broke. The laughter swelled, fueled by nerves and the need for distraction. And soon the deputies were laughing too.

From his nearby office, Sheriff Hooker bellowed, "What's so funny? There's nothing funny here!" It only made everyone laugh harder. The overhead lights came back on.

Sheriff Hooker was attempting to calm himself with knitting. The die was cast, but what now? A triumphant interview on television, or another mass panic? Repercussions were mounting. As word of the soccer game arrests spread, a flood of family and friends assembled outside the jail, blocking access to the media and the TV trucks arriving from Indianapolis and Louisville. The Sheriff and his deputies were, in fact, prisoners too. Knit one, purl two.

The Sheriff administered a self pat-down, searching for his phone. Several calls from his campaign manager and Mayor Rosewater and the Governor had gone unanswered. He had ignored them all, in favor of savoring his giddy apotheosis. He stuffed another stick of gum in his mouth and checked for messages, while surveying the crowd outside. His campaign manager urging him to hang tough. Mayor Rosewater, the sniveling chump, urging him to release the detainees or else the city could face lawsuits and a federal investigation. The Governor cravenly demanding to be given credit for his support of the Sheriff's immigration stance.

The phone record also displayed a series of calls from his home number. That would be Chica. What did she want? Probably the dragnet had pulled in some of her relatives. Craptastic. An onslaught of such calls at the switchboard from grumpy citizens demanding the selective release of their gardeners and nannies. Threats of withholding campaign donations, or even worse. The Sheriff stuffed another piece of gum into his mouth. What if little Chica was angry enough at actually witnessing the arrests to reveal something about Sheriff Hooker's frozen mother?

And what would Hazel be telling him to do now?

The crowd outside the jail climbed onto the retaining wall of the courthouse. They joined hands and swayed back and forth. "Freedom now," the crowd chanted, led by Dr. Rufus Crane. He was in his element.

The TV cameras loved it. The swelling mass soon spilled off the sidewalk and filled the street. Dr. Crane signaled for Chad and Night Snow to enlist volunteers to direct traffic around the courthouse square onto Elm Avenue. They waved 'Honk for Release' signs.

Sheriff Hooker observed the melee from his office window and began to consider the possibility that he would need an exit strategy, a face-saving plan. Something to disperse the liberal protesters so that the TV crews could get inside and he could proudly deliver the real story, the real truth, his firm message. Let this be a warning, citizens. Perhaps standing in front of the state flag, or with a rifle on his shoulder, or on his horse. But how could he get the horse into the building? He dialed his campaign manager's number and shoved more gum into his mouth. Both cheeks bulged.

"Izwanna makedis a strawng warneen. Iza strawng leeeder."

"What? Who is this? Sheriff, is that you?"

"Weezdoonit! Weezwarnem!"

"Excuse me? We *what*?"

Sheriff Hooker attempted to extract the giant wad of gum from his mouth. It got stuck on the phone and accidentally pressed down into the mouthpiece, which further garbled the transmission.

Across the square, Glodene Butz gathered the cabal inside the portico of St. Fernando the Fur Trapper to confer on the situation. She calmly outlined competing goals. On one hand, they needed to contain the surging crowd and secure the release of the detainees. "We could pressure the Mayor and the Chamber of Commerce with the threat of an organized business boycott." On the other hand, they needed to maximize the exposure to the Sister City cause. If somehow the crowd's roiling ire could be channeled into a broader awareness for the upcoming referendum.

"Hashtag 'OrphanSisters,'" Chad said, "Tell everyone you know to make a post."

"I'm on it," Night Snow said, punching her phone. "Frank usually runs the online show."

Glodene said, "Where is Frank?"

"I think we lost him at the stadium," Night Snow said.

"Where did he go?" Glodene asked.

"He's taking the kids home," Chad said, "Winnie is driving her mother to the airport to catch a plane this evening. In the mayhem at the game, Frank ended up with them and I ended up here."

Night Snow clapped him on the shoulder and said, "This is where you belong."

An official city vehicle, an SUV with police flashers pulled to a stop and honked, halted by the traffic crunch. Two figures emerged from the backseat and tried to push through the crowd toward the media trucks.

Glodene pointed and said, "Our absentee Mayor has finally arrived. Straight from his dinner table, and he's forgotten to pull his napkin out of his neck. Let's follow him."

The cabal moved off the portico and back into the street. Chad paused, hearing a noise from inside the church. He tugged on the wooden door to the chancel. Halfway to the altar, he saw a prostrate male figure, kneeling and banging his forehead against the stone floor. Chad moved down the aisle and knelt and grabbed the person's shoulders before more damage was inflicted. Blood and tears streamed down Ricky's beleaguered face.

Ricky, mistaking Chad for a priest in the dim light, launched into a disjointed confession. "I am the sinner. It should be me over there. Not my mother. They should put me back in that jail. Not *mi madre*. I'm the one who deserves deportation. Not *mi madre*. A saint who has worked herself to death to give her son everything. I squander it on spice. I am the sinner. I am the criminal. Release her and put me back in there. Punish me, Father."

"Sorry, not a priest," Chad said, offering his bandana from a back pocket for Ricky to swab his face.

Recognizing Chad, his mentor and catcher, Ricky collapsed again. "If they let her out, I promise to be a better son. I'll go to church and get a job and finish school and not diss Rosa and play baseball. I'll bunt. I'll be a great bunter. If they let her out, I promise to bunt."

They heard a chorus of excited cheers from the street. It echoed inside the empty church. "Be careful what you promise," Chad said, "I think there's a good chance that she will be released soon."

"For real?"

"Sheriff Hooker made a rash, impulsive move that he can't sustain. Mayor Rosewater and the president of the Chamber of Commerce just arrived. How about we get up and walk across the street and see what's happening?"

As Ricky lurched up off his knees and rose to his full height, another emotional cheer sounded outside. Chad gazed on Ricky's wet face. It was still taking on its fully adult cast. Chad noticed something new. He stepped back and noted a resemblance that he couldn't quite place yet, while Ricky swabbed the raw bruise on his forehead. A face of someone Chad had met recently. Ricky looked a lot like a younger version of the mayor of Ciudad de la Gruta. Why hadn't anyone else made that connection? Maybe they had, and no one wanted to admit it.

Chad said nothing, not exactly an appropriate topic for discussion at the moment. He put an arm around the kid's shoulders.

Chad and Ricky emerged from the church and embarked on the walk toward the jail, where the Sheriff was trying to negotiate an orderly release of the detainees, in exchange for the crowd allowing the TV crews to pass unhindered into the building and give him his big exposure.

With blood still oozing from Enrique's head wound and Chad leading the way, pleading for space, please, they managed to reach the front steps of the Justice Building complex just as Dolores and Rosa came forth.

"¡M'ijo!"

"¡Mamá!"

Ricky threw himself into her arms and collapsed onto his knees, pressing his forehead against his mother's breast. Everyone crying. And the photographers clicked away, scoring an iconic Pietà image that appeared in newspapers and newsfeeds, with Sheriff Hooker glaring in the background.

29.

The photo of Ricky curled in Dolores's embrace, his profile seen at the same angle that Chad had witnessed in the church, appears on the front page of the newspapers, *The Splinter* and *The Gruta Extra*, beside a file headshot of El Plástico with the same distinctive jaw line. *The Extra* runs a provocative headline: "Sister City - Mayor's Lovechild?" Identifying Dolores Sánchez as a former resident of Ciudad de la Gruta and demanding a paternity test, proposing that El Plástico's support of the Sister City plan could be a blackmail scheme to maintain the shameful secret.

Lines form at the kiosk on the *zócalo* and the newsstand in the bus stations. In the busy intersections downtown, hawkers scurry out into the street to deliver papers to motorists at stop lights. The morning edition sells out by 10 a.m. Bookies begin offering odds on how long the mayor can last. The limestone casements of the town hall receive a few more bullet pockmarks.

"The smart money knows not to bet against you," El Drone says on the phone, calling from his latest hide-out. "We can weather this."

El Plástico grumbles, "Why, Mister Drone, why do things keep going from bad to worse?

A pause for El Drone to reflect. "Because this is Mexico?"

"I forgot. I was thinking about my son in Cave City."

"Today's headlines could be a useful diversion from the soccer game topic."

"I'll be forced to give in to Ramón and TiendaMax," El Plástico says.

"Not necessarily. Hold on. I'll be down to City Hall in half an hour."

In his office, El Plástico steps over to the arched window and peers down through the prismatic bullet-hole at the hubbub in the street. His mood shifts slightly, a little surge of hope. He glances up at the portraits of his predecessors, who stare down at him in judgmental derision. "Let he who is without sin cast the first stone," El Plástico mutters.

He moves to his desk and leans back in his chair and hoists his feet up. Snaps open a crisp copy of *The Gruta Extra*. Feeling a subtle, emerging, protective buffer, he gazes at the photo of Dolores and Ricky. A loving mother and her son. Ignoring the flashing lights on his telephone and computer, El Plástico studies the photo with admiration and pride and a growing sense of relief. Dolores so enduringly beautiful, despite the wear and tear. Each age spot on her skin is a bittersweet indictment of El Plástico's denial. He wonders if deep down, he must have always known the truth. And the handsome mirror of Ricky's mug sparks a guttural, animal joy. "Hello there, my son, my boy."

El Plástico reaches for the old-style Rolodex at the edge of his desk. He flips through it and finds a number and dials. He closes his eyes and allows his face to be scoured by an onslaught of sun, as he listens to the phone ring. Finally, Milena Madero answers.

"I thought for sure I'd get a recording," El Plástico says.

"When I saw who it was, I felt it was my duty to pick up," Dra. Madero says.

"Thank you. I always liked how you were able to coat your harshest insights with a layer of humor. I need to schedule a session," El Plástico says.

"I can imagine. I just saw the newspaper."

"Yes, but it's not what you're thinking."

"There's a crystal ball on your desk?" Dra. Madero says.

"I need to talk about why I'm feeling so oddly peaceful right now. Is that common?"

"Is what common?"

"For there to be a sense of peace, when we stop living a lie," El Plástico states.

"Speaking of insights," she says.

"Do you have any time this week?

"Thursday at five."

"I'll be there," El Plástico says.

A petulant knock at his office door. El Plástico swallows and straightens his shirt and prepares for a parade of alarmed staffers and colleagues. Turns out to be a parade of a more personal sort. First up, Gonzalo Sánchez, waving the .22 pistol again. Watch out. Gonzalo barges in and tosses a newspaper on the mayor's desk.

"I should be shooting out more than your window," Gonzalo spouts.

"I'm sorry. I was afraid of that. I'm very sorry," El Plástico says.

"My sister, my poor sister."

"We were young. We were teenagers."

"No excuses. Be a man. She looked up to you and revered you, and you took advantage," Gonzalo says.

"I'm terribly sorry. Absolutely, you're right," El Plástico says.

Gonzalo paces in front of the large window. He thrusts the pistol back into his pocket.

"Listen, I understand and somehow I can't bring myself to stay angry," Gonzalo adds, "I'm hoping this could be a boost for Ricky. The boy needs something. Maybe this is it."

"You must have already suspected," El Plástico says.

Gonzalo shrugs. "I've been asking myself. And, yes, a few times when Enrique was little. It's not just his face. He carries himself like you too, the way he swings his shoulders, but I didn't want to upset Dolores by mentioning it."

"I suppose this explains why she wouldn't communicate with me all those years," El Plástico says.

"I tried calling this morning. She's not talking to anybody," Gonzalo says.

"When you do get through, please tell her that I want to speak with her. I owe her an apology. I owe her much more than an apology."

Gonzalo nods, "I have to warn you of something. Don't think this will get you two back together again."

El Plástico wags a finger and rises from his chair. "Is she with someone?"

"A woman. Her name is Rosa," Gonzalo says.

El Plástico says, "At least she's not alone."

Next up, Mercedes. Smoking a cigarette and also waving a copy of *The Extra*.

"You jerk! And don't think you can lie your way out of this like an American *presidente*. That boy is so obviously yours, that exact same look of fat and happy."

Waving her cigarette and flicking hot ashes around, Mercedes gasps and drops the paper, as the edge of the front section catches fire. Before another word is spoken, El Plástico and Mercedes are stomping on the smoldering newspaper, snuffing out an incipient blaze.

"This must mean something," El Plástico comments.

Mercedes snorts, "It's a hot story, spreading like wildfire. El Plástico exonerated in the court of infertility."

"You've come here to gloat? To blame me yet again for us not having children?"

"I'll probably get around to that," she says.

"How did you get in here, by the way? I told my secretary not to admit any unscheduled visitors," El Plástico asks.

"She was staring at the headlines too. And no woman would stop another woman in my position."

"I don't understand. What is your position exactly?"

"Stand-in. Substitute fuck," Mercedes says, "You were always still in love with her, and I was only a backup. I suppose it should be a gift to know why it felt like you were never there, never really my husband."

"I had no idea there was a child. I mean, that he is my child."

"Don't lie to me."

"Okay, maybe at some level."

"What are you going to tell Juan Pablo – your 'adopted' son, your substitute son, now that your real son is exposed. How do you think Juan Pablo is going to feel?"

"That he has a brother?"

"I don't think so. He's going to feel just like me – a substitute, a pawn."

"You've talked to him? Is he back from the soccer game?"

"Prepare yourself," Mercedes says.

El Plástico sucks in a deep breath and surprises himself and Mercedes with a measured response. "I just made an appointment with Dra. Madero for Thursday at five p.m. You're welcome to join me."

Mercedes struggles to suppress her tears. "Prepare yourself," she says again and turns and exits.

Next up, El Drone. With the requisite copy of *The Extra*, rolled up like a baton in a relay race that he hands off to El Plástico.

"As if I need another copy," El Plástico grunts.

"Just getting them off the street."

"Is it that bad?" El Plástico asks. "Should I be 'lawyering-up', as the gringos say?"

"I think the odds are starting to shift," El Drone says, "In the few stops I've made on the way into town this morning, I've been hearing an upswing, a surge of sentiment in your favor. People are impressed that their stolid, mastodon mayor is actually a flesh and blood creature of passion."

"Stopping where?"

"Various cantinas. Doing some research."

"Hair of the dog?"

"Me and those dogs," El Drone says.

El Plástico proffers his handkerchief. "You're bleeding."

El Drone's face is covered with shaving cuts from a shaky attempt at cleaning up, and also patches of missed whiskers that look like poppy seeds sprinkled on a bagel. Still hungover from yesterday's long session at La Sombra Azul, monitoring media reports and reactions rolling in from the soccer game and its aftermath. #OrphanSisters currently topping six thousand posts, including some solid, unsolicited advice: push a get-out-the-vote drive among the Hoosier retirees at Flamingo Estates.

"That's only a few hundred people out there," El Plástico says, "Do you think they'd support us?"

"Hometown sympathies. Maintaining a link. Every vote will help," El Drone says.

"If they're not citizens, how is it legal?" El Plástico asks.

"Fine print in the city charter. To vote in a referendum, a person only has to pay taxes here. You should know that, Mr. Mayor."

"So we stay the course. Is that it?" El Plástico says. "Can you tell that asshole Ramón to go find some other town to exploit?"

"Full steam ahead," El Drone says. "The rat be damned."

El Plástico returns to his spot at the arched window. "But what about us traveling to Cave City for the Orphan Sister festival? I'm not sure if Dolores and the boy could handle having me there now. And, frankly, I'm not sure I could handle it, for that matter."

El Drone insists, "We stay the course. We go to Cave City. The story of you being reunited with your son and his mother, it will be the feel-good story of the week. You all could end up on the Sunday talk shows."

El Plástico says, "First we have to win the referendum here, then we'll talk about it."

Another knock on the door. The secretary sticks her head in, "It's Mayor Rosewater on the phone for you, sir."

Cut to: both mayors videoconferencing. As predicted, Mayor Ralph Rosewater rallies to the cause. "Amigo, I am slow, but I do finally get it." He's about to be outflanked by the forces of reaction and a fresh set of headlines for tomorrow's newspapers. Mayor Rosewater contritely offers everything and the moon to make up for the soccer game arrests. Knowing that both cities must approve the referendum, Ralph Rosewater promises a live press conference apology to the people of Ciudad de la Gruta for the impertinent, unconstitutional and disrespectful actions of Sheriff Hooker. He calls for dialogue and televised debates. And, what's more, to right other wrongs, he promises to relocate the offensive Mexican War monument from the central square to a remote spot on Mount Trashmore.

30.

After her brief stint in jail, Dolores did not rebound so quickly. The revelation of Enrique's parentage did not bring any relief. Her heart felt perforated. Like some kind of lancing, a surgical removal of a deeply lodged tumor. But the suddenness and coarseness of the operation left her an invalid, on several levels. Literally, she felt unable to move. Collapsed on the musty fainting couch that Rosa had dragged home from the dump not two weeks ago, as if anticipating its need. Collapsed, immobile, fanning herself like her grandmother, a saintly invalid in Ciudad de la Gruta, who spent over two decades playing *lotería* in the kitchen. Not that Dolores felt any identification with her grandmother's status. If anything, she felt the opposite. As if she were paralyzed by a self-flagellating guilt over missing work, over not showing up at her jobs, over not volunteering time for the Sister City effort, captured by the intense shame that the archetypal caretaker churns up when she is the one needing care. The trailer dimly lit by the flicker of votive candles.

Figuratively, Dolores' invalid status also came from an internal collapse of any sense of justification for this life-on-the-run. Why did she move to Cave City? Who was she protecting? Her rationale for leaving Mexico with a baby in her womb these many years ago erased from conscious memory, especially after repeated grilling from Ricky. Why, Mom? Why did you do it? What was it about this Roberto guy? What were you trying to protect me from? Or were you just trying to protect yourself? From what? Why is my life here supposedly better than what I would have had in Mexico? Why, Mom? Why?

"I don't know."

"How can you not know?"

"I don't know."

And the unspoken grilling from Rosa about Dolores' intentions for their future together. Rosa also sensed that El Plástico would see this situation as an excuse to reenter the scene. Rosa fanned and massaged and swabbed Dolores' face and neck with a wet cloth. She tended to Dolores like one of their hospice patients. Her loving, mournful gaze pleading, "Don't leave me."

Ricky summoned Chad for daily pitch and catch sessions, despite the chilly winter gloom. Firing fastball after fastball, Ricky spoke obliquely and at length about topics such as birdsongs. More specifically, the high-pitched chirr of the robin. Its frequency stimulated something in his brain.

"The sound brings everything into perspective," Ricky said, pulling off his cap and gently rubbing the scab on his forehead.

"Um, how so?" Chad said, concerned that the kid might be using again, something heavier than pot. He stood up from his catcher's crouch and glanced over at Night Snow, swinging on the porch glider. She had just arrived with another casserole for Dolores.

"The robin is talking to me," Ricky said, "Encouraging me, encouraging the little bounce-back clown inside me that gets knocked down and usually pops back up just to get hit again, to instead stay down for a moment and realize, hey, everything is going to be cool."

"Right, good," Chad murmured, maintaining a curious and neutral tone. Like with his clients at the clinic who frequently lapsed into magical explanations for natural phenomena, maybe this was a positive sign coming from Ricky; a sign that he was trying to fulfill his bloody-forehead vow in the church by tapping into some indigenous wisdom.

"Say more," Night Snow urged.

Ricky slapped the palm of his glove. "Things are connected in ways that we don't always see at first," he said.

"Spoken like a good archeologist," Night Snow said.

Ricky slapped his glove again. "There's a web. There's an invisible web. And when we get a glimpse of it, suddenly things come into perspective."

Chad had been waiting to have this conversation with the kid until the right moment presented itself, which apparently was now. "You're talking about the discovery of your birth story," Chad said, "how it changes the way you see yourself."

"And also how you see your mom," Night Snow added.

"Totally," Enrique nodded.

"And speaking of birth stories," Night Snow said, moving off the porch to be closer to Chad, as they shifted into a familiar co-therapist role with each other, like after an AA meeting, co-counseling a newcomer to recovery. "Do you know what that says about you, Enrique?"

"What, what about me?" Ricky asked.

"Do you know who *always* has a birth story?" Night Snow said. "Heroes. All the big-time heroes, going as far back in history as you want. All the heroes have birth stories."

"Superheroes, even?"

"Totally," Chad confirmed.

Ricky paused and nodded, breathing in his newfound hero-hood, and slapped his glove again.

"I've been thinking about talking to my dad and eventually meeting him," Ricky said, "That should probably wait until my mom adjusts, you know. She's kind of struggling right now. Trying to figure things out. I know she feels bad about being laid up and not being active with you guys, what with this being such a critical time. Could I volunteer? Is there anything I can do to help out with the Sister City referendum?"

Chad and Night Snow turned and eyed each other.

"I'm sure we can find something for you to do," Chad said.

Night Snow concurred. "You can help build my float for the Orphan Sister festival."

"Your dad will be coming for the festival," Chad said. "Are you ready for that?"

"I'm ready," Ricky said. He stepped back into position and slowly began his wind-up, signaling to Chad to prepare for a fastball on the outside corner.

31.

Father Mike follows the worsening news of Cave City with a heavy heart, knowing that many of the families affected by the soccer game arrests and the political showdown aftermath that forced many people into hiding are his former parishioners.

Interviewed by Juan Pablo for a post-game feature in *The Gruta Extra*, Father Mike and Dotcom discuss the special collection plate they have established for the Sister City Legal Defense Fund. "A rather ironic role-reversal that we are now sending money north to our beleaguered compatriots," Dotcom says, "It's not much, but we'll do what we can."

The congregation of the Church of Planet Jesus is growing. During the busy holiday tourist season in the Yucatán, word has gotten out via Juan Pablo's article and postings on travel websites about a rad happening in an abandoned drive-in movie theater on the outskirts of Ciudad de la Gruta. Something involving a time-traveling Jesus and his previously unknown sister, Wifi, beaming down messages from another planet during a revival-style ceremony known as 'Love from Above.'

Local Mayans and holiday travelers and international tourists appear in clusters, a few more every week, wanting to see what is going on out there at the drive-in. Part carnival act, part savvy blend of Maya and Christian end-times perspectives. Dotcom, in her Federation robes and hair bow, preaches on top of a sawhorse dais, while the congregants lounge on the hoods of their vehicles or sit in scattered Chevy and Plymouth backseat banquettes, hauled over from the scrap yard. On the big screen behind her, Father Mike projects a loop of outer space footage. Twinkling stars beckon the congregants to visualize a Planet Jesus, a new home far away from all this rust and decay and corruption, waiting for them at the edge of the universe. On top of the screen, two spotlights shower the crowd in rosy beams during the 'Love from Above' liturgical dance, with percussionists banging on pots and pans.

Part of it is feeding the masses. Every service includes a 'loaves and fishes' communion, basically a big potluck during which new adherents are introduced in Biblical lineage style, unto the third generation. Afterwards, Father Mike hears confessions in the projection booth.

Dotcom preaches on the concept of 'morphic attunement,' an important aspect of Planet Jesus theology. The gist being that certain physical locations, including planets, can have a special relationship with another distant physical location, often via a mystical sisterhood. In the same way that Planet Jesus has a special relationship to Earth, likewise Ciudad de la Gruta has a special morphic attunement to Cave City.

In the last week before the election, Father Mike follows up with a direct message to the local residents and to "those folks watching via livestream back in Indiana" about the upcoming Sister City vote. This is not his usual style. Trained to believe that only redneck Bible-thumpers preach raw politics from the pulpit, Father Mike prefers to minister in a more metaphorical, around the barn approach.

But the Sister City vote is only a few days away, and all indications are that it will be close.

Everyone works hard to get the referendum across the finish line. El Drone plasters up directions to the polling places, and recruits drivers from the cantina to provide rides, along with Mercedes in her Galaxy and Juan Pablo in his blue VW Bug.

Ignacio and Señora Calatrova feature Juan Pablo on their radio show, ostensibly to talk music, but really to allow him to speak publicly about his experience at the soccer game in Cave City. He describes the crack-down and witnessing the terror of his teammates and realizing that, all personal matters aside, the situation is more complicated than he knew. He mentions two new clauses to the Manifesto on the theme of refugee rights and urban sanctuary.

El Plástico goes out early every morning to gather up plastic bottles and remind the citizenry of his signature efforts, and to hand out the traditional candy and bling. Gonzalo accompanies him with a soft, gray, jeweler's cloth, offering to clean people's eyeglasses, so they can see the ballot clearly, for a ten-peso donation.

Ramón Puentes persists in his efforts too, the indefatigable nemesis, like a piece of toilet paper stuck to a shoe. He reverts to old-style campaign tactics. Hiring people to wear sandwich boards and trucks with loudspeakers to drive around town broadcasting aspersions about El Plástico and the boondoggle of Sister City.

El Drone, operating round the clock now, is concerned about the tone of Ramón's personal attacks and fears that he is lapsing into a juvenile combativeness that might lead to trouble. He is also worried about Juan Pablo. The kid's thin beard is looking scraggly and sad.

Juan Pablo shows up unexpectedly at El Drone's corner table in La Sombra Azul. He reports that Ramón has renewed his bribe offer, along with a vague death threat, mistakenly believing that Juan Pablo's Cave City trip and the revelations about El Plástico's other son must have weakened Juan Pablo's support.

"A death threat? No, really?"

"We journalists are under attack these days, and he's taking advantage of that. He's probably not serious," Juan Pablo says, trying to appear calm. Beside him, the shadows of ceiba branches on the bright courtyard wall look like an X-ray printout of the root system below.

"Why did you come here to the cantina?" El Drone asks, "Why didn't you take this news directly to El Plástico?"

"Because every time I talk to him," Juan Pablo says, "he tries to drag me into a therapy session with him and Mercedes and Dra. Madero."

"You know that they're separated, but trying to get back together?"

"Yes, and if the discovery of this Ricky kid, his biological son in Cave City somehow forces them to confront their issues, that's fine and good, but I'm done being their glue. I'm done being the go-between," Juan Pablo says, "After the vote next week, I'm leaving. I'm moving to Mérida."

El Drone startles and spills his coffee. This announcement takes things to a different level. A waiter helps him mop the spill. El Drone peels an orange and places the peelings in his empty cup. He signals for more coffee and, with some trepidation, decides to reveal a recent private message from the mayor.

"Why would you want to leave town? You can write your own ticket here," El Drone says.

"To avoid being killed, for one," Juan Pablo replies, "I know journalists face danger everywhere in this country, but in Mérida, the City of Peace, at least there's safety in numbers. What did you mean about writing my own ticket?"

El Drone says, "You're a budding journalist, right, so you know what off-the-record means?"

"Of course."

"This is strictly off the record."

"*De acuerdo.*"

"I've been hearing from El Plástico about those therapy sessions too. And the latest is that, if the Sister City referendum passes, El Plástico is thinking about retiring. Hanging it up and returning to private life, perhaps with his biological son and the mother, perhaps back with Mercedes, who knows. Part of hanging it up means passing the torch, specifically to you. With his backing, you would become the youngest mayor in all of Mexico."

To his credit, Juan Pablo laughs. "Not if I'm dead," he says.

"Point taken. I'll see what I can do about Ramón."

El Drone hatches a safety plan at the next Monday meeting in the mayor's office. He and El Plástico discuss the ethics of installing personal surveillance cameras for Ramón Puentes, who has taken to only going out at night, scurrying on foot and not using his car, to avoid the drones. Technically, a judge's order is required for covert surveillance, and previously that could have been obtained from Mercedes' father, no questions asked, but not now.

El Plástico muses, "Do you think a leader is still a leader if he goes somewhere that his people cannot follow?"

"I assume you want my honest opinion on this?"

"No, I just answered it for myself. Let's do it."

El Drone says, "I could rig up a couple cameras on streetlamps by his hotel and we could call them 'traffic-calming devices.'"

"What if Ramón recognizes you?"

"We can ask Gonzalo to do the work. He's handy enough."

One camera goes up on the corner streetlight across from Ramón's hotel and the other above the colonnades near Juan Pablo's apartment. During a test-run monitoring session from the security office at City Hall, El Drone and El Plástico watch Ramón in action in real time, not realizing at first what they're seeing. They've both been up all night, catnapping for days really, preparing for the last hurrah of campaigning before the vote. Their jarring moment of awareness is like waking from a short, profound sleep and not knowing where or who or what, blobs of consciousness trying to decipher the external stimuli on the monitors.

It is just after dawn, still cool, and a white mist covers the city, like lather waiting for the sun's razor.

On the upper screen, Ramón exits his hotel, dragging a suitcase on wheels. He looks small. A tiny, random detail, like an ant trying to carry a crumb back to the nest. The streets around the *zócalo* are empty, still blocked off from the weekend's pedestrian-only status. The police have not yet removed the barricades and pylons.

"Where is Ramón going so early?"

"To find a taxi?"

"He walks like he's got water sloshing around inside him."

"Maybe he's still drunk."

El Plástico and El Drone peer over to the second monitor, where a different figure appears, a different ant, Juan Pablo Chayac stumbling toward his apartment across Centennial Park. From a night out doing whatever it is youths do all night long. Everything misty and dim, barely light enough to make out the shapes of the statues and trees.

El Drone sighs and produces a sound in his throat, like a straw searching for the bottom of a glass. "Something is about to happen."

"What kind of something?" El Plástico asks.

"Look back at the first monitor."

Ramón has become a smaller figure now, but they can still see him. He approaches a car, a VW Bug, parked on the street. Ramón pauses and opens his suitcase and pulls out a small hydraulic jack. He pulls out some tools and wires and a metal fuse box. It all vaguely reminds El Plástico of his Pickle Science routine, but he still doesn't get it. Ramón jacks the rear bumper and drops to the ground and crawls underneath the car.

On the other monitor, Juan Pablo, only a couple blocks away, stops to tie his shoe.

"Wait, what are we watching here?" El Plástico asks. "Is that Juan Pablo's vehicle?"

El Drone jumps up and says, "A slick desperado, probably lacking as much sleep as we are, trying to skew the Sister City vote by scaring people away from the polls with a bomb."

Both El Drone and El Plástico leap up from their chairs and hustle out of the office and City Hall into the street, clattering down the broad stone staircase.

"You go for Juan Pablo. I'll get Ramón," El Drone calls, jumping into action, after years of AWOL lethargy, feeling that he is off to rescue a part of himself too.

El Drone runs across the *zócalo*, yelling for Ramón to cease and desist. El Plástico cuts left toward the park. He turns at Speakers Corner, and races toward the basketball courts across from Juan Pablo's apartment. Juan Pablo stops and turns at the sound of footsteps and receives a sudden, surprising bear-hug tackle.

"Don't move. Wait here," El Plástico orders.

Juan Pablo instinctively knows who it is by the smell of the bay rum aftershave. "What's happening?"

"A car bomb."

A block away, Ramón is working underneath the VW. Hearing El Drone's calls, he tries to slide back out from under the vehicle, but accidentally detonates the device. A whoosh of flame and smoke and debris. A gasoline rainbow spreads across the pavement. Ramón moans and rolls sideways into the gutter.

El Drone arrives and bends over Ramón Puentes, still alive, badly singed and scraped, and drags him by the feet to safety. El Drone cradles Ramón's head in his arms. He wipes soot off his face. Footsteps approaching.

El Plástico and Juan Pablo hustle to his side. El Plástico drops to one knee. "Ramón, why this?" he says.

"It went wrong," Ramón whimpers.

"Don't talk. Juan Pablo is calling an ambulance."

El Plástico takes off his white *guayabera* and tears it into long strips for bandages.

32.

Fortunately, the bomb disruption did not scare away the thick-skinned voters of Ciudad de la Gruta. If anything, it increased turnout. Long lines of humanity spilled from the voting stations. The vote count went far into the night. Finally, it was announced that the referendum had passed, but there was going to be a recount. A day later, hurrah, it survived the recount. Barely, by a margin of four hundred and thirty-seven votes.

Ignacio telephoned Frank Vigo with the result.

"Of course, Sheriff Hooker will claim this is a half-hearted, pyrrhic victory that only shows how weak the Sister City agreement really is," Ignacio said.

"A win is a win is a win," Frank said, "Congratulations. Time for you to get some rest. It's our turn to kick into gear. Sheriff Hooker just threw us a curve ball by scheduling his big rally two days before the Orphan Sister festival and our vote next week."

"I'm glad to hear that Dolores has recovered enough to be present for El Plástico's visit to Cave City," Ignacio said.

"It will be tough on Dolores," Frank said, "I think Ricky, their son, is secretly excited. How is Juan Pablo doing?"

"Still a mess. Sleeping on the floor in Señora Calatrova's dressing room. We're trying to get him to talk to Dra. Madero," Ignacio said, "Stay in touch, and give my love to Glodene."

Frank was alone in his office, grading papers. He paused to post the good news on several sites and saw Sheriff Hooker's team was already tweeting vague accusations of ballot-tampering. #HicksForHooker. The social media wars had begun.

Frank tweeted, "A win is a win is a win. #SisterCityVictory."

He soon realized it was more than that. This was so much more. It was the triumph of the Spirit Tunnel. He danced over to the window. He held out his arms to an imaginary dance partner and slid across the floor in an exultant cha-cha-cha, and just as quickly, it all turned on him. He sat back down at the desk and held his head in his hands. The black hole of Nina and Paulo's absent and presumably dead parents consumed all the light. Something would have to be decided about the kids.

Right here, last August, with Winnie. Warning her against getting in too deep. The afternoon light embracing both of them. He realized that he had also been warning himself. Another tunnel ahead, he thought. The boy from New Madrid teaching himself to fish because he actually believes he might catch a fish that could turn into a Prince. Retroactive recognitions of hidden intents and desires. Nina and Paulo a fulfillment of unconscious hopes for a family that could have never been expressed. It all felt messy and wrong. It contradicted his smiling, Mr. Placid demeanor. A wriggling, wet fish trying to jump off the hook. Like another coming-out, and perhaps that is all life is: a series of messy comings-out.

Eyes itching, Frank finished grading his papers. He put on a coat and hurried over to the strategy meeting at the Elbow Room. The cabal was meeting to finalize the line-up for the Orphan Sister Parade. Glodene Butz leading off in her golf cart, followed by the floats, designed and built by Night Snow. Featuring the teenage Orphan Sisters in period costumes, selected by the same panel of experts who also choose the annual Corn Queen. The Southwest Hoosier State Marching Hundred, playing an arrangement of *El Salón Mexico*. Next up, per the requirement that all parades contain antique machinery, Brakeless Eddy had revived three of his old tractors. Also, per the uniforms rule, Dolores and Rosa were leading a contingent of home-health aide workers in their blue blouses. Still a question as to whether the sewing guild would field a color-guard entry.

Frank squeezed in with Winnie and Chad and Night Snow into their booth. They again voiced a celebratory "woo-hoo" for the election results from Ciudad de la Gruta and expressed gratitude for Juan Pablo's survival.

"And thank goodness for Dolores being able to leave home for the first time in a long while to babysit the kids," Winnie said, "I'm happy for her and for us. Frank and I don't have to feel guilty about taking a couple days in Boston."

"Remind me what that's about," Chad said, devouring an onion ring.

"The annual conference, the job fair thing," Frank said.

"My job search for next fall," Winnie said, "Why do you look so surprised? You've known about it for weeks. It's why we didn't go home for Christmas, because I'm taking this trip to Boston now. It's why I cut my hair."

In an effort to appear more serious and professorial for her interviews, Winnie had driven out to Timeless Hair Creations. The new 'do' haunted her like a phantom limb. No place to put a pencil. She was not yet comfortable with her pageboy and she thought everyone else was just pretending to like it.

"And Frank is going because…"

"I have to recruit someone to replace her," Frank said.

"There's no replacing Winnie," Night Snow said. "We're going to miss you two."

"Wait, let's slow down," Chad said and scooted over to make room for Dr. Rufus Crane, just arriving. He wore a trench coat lined with mohair over his scrubs. He rolled Glodene's wheelchair inside and parked her at the end of the booth.

They all sat squeezed together amid their coats and mufflers. Despite all the sizzle on the grill, what with the front door constantly opening, the heat from the kitchen at the Elbow Room only partially warmed the booths in January.

"Another round of root beers, on me," Chad said.

A ripple of their cozy togetherness and camaraderie manifested as a deep flush on Chad's face, even as its dissolution was being discussed. A welling up. A poignant nostalgia before the fact. Along with the recognition that he'd been wanting to broach this topic with Winnie, the idea of staying on another year. As usual, he'd stalled, thinking he needed to assemble an itemized argument, i.e. more experience for both of them at their jobs, more differentiation from their families, etc. Maybe the best argument was right here at this table. This shared connection, this joint engagement, this reason to get up in the morning that neither of them had much of back in Boston.

"What about Paulo and Nina?"

"Like I said, Dolores and Rosa are on board to stay at Frank's house. Hopefully, you'll want to spend some time with them too, while we're away," Winnie explained.

"No, what I meant was," Chad said, "if we leave permanently."

Winnie bit a lip and nodded. "That's bad. Much worse than having my hair cut off."

"And what about my dad's big trip to Indiana?" Chad said, "You'll miss Chief. He's coming for the Colts-Patriots game this weekend."

"We might get to see Chief in Boston," Winnie said, "My parents are hosting a dinner party."

"I'll buy him a cigar," Frank said.

"Hey, what are we talking about here?" Dr. Crane interjected.

Winnie smiled and said, "Chief O'Shaughnessy. The bull in the china shop. Chad, you should take your dad out to meet Brakeless Eddy. I would like to be a fly on the wall for that."

Enough sarcasm in her tone to irritate Chad. And granted, the bull-in-the-china-shop analogy was accurate, and Chad wasn't exactly looking forward to his visit either, but at least show a little respect. Chad stewed and decided, what the hell, to make his pitch publicly, playing for Frank and Night Snow and Dr. Crane's presence as leverage.

Chad said, "Winnie, I'm glad you're pumped about this job fair and that you feel confident about landing a position, but if you get an offer, are you allowed to defer it for a year or so?"

"What do you mean?" Winnie asked.

"I think there are some good reasons for us to consider staying on here."

Winnie laughed. "This I never would have predicted. Breaking news! Devoted New England Patriots Dude wants to stay in Colts-land."

"I'm serious," Chad said, "We could both benefit from another year in Cave City." Chad waited for Frank to step in and support his idea, and was surprised that he remained silent.

Under the table, Night Snow put a hand on Chad's knee. Glodene pressed the tips of her manicured fingers together.

Dr. Crane rode to the rescue. "Funny you should bring that up, because Chad will soon be due for his six-month job review, and I just applied for some grant money to study the work he's been doing. The ritual aspect of the technique is resonating with the patients and we're getting good outcome data, but to do that research we'd need you to stay on at least for another year."

"What about the wedding?" Winnie said.

"Nothing has to change with the wedding plans," Chad insisted, "We fly to Boston in June, do the deed, and come back here after the honeymoon."

"But that isn't the *deal*," Winnie said.

Chad, overplaying his hand, responded, "What deal, you mean the deal with your mother?"

Watch out, Winifred, slow down. She reached into her purse and pulled out a hand fan, folded tight like a wand. Her newest academic research project, antique hand fans and their secret language; the pioneer women's use of hand fans, coded flutters for communication. She held it tightly in her palm. Winnie did not want a repeat of the balcony meltdown, especially in front of Glodene. Up close and personal, and in her own way confirming their bond, Winnie spoke carefully, clutching the fan.

She leaned over to Chad and said, "Sorry, but I am tired of you trying to have it both ways with my mother. Claiming that you, oh wise one, can see exactly what's wrong with her and me. My mother made a good faith effort, coming out here and spending several days and connecting with us and the kids, and staying on for the soccer game, and then she gets traumatized by a riot. Almost crushed in a riot. And we don't come home for Christmas, because we're working on the Orphan Sister Festival. And, correct, the deal with her, with us, with both our families was that we come here for one year and then return to our hometown."

Winnie stopped herself and sucked in a sharp breath and looked around at her audience, which now comprised not only Frank and Night Snow and Glodene and Dr. Crane, but also several wide-eyed faces in the nearby booths. She said, "I need a break. Frank, get me out of here."

Glodene said, "Yes, go get some air."

Winnie slid sideways with her hip and Frank stood up and helped her out of the booth. Both of them waved their goodbyes. Frank saluted and said, "We'll see you all in a couple days. Have a good time at the Patriots game. We fly out early tomorrow. Back in plenty of time for the festival on Tuesday."

Night Snow nodded and pinched Chad's arm and said, "This too shall pass, oh wise one. Do you want to go to a meeting?"

"I'd rather go play Scrabble with Glodene."

"You're sure you don't need to go to a meeting?"

"Whether I *need* to go to a meeting is a different question than whether I *want* to go."

Dr. Crane sensed an opening. "Chad, are you saying there's a chance that you would stay even if Winnie doesn't?"

"Is that what it sounded like I was saying?"

"I'm just asking," Dr. Crane said.

"I guess there could be a chance," Chad said, not quite ready to entertain the possibility.

"Believe me, I know about long-distance relationships. It's a difficult call," Rufus Crane said, "That's what Milena and I tried. A long-distance thing. And it didn't work. She had all sorts of tricks. Self-soothing tricks that were supposed to make us feel like 'I'm with you even when I'm not with you.' None of it worked."

By pre-arrangement, Winnie was staying the night at Frank's house, because of the early departure to the airport and because she wanted to maximize her time with the kids. That was her weak point, and Chad had pegged it and she didn't want to admit to him or herself how much she was going to miss Nina and Paulo next year. After reading to them and putting them to bed, Winnie retired to the guest room and the rabbit-hole of her new research project: fan-talk. She had been introduced to this system of communication by accident, during one of Glodene's volunteer sessions at the Historical Society, sorting through a donation box that contained a collection of hand-fans. Glodene demonstrated some of the coded fluttering moves. An entire language from colonial and frontier times that crossed borders, spanned North and South, and the Old and New World. Spanish women and Mexican women and English women and pioneer women. Silenced by convention, they were able to communicate via a flick of the hand-fan. "What a prick." "This is so boring." "Let's go pick berries." Fan-talk was going to be Winnie's contribution to the field, her first published book. Long after midnight, when she should have been printing out boarding passes and preparing for her trip, instead she practiced and practiced the subtle gestures. It erased her worries about Chad and the return east. Even when Frank came in and said, "Don't you think you should get some sleep?" Winnie dexterously shook out her fan and fluttered it in a way that expressed, "Give me a hug."

Chad was playing Scrabble with Glodene in the parlor of her Victorian manse. Sycamore logs burned fast and hot in the fireplace, while outside, wind and snow flurries whipped around the porch. Once a week, Chad dropped by for a game and some infusions of her wry spirit. The old crone was an important feature of Cave City life that he would miss too. Tonight, he made the mistake of finally asking her true age. She answered, "Sorry, Chad. As they say, 'Age is just a number, and mine is unlisted.'"

Setting up the board, she dropped her tiles twice and refused Chad's help to gather them up. The second time, bending to the floor, she let out a chirrup of pain.

"The arthritis again?"

"Getting worse, but it's only pain. I can still untie knots in my shoelaces," Glodene said.

The Scrabble board had become a quasi-divination device. Glodene offered reflections on the symbolic significance of Chad's tiles, served up with her bedrock optimism. "You pick the tiles that you're meant to pick."

After the showdown with Winnie at the Elbow Room, instead of going to an AA meeting, Chad played Scrabble at Glodene's house until midnight. He picked the 'v' and built on her 's' and spelled 'travesty.' Next, combining the 'g' and the 'b,' he played an add-on and improvised 'gobsmack.' Glodene allowed it and murmured, "I understand your father is coming to town, and I hope you'll be as direct with him as you are with me tonight."

Fat chance of that. Chad poked at the fire and put on another log, while Glodene took her turn. She bingoed on the word 'abandon.' He should have known.

"I'm still not a good defensive player," he said.

"On the contrary, a bit too much," she said.

Chad picked the 'x' on his last draw and went out by playing 'ex.'

Glodene challenged it. "Is that actually a word in common usage, or just a pre-fix?"

"It is a word," Chad said.

She nodded. "One that you may be experiencing soon?"

No answer. No sound, except the fire and the snow being hurled like sand against the bay window.

"So what is your plan, young man?" Glodene smiled, "besides taking vitamins."

Chad smiled and shook his head.

"I've suffered a few losses in my life," Glodene said, "and it took several years of blaming myself to accept that there was nothing I could have done to prevent them."

She held out a trembling hand. A pitchfork prong of veins throbbed under her paper-thin skin. Chad took the old lady's hand and held it between both of his.

"A rematch, Madame?"

"Not just yet," she said.

They watched the fire burn down to embers.

The next Sunday, before the Orphan Sister Festival, Chad O'Shaughnessy and Night Snow drove the throaty Green Monster up to Indianapolis to meet Chief O'Shaughnessy at the Colts and Patriots game. Gameday traffic was notoriously bad, especially south of the city. Night Snow recommended a back roads route to avoid the traffic and because they had to pick up Chief at the airport. Cruising out through the wintry countryside, past Dr. Crane's clinic, Chad mulled over the strange feeling that his work with the *trabajadores* might actually be worth the risk of living apart from Winnie.

Yes, no, maybe. Pick one.

As he drove past the dirt road that fronted Brakeless Eddy's Brake Repair, Chad pondered the idea for a meeting between his father and Brakeless Eddy. An even more radical contribution to the healing of human divides: a meeting between two branches of the family separated for over a hundred years.

Yes, no, maybe. Pick one. Ideas raced around in his mind, like squirrels chasing each other up around the broad trunk of a tree.

Chad mulled over various scenarios. "Brakeless Eddy in his overalls and my dad in his three-piece suit kicking back together in the shop. Can you see it?"

"A pretty picture, but how can you be sure it will go well?" Night Snow asked. "A lot of those attempts go seriously awry, because people don't prepare enough. Don't you think you should check with Eddy first?"

"Eddy would be fine with it. My dad is more unpredictable. He's liable to make a crack about grease or cowpies. He's a buttoned-up guy with an unbuttoned filter, so he blurts out a lot of high-handed shit. You're right. I'd have to sell him on why it's important."

"Why *is* it important?" Night Snow asked.

Chad scratched his chin. "Hard to explain."

"Because there might be another angle on it," Night Snow mused, "What if, actually, a part of you knows it would be a disaster, and that part of you wants it to be a disaster, because a disastrous meeting between Eddy and your father would definitely prove that the historical split in the family is real and permanent, and likewise, it would confirm that your own split is real and permanent, and it would help legitimize a decision to stay in Cave City."

Chad said, "Who's the therapist here?"

"Think about it," Night Snow said.

They drove through miles of tract housing in the southern suburbs of Indianapolis and turned onto the Airport Expressway. The plan was to pick up Chief at the airport and head downtown to the stadium for the game and dinner afterwards at St. Elmo's Steakhouse, because Chief liked a good steak, and then drive back to Cave City. And maybe entice Chief to stay on for the Orphan Sister Festival.

When Chief lumbered off the airplane with a tipsy coterie of New England Patriots fans, some of whom Chad recognized as his dad's longtime road-game buddies, it became apparent that the plan would change. For Chief, the focus of the trip was not so much to visit his son as it was for Chad to have the opportunity to join Chief's crew in a typical football weekend debauch.

"Been there, done that, a few too many times, starting as a kid with the Boston College games," Chad whispered to Night Snow. He attempted to inhale a cleansing breath, as Chief stumbled towards them.

"There's my Chadski."

Chief O'Shaughnessy paused and reached down to zip up his trousers and button his vest, which had been loosened for a doze on the plane. He slapped Chad on the back and made a big show of pretending that Night Snow was Winnie with a much-needed makeover.

"Wonderful dye job. The black hair is perfect for you, and that Colts hat adds just the right touch of indecent."

"Dad, this is my friend, Night Snow," Chad said.

"I know. I know. Just fooling," Chief said, "As a matter of fact, we saw Winnie last night at a dinner party and, goodness, what happened to her hair? It looks like she cut it with garden shears. Don't you have any hair salons for the ladies out here in the sticks? Remember what your mother used to say about going down to the beauty salon for an estimate?"

Chad and Night Snow were saved from having to respond by an interruption from Chief's group. "You with us or you with them, Chief?"

The Patriots boosters, many clad in team jerseys, were mobilizing for a march toward the taxi stand and they wanted to know why Chief was dawdling.

"Tickets? We got a ticket for Chadski?" Chief demanded.

Chad said, "I told you on the phone. Night Snow has seats for us three. Great seats. Fifty-yard line. I told you on the phone last week."

This was news to Chief, who apparently now suffered from selective deafness. "Say what? You said what on the phone?"

Chad repeated his statement. "Great seats. You'll be able to look right across the field at your buddies making fools of themselves."

"No, the lucky charm crew has to stick together. We always sit behind the Patriots bench."

"Whatever you want, Dad."

Chief was flexible enough to accept a ride to the stadium. Twenty minutes together in the Pontiac, during which they discussed Chief's theory about the curse of the Colts. Chief expounded on his theory that the Indianapolis Colts would never truly rise to the top because of their shameful uprooting from their historic home in Baltimore. This caused a permanent stain and sense of dislocation in the team's identity and furthermore it is an accepted truth that a team's identity is a serious matter and another thing... what was the other thing... Chief dug at the inner recesses of his ears and wheezed on, but not with much clarity, about even more invidious sorts of uprootings and dislocations that prevent individuals from rising to the top. It was a garbled harangue that hinted that last night at the dinner with Winnie in Boston she had mentioned Chad's idea of staying on in Indiana. Chief was attempting to issue a statement of disapproval and an implicit warning about his bestowal of funding for the Indiana folly, warning that the fine print contained a time limit and a clawback clause.

All of which, regarding the question of where Chad would sit at the game, made it easier for him to decide to stick with Night Snow and her seats. A decision that Chief took surprisingly well, because it allowed him to avoid any further parental duty until dinnertime, and to freely descend to the level of his confederates without having to worry about making an impression.

For the next two hours, Chad and Night Snow sat directly across the field from Chief and his crew. While the teams wrestled between them, offense and defense, surging forward, surging back in the middle distance, Chad stared over at his father and imagined that the game between them was literally *the game between them*. All the years of back and forth headbutting and maneuvering for position, all for what? The goal was for Chief to bring his son into the fold and force him to accept the male heir's crown, thorny as it was with complications (under no circumstances does one ever sell the bank stock), causing Chad to question his idea for staying on in Cave City, because maybe it was just a stall tactic, an attempt to delay the inevitable Back Bay mortgage and membership at St. Botolph's Club. As for his goal in the bigger game, what was his goal, what had he been headbutting *for* all these years? Other than playing out the clock... whatever that means. Any tangible goal felt lost in a concussive clash of body memories. One in particular intruded now: waking in the middle of the night as a child to the insomniac groans from his father's bedroom, where Chief had to not-sleep because of his insomnia, at least three times a week. His teeth-grinding sounded like ghosts' footsteps. From those nocturnal gratings Chad, as a child, was able to intuit that the fine print in the male-heir crown deal hid dangerous traps.

"I bet you don't even know the score," Night Snow said at halftime.

Chad nodded. "I haven't really been paying attention."

"Or you've been paying attention to something else. Like how weird it is that our parents can continue to exert such influence on us, even when we're supposedly adults, or even from beyond the grave."

"Or even when *they're* acting like the kid," Chad said. They watched Chief hugging a cheerleader across the field with Night Snow's binoculars.

Chad winced, hesitant to admit the accuracy of her probe. He voiced a different, niggling concern. "Why didn't Chief mention meeting Frank at the dinner with Winnie?"

Night Snow said, "I don't know. Maybe Frank wasn't there."

"He must have been there, if Winnie's folks were hosting."

"Why does it matter?"

Chad cracked and re-cracked all his knuckles. "What is the score, by the way?"

"All tied up at seventeen."

The next alteration in the plan came at dinner, during the appetizers, with an offhand comment from Chief that an unexpected board meeting had forced him to switch his return flight to the next morning, very early, so it wouldn't really make sense for him to travel down to Cave City. He hoped Chad would understand, because, of course, nothing he could do really, and, besides, Chad would be back in Boston soon enough and they could spend a lot of time catching up. Chief, relaxed and magnanimous, thanks to the Patriots victory, undid his vest and ordered more wine.

Chad feigned appropriate regrets, relaxing a bit, now that he didn't have to struggle with how to engineer a meeting with Brakeless Eddy. He and Night Snow could settle into a good meal on the old man's dime and head home at their leisure.

Chad did gingerly bring up the topic of Brakeless Eddy and his family affiliation, but Chief rebuffed it again, claiming that his grandfather, Old Dribbleface, had made up that story as a cautionary tale about moodiness in the O'Shaughnessy clan.

"I forgot to tell you about Winnie's job. You've probably heard from her?" Chief said.

"A text or two."

"She's got an assistant professor spot at Brandeis. She and her colleague, Frank, both have interviews scheduled."

"You met Frank?" Chad asked.

"Very suave guy. Sharp dresser. He was wearing a pair of Cuban nose-pickers."

"Excuse me?"

"Pointy shoes, you know, with a buckle. That's what they call them at the club."

"That's rude, dad, and what did you mean about Frank having an interview?" Chad asked, "He's not looking for work. He's out there to hire a replacement for Winnie."

Chief laughed and showed blitz, waving his knife in the air. "Oh, Chadski, who knows anymore what's going on with you young things. Let me just tell you this, you'd better watch out for that Frank fellow." Chief nodded at Night Snow. "And it looks like Winnie better watch out for this fetching squaw."

One, two, three deep groans from Chad, repeatedly, in the car. They drove back south on I-69. Chad stuck to the speed limit. Night Snow burnt through a few cigarettes.

"On the bright side," Night Snow said, "I think your dad and Brakeless Eddy would probably get along fine."

Chad said, "Sorry. I hope that wasn't too painful for you."

"Not to worry," Night Snow said, "Wait till you meet my dad. It's worse. He truly believes he's a stand-up comic."

"One of those Delmar-like old guys, who's always joshing about everything?"

"No, literally. He lives over in Iowa, works the casino boats on the river, telling Indian jokes. Goes by the stage name of Pure Bull. *That* is painful."

Chad tried a diversion, returning to a recent debate about Night Snow's theory that people develop as adults until they get stuck in a certain year of their life, and they live that year over and over, while the world goes on.

"I'm becoming unstuck from my old year," Chad said, "and I'm looking for a new year to burrow into and it's this one, this year in Cave City."

Night Snow punched in the dashboard cigarette lighter and said, "I was really surprised that Frank didn't speak up in favor of you staying, when we were all together at the Elbow Room."

Chad added, "You didn't say much either."

"I said we'd miss you."

"That's all, that's it?"

Night Snow continued, "Frank and I are overly influenced by the fact that Cave City is a college town and you can't get too attached, because people are always moving on."

Chad signaled a lane change to take the exit for Cave City.

Night Snow said, "Of course what I really think is that I'd love to have you stay."

"Good to know," Chad said.

They cruised into town along the river road. Chad drove around Mound Park a couple times. And a couple more times. In the dim light from the streetlamps, the mounds appeared bigger and ominous, like something welling up from underground that was about to burst.

"Can I drive you home tonight?" Chad asked.

"That would be good," Night Snow said.

Chad had to ask for directions, because he'd never actually been to her place.

Turn left. Turn right. Turn left. Straight ahead. The neighborhood by the wharf on the river. They came to a stop in front of a low, shotgun-style bungalow, with a teepee in the side yard.

"This must be you," Chad said.

"Strictly speaking, historically, the teepee was not a local building type," she said, "Shawnees were more about wigwams and lodges, but all Indians build circle spaces. Gotta have a round room. Living in square spaces turns me into one."

Chad turned off the engine. "Are you going to invite me in?"

"Here's another factor that gets in the way of me telling you what I really think," Night Snow announced, "Supposedly, I'm your sponsor, but I've been failing at that and blurring the boundaries and you don't need me as a sponsor anyway, so I'm resigning. I'm resigning as your sponsor, so I can tell you what I really think and invite you into my house to see the parade float for the Sister City Festival."

Chad said, "Why couldn't you invite me to your house anyway? Why has it taken this long?"

"Because it's bringing you into a problem," Night Snow said, "A big problem that I need your help with." She slapped her forehead. "Watch out. You are about to experience some of my shady stuff, and I hope it doesn't make you run the other way."

Relieved to be out of the spotlight, Chad said, "This has been a very interesting day."

"It's about to get more so," Night Snow said. She led him up the limestone steps to the enclosed screen porch and unlocked the door. She waited until Chad stepped inside. She closed the door and locked it again. Flipped on the overhead light.

Bones, bones, and more bones. Human bones that were being used as material for a parade float.

"Excuse me, what am I looking at?" Chad asked.

"A craft project," Night Snow said, "I borrowed them from the lab. I didn't tell you because it's sort of against the law. The bones of my ancestors. I've been arguing with the department about using them for research and not reburying them. So, I figured, let's really put them on display. You'll notice the plywood base that fits perfectly into the flatbed of a truck. At first, it was just a small part of the float, about demonstrating a Mayan practice of digging up their ancestors' bones every five years and washing them, a cleansing practice. I thought it was a fine idea. But then it morphed into a diorama made entirely of bones. Accompanied on the float by the two live Orphan Sisters standing in the middle of the bone village, waving to the crowd. Last week, Ricky came over along with Nina and Paulo and they were all completely grossed out. I realized maybe I've gone too far. Like the assassination attempt against Juan Pablo. Everything is going too far."

Chad pressed his fingertips together and said, "Let's just take them back to the lab. I don't want you to get expelled or lose your job, or even worse."

"This is like the stunts I used to pull in college," Night Snow said, "I wasn't really thinking about consequences. The problem, however, is that the bones don't want to go back."

"What do you mean, they don't want to go back?"

"For the bones, it would be like going back to prison. I can't do it myself, but if you were to initiate the action, then I could assist," Night Snow said.

"You're telling me that you need a bones-buddy?"

"Yes, that would be the clinical description," Night Snow said.

33.

Before confronting the injured Ramón Puentes in the burn unit at the hospital, El Plástico and El Drone re-watch the video of the aborted bombing. They are trying to spot any accomplices or other witnesses. Misty, blurry dawn. They notice an old lady, hitherto unseen, out walking a Chihuahua puppy near the park. "An eyelash on a leash," El Plástico says.

"Our canine protector," El Drone says.

"I'm going to call Juan Pablo one more time," El Plástico says. "Should I try his cell directly, or call Señora Calatrova?"

"Try him direct."

El Plástico wants to invite Juan Pablo to participate in the interview with Ramón, as a sort of victim reconciliation gesture. "An interesting slant for a journalist," Juan Pablo responds, but he declines again. The phone call includes a lot of silence. Juan Pablo is not interacting with anybody, except Dra. Madero and Señora Calatrova. Although uninjured physically by the event, except for the bruises from El Plástico's bear-hug tackle, he is experiencing post-traumatic shock. Again.

On the way to the hospital, El Plástico and El Drone retrace their steps from City Hall past the site of the bombing. The street is mostly cleaned up now. Hard to tell anything ever happened. They are hoping to take advantage of Ramón's precarious situation to press him on the details. Were other people involved from corporate headquarters or the party? Did he receive any training or instruction? Was he promised a pay-off, and by whom? The doctors have reported that Ramón is hanging on by a thread, an oddly voluble thread. He is talking about anything and everything with the nurses and the other patients in the unit. If he's speaking, he must be alive.

The police guard jumps up and salutes when El Plástico and El Drone exit the elevator. And, oops, they slip and almost fall. El Drone catches the mayor's elbow. The hallway floor, sopping wet, has just been mopped. A janitor sets up several box fans, creating a noisy wind tunnel.

A nurse ushers them into the burn ward.

Inside a curtained cubicle, Ramón Puentes, hidden in bandages, is gabbing with a slim, elderly woman in traditional costume. They are reminiscing about the names of pets. She introduces herself as his great-aunt and launches into an emotional plea for understanding. "They made him do it, Señor Plástico. They drove him to it. He was always a good boy at heart."

"Who are you talking to?" Ramón says, unable to turn his head enough to see the new arrivals.

"The mayor is here," says the great-aunt, "with his henchman."

"Can you leave us alone for a few minutes, please?" El Drone asks.

"Don't leave," Ramón gasps. "These men are here to kill me."

El Plástico sighs and sits down beside his damaged nemesis. He is surprised to see the gallant, dashing Ramón in such a pitiable state. Entirely swathed in thick bandages, his face barely visible, small openings for eyes, nose, mouth. "Relax, Ramón. We'll do you no harm. We just want to ask a few questions."

El Drone ushers the great-aunt out of the cubicle, back into the wind tunnel. The three men breathe together, in a sort of raspy wallah. Ramón, still fearing the worst, mumbles prayers for his salvation. "Dear God, forgive me, an arrogant fool."

El Drone has seen this before. Previously powerful men, heretofore known as dangerous foes, reduced to moaning, repentant carcasses. And on occasion El Drone has felt something similar within himself when faced with his own deceits. He tries to reassure Ramón. "Seriously, we just want to clarify some things."

Ramón quiets and peers at the window and the opal sky. "I know exactly what you want. It was only me. It was only me trying to be a star. It was only me trying to impress them. And for proof, you don't have to go any farther than the amateur bomb I made. Never trust crap on the internet. If there'd been anyone else involved, it wouldn't have been such a poor job."

El Drone nods and says, "That's basically what we figured."

El Plástico jumps in, "Here's what I can't figure. Why would you want to hurt Juan Pablo? I understand your motivation for striking at me. I understand you wanted to stop Sister City. But why in God's name would you risk hurting Juan Pablo?"

Ramón twitches and gurgles, "I just wanted to frighten him. It was out of raw jealousy."

"Jealous of what?"

"I don't know… our lost youth."

El Plástico sits on his hands, to restrain them from retaliating. Witnessing Ramón's bandaged docility takes him in a different direction. An admission of an intense bond, like Ignacio and Delmar Butz, but with a negative twist. "I had a memory about us last night, Ramón. I remembered a school field trip when we were quite young, before our feud began. Our biology teacher took us out to see a bird-banding project in the *campo*. You, me, Dolores, Gonzalo, we were all there. Early morning, with those long nets. A few songbirds that we couldn't identify flew into the nets and we gently freed them and held them in our hands before the release. Even the teacher could not identify them. He thought they must be lost, that they flew down from the north by mistake."

"Before the release," Ramón echoes.

"Do you remember that trip?"

"Wait, what are you saying?"

"That somewhere on the journey, we all got lost," El Plástico whispers.

Ramón makes a swallowing noise.

"Somewhere along the way, we all got lost," El Plástico repeats, and turns toward El Drone, who nods slowly.

"Yes, and about Mercedes," Ramón continues in a confessional mode, "That was another kind of bomb that exploded in my face."

"It might have happened anyway."

"I'm very sorry for the trouble I caused you," Ramón says.

"A separate matter," El Plástico says, "It may have all been for the best."

"I don't know if that's true," Ramón says.

El Plástico shrugs, "In the end, I'm not sure we are meant for each other."

Ramón sputters through his bandages, "Correction, Roberto. I think she is meant for you. Her energy, her drive. Really, you need her. You're not the same without Mercedes."

El Drone nods and says, "Some of us have been trying to tell him that for months."

El Plástico slides to the window and scrutinizes the view across several blocks of rooftop patios. Potted plants and a lemon tree and, on the farthest one, a large, empty birdcage.

"Ramón, you seem to be in a very reflective mood," El Plástico says, "Would you like us to summon a priest?"

Ramón says, "Already arranged. They'll be here soon. They come every day to see me."

"They?"

"Dotcom and Father Mike. The Church of Planet Jesus has taken a real interest in me."

"Some ministerial ambulance chasing," El Plástico comments.

"Call it what you will," Ramón says, "They need talent. And I need an opportunity to redeem myself. When I recover from these burns, and get out of prison, I'm going to work for them as a marketing strategist. I've got an idea for reviving the practice of selling Indulgences. An old idea whose time may have come around again, a steady source of cash flow."

"Excuse us, please, gentlemen."

A thumping noise from Dotcom's cane on the wet hallway floor. The Church of Planet Jesus priests arrive. Dotcom and Father Mike enter the ward in full ceremonial garb with incense shakers and palm fronds waving behind them. Now El Drone and El Plástico are in the same position as the great-aunt was previously, being asked to leave so that something more important can happen.

"Praying with the patient. We'll just be a few minutes," Father Mike explains.

"No, I want them to stay. I want them to see this," Ramón Puentes wheezes.

"All right, Ramón," El Plástico says, "We'll stay a few more minutes."

Father Mike turns aside to El Plástico and whispers, "Even a devil like this deserves our pity. The doctors say he doesn't have long."

"We're singing him over. It's the least we can do," Dotcom says, "Oh, and listen, Mister Drone, I've been in touch with Priestess Dawn and Priestess Moon and they will intervene and do what they can for the Cave City vote."

"In touch with them how?" El Drone asks.

"It takes one to know one," Dotcom explains, showing off a new phrase.

At his next appointment in Dra. Milena Madero's office, El Plástico describes the meeting with Ramón, or he tries to. There is something about the experience that is hard to put a finger on. An uncomfortable feeling that reminds him of the black snake in his spleen.

"Do you think Ramón has really changed?" Dra. Madero asks.

"I never would have predicted it. Never in a million years. It might be possible."

"And if you no longer have a nemesis? What will that change in you?" Milena asks.

"That is a tough question," El Plástico nods, "That is a good question. What will change in me, if I don't have a nemesis? That is like asking what would happen if you and Rufus Crane got back together."

"Not exactly, no. Of course, I do miss Rufus, but that is beside the point here," Dra. Madero says.

She pauses and adds, "Señor Plástico, I must tell you, it has always been evident to me how open you can be to examining a question or an idea. You take it and hold it in your hand, examining it from different angles, pondering, if this, then that. But, honestly, I never really know if you have actually accepted or rejected the thought. I never really know where you're coming from."

"How can you say that? Everyone knows where I'm coming from," El Plástico sputters.

"Sorry, not me," Milena Madero says, "and I don't think Mercedes does either."

El Plástico winces and continues to describe the prayer ritual and its effect on him. "Dotcom was a sight to behold. At first I felt outside it all, an observer, but gradually I began to feel like she was praying for me too."

"How so?" Milena asks. She switches out the eyeglasses from the top of her head, and holds them in her lap, opening and closing the frames repetitively, like a hypnotic device.

"Praying for me and our upcoming trip to Cave City. Praying for me in the event it's a failure and the Sister City referendum losses the vote there. I don't think I've ever actually admitted that possibility to myself. I know we've been talking about the impact of the revelation around Enrique's existence, but I've never really thought it might be the end of Sister City."

He shifts around in his chair, crosses and re-crosses his legs. A spray of sun shooting down from the skylight engulfs the room and bounces back and forth off all the mirrors. The eyeglass frames in Milena Madero's lap open and close, open and close.

"What will you do if the referendum fails in Cave City?" she asks.

El Plástico grits his teeth. "If Sister City fails up north, I may think again about running for governor. Or I may retire. And if I do run for governor, truth be told, I will need Mercedes to be with me."

"In what sense?"

"In every sense."

"I often forget that I'm dealing with a political animal here," Dra. Madero says, "and not just any political animal..."

"One with some grit," El Plástico says, thumping his chest.

"Let's hope so."

Dra. Madero examines her wristwatch and shakes it and says, "Mercedes is coming today, you know. She must be late. She's picking up Juan Pablo."

"Juan Pablo will be here too?"

Dra. Madero says, "It was my idea. I thought it would be helpful to reconstitute the original family group, so to speak, what with Juan Pablo again recovering from a traumatic attack and you and Mercedes being his main source of support."

The political animal reaches for a tissue.

"Let's go back a few steps to the big trip to Cave City," Dra. Madero says, "When you describe the elaborate preparations, all the food and costumes and gifts that you plan to transport to the Orphan Sister Festival...to me, frankly, it sounds like the unstated goal is Dolores, your first love and the mother of Enrique. That's where you're coming from. That you want Dolores back, not Mercedes, that the unconscious goal of the trip is to win back Dolores and Enrique, whatever happens to the Sister City referendum. And have you considered the possibility that Dolores might refuse you?"

A knock on the door. "Hold that thought," Dra. Madero says, and rises from her chair to welcome the latecomers.

Mercedes and Juan Pablo step into the bright room of mirrors, both wearing Sister City sweatshirts. They shuffle forward cautiously toward Dra. Madero's open arms. "We're all here now," Mercedes says.

El Plástico seizes the moment. He jumps up and spontaneously initiates an embrace with Mercedes that becomes a group hug. Somewhat out of character. It catches everyone by surprise. Juan Pablo wiggles an arm toward Dra. Madero, inviting her to join in too. They stand together in a tight circle.

El Plástico continues the conversation with Dra. Madero, as if this interruption had not occurred. "I'm going to clarify my true intentions," El Plástico announces, "Here's where I'm coming from, Milena Madero. I want us all to go north to the Orphan City Festival. I want all my core family with me. I want *us* all to embrace Dolores and Enrique as part of *our* family. As part of the Sister City family."

Mercedes squints suspiciously at her therapist. "Is this a trick?" she asks.

"Are you serious? Are you for real?" Juan Pablo asks.

"One hundred percent serious," El Plástico says, "I'll arrange a special spot on the bow of the boat for Mercedes, just the way you used to like it. My bowsprit, my guide. Juan Pablo, you can fish off the stern, just the way you used to."

Mercedes again glances sideways at Dra. Madero, seeking her opinion.

Milena Madero raises her eyebrows and says, "It could be therapeutic."

"Yes, agreed. It could be," Mercedes says.

Juan Pablo weighs in, "I'll only do it if you come too." He gives Dra. Madero's arm a squeeze.

"I'll only come if you do," Mercedes echoes.

"Me? You really want me to come?" Milena Madero says.

"You count as part of the family," Juan Pablo says.

"Is there room on that boat for all of us?"

El Plástico answers, "The vessel is rated for drinking ten, feeding eight, and sleeping six. We'll make it work."

"And how long is this journey?"

"Two and a half days up, two days there, two and a half days back."

Dra. Madero switches her eyeglasses out again. Such a trip would be highly unorthodox, yet she prides herself on the unorthodox. She recalls the recent video consult with Dr. Crane's young therapist at the clinic and her advice about cutting the forest path, to be able to walk with his clients. Is this her version of cutting a new path?

"I don't know. I'm suspicious of happy endings," she says, "I'd have to make a few phone calls."

Cut to: El Drone and El Plástico and Juan Pablo loading a city truck with supplies. Food, baggage, party gifts, extra fuel. They drive to the port on the coast. Mercedes and Dra. Madero and Ignacio and the others follow in the red Galaxy. El Drone telephones an old contact in the customs office at New Orleans and reconfirms their authorized passage, and the refueling stops. The vehicles pull into the marina and stop dockside. They begin stowing all the boxes, carefully, below deck and above. El Plástico directs the loading to maintain seaworthiness, tying down crates and covering them with tarps. El Drone studies the charts. They check the weather report. Two and a half days, averaging twelve knots, if the weather holds, pretty much a straight shot north across the Gulf and up the Mississippi, with a short jog along the Ohio and Wabash. Refueling in New Orleans and Memphis. Mercedes and Milena, taking their positions at the bow of Xtabay, slather on sunscreen. El Plástico starts the engine and orders Juan Pablo to cast off. Ignacio, on the dock, uncleats the stern line and throws it aboard. Ignacio and Señora Calatrova and Gonzalo wave goodbye from the wharf.

34.

In the year 4 Pop 13 K'an, in the month of Kayab, a direct ancestor of Ignacio Morales, on his mother's side, stands on the beach with his fellow laborers and waves to the departing canoes, a flotilla of Maya royalty, paddling north to visit the Mound People. He bends and hoists a basket and winces from a sharp pain in his chest. He turns and directs the carts and animals to begin their march back to the village. In barely one week, he will fall dead from a heart attack.

A thousand years later, Ignacio Morales and Señora Calatrova and Gonzalo Sánchez stroll down to the same beach from the *malecón*. They wave farewell to El Plástico's vessel, easing forward out of the harbor channel. The boat starts to generate an undulant, white wake. Ignacio pauses and winces and puts a hand on his chest. He stumbles and falls against Señora Calatrova. Barely able to break his fall, she clutches him and they both slide down onto their knees. Gonzalo runs for the truck and backs it down the boat ramp onto the sand. Gonzalo and Señora Calatrova hoist Ignacio into the cab. That evening, back home, curled in his four-poster bed, Delmar's ashes on the night table and his longtime diva companion beside him, holding his hand… a massive coronary solves the Equation.

35.

In Cave City, the finale was happening. The intensity of the Sister City campaign spilled into all areas of civic life. Rude accusations were hurled back and forth by otherwise polite, mild-mannered citizens in letters-to-the-editor. Mrs. Regina Fenstermaker, a Worthy Matron of the Eastern Star, and the harpist in the community orchestra, described the portly Mr. Horton Killibrew of Killibrew Kitchen Supply, who had written a letter in support of Sheriff Hooker, as "a clumsy, pot-bellied stove." He wrote in and called her a "testy, tin-eared harpy."

Mayor Rosewater's task force spearheaded a get-out-the vote campaign with public interest radio ads, using Ricky's Latin bluegrass jingles. Three rounds of direct-mail flyers brought a flock of Florida snowbirds north to vote early. Mayor Rosewater ordered the parks department to construct a temporary bandshell at the town wharf on the river so that El Plástico's boat could be met with appropriate fanfare. A new round of polls conducted by the Indianapolis Star showed the referendum to be a dead heat.

Sheriff Hooker's campaign scheduled a tiki-torch rally on the Sunday before the Orphan Sister Festival, along with a speech from a national *candy-date*. The Sheriff's TV ads ran footage from the soccer riot intercut with shots of scurrying termites and a scary voice-over about rotting foundations. In one ad, highlighting his many qualifications, Sheriff Hooker sang 'America the Beautiful' from atop his horse.

"Sheriff Hooker is a metaphysical swindler," Glodene Butz wrote in her letter to the op-ed page. She publicly invited all Sister City supporters to her house, round the clock, for sodas and doughnuts and naps. The cabal members rotated in and out of her parlor and kitchen, while canvassing and re-canvassing the campus and surrounding neighborhoods.

The pace increased after Winnie and Frank's return from Boston. She and Chad had no time to fully discuss her job offer from Brandeis University and whether they might be staying on or not. Winnie and Frank appeared to be using the frenzied pace to avoid the discussion. A few odd exchanges occurred. One afternoon while stuffing envelopes together, Frank commented to Chad, "You know, looking back on this year, one of my biggest regrets is not going fishing more often with you. The official season is still closed, but, when it opens up, I'll show you the spots, so you'll know how to find them." And Winnie to Night Snow, while hanging banners at the band shell, "By the way, Chad's skin is really sensitive and he gets sunburned a lot and he needs to be reminded to wear a hat."

Another puzzler was an overnight letter from a Boston law firm addressed to Winnie that Chad 'accidentally' opened. Winnie had consulted an adoption lawyer about Nina and Paulo. While loading the dioramas onto flatbeds for the parade, Chad mentioned the letter and said, "I can understand your feelings for Paulo and Nina, but why wouldn't you talk to me about an adoption?"

Winnie replied calmly, as if the subtext didn't need to be explained, "It was spur of the moment. Frank heard a rumor that Sheriff Hooker was planning to raid Frank's house and put the kids in foster homes as retaliation if he lost the vote."

On the day of Sheriff Hooker's tiki-torch rally, the tension escalated. Church buses began arriving early, unloading flocks of flag wavers. The ranks of Sheriff Hooker's supporters increased through the afternoon, in eager anticipation of the national candidate's appearance at dusk. Loudspeakers on the rally platform at the square played clips from the Sheriff's commercials, interspersed with a tape loop of horse's hooves on cobblestones. The temperature turned unseasonably warm. Almost tornado weather.

A number of rowdy counter-demonstrators assembled in the parking lot of St. Fernando the Fur Trapper, led by Ricky. He was ignoring Mayor Rosewater's maintain-the-peace orders. The stated strategy of the Sister City task force was to observe the rally and hand out leaflets and flyers, and otherwise allow Sheriff Hooker and his candidate friend to embarrass themselves with their tiki-torch hate speech.

Ricky was going rogue. He wanted to avenge his Uncle Gonzalo's deportation. Ricky's faction believed that Sheriff Hooker had upped the ante by bringing in the celebrity candidate and that the Sister City referendum would be lost if their seductive, supremacist spiel went unchallenged. Dolores and Rosa were terrified and took refuge, along with Nina and Paulo and several other families, in the sanctuary chamber of the church.

The rest of the cabal positioned themselves around the square, handing out Orphan Sister buttons and printed material. They tried to maintain visual contact with each other, but as soon as Sheriff Hooker and the candidate and his security guard strode onto the podium, the milling crowds surged. Customers inside the downtown bars and restaurants flowed out into the street to get a glimpse. It was every person for him or herself. Chad hallooed for Night Snow. He heard a faint reply from behind, drowned by the loudspeakers.

Chad, buffeted in the mass, saw a hulking Brakeless Eddy in coveralls, holding a baseball bat. Brakeless Eddy was part of the crush of counter-demonstrators, now trying to push forward from St. Fernando the Fur Trapper toward the main square. Oh, no, no, no, Chad thought. Either Brakeless Eddy was off his meds, or something was going very wrong. Chad closed his eyes and squeezed his temples and tried to remind himself about the complexities of crowd psychology and disassociation being a form of self-protection. But this was not an internal split. This split was out there in the universe, out there in time, before and after. This little town was a place apart no more. Chad listened to the microphones squeal and Sheriff Hooker spew a rabble-rousing introduction to the national candidate and heard the crowd roar in response. Chad felt kneecapped by a strong, receding wave of denial that exposed a last, fragile bubble of fantasy about this rural haven and his short residence here being somehow separate from the greater mess of the world.

The candidate thanked Sheriff Hooker and yanked off his fat, silk tie and waved it around his head and threw it into the crowd. His face plastered with makeup, the guy looked like he'd had a couple bad experiences on Broadway. He started his speech with, "Howdy there, Jasper!" Creating an awkward moment, because Jasper was Cave City's arch-rival in high school sports and Sheriff Hooker had to lean in and whisper a clarification as to the candidate's actual location.

The candidate recovered by explaining that he wanted the people of Jasper to hear the noise from Cave City tonight. That he wanted the people of Louisville to hear the noise from Cave City tonight. That he wanted the people of Indianapolis to hear the noise from Cave City tonight. That he wanted all of America to hear the noise of Cave City rejecting this phony Sister City baloney.

His call-and-response shtick generated a lot of noise, both pro and con. The pushing and shoving between the supporters and demonstrators worsened. Sheriff Hooker called for order, without any success. The Sheriff looked worried too.

Providentially, some rain started to fall and the wind picked up. A stinging shower that doused a few tiki-torches. The crowd began to thin, and Chad spotted Night Snow on the steps of the Justice Building. He made his way over to her. They found Glodene with Dr. Crane under the cover of the old Woolworth arcade. No sign of Winnie and Frank. The rain showers increased. Chad and Night Snow decided to make a run to his apartment, only a few blocks, to retrieve a couple ponchos and umbrellas. Items that could double as weapons, if necessary.

In the Buena Vista lot, directly underneath the balcony of his apartment, Chad encountered a moving van parked on the diagonal. Not necessarily an uncommon sight on a college campus. Chad saw it before he comprehended it, before he actually read the words 'Pilgrim Relocation Experts' on the side of the van. He saw a man leaning against the cab smoking a cigarette before he realized who it was. A person out of context, a person from another dimension. Vincent, the little punk, frigging Vincent. With another guy in overalls carrying furniture from the back of the moving van up the fire stairs and into Chad's apartment.

"Vincent, you scumbag."

"Chad, good to see you. I finally made it. I told you it was just a matter of time," Vincent said. He threw down his cigarette and approached Chad for a handshake.

"Right, six long months," Chad said.

"My bad. A few complications with the consignment shops. I got all your stuff back, man. Most of your stuff is here."

"Thanks, but why didn't you give me a heads-up call?"

"I tried, but you didn't answer, so I called Winnie. She's upstairs, with some dude." Vincent pointed at the balcony with his two forefingers, like he sensed something was up and he was rubbing it in.

Chad and Night Snow turned to face each other, shifting weight from one foot to the other, dancing around an honest appraisal of the situation. It took a moment for Chad to realize that only his possessions were being unloaded from the van.

Vincent focused his squinty eyes on Night Snow. "Who is this lady?"

"None of your business."

"I'd like to go to a powwow with her."

"Vincent, why are you only unloading my stuff?" Chad said. All Winnie's furniture was still in the van. The sleigh bed, the armoire, the rocking chair.

Chad said, "What gives?"

"Winnie and the other guy, that's what they told us. Winnie told us to take just her things back to her folks' house in Boston, and she said to unload your stuff, because you're staying here."

"That's what she said, that I'm staying?"

"I thought it was weird too," Vincent said, "I don't really see you living in this burg, man, but I do what I'm told."

"WINNIE!" Chad shouted.

Winnie and Frank stepped out on the balcony. The jig was up. A little defiant, a little humbled, they stood and nodded and shrugged the truth. And it was all happening in a rainstorm during Sheriff Hooker's rally. O, Mary, Joseph, and all the saints. At least nobody felt the need to yell or curse.

Frank called down, "I think it would be best if all four of us just acknowledge the transition. Let's just make it to the end of the semester. I hope we can all remain friends, Chad."

Other than a few details like cancelling the wedding, and who gets the dog, all of which could be worked out later, nothing much had to be negotiated actually. It all happened quickly and peacefully. Chad scratched his head and exhaled a breath that seemed to keep coming from somewhere deep inside and that had been held for a long time. Night Snow put a hand on his shoulder. He shifted his gaze and sent a pointless, nonverbal inquiry up to Winnie, "Um, I thought he was gay?" Winnie shrugged back a conciliatory reply, "Turns out otherwise."

Vincent said, "Let's all order some pizza. You have pizza out here, right? I'll buy."

He reached into his jeans and dug out two crumpled twenty-dollar bills that he handed toward Night Snow. She stared down at the money fluttering in his dirty fingers. "Is that not enough?" Vincent said, "or are you one those Indians who never uses a Jackson?"

Thunderclap. The downpour worsened. Night Snow shook her head and turned decisively on one heel. She said to Chad, "You can find me later at home, in the teepee. I'm going to get some time in the teepee, in a circle, to get myself unsquared."

Night Snow walked off backwards, as if trying to rewind the movie, in the opposite direction from the rally.

Chad approached the balcony and called up, "Winnie, could we get a moment to talk?" She nodded and Frank nodded, and she padded carefully down the wet fire stairs.

"Where are we going?" Winnie asked.

"To the same place Dolores took me on the morning we discovered the van was missing."

Chad led her around the corner of the apartment building to the storage room for abandoned furniture. He jiggled the padlock on the garage-style door. It opened. They sat together on a torn leather sectional and listened to the rain on the roof. It was both peaceful and tense. Chad resisted the urge to reach down between the cushions and search for a roach tin. In the old days, it was occasionally possible to mollify Winnie with a toke or two.

Winnie said, "You wanted to discuss something?"

Chad said, "This is all kind of sudden, kind of a shock. I mean, we never even got a chance to go bowling together."

"And your point is?"

"What are the living arrangements until the end of the semester?" Chad said.

"You can have the apartment. I'll stay at Frank's."

"Winnie, you Marsh women are not known for behaving like this. Marsh women do not typically run with the wolves and grab for the brass ring."

"Oh, we're speaking in parables now?"

"I didn't know you had it in you," Chad said.

Winnie said, "Chad, your faux-astonishment is wearing thin. It should have been obvious."

Chad punched his leg and nodded and said, "I knew it, but I didn't know it. Just tell me that you'll be okay. I need to know that this is really your plan, not Frank's. When we first came out here, I felt like it was my job to make sure that you survived. I want to hear that this is your choice."

"I promise it is, Chad, and I'm sorry for everything I've done to play into the impression that I needed your protection," Winnie assured him. "Frank was serious about wanting us all to stay connected. You will always be tío Shad to the kids, and Night Snow will always be their Tía."

In her dim teepee, Night Snow sat cross-legged on the ground. She surrounded herself with a circle of stones and lit a candle, an attempt to create some *heyoka* space. She needed to get rid of the guilt. Usually, there was no guilt. This was not the first time she'd played a part in breaking up a paleface relationship. Perversely preying on their fantasies about going native and therefore, in a small way, revenging the domestic destruction inflicted on many Indian unions. "Creator, take it away," she prayed. And, honestly, everyone in town could see that it was only a matter of time for the mismatched Bostonians. She lit another candle. Now she had to get rid of the wanting, the desire. Wanting to hear Chad's footsteps through the raindrops outside the teepee, desiring another long drive in his Pontiac. It was never productive for an Indian to want anything like this, or else it would be robbed, outlawed. Perhaps this not-wanting was the reason why she had never finished her dissertation. Far safer to reside in the limbo of neither this nor that. She listened closely to the drumbeat of rain on the canvas, louder and louder. She breathed, "Creator, wash it all away." When the groundwater began to run in under the edge of the teepee, first in rivulets and then a half-inch sheet, Night Snow lay back flat and allowed the water to flow over and around her scars.

36.

The rain did not stop for seventy-two hours and fifteen inches. I'd like to think that Priestess Moon and Priestess Dawn had something to do with the weather onslaught. I want to believe that they were acting as genus loci across time, acting on behalf of their connected communities, that they summoned their rain gods and directed the deluge to occur in fast-forward time, such that Sheriff Hooker's rally was defused without violence. And, blessed be, that the Sister City referendum subsequently passed on the following Tuesday. Good to go for another twenty years.

The people of Cave City, after several days of being cut-off by flooding and seemingly ignored by helicopters flying overhead to Vincennes and Terre Haute, welcomed our little boatload of friends and fiesta supplies as if we were angels from heaven. It was a long trip.

El Plástico and I traded off eight-hour shifts at the helm of Xtabay. Milena Madero and Mercedes and Juan Pablo traded stories about *aluxes*, the little people, the Maya version of leprechauns. We lounged on deck and watched pelicans dive for fish. Pelicans have bad eyesight, so, splash, they try and try again. At one point, bump! We ran into something. El Plástico threw the throttle into reverse, and then neutral. We all scurried up to the bow and looked down on a large, ocean sunfish. A *Mola mola*. Ten feet in diameter. An ocean sunfish can weigh up to 2,000 pounds. A relic from the Pleistocene that lollygags around on the surface, feeding on jellyfish, occasionally emitting 30 million eggs, very few of which will survive. This gelatinous specimen was unharmed by our bump. A friendly, funny creature, its one dorsal fin, in the middle of its trampoline body, flopped back and forth in the air, as if waving hello. El Plástico had seen these oddities before in the Navy, and he described a group of recruits jumping in to swim with the gentle sunfish. Not to be outdone, Mercedes pulled off her robe and, already wearing her bathing suit underneath, leapt into the water. Juan Pablo took out his phone to take photos and we cheered her on, sensing that this was a part of our passage, that this creature was a spirit guide from the depths. Mercedes rolled across the flat, expansive top of the fish and she rolled underneath it and she tickled its fin. The fin flopped back and forth. After a few more minutes, El Plástico signaled for Juan Pablo to hang out a swim ladder, so she could climb back onboard. Mercedes shook out her hair and wrapped herself in a towel and joked, "Sort of like making love to my husband."

The closer we got to landfall, the more excited I felt. It had been almost twenty years since I'd been in the States. It started to feel like no time at all, a blink of an eye, like I was waking from a short dream. During my first shift at the helm, a rusty American shrimper passed us off to starboard, and I could see the captain gazing at our flag and name and ID number and debating whether to radio it in. I tried to imagine how I would answer his questions. How would I tell him or anyone who we were and where we were going and why? In my mind, I actually heard the words, "Once upon a time…" I waved and, fortunately, nothing happened.

We cruised across the Gulf and up the Mississippi without further incident, giving the oil tankers and coal barges a wide berth. Stopped twice for fuel. The skies stayed mostly clear, until we hit the edge of the storm system somewhere up near Paducah. Pine-needle size raindrops fell from the low clouds. Juan Pablo handed out ponchos and life jackets. Being the only gringo aboard, I acted as tour guide, offering some historical commentary along the way, as we motored by Natchez and Vicksburg.

"If we were going overland and following the ancient trade route, we could pick up the Natchez Trace and walk it all the way to Nashville…"

In response to a question from Dra. Madero, I shared the backstory on St. Fernando the Fur Trapper, who originally came up the river with DeSoto, before his epiphany, his vision of going solo to minister among the Potawatomi and the Miami and the Shawnee.

On we continued up the surging Wabash, hugging the shore and dodging logs and debris. "The river has quite a boil on," El Plástico said. Down below, Mercedes and Milena rustled up a last popcorn snack and closed the galley and everyone took positions on deck. The Xtabay made a wide turn around the sandbar as we approached the town wharf in Cave City.

Common sense told me that El Plástico should abandon his political welcoming speech. A crowd of forty or so awaited us under umbrellas and yellow raincoats and ponchos. Dolores was at their head. Nobody on the wharf appeared to be in the mood for a political speech. Dolores stood proudly beside her son. She looked ready for anything, her strength restored. She blew kisses and stepped forward and signaled for the Xtabay to enter the first berth.

Having trained for this kind of disaster relief in the Navy, El Plástico shifted into practical mode. He reversed the engines and directed me to toss a line to Ricky on the float, as we eased in against the bumpers. He ordered Juan Pablo to toss another line to Frank Vigo at the stern.

All eyes, of course, were on Dolores and El Plástico. After a moment of hesitation, they moved together into a seamless, wordless dance, tying the boat safely against the pilings. As if they were picking up with their relationship, not where they left off, but earlier, as teen adventurers exploring the caves. This was simply the next adventure. They were starting a new adventure together. All of us watching sensed that it would be okay. And, okay now, we disembarked and joined a group of volunteers stacking sandbags near the launch ramp, where the river was near cresting and threatening Night Snow's neighborhood.

All the personal stuff between us and our greeters was temporarily subsumed by a spirited all-hands-on-deck effort to pass sandbags and finish securing the boat and unload the supplies onto the band shell platform, which had remained relatively dry.

Other adventurous citizens began wading through the flooded streets to assist. People tired of bailing out their basements and hunkering down indoors, happy to get out of the house, even if it meant getting a little wet. Soon we had camp stoves lit and the coffee was on and the Orphan Sister Festival was up and running, in a form no one had planned, essentially a community kitchen event. Coffee, eggs and salsa, beans, tamales, Glodene's brownies. Ricky played his banjo and Juan Pablo accompanied him with improvised washboard percussion.

Winnie and Night Snow served up the hot food, calling out waitress lingo from Happy Dan's. "One coffee - topless!" Meaning, 'for here.' "Two eggs wrecked!" Meaning, 'scrambled.'

"You need to get to know your vinegars," Dolores said, in response to a question about the secret ingredient in her hot sauce.

More water-logged citizens appeared, including Sheriff Hooker and Chica on horseback. Unable to resist the smell of the food. Chica rode hunched-up behind him, wearing a baggy, brown sweater, all elbows and knees, part grasshopper. Conversation stopped momentarily, until El Plástico waved for the Sheriff and Chica to climb down off the horse. Having reluctantly accepted the imminent passage of the Sister City referendum, Sheriff Hooker approached El Plástico and offered his hand. "Congratulations. There is still a slim chance of me winning the mayoral election in the fall and, if so, we two mayors would have to be able to work together."

El Plástico snorted and pulled Juan Pablo to his side for support. But, before shaking the Sheriff's hand, El Plástico nailed Hooker with a double barrel, point blank, damning glare. It elicited an awkward, scriptural apology. Sheriff Hooker lowered his head and mumbled, "Guilty as charged. I have done things I ought not to have done and there is no health in me."

El Plástico cleared his throat and squeezed Juan Pablo's shoulder and redirected the topic to horses. Acknowledging the Sheriff's horsemanship and sharing an idea for developing horse-drawn Sister City carriage tours in both Ciudad de la Gruta and Cave City, Juan Pablo and El Plástico chatted up the development of equine therapy programs and the resurgent use of horses in organic farming; perhaps the two cities could work together to foster more local horse breeding as a way to create jobs in these related fields. The Sheriff was soon offering horseback rides, clip-clop through the water along the river-walk, to all the children, including Nina and Paulo.

As the impromptu party settled into a groove, I was able to step back with a plate of beans and ponder my return to the homeplace. I didn't have to be the tour guide anymore. Or even El Drone for that matter. All that identity viscera bobbed away like the logs and debris in the green river. I could see the dome of the courthouse, with the tip of the tree growing out of it, and the neon lights on the mound-shaped sign outside the Indian Mound Motel, and a brick warehouse across from the wharf that used to be the roller rink. Now converted to self-storage units. Maybe that's what I needed, a self-storage unit.

My nostalgic pangs were buffeted by the wet, cool air and periodic surges of white daylight. Like a rheostat in the sky, the sun attempted to poke through the thick clouds. Instead of a personal telescoping, however, instead of Cave City suddenly reclaiming its status as the center of the universe, the opposite happened. A vortex opened into a spinning immensity. I offered up a toast to friends not with us, Father Mike and Dotcom and Ignacio and Señora Calatrova. This was before we had received news of Ignacio's heart attack.

"And Uncle Gonzalo!" Ricky added. Everyone mustered a clink of coffee mugs.

I noticed Dra. Madero and Dr. Crane sneaking away from the pavilion toward the Indian Mound Motel. I gave them a sharp, appreciative whistle.

"Where are you two quacks off to?"

"We're going to a medical meeting," Dr. Crane called.

"He needs some continuing education credits," Dra. Madero said.

"Back in a couple hours," Dr. Crane called.

I watched El Plástico excuse himself from Sheriff Hooker and Chica. He eased away and picked up a plate of brownies and handed it to Dolores. She scooted and made room for him in the circle with Rosa and Mercedes. They passed around the brownies plate and listened to Ricky pluck the banjo.

I felt myself being pushed toward a decision. Watching them sway to the music, and watching the others kicking a soccer ball around the puddles with Nina and Paulo and Bongo, I felt pushed toward a decision to stay. And, no, it did not feel like a new adventure. For me, it was more that the adventure was over, and it was time to breathe again.

El Plástico sidled over to me and said, "I am going to miss our Monday morning meetings. I can ask Juan Pablo and his friends to figure out how to keep the drones flying. Juan Pablo can help me pilot the boat back too. He's driven it before."

"I'm sorry, boss."

"I know what you're thinking, and I understand and support it."

"Good, because I'm not sure I do. It could be a big mistake."

"One well worth making."

I said, "Have you spoken with Enrique?"

"Believe it or not, he asked me if he could catch a ride with us and visit his mother's hometown," El Plástico said.

"What did you tell him?"

"Of course, I would welcome it, if we have bunk space. He might have to sleep on deck."

"He can have my bunk."

"Listen, won't there be a few legal difficulties for you?" El Plástico asked, "The DEA trying to track you down?"

"I'll have to go incognito for a while. I'll have to become a John Doe. I can live in one of the caves, like I always wanted to do as a kid."

"Living in a cave, what would you do with your time?"

"Don't know, maybe write a memoir."

El Plástico nodded. "You gringos like to say that everyone has a book inside."

"Could be the reason for this pain in my gut," I said, mock-clutching my belly, "It's been bothering me for a long time."

"You mangy dog, you're pregnant," El Plástico joked, "with a litter of books. What are you going to say about me?"

"Oh, nothing actionable, nothing that you'll lose sleep over."

"My dear Drone, I hereby authorize you to say whatever you want."

"He knew when to hold 'em and he knew when to fold 'em."

"I hope that's a good thing."

"Yes, it is."

We stumbled into each others' arms, as men do, for a long *abrazo*. The same way I imagined Ignacio and Delmar embracing the last time they were together. A collective murmur caused us to shift our attention toward the river. Everyone turned and looked skyward, out beyond the sandbar, to the clouds parting and revealing a radiant light show. The sun reasserting its presence. Streaked, bent, rainbow-like arches extended down from the sky to earth. Hoops of light over the water and the trees, a shining orb connecting all things and all beings and all time.

More on that later.

End.

About the Author

Ian Woollen lives and works in Bloomington, Indiana, home to several limestone quarries, and not far from the mythical Cave City. His short fiction has appeared in a variety of journals, including *The Mid-American Review*, *Split Lip*, *Juked*, *SmokeLong Quarterly*, and *Fiction Southeast*. His last novel from Coffeetown Press, *MUIR WOODS OR BUST*, won a 2017 INDIES Prize (for Humor/Satire).